WELCOME TO THE NOVELS OF

JULIE JAMES

~A *Booklist* Top 10 Romance of the Year~
~American Library Association Reading List for Top Genre Novels~
~Best Contemporary Romance, *All About Romance* Reader Poll~
~RomCon Readers' Crown Award Winner~

"An addictively readable combination of sharp humor, sizzlingly sexy romance, and a generous measure of nail-biting suspense."
—*Chicago Tribune*

"One of the most sophisticated contemporary romances out there," and James writes a smart, tough yet extremely appealing heroine...A must-read for those searching for a smart romance with great characters and a no-holds-barred plot."
—*San Francisco Book Review*

"A delicious, delightful read that all hopeless romantics will enjoy."
—*Chicago Sun-Times*

continued . . .

Something About You

"Smart, snappy, funny yet realistic. I can't count the number of times I laughed while reading the book . . . This is one book I can totally recommend."
—*Dear Author*

"From first impressions to the last page, it's worth shaking your tail feather over . . . This is a contemporary romance well worth savoring, and laughing over, and reading all over again."
—*Smart Bitches, Trashy Books*

"Just plain fun! James is a master of witty repartee."
—*RT Book Reviews*

Practice Makes Perfect

"A tantalizing dessert—a delicious, delightful read that all hopeless romantics will enjoy."
—*Chicago Sun-Times*

"A fast-paced romantic comedy, packed with hilarious situations and sharp dialogue . . . A talented writer . . . Expect a lot of sparks to fly."
—*San Francisco Book Review*

"A sophisticated contemporary romance . . . proves that [James] is a master at conveying both courtroom and behind-the-scenes maneuvering."
—*Booklist* (starred review)

Just the Sexiest Man Alive

"Fantastic, frolicking fun . . . Read *Just the Sexiest Man Alive*, and you will be adding Julie James to your automatic-buy list!"
—Janet Chapman, *New York Times* bestselling author

"Witty banter and an amazing chemistry . . . bring this delightful story to life."
—*Chicago Sun-Times*

"Remind[s] me of Katharine Hepburn and Spencer Tracy movies: they have that funny edge."
—Eloisa James, *New York Times* bestselling author

"Witty and romantic."
—*Publishers Weekly*

About That Night

JULIE JAMES

BERKLEY SENSATION, NEW YORK

THE BERKLEY PUBLISHING GROUP
Published by the Penguin Group
Penguin Group (USA) Inc.
375 Hudson Street, New York, New York 10014, USA

Penguin Group (Canada), 90 Eglinton Avenue East, Suite 700, Toronto, Ontario M4P 2Y3, Canada
(a division of Pearson Penguin Canada Inc.) • Penguin Books Ltd., 80 Strand, London WC2R 0RL,
England • Penguin Group Ireland, 25 St. Stephen's Green, Dublin 2, Ireland (a division of Penguin
Books Ltd.) • Penguin Group (Australia), 250 Camberwell Road, Camberwell, Victoria 3124, Australia
(a division of Pearson Australia Group Pty. Ltd.) • Penguin Books India Pvt. Ltd., 11 Community
Centre, Panchsheel Park, New Delhi—110 017, India • Penguin Group (NZ), 67 Apollo Drive,
Rosedale, Auckland 0632, New Zealand (a division of Pearson New Zealand Ltd.) • Penguin Books
(South Africa) (Pty.) Ltd., 24 Sturdee Avenue, Rosebank, Johannesburg 2196, South Africa

Penguin Books Ltd., Registered Offices: 80 Strand, London WC2R 0RL, England

This is a work of fiction. Names, characters, places, and incidents either are the product of the author's
imagination or are used fictitiously, and any resemblance to actual persons, living or dead, business
establishments, events, or locales is entirely coincidental. The publisher does not have any control over
and does not assume any responsibility for author or third-party websites or their content.

ABOUT THAT NIGHT

A Berkley Sensation Book / published by arrangement with the author

PUBLISHING HISTORY
Berkley Sensation mass-market edition / April 2012

Copyright © 2012 by Julie James.
Excerpt from *A Lot Like Love* by Julie James copyright © 2011 by Julie James.
Cover art by Claudio Marinesco. Cover design by Rita Frangie.
Interior text design by Laura K. Corless.

ISBN: 978-0-425-24695-5

BERKLEY SENSATION®
Berkley Sensation Books are published by The Berkley Publishing Group,
a division of Penguin Group (USA) Inc.,
375 Hudson Street, New York, New York 10014.
BERKLEY SENSATION® is a registered trademark of Penguin Group (USA) Inc.
The "B" design is a trademark of Penguin Group (USA) Inc.

PRINTED IN THE UNITED STATES OF AMERICA

10 9 8 7 6 5 4 3 2 1

ALWAYS LEARNING   **PEARSON**

For Charlene—
I know you're watching,
and I'm keeping that promise.

Acknowledgments

First and foremost, I owe tremendous thanks to John and Chris, two assistant U.S. attorneys who were unbelievably generous with their time in answering my many, *many* questions about federal criminal procedure and life as an AUSA. Since my days as a federal appellate clerk, I've had the utmost respect for the talented prosecutors who serve in those positions.

Special thanks as well to Special Agent Ross Rice and Assistant U.S. Attorney Russell Samborn, who opened the doors to their offices and gave me glimpses of day-to-day life at both the Chicago division of the FBI and the U.S. Attorney's Office for the Northern District of Illinois. I'm grateful also to Dave Scalzo for sharing his business expertise and to Jen Laudadio for, well, you know what.

To Elyssa Papa and Kati Dancy—thank you so much for your wonderful feedback and insights, and for working with some really tight deadlines. Simply put, you ladies rock.

Thanks as well to my editor, Wendy McCurdy, and my agent, Susan Crawford, for their understanding, helpfulness, and patience during what turned out to be a very eventful year for me. I also want to express my gratitude to the entire team at Berkley—all of whom do such a fantastic job—including my incredible publicist, Erin Galloway, and Christine Masters, copy editor extraordinaire.

Finally, to my husband: I know I always thank you in my books, but—wow—I think I may actually owe you my first-born child after this one. Good thing he's already yours, or I'd probably be in a lot of trouble with DCFS for that arrangement.

One

May 2003
University of Illinois, Urbana–Champaign

SHE HAD SURVIVED.

Pressed against the wood-paneled wall of the bar, her chin resting on her hand, Rylann Pierce listened as her friends chatted on around her, quite content for the first time in a month to think about nothing whatsoever.

Along with five of her law school classmates, she sat at a crowded table on the second floor of the Clybourne, one of the few campus bars frequented by highbrow graduate students who demanded that their watered-down, four-dollar drinks be served in actual glasses instead of plastic. Everyone in the group was in the same section as Rylann, which meant they'd all completed their last final exam, Criminal Procedure, late that afternoon. Spirits were high and boisterous—at least boisterous by law-student standards—punctuated only by occasional lows when someone realized a point they'd missed during the obligatory post-exam recap.

Someone nudged her elbow, interrupting her reverie. "Hello? Anyone there?"

The question came from Rylann's roommate, Rae Mendoza, who was seated at her right.

"I'm here. Just . . . picturing myself at the pool." Rylann tried to hold on to the mirage for a few moments longer. "It's sunny and seventy-five degrees. I've got some kind of tropical drink with one of those little umbrellas in it, and I'm reading a book—one I don't have to highlight or outline in the margins."

"They make those kinds of books?"

"If memory serves." Rylann exchanged a conspiratorial smile with Rae. Like many of their classmates, they'd both spent nearly every waking hour of the last four weeks outlining class notes and textbooks, taking practice exams, staring bleary-eyed at *Emanuel Law Outlines* into the wee hours of the night, and meeting with study groups—all in preparation for four three-hour tests that would help determine the course of their future legal careers. No pressure there.

The rumor was that the second and third years got progressively easier, which would be nice—there was this interesting activity called *sleep* Rylann had heard of, and she was thinking about trying it out. Perfect timing, too. She had a week off before her summer job started, during which she planned to do nothing more strenuous than roll herself out of bed every day by noon and mosey over to the university's outdoor pool, which was open to students.

"I hate to burst the bubble on your daydream, but I'm pretty sure they don't allow alcoholic drinks at IMPE," Rae said, referring to the university's Intramural Physical Education building, which housed said pool.

Rylann waved off such pesky details. "I'll throw a mai tai in my College of Law thermos and tell people that it's iced tea. If campus security gives me any trouble, I'll scare them off with my quasi-legal credentials and remind them of the Fourth Amendment's prohibitions against illegal searches and seizures."

"Wow. Do you know how big of a law school geek you just sounded like?"

Unfortunately, she did. "Do you think any of us will ever be normal again?"

Rae considered this. "I'm told that somewhere around third year, we lose the urge to cite the Constitution in everyday conversation."

"That's promising," Rylann said.

"But seeing how you're more of a law geek than most, it might take you longer."

"Remember that conversation last night when I said I was going to miss you this summer? I take it back."

Rae laughed and slung her arm around Rylann's shoulders. "Aw, you know you're going to be so bored here without me."

Rylann was overcome by a sudden pang of sentimentality. Now that finals were over, Rae and nearly all their law school friends were heading back home. Rae would be in Chicago for the next ten weeks, working double shifts at a bartending job that sounded glamorous and fun and that would pay her enough money to cover nearly a year of tuition. Rylann, on the other hand, had scored a summer law internship with the U.S. Attorney's Office for the Central District of Illinois. While the internship was a prestigious and coveted position among law students—particularly among first-years—she would be paid at the not-so-glamorous GS-5 salary, which would earn her little more than what she needed to cover her rent and living expenses for the summer. Perhaps, if she were particularly frugal, she'd have enough left over for next semester's textbooks. Or at least one of them. Those darn things were expensive.

But despite the meager GS-5 wages, she was thrilled about the internship. As much as she grumbled about her student loans, she wasn't going to law school for the money. She had a six-year academic and career plan—she was big on having plans—and her summer internship was the next step in it. After graduation, she hoped to land a clerkship with a federal judge, and then she'd apply to the U.S. Attorney's Office.

Although many law students had no clue what type of law they wanted to practice after graduation, this was not the case with Rylann. She'd known since she was ten that she wanted to become a criminal prosecutor and had never wavered in that, despite the lure of money offered by big law firms. Sure, that paid the bills—and then some—but civil litigation seemed too dry and impersonal for her tastes. Corporation X suing Company Y for millions of dollars in a lawsuit that could go on for years without anyone giving a damn except for the lawyers who billed three thousand hours a year working on it. No thank you.

Rylann wanted to be in court every day, in the thick of things, trying cases that meant *something*. And in her mind, not much could be more meaningful than putting criminals behind bars.

A male voice coming from across the table interrupted her thoughts. "Three months in Champaign-Urbana. Remind me how the girl who's second in our law school class couldn't work herself a better deal."

The voice belonged to their friend Shane, who, like everyone else at the table, had a drink in his hand and a good-humored glow about him. Rylann could guess the reason for the glow. In addition to being done with finals, summer break meant that Shane got to return home to Des Moines and see his girlfriend, with whom he was adorably smitten—although being a guy, he naturally tried to conceal that fact.

"It's not the place that matters, Shane," Rylann said. "It's how good you are when you get there."

"Nicely said." Rae laughed, high-fiving her.

"Scoff if you want," Shane replied. "But my car is packed, gassed up, and stocked with snacks for the road. At seven A.M. tomorrow, come rain or shine, I'm blowing this popsicle joint."

"Seven A.M.?" Rae looked pointedly at the drink in Shane's hand, his third so far that evening. "I'm thinking that's not going to happen."

He waved this off, the drink spilling slightly. "Please. Like a little hangover's going to get in the way of a man in love."

"Aw. That's very romantic," Rylann said.

"Plus, I haven't gotten laid in two months, and the reunion sex is *awesome*."

"And there's the Shane we know and love." Rylann took the last sip of her drink and shook the ice in her glass. "Speaking of hangovers, I think the next round is mine." She collected orders from the group, then scooted around the crowded table and headed over to the bar.

"Three Amstel Lights, one rum and Diet Coke, one gin and tonic, and a Corona with two limes," she told the bartender.

A voice, low and masculine, came from her right.

"Sounds like a party."

Rylann turned in the direction of the voice, and—
Whoa.

Guys like the one leaning against the bar next to her did not exist in Champaign-Urbana. Actually, guys like the one next to her didn't exist anyplace she knew of.

His dark blond hair was thick and slightly on the longer side, just brushing against the collar of his navy flannel shirt. He was tall, with piercing blue eyes and an angular jaw that was slightly scruffy, as if he hadn't shaved for a couple days, and had a leanly muscular body. He wore dark jeans and well-worn construction-type boots and, together with the flannel, looked ruggedly masculine and wholly, undeniably sexy.

Undoubtedly, she was not the first woman to blink twice at the sight of him, nor would she be the last. And he appeared to be fully aware of this fact. His blue eyes sparkled with amusement as he rested one elbow against the bar, all confidence as he waited for her response.

Run.

It was the first thought that popped into Rylann's head.

Her second thought was that her first thought was *ridiculous,* and she nearly laughed out loud at herself. *Run.* Really? He was just some guy in a bar; having spent five years in a college town that allowed people to enter bars at the age of nineteen, she'd seen plenty of those.

She gestured to the crowd around them. It was after eleven o'clock, and the place was packed to the gills. "Last day of finals. It's a party for everybody."

He looked her over with assessing eyes. "Let me guess. You're graduating this weekend. You just took your last exam, and tonight you're celebrating your entry into the real world." He cocked his head. "I'd say . . . advertising major. You scored a job with Leo Burnett and are about to move into your first apartment in Chicago, a quaint and overpriced two bedroom in Wrigleyville that you'll share with your roommate over there." He nodded in the direction of Rae, obviously having noticed which table Rylann had been sitting at.

She rested her arm on the bar. "Is this 'guess my major'

routine your typical opening line or something you break out only on graduation weekend, hoping most women are too drunk to notice how generic it is?"

He looked offended. "Generic? I was going for confident and perceptive."

"You ended up somewhere around clichéd and smug."

He grinned, revealing two small dimples that added a hint of mischief to his angular jaw. "Or maybe I was just so dead-on perceptive that it scared you."

The bartender pushed the six drinks Rylann had ordered in front of her. She handed over two twenties and waited for her change. "Not even close," she said to Smug Dimples, happy to prove him wrong. "I'm a grad student. Law school."

"Ah. You're putting off the real world for another three years, then." He casually took a swig of his beer.

Rylann fought the urge to roll her eyes. "I see. Now you're going for clichéd *and* condescending."

Smug Dimples looked her over slyly. "I didn't say there was anything wrong with putting off the real world, counselor. You inferred that part."

Rylann opened her mouth to respond, then shut it. Okay, fair enough. But he wasn't the only one who could make quick assessments, and she'd bet that hers would be a lot more accurate than his had been. She knew his type—*every* woman knew his type. Blessed by an abundance of good looks and a corresponding amount of overconfidence, guys like him typically compensated by being short on personality. It was nature's way of keeping things fair.

The bartender handed back her change, and Rylann grabbed two drinks to make her first trip back to the table. She was about to throw out a sassy parting remark to Smug Dimples when Rae suddenly appeared at her side.

"I'll help you out with those, Rylann." With a wink, Rae skillfully grabbed four drinks with both hands. "Wouldn't want you to interrupt your conversation on our account."

Before Rylann could utter a word in protest, Rae had already begun to ease her way through the crowd back to their table.

Smug Dimples leaned in closer. "I think your friend likes me."

"She's known for her exceptionally poor taste in men."

He laughed. "Tell me how you really feel, counselor."

Rylann glanced at him sideways. "It's not 'counselor' until I graduate and pass the bar, you know."

Smug Dimples's eyes met hers and held them. "Okay, we'll do first names instead. Rylann."

She said nothing at first as she looked him up and down, coming to one inescapable conclusion. "You're used to getting your way with women, aren't you?"

He paused for a second. "Far more than I'd like, actually."

He suddenly looked serious, and Rylann wasn't sure what to say in response. Perhaps that was her cue.

She tipped her glass with a polite smile. "I think I'll head back to my friends now. It's been a pleasure . . . not quite meeting you."

She walked back to the table, where her friends were engaged in a heated debate over the scope of the Fifth Amendment's right to counsel during custodial interrogations. The guys in their group, including Shane, kept right on arguing as Rylann squeezed by, either not having noticed—or not caring about—her interaction with the guy at the bar. Rae, however, practically yanked Rylann into her seat.

"So? How did it go?" she asked eagerly.

"Assuming you're talking about Smug Dimples over there, it didn't go anywhere."

"Smug Dimples?" Rae looked ready to smack her upside the head. "You know who that is, right?"

Surprised by the question, Rylann stole a glance back at Smug Dimples, who'd already joined his friends over at the pool table. Well, she'd had a theory up until that moment. Judging from the no-fuss jeans, flannel shirt, and work boots, along with the slightly too-longish hair, she'd pretty much assumed he was a townie, likely one of those guys in his twenties from Champaign who hung out with his friends at campus bars looking for easy pickings among the co-eds.

But now, given Rae's implication that he was somebody she should know, she needed to rethink that assumption.

An athlete perhaps. He was tall enough, easily over six feet, and certainly had the body—not that she'd paid attention to that, of course.

Maybe he was the Fighting Illinis' new quarterback or something. Rylann had been living in the insular world of law school for the past nine months and, frankly, didn't have much of an interest in college football, so that could easily be the case. Although he seemed a bit older than she would expect for an undergrad.

"All right, I'll bite. Who is he?" she asked Rae. She prepared to be wholly unimpressed.

"Kyle Rhodes."

Rylann stopped her drink midway to her mouth. *Well.* She actually did know that name. Virtually everyone at the university knew that name.

"The billionaire?" she asked.

"Technically, the billionaire's son—but yes, the one and only," Rae said.

"But Kyle Rhodes is supposed to be a computer geek."

Rae shifted her position to check out the object of their discussion. "If that's the new face of computer geek, sign me up. He can push my keyboard buttons any day."

"Nice, Rae." Rylann resisted the urge to look over again. She wasn't familiar with all the details of his story, but she knew enough from the *Time*, *Newsweek*, and *Forbes* articles she'd read about his father, a Chicago businessman hailed as the epitome of the American dream. From what she recalled, Grey Rhodes had come from modest roots, graduated from the University of Illinois with a master's degree in computer science, and eventually started his own software company. She didn't remember much about his career, except for the one detail that really mattered: about ten years ago, his company had developed the Rhodes Anti-Virus, a software security program that had exploded worldwide to the ultimate tune of over one billion dollars.

She also knew that Grey Rhodes made generous donations

to his alma mater, at least, she assumed that was the case, since the university had named an entire section of the campus after him—the Grey Rhodes Center for Computer Science. With his billion-dollar empire, he was easily the most wealthy and famous of the school's alumni. And thus Kyle Rhodes, a grad student in computer science and the heir apparent, was also a name people knew.

So Smug Dimples had a name now, Rylann thought. Well, good for him.

She watched surreptitiously as Kyle Rhodes leaned across the pool table to take his shot, the flannel shirt stretching tight across his broad, seemingly very toned chest.

"You could always go back over there," Rae said slyly, her eyes trained in the same direction as Rylann's.

Rylann shook her head. *Not a chance.* "Didn't your mother ever warn you about that kind of guy, Rae?"

"Yep. On my sixteenth birthday, when Troy Dempsey pulled into my driveway and asked if I wanted to go for a ride on his motorcycle."

"Did you go?" Rylann asked.

"Hell, yes. I was wearing a denim miniskirt, and I burned my calf on the exhaust pipe. Still have the scar to this day."

"There's a lesson to be learned there," Rylann said.

"Never wear a denim miniskirt?"

Rylann laughed. "That, too." *And stay away from bad boys.*

They moved on from the subject of Kyle Rhodes and joined their friends in the Fifth Amendment fracas. Before Rylann realized it, over an hour had passed, and she was surprised when she checked her watch and saw that it was after midnight. She caught herself glancing in the direction of the pool table—her treacherous eyes seemed to have a will of their own that night—and noticed that Kyle Rhodes and his friends were gone.

Which was just fine with her.

Really.

Two

THE BAR LIGHTS came on, a signal that it was time for everyone to clear out.

Rylann checked her watch impatiently, saw that it was a quarter past one in the morning, and wondered what could be taking Rae so long in the bathroom. She didn't think her friend was sick—sure, they'd both had a few drinks that night, but they'd spread them out over several hours.

When another person, the third in the last five minutes, bumped into Rylann in the half stampede/half stumble of drunk patrons to the door, she figured she should check on what was keeping Rae. Moving against the herd, she waded deeper into the bar. Without warning, a guy slammed into her from the left, spilling his beer down the front of her black V-neck shirt.

Rylann cringed as the cold, sticky liquid trickled between her breasts and down her stomach. She glared at the culprit, a guy wearing a Greek-lettered baseball cap low on his forehead. "That's just great," she said dryly.

He managed a lopsided grin. "Sorry." He turned around and pushed his friend. "Look what you made me do, asshole!"

As Asshole & Co. made their way out of the bar without another glance in her direction, Rylann shook her head. "Undergrads," she muttered under her breath. No more campus bars, she decided. Sure, the drinks were cheap, but they clearly needed to find someplace with a more *cerebral* crowd.

"Now, now, counselor. Not so long ago, that could've been your pledge-dance date."

Rylann recognized that teasing tone. She turned around and saw Smug Dimples, aka Kyle Rhodes, relaxing against the bar, his long legs stretched out in front of him.

She walked over, resolved to remain cool in the face of such undeniable attractiveness, and tried to decide how annoyed she was that his assessments of her were getting more accurate. She *had* been in a sorority and had, in fact, gone to pledge dances and several other functions with inebriated frat guys in baseball caps who inevitably ended up spilling beer on her at some point in the night. Good times.

She stopped alongside Kyle at the bar and pointed to the stack of cocktail napkins behind him. "Napkin, please."

"You're not going to tell me that I'm wrong about your pledge-dance date back there?"

"It was a lucky guess." Rylann held out her hand and repeated her request. "Napkin."

Kyle looked her over, then turned to the man standing behind the bar. "Think we could get a towel, Dan?"

"Sure, no problem, Kyle." The bartender opened a cabinet underneath the bar and pulled out a fresh towel. He handed it to Kyle, who passed it over to Rylann.

"Thank you. They seem to know you around here, Kyle." She pointedly repeated his first name so that she didn't need to feign cluelessness if he offered it. For some reason, she didn't want him to know that Rae had told her who he was.

"The manager is a friend of mine." Kyle gestured to his two friends, who were playing pool in the corner of the bar. "He gives us free drinks. Can't beat that deal."

Rylann bit back a laugh. She wouldn't have thought that a billionaire's son would care about getting a *deal* on drinks. Then again, having never met a billionaire's son before, she really didn't know what they cared about.

She dabbed at her wet shirt with the towel, grateful that she'd worn black and didn't have to worry about see-through issues. She half-expected Kyle to make some kind of smirky remark about the way the material clung to her chest, but he said nothing. And when she'd finished with the towel and set it on the bar, she looked up and found his eyes on hers, not zoned in on her boobs.

"So where are your friends?" he asked.

Shit! Rae. Rylann had completely forgotten about her after Frat Boy had dumped the beer down her shirt. "That's a good question." She looked around the bar and noticed that it was empty except for a few stragglers. Neither Rae nor her other law school friends were among them.

This was starting to get odd.

"She was supposed to meet me by the front door after she went to the bathroom, but she never came back . . . Excuse me for a moment." Rylann left Kyle standing at the bar and strode into the ladies' room. A quick check of the stalls revealed they were all empty.

After exiting the ladies' room, she headed toward the wide wooden staircase that led to the second floor. A bouncer promptly cut her off at the pass.

"Bar's closed," he said. "You need to make your way to the door."

"I'm looking for my friend who said she was going to the bathroom. There's one upstairs, right?"

"Yes, but there's no one in it. I just checked," the bouncer said.

"Is there anyone still hanging out by the bar? Tall girl, light brown hair, wearing a red shirt?"

The bouncer shook his head. "Sorry. The whole floor's empty."

Kyle appeared at Rylann's side as the bouncer walked off.

"Okay, now I'm worried," she said, more to herself than to him.

"Does she have a cell phone?" Kyle asked.

Rylann frowned. "Yes, but I don't." She caught Kyle's look and went on the defensive. Rae, and pretty much everyone else she knew, had been nagging her to get a cell phone all year. "Hey, those plans aren't exactly cheap."

He pulled a black cell phone out of his jeans pocket. "It's called 'free evening minutes.' Welcome to 2003."

"Ha, ha." Rylann thought about leveling him with a

withering stare but decided against it—she really could use that cell phone. The sass could wait.

She took the phone from Kyle, realizing that this was the second time she'd accepted help from him in the last five minutes. Common courtesy meant this obligated her to be at least somewhat pleasant to him.

Crap.

She dialed Rae's number and waited as the phone rang.

"Hello?" her friend answered in a perplexed tone.

Rylann breathed a sigh of relief. "Rae, where are you? I'm standing here like an idiot waiting for you to come out of the bathroom. But you're not *in* the bathroom."

"Carpe diem."

Rylann scooted a few feet away from Kyle. "'Carpe diem'? What do you mean by that?" She had a funny feeling she wasn't going to like whatever her friend was about to say next.

"It's Latin for 'Don't kill me.'"

Oh boy.

"What did you do, Rae?"

"Okay, here's what happened: when I came out of the bathroom, I saw Kyle Rhodes at the bar, checking you out," Rae said. "I decided that if you aren't going to treat yourself to a little fun after the long year we've had, then I'm going to make the fun come to you. So I grabbed the guys, and we all sneaked out the back door."

"You didn't."

"I did. He's the son of a billionaire, Rylann. And he's gorgeous. You should be thanking me, actually. We're already a block away from Shane's apartment, and I think I'll hang out here for a while. Give you some space."

Rylann lowered her voice further. "This goes against the woman code, Rae. We never leave one of our own behind. Now I have to walk home by myself."

"Not if everything goes as planned . . ." Rae sounded very evil genius–like before her tone turned coy. "Whose phone is this, anyway?"

No way was Rylann going to answer that. "Come to think of it, I am going to kill you. And then I'm going to steal the black Manolos you bought last winter and dance in them at your funeral." She hung up the phone with emphasis.

She walked over to Kyle and handed the phone back to him.

"So?" he asked.

Rylann quickly thought up an excuse. "One of our friends got sick, so Rae and the others had to get him home fast."

"Or maybe she left you here so that you'd be stuck with me."

Rylann threw up her hands. "Okay, that's freaky. How would you know that?"

Kyle shrugged. "I heard the 'carpe diem' part and guessed. I have a twin sister. I've seen how her and her friends' scary matchmaking minds work."

Rylann blushed. "I hope you know that I had nothing to do with this."

Kyle seemed more amused than bothered by Rae's schemes. "Don't worry, counselor, I won't have you charged as a co-conspirator." He nodded toward the door. "Come on. I'll walk you home."

Rylann began making her way toward the exit. "Thanks, but that's not necessary. I only live eight blocks away."

Kyle scoffed as he followed her to the door. "Like I'm going to let a woman walk home by herself at one thirty in the morning. My mother raised me better than that."

"I won't tell her if you don't." Not that it was Rylann's first choice to walk home alone, but she'd be lying if she said she hadn't made similar late-night treks across campus as an undergrad. Besides, Kyle Rhodes was a virtual stranger himself. Who said *he* was safe?

Kyle stopped her just as she reached the front door. "It's not only what my mother would say; it's what I think. My sister is a grad student at Northwestern. If I found out that some jerk let her walk home alone this late, I'd kick his ass. So it looks like you're stuck with me. Like it or not."

Rylann thought through her options. The speech about his sister seemed genuine enough. From what she could tell, Kyle Rhodes was cocky and trouble, but not *that* kind of trouble.

"All right, fine. You can walk me home." She paused. "Thank you."

"See? Was it that hard to be nice to me?"

Rylann pushed the door open and stepped outside. As usual, the crowd was thick in front of the bar as students discussed the all-important questions of which after-hours party to go to and whether to make a pit stop at La Bamba for burritos along the way. "I'm sure there are plenty of women who are more than happy to be nice to you," she said to Kyle while navigating her way through the crowd. "I figured I'd buck the trend."

Kyle followed her. "Who's making assumptions now?"

"You hang out at a bar preying on random women buying multiple drinks. It doesn't take a genius to figure out that this isn't the first time you've 'escorted' a girl home."

"First of—" Kyle was cut off as he became momentarily separated from Rylann by a group of women walking in the opposite direction. Ignoring the women's interested looks, he continued. "First of all, I don't *prey* on anyone. Second of all, I don't, as a habit, hang out at bars picking up women. Tonight was an exception. I saw you at the table with your friends and followed you to the bar when you walked over."

"Why?"

He shrugged matter-of-factly. "I thought you were hot."

"Thanks," Rylann said dryly.

An inebriated undergrad stumbled obliviously as he walked past them. Kyle took Rylann by the waist and pulled her out of the man's path just before they collided.

They stopped at the street corner, keeping a safe distance from the drunk guy, and waited for the light to change. Kyle looked her over. "I didn't know then that you'd also be this . . . spicy."

"You're free to rescind your initial offer of interest."

Kyle laughed. "Christ, you *are* a law geek. I'm not rescinding anything. I don't mind hot and spicy. Actually find that appealing in a girl." He cocked his head, thinking this over. "And chicken wings."

Rylann turned her head and stared at him. "Did you really just compare me to chicken wings?"

"You say that like it's a bad thing. Chicken wings are the bomb."

Rylann had to fight not to smile at that one. "Why do I get the feeling you're never serious?"

Kyle gestured with his arm to the surrounding crowd milling on the sidewalk and spilling into the street. The feeling in the air was tangibly ebullient. "Who wants to be serious tonight? Law school's over for the year, counselor. Live a little."

Frankly, she wasn't quite sure what to make of Kyle Rhodes. The logical part of her knew that with the whole hot-billionaire-heir-wearing-work-boots thing he had going for him, she was likely one in a parade of women he'd hit on. Still, she'd be lying if she didn't admit she found the attention at least somewhat flattering. This was a guy many women would chase after, and he was chasing after her.

At least for five minutes.

"Look," she said to Kyle. "I appreciate you walking me home. Really. But just so we're on the same page, that's all this is. A walk."

The light turned green, and they crossed the street in tandem.

"No offense, but you seem a bit uptight about the rules here," Kyle said. "Don't you ever just go with the flow?"

"I'd say I'm more of a planner than a fly-by-the-seat-of-my-pants type."

He groaned. "I bet you're one of those people with a five-year plan."

"Mine's six." Rylann caught his look. "What? That's how long it will take to get where I want to be," she said with a touch of defensiveness. "Not all of us have the luxury of ambling our way through our twenties until we decide it's time to grow up, Kyle *Rhodes*."

Kyle spun around and stopped in front of her, so abruptly that she nearly barreled into him. "Listen, I'm going to fast-forward through the whole give-the-rich-guy-his-comeuppance speech. I've been dealing with that routine since high school." He pointed emphatically. "And I don't amble my way through anything. As a matter of fact, the reason I was out celebrating tonight is because I just took my qualifying exam to become a PhD candidate."

She stood corrected. "Impressive. In the future, you might want to open with that line instead of the lame guess-my-major routine." She smiled charmingly. "Just a suggestion."

Kyle threw up his hands. "I swear, never again. This is what I get for approaching a strange girl in a bar. I pick the sarcastic one." He stalked away in frustration.

Rylann let him go for a few feet before calling out, "You're headed in the wrong direction." When he turned around, she pointed innocently. "My apartment's that way."

He switched directions and coolly breezed past her.

Rylann watched with amusement as he walked by. She kind of liked this cranky side of Kyle Rhodes. It felt much more real than the Smug Dimples pseudo-charm routine. "I don't think it counts as walking me home if you're a half block ahead of me," she called out to him. "I'm pretty sure there's a five-foot rule or something."

Kyle stopped but didn't turn around. He waited in silence for her to catch up.

When she did, she paused before him, standing a little closer than before. "I suppose congratulations are in order. Tell me more about your PhD exam."

"Oh, *now* you want to be nice," he said.

"I'm considering it."

They continued walking in the direction of her apartment. "I'm in the computer sciences grad program," Kyle said. "My focus is on systems and networking research, specifically security. Protections against DoS attacks."

"That sounds very . . . technical."

Seeing her cluelessness, he explained. "*DoS* means "denial of service." In basic terms, a type of computer hacking. Companies view them mostly as nuisances, but my prediction is that these types of attacks will continue to grow more advanced over the next few years. Mark my words, one day somebody is going to cause a lot of panic and mayhem if websites don't start taking these threats seriously."

"Your father must be very proud that you're going into the family business," Rylann said.

He grimaced. "Actually, that's a bit of a sore subject. I'm not planning to work for him. I'd like to teach instead." He caught Rylann's look of surprise and shrugged casually. "Can't beat a gig that lets you have summers off, right?"

"Why do you do that?" she asked.

"Do what?"

"Put out this whole laid-back, don't-take-me-too-seriously vibe. I assume that's the reason for the work boots and flannel getup."

"No, I wear work boots and flannels because they're *comfortable*. In case you haven't noticed, we go to school in the middle of a cornfield. Black tie isn't exactly required around here." He cocked his head. "Besides, why do you care what kind of vibe I put out?"

"Because I suspect there's more to the illustrious Kyle Rhodes than meets the eye."

They paused at a street corner, only two blocks from Rylann's apartment. A cool breeze served as a quick reminder that she was wearing a damp shirt. With a slight shiver, she folded her arms over her chest and rubbed them to stay warm.

"Nope. I'm still the same jerk you thought I was with the lame pickup line." Without discussion, Kyle pulled off his flannel shirt and handed it to Rylann. Underneath, he wore a gray fitted T-shirt that hugged the toned muscles of his chest, abs, and biceps.

Rylann waved off the shirt, trying not to stare at his body. And failing miserably. "Oh, no thanks. We're only two blocks from my apartment. I'll be okay."

"Just take it. If my mother knew I let a woman walk home shivering in a wet shirt, she'd kill me."

Rylann took the shirt from him and slid her arms into it. It was warm from his body. "Twenty-three years old and still listening to Mom. That's cute."

Kyle stepped closer and adjusted the collar of the shirt, which was caught underneath the neckline. "Twenty-four.

And my mom's pretty kick-ass—you'd listen to her, too." He nodded, satisfied with the collar. "There."

When his hand brushed against Rylann's neck, her stomach did a little flip-flop.

Major sparks.

Dammit.

"Thank you," she said. *Not this one*, she firmly reminded herself. This guy had no place in her six-year plan. Hell, he had no place in her six-*day* plan.

Kyle gazed down at her. "I lied when I said I followed you to the bar because you're hot." He touched her cheek. "I saw you laughing with your friends, and your smile sucked me right in."

Oh . . . *man*. Rylann's heart did this strange skipping thing. She debated for a moment as she peered up into those incredible blue eyes of his, then decided, what the hell? After the year she'd been through, she had earned a little treat.

She stood up on her toes, lifted her lips to his, and kissed him.

The kiss was teasing and gentle at first, and he cupped her cheek as he slowly, seductively, claimed her mouth with his. She slid one hand up his chest, momentarily forgetting—or not caring—that they were standing on a street corner where anyone could pass by. She pressed up against him, and the kiss deepened as his tongue swirled around hers, hot enough to make her body feel like it was melting.

It felt like an eternity before she managed to slowly pull her lips away.

His hand was still on her cheek as their mouths hovered inches from each other. His eyes were a deep, burning blue. "What made you do that?"

"I thought I'd fly by the seat of my pants for a change," she said, a little out of breath.

He raised an eyebrow. "And?"

Exhilarating. Rylann smiled to herself, having a sneaking suspicion that Kyle Rhodes had already heard enough compliments about his kissing to last a lifetime. So she shrugged noncommittally. "Not bad."

Kyle scoffed. "Not bad? Counselor, there are two things I've got mad skills at. And computer science is the other one."

All righty, then. Rylann rolled her eyes. "Seriously, where do you come up with these lines?" She turned away and began walking the remaining two blocks to her apartment, figuring there wasn't enough room for her, Kyle Rhodes, and his ego on the sidewalk.

She'd gone a few feet when she heard him calling after her.

"It doesn't count as a walk home if you're half a block ahead of me," he said, teasingly echoing her earlier words.

"I'm releasing you of all your obligations," she shouted without looking back. She could hear his laughter, warm and rich, following behind her.

When she reached her building, she cut through the court-yard and walked straight to the weather-faded wooden stair-well that would take her to the second-floor apartment she shared with Rae.

"Rylann."

She turned around and saw Kyle standing at the bottom of the stairs.

"I was wondering if you're sticking around this cornfield for the summer?" he said.

"Not that it matters, but yes." She sniffed. "I've got an internship with the U.S. Attorney's Office."

Kyle climbed up the steps to meet her midway on the staircase. "In that case, have dinner with me tomorrow."

"I don't think that's a good idea."

He tugged the collar of the shirt she was wearing. "You're just going to take my shirt and run?"

She'd completely forgotten about that. She began to slide the shirt off. "Sorry. I—"

Kyle put his hand over hers. "Keep it. I like the way it looks on you."

Darn sparks shot right down to her toes. She gave him her best no-nonsense stare. "This was supposed to be just a walk."

"It's only one date, counselor. We'll get chicken wings and beer and bitch about how bored we're going to be living here this summer."

Actually, that didn't sound half-bad. "And what if I'd said that I wasn't sticking around for the summer?" Rylann asked. "What if you'd been right, and tomorrow I was leaving for Chicago to move into my quaint and overpriced two-bedroom apartment in Wrigleyville?"

He grinned, a smile that could melt the polar ice cap. "Then I guess I'd be driving two hours to pick you up for those chicken wings. See you tomorrow, counselor. Eight o'clock." With that, he turned and strode back down the staircase.

A few minutes later, safely ensconced inside her apartment, Rylann leaned her head against the front door, musing over the evening's turn of events. She closed her eyes, a smile curling at the edges of her lips despite all her attempts to fight it off.

Wow.

AS FATE WOULD have it, however, the good feeling didn't last.

Rylann waited until ten o'clock, two hours after the time Kyle had said he'd be at her apartment. Then she finally gave up and slid out of her jeans and heels.

He'd stood her up.

This was okay, she assured herself. Her internship, which she'd been looking forward to for months, started in a week, and she didn't need to be distracted by first dates with a sometimes-charming sexy billionaire computer geek and the whole will-he-call rigmarole.

Poor Rae would be crushed, she thought. Before leaving for the summer, she'd left Rylann her black Manolos specifically for the occasion.

"I can't have you running around in flip-flops for your date with a billionaire," Rae had lectured, playing it cool and trying not to appear too sentimental as she'd handed over the shoe box to Rylann before getting into her car.

Rylann had hugged her friend. "You and the rest of your shoes need to get back here soon."

"Call me tomorrow and let me know how the date goes,"

Rae had said. "Maybe he'll fly you to Italy for pizza or rent out a restaurant for your first date."

Or maybe he'll just forget the whole thing.

Resolved to ignore the disappointment she felt, Rylann changed into a camisole and drawstring pajama pants. No sense in being dressed up if she had no place to go.

She got comfortable on the couch and absentmindedly flipped through the television channels. It struck her how quiet her apartment was, and in the next moment, she realized how dangerously close she was to wallowing in self-pity.

No way, she told herself, refusing to go down that road. It wasn't as though Kyle Rhodes was *that* great. For starters, he was cocky and too confident, and he dressed as if he'd just fallen off a tractor. And the whole computer thing? That was a snooze-fest of a conversation topic if she'd ever heard one.

Honestly, she hadn't even liked the guy much.

Really.

THE NEXT MORNING, Rylann came out of her bedroom dressed and ready to go for a run. With all the studying she'd done over the last few months, she'd barely worked out and felt the need to rectify that situation. She suspected this enthusiasm would last for about fifteen minutes, until she collapsed in a gasping heap somewhere in the middle of mile two.

She was in high spirits for a woman who'd been stood up the night before. Most of this stemmed from the fact that she intended to toss Kyle Rhodes's flannel shirt in the Dumpster on her way out, and also from the fact that she had this great one-liner planned in the event she ever did run into him again, about how she hadn't gotten the chance to put his shirt where she'd really wanted to, so she'd stuck it in the other place the sun didn't shine.

When she stepped outside her apartment—MP3 player in one hand and the soon-to-be-forgotten flannel shirt in the other—she saw the newspaper lying in front of her door. As she picked it up, the early morning sun made her blink, and somewhere in the back of her mind she was thinking about how it was going to be a warm, gorgeous May day. *A perfect day for the pool*, she thought. *Maybe I'll—*

It took a moment for the newspaper's headline to register. At first it seemed like any another tragic headline, the kind that makes a person pause at the brief sadness one feels when hearing such things. Then it dawned on her.

WIFE OF BILLIONAIRE ALUMNUS KILLED IN CAR ACCIDENT

Marilyn Rhodes.

Kyle's mother.

Without looking up from the newspaper, Rylann shut her front door, sat down at her kitchen table, and began to read.

Three

Nine years later

THE CHILLY MARCH wind cut across Lake Michigan, an icy sting that could easily bring tears to one's eyes. But Kyle barely noticed. When he was running, he was in the zone.

It was dark outside, after seven P.M., and the temperature hovered right around forty degrees. Every day for the past two weeks, he'd hit the jogging trail that ran along the lake and run a twelve-mile circuit from his apartment and back. His doorman, Miles, had commented yesterday on the routine, and for simplicity's sake, Kyle had said he was training for a marathon.

In truth, he just liked the quiet solitude of running. Not to mention, he reveled in the freedom he'd come to appreciate while running. Ah . . . such glorious freedom. The knowledge that he could keep going, with nothing but physical exhaustion to stop him.

And, of course, a team of armed U.S. marshals if he went more than ten miles from home.

A minor technicality.

Kyle had quickly realized there was one drawback to his running routine, something he'd figured out around mile three the first morning: the electronic monitoring device strapped to his ankle chafed like a bitch while jogging. He'd tried sprinkling some talcum powder on it, but all that had gotten him was a white mess that left him smelling like a baby. And if there was anything a committed bachelor in his thirties did not need to smell like, it was babies. A woman got one whiff of that and suddenly all sorts of biological clocks came out of snooze mode and started ringing with a vengeance.

But, as Kyle knew full well, a man could have worse problems than chafing and baby powder. A man could get arrested, say, and be indicted on multiple federal charges and end up in prison. Or a man could find out that his stubborn, pain-in-the-ass twin sister had nearly gotten herself killed while working with the FBI as part of an agreement to secure his early release from said prison.

He still wanted to throttle Jordan for that one.

Kyle checked his watch and picked up the pace for the last half mile of his run. According to the terms of his home detention, he was allowed ninety minutes per day for "personal errands," as long as he stayed within a ten-mile radius of his home. Technically, he was supposed to use those ninety minutes for food shopping and laundry, but he'd figured out how to game the system: he ordered his groceries online and had them delivered to his front door, and he utilized the dry cleaner located in the lobby of the high-rise building in which he lived. That gave him ninety minutes a day outside his penthouse, ninety minutes when life seemed almost normal.

On this evening, he made it back to his building with eight minutes to spare. He may have been gaming the system, but he wasn't about to test it. God forbid he got delayed with a leg cramp and an alarm was triggered from his ankle monitor. All he needed was a SWAT team storming the beach and slapping him in handcuffs just because he hadn't stretched properly.

The rush of warm air that hit Kyle as he entered the building felt stifling. Or perhaps it was just the knowledge that his return through those doors meant he would be trapped in his apartment for the next twenty-two hours and thirty-two minutes.

Only three more days to go, he reminded himself.

In little more than seventy-two hours—he'd started thinking in terms of hours ever since his prison days—he would officially be a free man. Assuming, that is, that the U.S.

Attorney's Office upheld their end of the bargain, which was a big assumption. It was safe to say that he and the U.S. Attorney's Office were not on the best of terms these days, despite whatever deals they'd made with his sister regarding his early release from Metropolitan Correctional Center, the federal prison where he'd served four months of an eighteen months' sentence. They had, after all, called him a "terrorist" both in open court and directly to the media, and in Kyle's book, that got people a one-way ticket onto his shit list. Because a "terrorist," as any moron with a dictionary knew, was a person who engaged in violence, terror, and intimidation to achieve a result.

He, on the other hand, had just engaged in stupidity.

Miles the doorman checked his watch as Kyle passed by the front lobby desk.

"Can't even give yourself a break on a Saturday night?"

"No rest for the wicked," Kyle said with an easy grin.

He caught an elevator and pushed the button for the thirty-fourth floor, the penthouse. Just before the doors shut, a man in his late twenties wearing jeans and a ski pullover scrambled in. He blinked in recognition when he saw Kyle but said nothing as he pushed the button to the twenty-third floor.

They rode the elevator in silence, but Kyle knew it wouldn't last. Eventually, the other guy would say something. Some people cussed him out, others high-fived him, but they always said something.

When the elevator arrived at the twenty-third floor, the guy glanced over before stepping out. "For what it's worth, I thought the whole thing was pretty funny."

One of the high-fivers. "Too bad you weren't on the grand jury," Kyle said.

He rode the elevator to the top floor, space he shared with two other penthouse apartments. He let himself into his apartment, peeled off the sweaty nylon jacket he wore, and tossed it over the back of one of the bar stools in front of his kitchen counter. Per his instructions, his place had been designed with an open floor plan, with all of the living space except the bedrooms flowing together for an airy feel that complemented the floor-to-ceiling windows that ran along two walls. He had a spectacular view of the lake, although on most days everything outside looked gray and dull. Par for the course for Chicago in March.

"If you ever have to work a deal for me to serve home detention again," he'd joked to his sister, Jordan, when she and their father had been visiting the week before, "make sure the Feds include a provision that says I get to spend the cold months on a beach in Malibu."

Their father, apparently unamused, had walked out of the room to take a phone call.

"Too soon," Jordan had said, shaking her head.

"You have no problem making prison jokes," Kyle pointed out defensively. In fact, his sister had developed quite an annoying knack for them lately.

Jordan had waved around a Mrs. Fields cookie she'd pilfered from a tin in his pantry. "Yeah, but I've known since we were three that you're a moron. Strangely, it took Dad this long to figure it out." She'd smiled sweetly as she took another bite.

"Thanks. Hey, genius—that cookie's five months old." Kyle had chuckled as his sister scrambled for a paper towel.

Later, on her way out the door, Jordan had revisited the issue, more seriously this time. "Don't worry about Dad. He'll get there eventually."

Kyle hoped Jordan was right. For the most part, their father had handled Kyle's very public arrest and conviction as well as could be expected. Like Jordan, Grey had been at all of Kyle's court appearances and had visited him in prison every week. Still, things were a little awkward with his dad these days, and there was no doubt that a man-to-man conversation was in order.

Eventually.

Pushing that issue temporarily aside, Kyle stripped out of his running clothes and took a quick shower. He checked his watch and saw that he had a good half hour before his visitors arrived, so he settled in at the desk in his office to read the evening news on his thirty-inch flat-screen monitor.

After perusing the national news, he skimmed the Tech

section of the *Wall Street Journal*. He exhaled in annoyance when he saw that his upcoming court appearance was the second story on the page.

At least he hadn't been one of the headlines, although he had no doubt that his picture would once again be plastered all over the papers come Tuesday, when the judge ruled on the government's motion. It was ridiculous, really, that one screwup—yes, he'd screwed up, he fully admitted that—had gotten this much attention. People broke the law every day. Okay, several federal laws in his case, but still.

Kyle ignored the *Wall Street Journal* story, not needing to go over the lurid details. He knew full well what he'd done—hell, half the free world knew what he'd done. In legal terms, he'd been convicted of multiple counts of electronic transmission of malicious codes to cause damage to protected computers. In tech terms—language he preferred over all that lawyer-speak—five months ago he'd orchestrated a distributed denial of service attack against a global communications network through the use of a "botnet," a network of computers infected via malware without their owners' knowledge or consent.

Or, in the common vernacular, he'd hacked into Twitter and crashed the site for two days in what was undoubtedly the most boneheaded move of his life.

And the whole thing had started over a woman.

He'd met Daniela, a Victoria's Secret model who lived in New York, at a friend's art show in SoHo, and they'd hit it off instantly. She was beautiful, she had a genuine appreciation for art and photography and could talk passionately about the subject for hours, and she didn't take herself too seriously. They'd spent the entire weekend together in New York, a whirlwind of sex, restaurants, bars, and fun—which was all that Kyle had been looking for at the time.

They had begun casually dating long distance after that, with Kyle flying out to New York a few times over the next several months to see Daniela, and the tabloids had begun to gossip about their relationship. The supermodel and the billionaire heir.

"Imagine that. My brother's dating another model," Jordan had called to say after seeing him and Daniela mentioned in the Scene and Heard column of the *Tribune*. "Ever think about diversifying your portfolio?" she'd asked dryly.

"Why?" he'd said matter-of-factly. "I like dating models."

"Not enough to introduce any of them to me or Dad," she'd shot back.

His sister always did have the most annoying way of pointing out things like that.

It was true, he'd never been in a long-term relationship, and there was one simple reason for that: he *liked* being single. As well he should. Over the course of the last nine years, he'd settled into his life at Rhodes Corporation, climbing up the corporate ladder all the way to executive vice president of network security. He worked hard, but he also liked to play hard, and he saw no reason to tie himself down to one woman. He always kept things light and easy, never promising anything more than a good time for however long things lasted.

Still, Jordan's comment nagged at him. The bachelor scene had begun to feel a little . . . old at times. Sure, a man in his position generally never had problems meeting women, but he was starting to wonder whether casual dating and hot hookups were enough. He'd always assumed he'd settle down at some point—he'd grown up in a happy, loving family and knew that was something he wanted for himself eventually—so he figured, perhaps, it was time he started taking some steps toward that.

With that in mind, he'd begun to spend more weekends with Daniela, either flying out to New York to visit her or paying for her to come to Chicago. He wasn't naïve enough to think their relationship was perfect, but in the nine years he'd played the field, he'd yet to find this so-called "perfect fit" with any woman. So he ignored those concerns—after all, a man could do a lot worse than having a Victoria's Secret model in his bed on a regular basis.

But about six months into their relationship, when Daniela asked about meeting his family, Kyle hesitated. Because he'd never introduced them to a woman before, it seemed like a

huge step. Gigantic. For years, it had been just the three of
them: him, his dad, and Jordan. Together they'd navigated the
often-surreal spotlight they'd been thrust into because of his
father's wealth and, miraculously, had come out mostly normal on the other side. So despite the fact that he'd been dating
Daniela longer than anyone else, and had even twice used the
word *girlfriend* when describing her, he'd hemmed and hawed
and changed the subject without giving her a direct answer.

Perhaps that had been the first sign of trouble.

The following week, Daniela had called him, speaking so
fast that he could barely understand her with her Brazilian
accent. She told him that she'd been cast in a music video—
something she was very excited about, since she wanted to
transition into acting. On her way to Los Angeles, she'd surprised Kyle by stopping in Chicago for a night to celebrate.
A sweet thought, but unfortunately, he had a work conflict
that evening.

"You should've called me first—I'm having dinner tonight
with my entire management team," he'd told her apologeti-
cally. As executive vice president of network security, he liked
to meet at least twice a year with his managers in a nonwork
environment. "We're discussing intrusion prevention, network
access control, and threat response products." He'd winked.
"Very sexy stuff."

Daniela showed zero interest in the subject, which was not
unusual. Actually, Kyle had yet to find a girl who showed any
genuine interest in his job—although many of them were
plenty captivated by the penthouse and Mercedes SLS AMG
it afforded him.

"But if I'd *told* you, it wouldn't have been a surprise." Daniela pouted. "Can't you skip it? What will your father do?
Ground you for not going to some boring meeting with a
bunch of computer nerds?"

Not surprisingly, that comment hadn't gone over so well
with Kyle.

Perhaps their conversations were getting lost in translation,
or maybe she truly didn't care. But Daniela had never seemed
to grasp that his job at Rhodes Corporation was a *real*

position. Not to toot his own horn, but he was a shining star at the company—and it wasn't because he was the boss's son. He was, simply, just that good at what he did.

Nine years ago, Kyle had had his reasons—very private, personal reasons—for dropping out of his PhD program and joining Rhodes Corporation, but the reason he'd stayed at the company for so long was because of the work experience. In his industry, there was no better man to learn from than Grey Rhodes—the billion-dollar empire he'd built from the ground up was concrete proof of that.

That being said, it wasn't all smooth sailing. His father may have been CEO of the company, but Kyle was in charge of network security and insisted on autonomy: he ran his department the way he wanted. True, every now and then he and his father butted heads and stepped on each other's toes . . . well, actually, that happened a lot. But they were professionals, and they worked through it the same way any other CEO and executive VP would work through their issues. His father respected his opinions and had come to see Kyle as his right-hand man.

The problem was, Kyle didn't want to be the right-hand man anymore. He was good, he was ready, and he was driven. But at Rhodes Corporation, there could only be one man at the top. And that spot was taken.

He had ideas. Plans for the future that likely did not match up with those of his father. And the time to put those plans into motion was quickly coming.

That evening, he and Daniela had argued over her comment for almost an hour. In the end, however, Kyle had tried to make amends. She had flown into Chicago to surprise him, after all. He didn't want to spend the entire night fighting, especially since they wouldn't see each other for a couple weeks.

"I'll tell you what," he'd said, putting his arms around her and pulling her closer. "I'll pick up a bottle of champagne on my way home from dinner. We can have a private celebration when I get back."

"Aw, babe, you tempt me," she'd said, kissing his cheek

affectionately. "But I feel like . . . what's the expression? Living it up tonight. I think I'll give Janelle a call. She's in Chicago for a shoot with Macy's. You remember Janelle, don't you? You met in New York that night we had drinks at the Boom Boom Room . . ." her voice trailed off as she strolled into his bathroom, toting her enormous makeup bag.

That night, Daniela didn't get back to Kyle's place until five A.M., only a half hour before he normally woke up to go for his daily run. She let herself into his place with the key he'd given her and passed out cold on his bed, on top of the sheets and snoring, with her Christian Louboutins still on. Kyle didn't bother to wake her, and she was gone, having left for L.A., by the time he came home from work.

That was probably the second sign of trouble.

He didn't hear from Daniela for the next four days. At first, he assumed she was busy with the music video shoot, but when she didn't return any of his calls or text messages, he began to get worried. He knew she sometimes partied hard with her friends, and he'd begun to have nightmare visions of her becoming one of those tragic tales reported on *Access Hollywood*, the supermodel who drank too much and died when she slipped in a hotel bathroom and dropped her five-ton makeup case on her head.

On the fourth night of her trip, he finally got a response.

Via Twitter.

@KyleRhodes Sorry not going 2 work out 4 us. Going 2 chill in LA with someone I met. I think U R sweet but U talk too much about computers.

Kyle had to give her credit; it took skill—plus no heart and a serious abuse of the English language—to break up with someone in fewer than 140 characters. She didn't even have the decency to send him a private message; nope, she'd just tweeted that sucker for anyone and everyone on Twitter to see. But that wasn't the worst of it. Twenty minutes later, Daniela posted another tweet, this time with a link to a video of her making out with movie star Scott Casey in a hot tub.

That sucked.

Kyle felt like he'd been punched in the gut when he saw

the video. He knew they'd had their problems, but what Daniela had done was just so . . . heartless. Particularly since she'd managed to make him look like a complete and utter fool. He could just see the tabloids:

STEAMY SAUNA SCANDAL!!!
Supermodel Cheats on Billionaire Heir

He worked in computers, he knew what would happen—the video would go viral within minutes. Between the wet supermodel in her skimpy bikini, the movie star, and the fact that the damn thing was even cinematically pleasing with the sweeping views of the Hollywood Hills in the background—*everyone* was going to see it.

Not on his watch.

Kyle grabbed the bottle of Scotch from the bar he kept in his home office and slammed a shot. And four more after that for good measure. One thought kept ringing through his head.

Fuck Daniela.

He may not have been a movie star, or the CEO of a billion-dollar corporation, or on the cover of *Time* and *Newsweek*, but he was not some also-ran. He was Kyle Rhodes, and he was a tech god. His specialty was network security, for chrissakes—he could simply hack into Twitter and delete Daniela's tweets and the video from the site, and no one would ever be the wiser.

And he might have gotten away with the whole thing if only he'd stopped there.

But somewhere along the way, as he sat at his computer with his glass in hand, intoxicated and furious, staring at that tweet—that stupid it-was-fun-while-it-lasted-but-fuck-you of a tweet—he had a moment of Scotch-induced clarity. He realized that the true problem lay with social media itself, the perpetuation of a world in which people had become so wholly *un*social that they believed 140-character breakups were acceptable.

So he took down the whole site.

Actually, it wasn't all that difficult. For him, anyway. All he needed was one clever computer virus and about fifty thousand unknowingly infected computers, and he was good to go.

Take that, tweeple.

After he crashed the site, he decided to cut loose. He threw his laptop, his passport, and a change of clothes into a backpack, hopped on a red-eye flight to Tijuana, and proceeded to get shit-faced drunk on cheap tequila for the next two days.

"Why Tijuana?" Jordan had asked him during the brouhaha that followed his arrest.

"It seemed like the kind of place a person could go without being asked any questions," he'd explained with a shrug.

And indeed, it was that. In Tijuana, no one knew, or cared, who he was. He wasn't a guy who'd been cheated on by his supermodel ex-girlfriend. He wasn't an heir, a tech geek, a businessman, a son, or a brother. He was no one, and he loved all forty-eight hours of the anonymity—being the son of a billionaire had deprived him of that freedom long ago.

On the second night of his trip, Kyle had been sitting at the bar he'd made his home for the last two days, nursing what he had decided would be his last shot of the night. He'd never been on a bender before and, like most men, had found it to be an effective way to deal with his problems. But sooner or later, he had to get back to the real world.

The bartender, Esteban, shot Kyle a sideways look as he cleaned some glasses. "You think they're going to catch this guy?" he asked in a heavy Mexican accent.

Kyle blinked in surprise. That was more words than Esteban had uttered to him in two days. He momentarily debated whether this query violated his no-questions policy, then ultimately found it to be acceptable. After all, it wasn't like they were talking about *him*.

"What guy?" he asked.

"This tweeder terrorist," Esteban said.

Kyle waved his glass in front of him. "No clue what a tweeder is, or how you terrorize one, but it sounds like a hell of a story, amigo."

"Oh, you're a funny guy, eh?" Esteban pointed to a television mounted to the wall behind Kyle. "Twee-ter, *pendejo*."

Out of curiosity, Kyle looked over at the television and saw a Mexican news program. His four years of high school Spanish was little help; the female reporter was speaking too fast for him to understand what she was saying. But three words written in bold letters across the bottom of the television screen needed no translation.

El Twitter Terrorista

Kyle choked on his tequila.

Oh . . . *shit*.

He stared at the television screen with growing frustration as he tried to understand what the reporter was saying. It was tough, particularly given the fact that he was about six sheets to the wind, but he did manage to catch the words *policia* and *FBI*.

His stomach churned, and he barely made it out of the bar before he bent over and threw up seven shots of tequila, impaling his forehead on a heretofore unseen cactus in the process.

That sobered him up right quick.

In a panic, he made his way back to the cheap posada that had rented him a room on a cash, no-ID-required basis, and called the one person he could count on when shit-face drunk in Tijuana, bleeding from his forehead, and wanted by the FBI.

"Jordo, I fucked up," he said as soon as she answered the phone.

Likely hearing the anxiety in his voice, she'd gotten right to the heart of the matter. "Can you fix it?"

Kyle knew he had to—ASAP. So as soon as he hung up the phone, he fired up his laptop and stopped the botnet's denial of service attack.

There was only one problem: this time the FBI was waiting for him.

And they had computer geeks, too.

The next morning, sobered and chagrined, Kyle loaded up his backpack and took a taxi to the Tijuana airport. There was a moment before boarding, as he handed over his ticket to the Aeromexico flight attendant, when he thought, *I don't have to go back*. But running wasn't the answer. He figured a man needed to own up to those moments in life when he acted like a complete dickhead, come what may.

When the plane landed at O'Hare Airport, the flight attendants asked the passengers to remain in their seats. Sitting eight rows back, Kyle watched as two men wearing standard-issue government suits—clearly FBI agents—boarded the plane and handed over a document to the pilot.

"Yep, that would be me," Kyle said, grabbing his backpack from underneath the seat in front of him.

The elderly Hispanic man sitting next to him lowered his voice to a whisper. "Drugs?"

"Twitter," Kyle whispered back.

He stood up, backpack in hand, and nodded at the FBI agents that had stopped at his row. "Morning, gentlemen."

The younger agent held out his hand, all business. "Hand over the computer, Rhodes."

"I guess we're skipping the pleasantries," Kyle said, handing over his backpack.

The older agent yanked Kyle's arms behind his back and slapped handcuffs on him. As they read him his rights, Kyle caught a glimpse of what had to be fifty passengers taking photos of him with their camera phones, photos that would later be blasted all over the Internet.

And from that moment on, he ceased being Kyle Rhodes, the billionaire's son, and became Kyle Rhodes, the Twitter Terrorist.

Probably not the best way to make a name for himself.

They brought him to the FBI's offices downtown and left him in an interview room for two hours. He called his lawyers, who arrived posthaste and gravely laid out the charges the FBI planned to bring to the U.S. Attorney's Office. A half hour after his lawyers left, he was transferred to Metropolitan Correctional Center for booking.

"You've got a visitor, Rhodes," the guard said later that afternoon.

They led him to a holding cell, where he waited at a steel table while trying to get used to the sight of himself in an orange jumpsuit and handcuffs. When the door opened and his sister walked in, he smiled sheepishly.

"Jordo," he said, his nickname for her since they were kids.

She hurried over and hugged him tightly, a somewhat awkward exercise with the handcuffs. Then she pulled back and thunked him on the forehead with the palm of her hand. "You *idiot.*"

Kyle rubbed his forehead. "Ouch. That's right where the cactus got me."

"What were you thinking?" she demanded.

Over the course of the next couple weeks, that was the question Kyle would be asked hundreds of times by friends, family, his lawyers, the press, and just about anyone who passed him in the street. He could say that it had something to do with pride, or his ego, or the fact that he'd always been somewhat hot-tempered when provoked. But in the end, it really came down to one thing.

"I just . . . made a mistake," he told his sister honestly. He wasn't the first man to overreact when he discovered his girl was cheating on him, nor would he be the last. Unfortunately, he'd simply been in the unique position to screw up on a global level.

"I told the lawyers that I'm going to plead guilty," he said. No sense wasting the taxpayers' money for a sham of a trial, or wasting his own money in extra legal fees. Especially since he didn't have a defense.

"They're saying on the news that you'll probably go to prison." Jordan's voice cracked on the last word, and her lip trembled.

Hell, no. The last time Kyle had seen his sister cry was nine years ago after their mother's death, and he'd be damned if he let her do that now. He pointed for emphasis. "You listen to me, Jordo, because this is the only time I'm going to say this. Mock me, make all the jokes you want, call me an idiot, but you will not shed a tear over this. Understood? Whatever happens, I will handle it."

Jordan nodded and took a deep breath. "Okay." She looked him over, taking in the orange jumpsuit and handcuffs. Then she cocked her head questioningly. "So how was Mexico?"

Kyle grinned and chucked her under the chin. "That's better." He turned to the subject he'd avoided thinking about since his arrest. "How's Dad taking the news?"

Jordan threw him a familiar you-are-so-busted look. "Remember sophomore year, the night you climbed out the kitchen window to go to Jenny Garrett's party?"

Kyle winced. Did he ever. He'd left the window open so that he would have easy access back in, and their dad had come downstairs to investigate after hearing a strange noise. He'd found Kyle missing and a raccoon eating Cocoa Puffs in the pantry. "That bad, huh?"

Jordan squeezed his shoulder. "I'd say about twenty times worse."

Damn.

AFTER FINISHING HIS review of the evening news, Kyle made the mistake of checking his e-mail. His e-mail address at Rhodes Corporation had been accessible via the website, and though he no longer worked for the company—having turned in his resignation the day he'd been released on bond and thus sparing his father the awkwardness of having to fire him—the messages he received there were forwarded to his personal account.

Every day since he'd been released, he had received hundreds of messages: interview requests from the press, hate mail from some very angry people who seriously needed to take a break from Twitter (*Hey @KyleRhodes—you SUCK, dickwad!!!!!*), and oddly flirtatious overtures from random women who sounded a tad too interested in meeting an ex-con.

After checking to make sure there was nothing of actual importance he needed to respond to, Kyle deleted the entire lot of e-mails. He didn't do interviews, the hate mail wasn't worth answering, and although he may have been in prison for four months and thus in the midst of the longest period of

celibacy of his adult life, he found it generally prudent to avoid
having sex with *crazy* people.

His home phone rang, interrupting his thoughts. It was a
double ring, indicating that the call came from the security
desk in the lobby downstairs.

"Dex is here to see you," Miles the doorman said when
Kyle answered the phone, referring to Kyle's best friend,
Gavin Dexter. Dex was a frequent visitor to Casa Rhodes,
and Miles had consequently dropped the "Mr. Dexter" routine
ages ago.

"And he has several friends with him," Miles continued
with a note of amusement.

"Thanks, Miles. Send them up."

Two minutes later, Kyle opened the door and found his
best friend and a group of at least twenty people standing on
his doorstep. The crowd let out a loud cheer when they saw
him.

Dex grinned. "If Kyle Rhodes can't come to the party, then
the party will come to Kyle Rhodes." He slapped Kyle on the
shoulder, hearty man–style. "Welcome home, buddy."

SOMEWHERE AROUND MIDNIGHT, Kyle finally got a
chance to slip away from the crowd. His twenty-one guests
had nearly tripled, and the penthouse was now packed.

Needing a few moments alone, Kyle stole away to his
office, where he kept a small bar, and poured himself a glass
of bourbon. He took a sip and closed his eyes, savoring the
time before he needed to return to the party. To his so-called
friends.

Not a single one of whom, except Dex, had once bothered
to visit him in prison.

Metropolitan Correctional Center—or MCC, as the
inmates referred to it—was conveniently located in the middle
of downtown Chicago, and Kyle had been there for *four*
months. Yet the entire time, only three people had come to
visit him: his father, his sister, and Dex. For everyone else,
he'd been out of sight, out of mind.

Apparently, Kyle Rhodes wasn't the proverbial man of the hour when he lived in the Big House instead of a penthouse.

Those four months he'd been locked up had been a real eye-opener. At first he'd been angry, then later he'd decided it wasn't worth the effort. He understood now the type of friends they were—people he had fun with and partied with, but it didn't get any deeper than that. Going forward, he would never again make the mistake of thinking anything else.

So much had changed since the day Kyle had been arrested, and frankly, he wasn't sure he'd processed all of it yet. Five months ago, he'd had a successful career at Rhodes Corporation, been dating a Victoria's Secret model, and thought he had a circle of friends he could count on. Now he had no job, no prospects—since no one in his field would ever consider hiring a convicted hacker—and a prison record.

And it didn't take a tech genius to see where he'd taken his first misstep.

Clearly, he and relationships did not mix well. His first— and only—real attempt at a serious commitment and he'd been cheated on, been publicly dumped, and ended up in prison. But as much as he was tempted to blame Daniela for everything, he couldn't blame her for his own stupidity. *He* had been the idiot who'd hacked into Twitter; no one had made him do that. Nor could he entirely fault her for the demise of their relationship. Yes, she was a coldhearted bitch for the way she'd chosen to end things. But he'd realized, as he'd lie awake on those long, cold prison nights, that he'd only had one foot in the relationship from the very start. He'd convinced himself that he was ready for a commitment, but he— and half the free world—had seen just how wrong he'd been about that.

It was a mistake he would not be repeating. At least, not for a long, long time.

But there was an upside: he was awesome at noncommitment. Casual flings? He rocked that scene. Sex? He sure as hell had never had any complaints. So from now on, he was going to stay in his lane. Do what he did best. Trysts, flirtations, seductions, no-holds-barred monkey sex, it was all on the table. But any feelings deeper than a contented afterglow were out.

Just then, Dex popped his head into the office. "Thought you might be in here," he said, stepping into the room.

Kyle held up his glass. "Came in for a refill. Figured it's better than fighting through the crowd out there."

"Is the party too much?"

Kyle pushed away from his desk and headed toward the door. Maybe the party was a *little* much, but he knew Dex meant well. "Not at all," he fibbed with an easy grin. "The party's just what I needed."

"What do you think your friends at the U.S. Attorney's Office would say if they got word of this?" Dex asked with a chuckle.

"Hey, it's called home detention. I'm in my home, aren't I?" And as long as he was abiding by the terms of his supervised release, he didn't give a rat's ass what the U.S. Attorney's Office thought. In three days, he would be free and clear of them.

"Speaking of your friends . . . Selene Marquez just got here," Dex said. "She's asking about you."

"Is she now?" Kyle knew Selene well—quite well. She was twenty-five years old, was a Chicago-based fashion model who did local work while trying to break into the New York scene, and had legs that reached the sky. Pre-Daniela, he and Selene had hooked up occasionally and had always had a good time.

"Maybe I should go say hello. Be the good host and all." Kyle raised a curious eyebrow. "How does she look?"

"Well, if I were a sex-deprived ex-con who'd been locked in prison for the last four months, I'd say she looked pretty damn good." Dex thunked his head. "Oh . . . wait."

"That's real funny, dude. Making jokes about a place where I lived in perpetual fear that I was going to get shanked."

Dex's expression changed, and he looked instantly chagrined. "Shit, I'm an ass. I shouldn't have said . . ." he paused, noticing Kyle's smile. "And . . . you're totally messing with me, aren't you?"

"Yes. Now, as an ex-con who's been locked in prison for

the last four months, I think I'll see for myself how Selene looks." Kyle grabbed Dex's shoulder on the way out. "Thanks, Dex. For everything. I won't forget it."

Dex nodded, knowing exactly what he meant. They'd been friends since college, and nothing further needed to be said. "Any time."

Kyle left the office and worked his way through the crowd. He found Selene in the foyer by the front door, looking spectacular in a silver minidress and three-inch heels.

She smiled when she saw Kyle approaching. "This is some party."

Kyle's eyes skimmed over her. "That's some dress."

"Thanks, I wore it especially." She stepped closer, lowering her voice to a husky whisper. "Maybe later, I can show you what's underneath it." She slid past him, her hand brushing suggestively against his, and headed into the party.

Kyle looked over his shoulder, watching the sway of her hips as she walked away.

This was how things should be. Simple. Easy. No messy feelings or entanglements.

He may not have figured everything out since getting out of prison, but he at least knew that much.

Four

RYLANN HAD NEARLY finished unpacking her suitcases before she realized that she'd been hanging her clothes in only half of the closet.

Clearly, her subconscious needed to get with the program.

Her new Chicago apartment came with exactly *one* of everything: one bedroom, one den, one walk-in closet, one parking space, one set of dishes, one toothbrush, and, most important, one owner. There was no other half.

She grabbed several of her suits off the top rack and hung them in the empty side of the closet. Then she thought they looked sad and pathetic all by themselves, so she stuffed some sweaters on the rack above them. Then her yoga pants and workout gear.

Still not enough.

She hurried back into her bedroom, where a suitcase lay open on the queen bed, and pulled out two black cocktail dresses that were her standard attire at work-related evening events. Back in San Francisco, she'd been active in the California bar association—she'd even served on the ethics committee—and as part of that she'd often attended cocktail parties and dinners with the movers and shakers of the city's legal community. As one of San Francisco's assistant U.S. attorneys—prosecutors who handled federal crimes and were considered to be among the most elite trial lawyers in the criminal justice system—it was a circle she had moved comfortably in.

But she was finding new circles these days. That was, after all, what this move to Chicago was about.

Rylann hung the cocktail dresses on a rack next to her suits and stepped back to survey the results. With the eclectic mix of sweaters, suits, workout clothes, and dresses, it wasn't the most organized closet she'd ever seen, but it would do.

Twenty minutes ago, there'd been a brief moment in her unpacking when she'd faltered a bit. She'd stumbled upon *the* dress, the scarlet V-neck dress she'd been wearing on the night of The Proposal That Never Was, a dress that she probably should've burned for its bad karma except for the fact that it made her chest look a full size bigger. Bad karma or not, that was a pretty magical dress.

Besides, Rylann doubted that Jon, her ex-boyfriend, ever got misty-eyed in his Rome apartment over the clothes he wore on their last night as a couple, so why should she? In fact, given their complete lack of contact over the last five months, she'd hazard a guess that he didn't even remember what he'd been wearing.

Rylann paused, suddenly realizing that she didn't remember what he'd been wearing, either.

Yes. Progress.

She had a six-month plan to get over her ex and was pleased to see that she was on schedule. Actually, she was ahead of schedule—she'd slotted in two days for a temporary relapse after her move to Chicago, but so far she appeared to be doing just fine.

Dark gray suit, light blue shirt, the striped tie she'd bought him "just because" the day after they'd moved in together.

Damn. She did remember what he'd worn that night.

Per her six-month plan, she was supposed to be forgetting details like these. The way that same lock of hair stuck out from the back of his head every morning. The gold flecks in his hazel eyes. How he'd squirmed in his seat when he'd said he didn't know if he wanted to get married.

Actually, she'd probably remember that particular detail for a long time.

They were having dinner at Jardinière, a romantic restaurant in downtown San Francisco. Jon had planned the dinner as a surprise, not giving her any clues. But when they'd been seated and he'd ordered a bottle of Cristal champagne, she'd known. True, they both enjoyed wine, and had bought nice bottles of wine and champagne in the past, but Cristal went beyond their usual splurge. Which could only mean one thing.

He was going to propose.

Perfect timing, had been Rylann's first thought. It was September, which meant she'd have nine months to plan a June wedding. Not that she particularly cared about June, but there were work issues to think about: two of the female assistant U.S. attorneys in her office had just sprung the news that they were pregnant and planned to be off on maternity leave until May. If she and Jon got married in June, after the other AUSAs returned to the office, she'd be able to take two full weeks off for her honeymoon without feeling guilty about sticking someone else with the extra caseload.

After the waiter had poured their champagne, Jon clinked his glass to hers. "To new beginnings," he said with a mischievous look.

Rylann smiled. "To new beginnings."

They each took a sip, then Jon reached across the table and took her hand. As always, he looked handsome in his suit and with his dark hair perfectly styled. On his wrist he wore the watch she'd bought him for his last birthday. She'd spent more money on the gift than she'd intended, but he'd seemed oddly down about turning the big three-five, and she'd decided to splurge to cheer him up.

"So there's something I want to ask you." He stroked her fingers with his thumb. "You know that this last birthday got to me. Since then, I've been doing a lot of thinking about the direction my life is headed. And even though I know what I want, I think I freaked out because it's such a big step." He paused and took a deep breath.

Rylann squeezed his hand reassuringly. "You're nervous."

He chuckled. "A little, maybe."

"Just come out with it," she teased. "We already have the champagne."

With that, Jon looked into her eyes.

"I want to move to Italy."

Rylann blinked.

"Italy?" she repeated.

Jon nodded, the words coming easier for him now. "A spot opened up in our Rome office, and I put my name in." He threw out his hands and laughed like a kid who'd just been told he was going to Disney World. "Italy! How great is that?"

"That is . . . something." Rylann did a mental headshake, trying to make sense of things. Jon was a partner at McKinzey Consulting, and he'd worked his butt off to get there. At times, recently, he'd seemed a bit apathetic about his job, but not once had he ever mentioned transferring to *Italy*.

"What brought all this on?" she asked, feeling as if she were talking to a casual acquaintance and not the man she'd been dating for the last three years.

Jon took a hearty sip of champagne. "It's been on my mind for a while. I don't know . . . I'm thirty-five years old, and I've never really *done* anything. I went to school; I got a job. That basically sums up my life." He gestured offhandedly to her. "Same with you."

Rylann felt a flash of defensiveness at that. "I moved to San Francisco after law school, not knowing a single person out here. I'd say that was pretty adventurous."

"Adventurous?" Jon scoffed. "You moved here because you'd landed a clerkship with a federal appellate judge. Besides, that was seven years ago. Maybe it's time for a new adventure." He grabbed her hand again. "Think about it. We can get an apartment near the Piazza Navona. Remember that trattoria we found there, the one with the yellow awning? You loved that place."

"Why, yes, I did. As a nice place to visit on *vacation*."

"And here comes the sarcasm," Jon said, sitting back in his chair.

Rylann stopped another quip from rolling off her tongue. Fair enough—sarcasm wasn't going to help the situation right then. "I'm just trying to catch up here. This Italy plan seems to be coming out of left field."

"Well, you had to know something was up, with the champagne and everything," Jon said.

Rylann stared at him. Wow. He really had no clue. "I thought you were going to propose."

The silence that followed had to be one of the most awkward and embarrassing moments of her life. And suddenly, she knew that Italy was the least of their problems.

"I didn't think marriage was something you wanted," Jon finally said.

Rylann pulled back in disbelief. "What do you mean? We've talked about getting married. We've even talked about having kids."

"We've also talked about getting a dog and buying a new couch for the living room," Jon said. "We talk about a lot of things."

"That's your answer?" Rylann asked. "We talk about a lot of things?"

Safe to say the sarcastic tone was back.

"I thought you were focused on your career," Jon said.

Rylann cocked her head. Boy, she was really learning all sorts of interesting things tonight. "I wasn't aware that having a family and a career were mutually exclusive."

Jon shifted awkwardly in his chair. "I just meant that I figured marriage and kids were something we'd get around to later. Maybe."

Rylann caught the last word he'd added in there. True, she had focused on her career over the last seven years, and didn't have any regrets about that. Nor, frankly, did she plan to stop being career oriented. And as much as she typically liked plans, she hadn't felt the need to rush things with Jon. She didn't have a specific timeline in mind; she'd simply assumed that they would get married and start a family somewhere in her midthirties.

But now, seeing the way he toyed uncomfortably with his champagne flute, she realized this had become an "if"—not a "when"—situation. And she wasn't willing to settle for that.

"Maybe?" she asked him.

Jon waved his hand, gesturing to the crowded restaurant. "Do we really need to have this conversation now?"

"Yes, I think we do."

"Fine. What do you want me to say, Ry? I've been having second thoughts. Marriage takes a lot of work. Kids take a lot of work. I already kill myself at my job. I make good money, but I never have time to enjoy it. I'm not going to quit or take a leave of absence in this economy, so this transfer seemed like the perfect opportunity to do something for myself."

He leaned in, his expression earnest. "Don't make a bigger deal out of this than it has to be. I love you—at the end of the day, isn't that all that truly matters? Come with me to Italy."

But as Rylann sat there, staring into his dark hazel eyes, she knew it wasn't that simple. "Jon . . . you know I can't go."

"Why not?"

"For one thing, I'm an assistant *United States* attorney. I'm thinking they don't have a lot of job openings for those in Rome."

He shrugged. "I make plenty of money. You don't need to work."

Rylann's gaze sharpened. "If I'm supposedly so focused on my career, that's not really going to sell me on this trip, is it?"

Jon sat back in his chair, saying nothing for a moment. "So that's it?" He gestured angrily. "Going to Italy doesn't fit into your ten-year plan or whatever, so you're just going to choose your job over me?"

Actually, it was a twelve-year plan, and scrapping everything to move to Rome with no job and no prospects definitely wasn't in it, but Jon was conveniently sidestepping the issue. "Moving to Italy might be your dream, but . . . it isn't mine," she said.

"I'd been hoping it could be *our* dream."

Had he now? Rylann rested her arms on the table. Somewhere along the way, this had begun to feel like a cross-examination. "You said you asked for this transfer. Did you tell them you needed to discuss it with me before you committed to going?"

Jon met Rylann's eyes with a look of guilt she recognized well, one she'd seen numerous times on the faces of the criminal defendants she prosecuted.

"No," he said quietly.

She rested her case.

NEARLY SIX MONTHS after that night, Rylann was sitting on her living room floor, unpacking a box that contained half of the Villeroy & Boch dinnerware she and Jon had bought for entertaining. Jon had insisted she have the entire set of ten, but as a final "screw you and your pity," she'd taken only her fair share. Now, however, she was wondering what the heck she was going to do with an incomplete set of china.

Darn pride.

Her cell phone rang, so she put the dinnerware conundrum on hold. She rummaged around on the floor and finally located her phone under a pile of packing paper. She checked the display and saw it was Rae. "Hey, you."

"How's the new apartment?" Rae asked.

Rylann tucked the phone against her shoulder, freeing her hands so she could continue unpacking the box as she talked. "Mostly a disaster right now, since I got a late start. I spent the afternoon walking around, checking out the neighborhood." And she'd nearly frozen her ass off in her trench coat. Apparently, somebody hadn't told the city of Chicago that it was *spring*. "If I remember correctly, somebody had volunteered to come over and help me unpack," she said teasingly.

Rae sounded guilty. "I know. I'm the worst friend in the world. I'm still stuck at work. I've got a summary judgment motion due next week, and the draft this second-year sent me is a piece of crap. I've been rewriting the statement of facts all afternoon. But I think I can be there in about an hour. On the bright side, I've got cupcakes."

Rylann pulled a dessert plate out of the box. "Ooh—nice. We can eat them on my very fancy and incomplete set of china." She looked around. "Seriously, what am I going to do with five sets of dinnerware?"

"You could . . . throw an elaborate dinner party for my imaginary boyfriend, your imaginary boyfriend, and their imaginary third-wheel friend who seemingly never has anything better to do?"

Ouch. "Don't laugh. After Jon and I broke up and he moved to Rome, I *was* that third-wheel friend," Rylann said. Their closest friends in San Francisco had been "couple" friends, and after the breakup, she simply hadn't fit in anymore. One of the many reasons she'd been looking for a fresh start in Chicago. "At least in this city, I'm a first wheel. A unicycle."

Rae laughed. "Very tricky business, unicycling. Particularly in your thirties."

"It's not like I never dated before Jon. How different can it be?"

"Oh, such naïveté." Rae sighed dramatically. "I remember when I, too, was once so hopeful and unjaded." Her tone turned a touch more serious. "Think you're ready for all this?"

As Rylann took in the chaotic state of the apartment—*her* new apartment—Jon's words popped into her head.

Maybe it's time for a new adventure.

"I think I have to be," she told Rae.

Because there was one final piece of the sixth-month plan she was absolutely determined to follow through on.

No regrets, and no looking back.

Five

MONDAY MORNING, WITH her briefcase swinging by her side, Rylann got off the elevator at the twenty-first floor of the Dirksen Federal Building. She made her way to a set of glass doors bearing the familiar Department of Justice seal: an eagle carrying the United States shield with the motto *Qui Pro Domina Justitia Sequitur*, "who prosecutes on behalf of justice."

Seeing that seal helped put Rylann at ease. Sure, she was a little nervous about her first day at the Chicago office, and it felt odd being the new kid on the block again, but she wasn't a junior litigator fresh off a clerkship anymore. She'd prosecuted cases as an assistant U.S. attorney in San Francisco for the last six years; she'd advanced her way up to the special prosecutions division, and she'd had one of the best trial records in the district.

She belonged behind those glass doors, she reminded herself. And the sooner she proved that to everyone else, the better she'd feel. So she took a deep breath—silently vowing to knock 'em dead—and stepped into the office.

The receptionist behind the desk smiled in greeting. "Good to see you again, Rylann. Ms. Lynde said that you'd be starting today. I'll let her know you're here."

"Thanks, Katie." Rylann stepped off to the side, standing before a panoramic photograph of the Chicago skyline. She was somewhat familiar with the office, having gone on a tour last month when she'd flown in to interview for the open AUSA position. Spanning across four floors of the Federal

Building, the office employed approximately 170 lawyers, two
dozen paralegals, and a large administrative and support staff.

Timing-wise, Rylann had gotten lucky with this transfer.
She'd been looking for a fresh start after her breakup with
Jon, and thus had been relieved when she'd heard that the
Department of Justice had opened up a new AUSA slot for
the Northern District of Illinois. Since she'd grown up in the
Chicago suburbs and had always considered the possibility
of returning one day to be closer to her family and Rae, she'd
leapt at the chance.

Rylann smiled when she saw an attractive woman with long,
chestnut-brown hair and a welcoming look in her aquamarine
eyes coming down the hallway. As she had been during her
interview, she was struck by how relatively young Cameron
Lynde was for a U.S. attorney—thirty-three, only a year older
than Rylann herself. Formerly the top AUSA in Chicago, Cameron had been appointed to the position after the former U.S.
attorney, Silas Briggs, had been arrested and indicted on public
corruption charges. The arrest of such a prominent political
figure had caused quite a stir—both within the Department of
Justice and in the media—and had been the topic of gossip
among all the assistant U.S. attorneys for weeks.

When interviewing, that had been Rylann's one concern—
transferring to an office that had recently experienced such
significant upheaval—but she'd walked away from the meeting with only positive impressions of Cameron. From what
she surmised, the new U.S. attorney was driven and ambitious
and eager to restore a good name to the Chicago office.

Cameron stuck out her hand. "It's good to see you again,
Rylann," she said warmly. "We've been counting down the
days to your arrival." She gestured to the stack of case files
she carried in her other hand. "As you can see, we're swamped
around here. Come with me—I'll show you to your office."

While making small talk, Rylann followed Cameron down
an internal staircase to the twentieth floor. The setup of the
office was similar to that of the one in San Francisco, with the
assistant U.S. attorneys in the exterior offices, and the support
staff and paralegals working from desks and cubicles in the

interior space. If she recalled correctly, all twenty-seven AUSAs in the special prosecutions division were located on this floor.

"So when I spoke to Bill after your interview," Cameron led in, referring to Rylann's former boss, the U.S. attorney for the Northern District of California, "he said that I'm supposed to ask why the San Francisco FBI agents call you 'Meth Lab Rylann.'"

Rylann groaned. Although, secretly, she didn't mind the moniker *that* much. "They gave me that nickname my first year on the job, and I've never been able to shake it."

Cameron looked curious. "So? Let's hear the story."

"I'll give you the abridged version. I was the second chair on a multiple-count organized crime and drug case, and was scheduled to meet the two FBI agents who'd handled the investigation at this underground meth lab. What the agents failed to mention before I got there was that the only way to get into the meth lab was to climb through a hatch in the ground and climb down a rusty, rickety fifteen-foot ladder. And since I'd been in court earlier that morning, I happened to be wearing a skirt suit and heels. Most inconveniently."

Cameron chuckled. "Come on. The agents had to be messing with you—how could they forget to mention that?"

Walking side by side with Cameron, Rylann didn't disagree. "I think they might have been testing the new girl, sure."

"What did you do?"

"The only thing I could do," Rylann said matter-of-factly. "I climbed through the hatch in my skirt suit and went down that rusty, rickety fifteen-foot ladder."

Cameron laughed. "Good for you." She stopped in front of a midsized office. "Here we are."

The bronze nameplate outside the door said it all:

RYLANN PIERCE
ASSISTANT U.S. ATTORNEY

Rylann stepped inside. It wasn't a glamorous office, with dark blue carpeting and fairly inexpensive furniture, but as a senior AUSA, she at least had a view of the Hancock building and Lake Michigan.

"Everything should be virtually the same as your old office," Cameron said. "Luckily, we don't have to waste time training you on the phones and computer, since you're familiar with those already. Oh, one thing I wanted to be sure of: you're on active status with the Illinois bar, correct?"

Rylann nodded. "Yes. I'm good to go." She had taken the Illinois bar exam the summer after graduating from law school and had gone back on active status as soon as she'd learned she'd gotten the job in Chicago.

"Perfect. With that said . . ." Cameron handed the stack of files over to Rylann. "Welcome to Chicago." She cocked her head. "Am I going too fast?"

"Not at all," Rylann assured her. "Just point me in the direction of the courtrooms, tell me where the nearest Starbucks is, and I'll be all set."

Cameron grinned. "The Starbucks is right across the street—follow the herd of people sneaking out of the office at three o'clock every afternoon and you'll find it. The courtrooms are on the twelfth through eighteenth floors." She gestured to the stack of files Rylann held. "Why don't you take the morning to review the case files? Feel free to swing by my office this afternoon with any questions you might have."

"That sounds great, Cameron. Thank you."

"You're actually the first AUSA I've hired since taking over. How am I doing so far with the welcome speech?"

"Not bad. The part where you softened me up by asking about the meth lab story was a nice touch."

With a laugh, Cameron looked her over approvingly. "I think you're going to fit in just fine around here, Rylann." She paused in the doorway before leaving. "I almost forgot. You should probably check out the top file first—there's a motion call tomorrow morning. The AUSA who'd originally handled the case had a trial unexpectedly rescheduled for this week, so I needed somebody in special prosecutions to cover for him. It's an agreed motion, so I don't expect you'll have any trouble. There'll be reporters, but just go with the usual response—that we're satisfied with the resolution of the matter, have no further comment, that kind of thing. You've been doing this for a while now, so you know the drill."

The prosecutor in Rylann was instantly intrigued. "Reporters for an agreed motion? What kind of case is it?" Curious, she opened the file folder on top of the stack and read the caption.

United States v. Kyle Rhodes

Thank God her six years as a trial lawyer had given her one damn good poker face; otherwise, her jaw would've hit the floor right then.

You've got to be shitting me.

Just seeing the name brought forth a sudden rush of memories. The amazing blue eyes and sexy smile. The lean, muscular, made-for-sin body. His mouth covering hers as she pressed closer to him in the moonlight.

Probably not the best time to let her new boss know that she'd *kissed* the defendant in her first case.

"The Twitter Terrorist case," Rylann said casually. Sure, she may have been taken aback by this unexpected turn of events, but no one else would ever know that. Once upon a time, Kyle Rhodes had made her heart skip a beat with just a kiss, but that had been nearly a decade ago. Now she was Meth Lab Rylann—and on the job, she never let anyone see her flustered.

"I figured that would be a fun one to give the new girl." Cameron paused on her way out the door. "Feel free to stop by my office anytime. My door is always open."

After she left, Rylann peered down at the mug shot of Kyle that was paper-clipped to the top of the file. Not surprisingly, he looked serious and chagrined in the photograph, a far cry from the devil-may-care charmer who'd once walked her home on a warm May night in Champaign.

She wondered if he would even remember her.

Not that this mattered much, obviously. She had no doubt that Kyle Rhodes had kissed many a woman in the last nine years—and done a helluva lot more than that—so she considered it quite probable that he wouldn't so much as blink when she walked into the courtroom tomorrow. Which was just fine with her. After all, what *she* remembered about that night was that her first impression of him hadn't been all that favorable.

And if her second and third impressions had been any different . . . well, she would forever plead the Fifth on that one. Because a serious federal prosecutor like herself did not get all hot-and-bothered over the criminal defendants she faced off against in court.

Not even a criminal defendant who'd once said he would drive two hours to take her out for chicken wings.

Luckily, that was ancient history. Yes, the circumstances of their "reunion" were ironic, perhaps even laughable, but at the end of the day she would treat Kyle Rhodes no different from the many other felons she'd encountered during her career as an assistant U.S. attorney. She was a professional, after all.

And tomorrow, she would prove just that.

Six

"KYLE! KYLE! WHAT are your plans for the future now that you're a convicted hacker?"

"Have you spoken to Daniela since your arrest?"

Seated at the defense table in the front of the courtroom, Kyle ignored the questions and the flashes of the cameras behind him. They would get bored with him eventually, he told himself. In less than an hour, he would have his freedom, and then this would all be over.

"Do you plan to make Facebook your next target?" another reporter screamed out.

"Would you like to make a statement before the judge comes in?" someone else yelled.

"Sure, here's a statement," Kyle growled under his breath, "let's get this show on the road so I don't have to listen to anymore dumbass questions."

Sitting next to him, one of his lawyers—inexplicably, there were five of them today—leaned over and spoke in a hushed tone. "Maybe we should handle all inquiries from the press."

The courtroom door suddenly opened, and cameras began flashing wildly. A low murmur spread through the crowd, and Kyle knew it could mean only one thing: either his sister or his father had walked in.

He looked over his shoulder and saw Jordan walking up the aisle in her oversized sunglasses and cashmere coat. She wore her blond hair—which was several shades lighter than his—pulled back in some sort of knot or bun thing and coolly ignored the reporters as she took a seat in the front row of the gallery, directly behind Kyle.

Kyle turned around to face her and blinked at the multitude of flashes that instantly exploded in his eyes. "I told you not to take off work for this," he grumbled.

"And miss your big finale? No way." Jordan grinned. "I'm all *atwitter* to see how things turn out."

Ha, ha. Kyle opened his mouth to retort—five months ago he'd given his sister free license to make jokes and, boy, had she ever run with that—when she took off her sunglasses, revealing a big, ugly yellow bruise on her cheek.

Aw . . . hell.

No way could he say anything sarcastic now. Kyle doubted he would ever stop feeling guilty over the fact that his sister had gotten that bruise and a broken wrist—and had nearly been *killed*—while working with the FBI as part of a deal to get him out of prison.

His fingers curled instinctively into a fist, thinking it was a good thing that the dickhead who'd caused those injuries was behind bars. Because a bruised cheek and a broken wrist would be the least of Xander Eckhart's problems if Kyle ever got five minutes alone with the guy. Yes, Jordan was a pain in the ass, but still. Kyle had clearly set the rules back in sixth grade, when he'd given Robbie Wilmer a black eye for de-pantsing Jordan on the playground in front of the whole school.

No one messed with his sister.

So he humored Jordan's Twitter joke with a smile. "That's cute, Jordo." Then he frowned as a dark-haired, well-built man wearing a standard-issue government suit walked into the courtroom.

"You invited Tall, Dark, and Sarcastic?" Kyle asked Jordan as Special Agent Nick McCall approached them. Despite the fact that his sister was now practically living with the guy, he and Nick were still circling each other warily. Since Kyle had been in prison the entire time Jordan and the FBI agent had been dating, he hadn't been around to see their relationship develop. All he knew was that Nick McCall was suddenly *there*, in their lives, and Kyle was therefore being a little . . . cautious before welcoming him into the family.

"Be nice, Kyle," Jordan warned.

"What?" he asked innocently. "When have I ever not been nice to Tall, Dark, and You Can't Be Serious About This Guy?"

"I like him. Get used to it."

"He's FBI. The guys who arrested me, remember? Where's your sense of family loyalty?"

She pretended to think. "Remind me again—why was it that they arrested you? Oh, right. Because you broke about eighteen federal laws."

"Six federal laws. And it was *Twitter*!" he shot back, perhaps a bit too loudly.

Seeing his five lawyers exchange if-this-guy-implodes-do-we-still-get-our-five-thousand-an-hour looks, Kyle sat back in his chair and adjusted his tie. "I'm just saying that we could all use a bit of perspective here."

"Hey, Sawyer—I'd recommend not using the 'It was Twitter' argument when the judge comes out," Nick said with a confident grin as he took a seat next to Jordan.

Kyle looked up at the ceiling and counted to ten. "Tell your FBI friend that I don't answer to that name, Jordo." In fact, he hated that nickname—one he'd earned in prison because of a resemblance he supposedly bore to a certain character on *Lost*.

"But the 'Rhodes' nickname was already taken," Nick said. He took Jordan's hand, the one with the cast, and gently stroked her fingers as their eyes met.

When Kyle saw Jordan smile at the FBI agent—some sort of secret, inside-joke-type smile—he reluctantly had to admit that the two of them appeared very into each other. It was weird to have to watch them being all affectionate—and kind of gross, actually, seeing how she was his sister—but sweet nonetheless.

Just then, another murmur flowed through the crowd, and everyone stopped and stared as business entrepreneur and billionaire Grey Rhodes strolled in wearing a tailored navy suit.

He took a seat on the other side of Jordan. "Hope I didn't miss anything. I've been *twittering* with excitement all morning."

Jordan laughed. "Good one, Dad."

Shaking his head, Kyle turned around in his seat and faced the front of the courtroom. Seriously, there were times when he thought that his family would actually be disappointed when this whole debacle was over. He half-expected to see them pull out popcorn and Cokes while they waited for the That Kyle Sure Is a Funny Asshole show to get started.

Speaking of assholes, Kyle checked his watch and looked over at the empty prosecution table. "Where's Morgan?" he asked his lawyers, referring to the assistant U.S. attorney who'd called him a terrorist and demanded the maximum sentence. Not that Kyle had expected a mere slap on the wrist for his crimes. But he was no fool—the U.S. Attorney's Office had sensationalized his case, seizing on the chance to make a name for themselves by dragging *his* name through the mud. He highly doubted they would've demanded the maximum prison sentence if he hadn't been the son of a billionaire—and his lawyers had said the same exact thing.

"Actually, Morgan's not coming today," said Mark Whitehead, the lead defense attorney, in response to Kyle's question. "He had a conflict with another trial. A new guy filed an appearance yesterday afternoon; I don't remember his name. Ryan something."

"So I don't get to say good-bye to Morgan in person?" Kyle asked. "Aw, that's a shame. We had such a special connection— it's not every day a man calls you a 'cyber-menace to society.'"

The door to the courtroom slammed open.

Kyle turned around, curious to check out this mope the U.S. Attorney's Office had rustled up on short notice, and—

Well, hello.

Those certainly didn't look like a mope's legs.

Sitting in his chair at the defense table, Kyle's gaze traveled from the ground up, taking in the high heels, sleek legs, black skirt suit and naughty good-girl pearls, and finally came to rest on a pair of gorgeous—and shockingly familiar— amber eyes.

Eyes that held his with bemusement.

Ho-ly fuck.

Rylann.

Kyle watched as she strode up the aisle toward him, looking criminally sexy in her suit and heels. She'd changed her hair—gone was the cute chin-length bob. Now she wore it long, tumbling over her shoulders in thick, raven-colored waves.

"Good morning, gentlemen," she said, stopping at the defense table. "Only the six of you today?"

Kyle fought back a grin. Yep, still as sassy as ever. His five lawyers immediately sprang to attention and rose to their feet. Slowly, he stood up as well.

Rylann introduced herself as she shook Mark's hand. "Rylann Pierce."

Pierce. After nine years, Kyle finally had a last name.

She shook hands with the rest of his lawyers, then made her way to him. With the edges of her lips turned up in a smile, she held out her hand. Her voice was low and throaty, with the same teasing note as the night they'd met. "Mr. Rhodes."

Kyle slid his hand around hers. The most innocent of touches, but with her it felt downright sinful. "Counselor," he said in a low voice, as intimate as he dared given their surroundings.

She cocked her head. "Shall we do this?"

It was only after she turned and walked to the opposite side of the courtroom that Kyle realized she'd been talking to his lawyers, not him.

She set her briefcase on the prosecution table just as the door to the judge's chambers flew open. "All rise!" called the clerk. "This court is now in session, the Honorable Reginald Batista presiding."

Everyone in the courtroom rose to their feet as the judge took his seat and the clerk called his case. "United States versus Kyle Rhodes."

Rylann stepped up to the podium along with Kyle's lead attorney.

"Rylann Pierce, representing the U.S. Attorney's Office, your honor."

"Mark Whitehead, for the defense."

The judge looked up from the motion he held in his hands.

"Since both parties and what appears to be the entire Chicago press corps are in attendance, we might as well get right down to business." He set the papers off to the side. "We're here on a rather unusual Rule 35 motion filed by the U.S. Attorney's Office, a motion to reduce the sentence of the defendant, Kyle Rhodes, to time served. My understanding is that Mr. Rhodes has served four months of the eighteen months' incarceration ordered by this court." The judge turned to Mark for confirmation. "Is that correct, counselor?"

"Yes, Your Honor," Mark said. "Two weeks ago, per an arrangement with the U.S. Attorney's Office, Mr. Rhodes was released from Metropolitan Correctional Center and has been serving his sentence in home detention."

The judge took off his reading glasses and turned to Rylann. "Ms. Pierce, I've seen the appearance you filed yesterday with the clerk's office, and I appreciate that you haven't been involved in this case prior to these proceedings. But I have to say, I'm a little surprised by this motion. During the sentencing hearing, your office argued—quite vehemently—that I should order Mr. Rhodes to serve the maximum sentence. I believe *terrorist* and *cyber-menace to society* were two of the terms Mr. Morgan used to describe the defendant. Now, four months later, you want to reduce that sentence to time served."

Kyle shot a nervous glance at the four lawyers sitting at his table, not liking the sound of that. He'd been under the impression that this motion was a done deal.

Then a beautiful voice spoke out on his behalf.

"The circumstances have changed, Your Honor," Rylann said. "The U.S. Attorney's Office, in conjunction with the Federal Bureau of Investigation, made an arrangement with the defendant's sister, Jordan Rhodes. In exchange for Ms. Rhodes's assistance in an undercover investigation, our office agreed to petition this court for the reduction of Mr. Rhodes's sentence. Ms. Rhodes upheld her end of the deal, and now we would like to honor ours."

"And while I note that this court is not bound by any agreements the government has made pertaining to the defendant,

I'm going to grant your motion, counselor," the judge said. "The defendant's sentence is hereby reduced to time served."

Kyle blinked. Just like that, he was free.

Then the judge turned to him, peering down sternly from his bench. "But do us all a favor, Mr. Rhodes: stay off of Twitter. Because if I see you in my courtroom again, there won't be any deal that can save you." He banged his gavel. "This court stands in recess."

"All rise!" the clerk shouted, and the entire courtroom rose to its feet.

Pandemonium ensued as an excited roar rippled through the crowd. Cameras flashed in Kyle's eyes as a mass of bodies, including his lawyers, Jordan, and his dad, swarmed him. Reporters surged forward, eager for a quote, but Kyle pushed past them, catching sight of Rylann as she grabbed her briefcase and turned to leave.

They met in the center of the aisle just as several reporters shoved microphones in both their faces.

"Ms. Pierce! Does the U.S. Attorney's Office have any comment about the fact that Kyle Rhodes is once again a free man?"

When Rylann's eyes met his, Kyle felt as if every nerve in his body had been zapped with a body Taser.

He peered down at her boldly, remembering well this woman who'd managed to get under his skin—in more ways than one—with only a walk home. He waited for her to say something, any kind of quip or wink or subtle nod to the fact that they had a prior history. But just as her lips parted, undoubtedly ready with what he assumed would be some sort of saucy zinger, another camera flashed.

She blinked—and the sparkle was gone from her eyes, replaced by an all-business expression as she turned to the reporters. "Only that we are satisfied with the resolution of this case."

Then, without so much as a glance back in his direction, she brushed past the reporters and walked out of the courtroom.

Seven

THURSDAY EVENING AFTER work, Rylann met Rae for dinner at RL Restaurant on Michigan Avenue. It had been a busy couple of days for both of them, with Rylann settling into her first week at her new office and Rae scrambling to get a motion on file, so this was the first chance they'd had to get together since Rylann's in-court reunion with Kyle.

A reunion she'd thought about more these past couple days than she cared to admit.

"I can't believe you haven't said anything yet," Rylann led in after the waiter brought their drinks. "Have you been following the news at all this week? Perhaps you heard a little something about a certain smug-dimpled ex-con?" She'd been dying to talk to somebody about the court appearance, and naturally that person was Rae.

Rae put down the menu she'd been reading. "Oh my God, yes—I've been meaning to ask you about that since Tuesday. I've just been so swamped with this summary judgment motion. I saw that the judge reduced Kyle Rhodes's sentence to time served."

Rylann smiled to herself, savoring the deliciousness of the gossip she was about to share. "This is true. But I take it you didn't see any of the billion photographs from the court hearing?" There'd been one particular photograph that had been blasted all over the media that had slightly concerned her, a shot of her and Kyle right at that very moment when they'd met in the courtroom aisle. Maybe she was being overly paranoid, but something about the way Kyle was peering down at her looked a little . . . intimate. As if they shared a secret.

Which, of course, they did.

"Sorry. I missed it," Rae said sheepishly. "I've been living in a hole since Monday."

"A hole that also kept you from noticing the name of the assistant U.S. attorney who handled the motion, obviously," Rylann said.

She was *so* enjoying this.

Rae shrugged. "I assume it's the same lawyer who handled the rest of the case."

Rylann casually took a sip of the pinot noir she'd ordered. "One would assume that, yes. Except—oh, small problem— the original lawyer assigned to the case had a last-minute trial conflict, and my office needed to send in a replacement." She smiled mischievously.

Rae stared at her for a moment, then her eyes went wide. "Shut up. They sent *you*?"

"Indeed they did."

"You went up against Kyle Rhodes in court?" Rae laughed. "Well, that's certainly an interesting way to reconnect after nine years. What did he say when he saw you?"

"He called me 'counselor.'"

Rae sat back in her chair, disappointed. "That's it? What did you say?"

"I said, 'Mr. Rhodes,' and shook his hand."

"Ooh . . . scintillating stuff."

Rylann threw her a pointed look. "We were in court, in front of a hundred reporters. What was I supposed to do? Write my phone number on his hand and tell him to call me?"

Rylann smiled. "Now that would've been cute."

"I don't do cute. Especially not in court." Rylann paused. "Although the 'counselor' thing is sort of an inside joke between him and me."

"Is it now?" Rae's tone turned suddenly sly. "So how did he look, counselor?"

Like sin in a suit. Rylann held her tongue, playing it cool.

"He's wearing his hair a little longer. Other than that, I didn't notice. I was in the zone."

"Which zone is that?"

"The prosecutorial zone, naturally."

"Then why are you blushing?"

Because, in addition to being cursed with fair skin from her Irish mother, she doubted there were many women in existence who wouldn't have some basic, instinctive physical reaction to Kyle Rhodes. With that devilish smile and those roguish good looks, any girl would be hard-pressed not to get a little flushed when thinking about him.

Still, Rylann covered by gesturing to her glass. "It's the antioxidants in the red wine. They open up the pores."

Rae smiled, not buying that for one second. "Right. So what happens next?"

"Nothing happens next. He's the Twitter Terrorist. I'm a prosecutor from the office who convicted him. I think that pretty much ends the story."

Rae thought about that. "Kind of an anticlimactic ending."

Rylann shrugged, adopting a matter-of-fact expression. "He walked me home, and we kissed once. Forever ago. I barely even remember that night."

Rae raised an eyebrow knowingly. "There are some things a girl never forgets, Ry. And one of those is a kiss from the right guy."

WHEN RYLANN GOT back to her apartment later that evening, she dropped her briefcase on the living room couch and unbuttoned her trench coat as she made her way to the bedroom. As she stepped into her walk-in closet and hung up the coat, Rae's words echoed through her head.

There are some things a girl never forgets, Ry. And one of those is a kiss from the right guy.

The notion was a little sentimental for her tastes.

She was a grown woman—thirty-two years old, not thirteen. Meth Lab Rylann did not get all weak in the knees over one measly kiss, no matter how irritatingly charming Kyle Rhodes had been that night.

Still . . . instinctively, her eyes went to the top shelf of the closet.

Shoved near the back was an old shoebox, one she'd had for years. On the day they'd moved in together in San Francisco, Jon had asked her what was inside.

"Just some old letters my mom sent me when I went away to college," she'd told him, perhaps the only time she'd lied to Jon the entire time they'd been dating.

Reaching up, Rylann grabbed the box off the shelf and removed the lid.

Inside was the navy flannel shirt Kyle had given her nine years ago.

She ran her fingers over the collar, remembering that moment when he'd handed the shirt over to her. The way her stomach had done a little flip as his hand brushed against her neck.

Okay, fine. Maybe she remembered a few teeny, tiny details about that night.

Rylann shook her head, wanting to laugh at herself as she stared down at the flannel. It was just so . . . silly. It was a *shirt*. Really, she had no idea why she'd kept the darn thing all this time. She'd moved from Champaign to San Francisco, and then into a different apartment when her and Jon had decided to live together, and each time she'd contemplated tossing it in the garbage. But something had held her back.

I saw you laughing with your friends, and your smile sucked me right in.

There'd been a spark between her and Kyle, whether she'd wanted to admit it or not. They'd spent less than thirty minutes together, but she'd felt it. Instant butterflies. Not with any other man, including Jon, had she ever experienced that.

"Pull it together, Pierce," she whispered to herself. This was not a road she needed to go down.

Because, simply, it didn't matter now.

They weren't fresh-faced grad students anymore. Kyle

Rhodes was an ex-con, and she was an assistant U.S. attorney. There was no place to go from there. She wasn't going to reach out to him, and after the way she'd brushed him off in the courtroom, she highly doubted that he would try to get in touch with her, either. So that was . . . that.

Slowly, Rylann put the lid back on the shoebox and returned it to its place on the back of her shelf. Out of sight.

And this time, out of mind. For good.

Eight

THE FOLLOWING MORNING, Rylann knocked on Cameron's door, pausing when she saw that the other woman was on the phone. With a welcoming look, Cameron gestured for Rylann to take a seat in one of the chairs in front of her desk.

"I've got to run, Collin, I've got some people in my office," Cameron said to the person on the other end of the line. "Yes, I am a very important person. I know it kills you to share the spotlight." She smiled at Rylann as she hung up the phone. "Sorry about that. Old friend."

She folded her hands on top of her desk. "So. I have an interesting matter I'd like to discuss with you. But first, I wanted to check in and see how your first week has been going."

"It's going well," Rylann said. "I think I've met almost all of the AUSAs in special prosecutions, and they seem like a great group." In fact, the only one she hadn't met yet was the elusive Cade Morgan, the prosecutor who had originally handled the Twitter Terrorist case.

"It is a great group," Cameron agreed. "I used to be in special prosecutions before they moved me up."

Rylann held back a laugh at that, appreciating the modesty. Cameron had been appointed to the position of U.S. attorney by the president of the United States—that was a bit of a bigger deal than simply being "moved up."

Cameron switched gears, ready to get down to business. "The FBI has recently briefed me on an investigation that I'd like you to handle. It's a somewhat sensitive matter, and one that I suspect will require an experienced AUSA in light of certain circumstances that I'll get to in a few moments."

Rylann was already interested. "What kind of case is it?"

"A homicide case. Two weeks ago, an inmate named Darius Brown was found dead in his cell at Metropolitan Correctional Center. Apparently, Brown was attacked in the middle of the night by his cell mate, a man named Ray Watts, who beat Brown to death with a makeshift weapon—a padlock attached to a belt. By the time the guards became aware of the attack and got to the cell, Brown was already unconscious. They rushed him to the medical facilities, where he died shortly thereafter."

Cameron reached into a file on her desk and tossed a mug shot of a man with close-cropped blond hair in his late twenties. "That's Watts, the cell mate. Currently serving two life sentences for first-degree murder and arson. He's a member of the Brotherhood, a local white supremacist group, and was convicted four years ago after he and two other members of the group firebombed the home of an African American man who'd recently opened a convenience store in Watts's neighborhood. Both the store owner and his wife were killed."

"Sounds like Watts is a real model citizen," Rylann said humorlessly. No matter how many times she heard stories like this, they still got to her. And if the day ever came when that stopped happening, it would be time to hang up her briefcase.

"He's a model inmate, too," Cameron said, just as dryly. "Apparently, he has a reputation of being very violent at MCC. Because of that, he'd been in a cell by himself for three months before Brown was transferred in with him."

She rested her arms on the desk, continuing. "Here's how this ended up on *my* desk. The FBI has a man, Agent Griegs, who's been working undercover as an inmate at MCC in an unrelated investigation. During this time, he's been passing along any information related to the goings-on at the prison that he believes the FBI might want to know about. After Brown was killed by Watts, the undercover agent told his contact that the attack seemed suspicious. Another agent,

Special Agent Wilkins, was subsequently brought in to take charge of the investigation.

"What immediately jumped out at Agent Wilkins was the timing of Brown's death. Brown, who is African American, had been moved into Watts's cell just two days prior to the attack—a transfer that had been arranged by a prison guard named Adam Quinn. Naturally, Agent Wilkins interviewed Quinn, and that's where things got really interesting.

"During the interview, Quinn became nervous and agitated when asked why Brown had been transferred to Watts's cell. The prison guard claimed that he'd set up the transfer because, per policy, inmates weren't supposed to get cells to themselves. But Quinn was unable to offer any reason why—when the prison had previously allowed Watts to be in a cell by himself for three months—he suddenly decided to follow this alleged policy. Nor did Quinn have an explanation as to why he'd chosen Brown to be Watts's cell mate."

"Which is suspicious in and of itself given Watts's history of racially motivated violence." Rylann paused, her mind already working through the fact pattern. "Did Agent Wilkins confirm whether there is a policy that inmates can't be in cells by themselves?"

"The warden said that while that is the general rule, they have made exceptions in the past for inmates like Watts who are particularly aggressive." Cameron proceeded on. "Not surprisingly, Agent Wilkins decided to dig a little deeper. In reviewing Brown's prison records, he found something very unusual. As it turns out, Quinn, the *guard*, had been attacked by Brown two weeks before Brown was killed."

Rylann's prosecutorial radar went on high alert. "What were the circumstances of that attack?"

"Apparently, Brown grabbed Quinn's forearm when he was collecting Brown's food tray and pulled it hard enough to dislocate the guard's wrist."

Rylann sat back in her chair. "Let me summarize to make sure I have this all straight. Brown attacks a prison guard and dislocates the guard's wrist. Two weeks later, Brown is transferred by that guard into the cell of one of the most violent inmates in the prison, a white supremacist no less, and is beaten to death." She looked at Cameron across the desk. "I assume we're thinking the same thing here: that Quinn engineered this attack in retaliation."

"That's exactly what Agent Wilkins suspected, so he kept digging," Cameron said. "Not surprisingly, Brown had been put in disciplinary segregation for a week after he attacked Quinn. When he came out, he told some of his inmate friends that the guard came to his cell one night and threatened him."

Rylann cocked her head. "What was the threat?"

"Brown claimed that Quinn said, 'You're gonna pay for what you did to my wrist, you piece of shit.'"

"Do we know if anyone heard that threat?" Rylann asked.

"We don't know yet. But I'll circle back to that in a minute," Cameron said. "After that, Agent Wilkins took a look at Quinn's personnel files and discovered that in the last year, the prison guard had been involved in two other altercations with inmates. And on both of those occasions, shortly thereafter the inmate was attacked and beaten by another prisoner."

She gave Rylann a moment to process this.

"So we've got a prison guard who doesn't like it when inmates step out of line," Rylann said. "But instead of getting his own hands dirty to retaliate, he uses other inmates to do the job for him. This time, however, he got carried away, picked the wrong inmate, and a man ended up dead."

"Thankfully, the undercover agent tipped us off. Otherwise, this might have gone unnoticed, just a fight between two inmates gone wrong." There was a gleam in Cameron's eye. "Which brings me back to your question—whether anyone heard Quinn threaten Brown."

Rylann had a feeling she knew what that look meant. "I'm guessing we have a witness."

"We *may* have a witness," Cameron said. "The FBI has identified an inmate who was also in disciplinary segregation on the night Brown claimed Quinn threatened him. In the cell right next to Brown, as a matter of fact. Unfortunately, we don't yet know what, if anything, this other inmate actually heard."

"Why not?" Rylann asked. "Is he refusing to talk?"

"For starters, this inmate isn't actually an inmate anymore. He was released from MCC just before Brown was killed. It's likely he doesn't even know that Brown is dead."

Rylann was still missing something here. "Why didn't the FBI simply talk to him at home?"

"They tried," Cameron said. "So far, they haven't been able to get past his lawyers. Which is why they brought the case to us. If we want to talk to this man, we're likely going to need a grand jury subpoena to do it. I doubt he'll cooperate voluntarily." She peered across the desk at Rylann, looking slightly amused. "He's probably feeling a little prickly toward the U.S. Attorney's Office these days. Especially since we called him a 'terrorist' and a 'cyber-menace to society.'"

Rylann blinked. "*Kyle Rhodes* is potentially our key witness?"

"Potentially *your* key witness," Cameron emphasized. "Starting now, Rylann, the case is all yours. One Twitter Terrorist included."

So much for out of sight, out of mind.

"Strange, how he keeps popping up in my cases these days," Rylann said. She hadn't seen the guy for nine years, and now he kept turning up like a bad penny. A *very* bad penny.

Wickedly, dangerously bad.

Cameron acknowledged this with a nod. "The motion call was pure happenstance. I needed a senior AUSA in special prosecutions to cover for Cade, and you, being the new kid on the block, had an open schedule. But when the FBI brought the Brown matter to me yesterday, admittedly, yes, you were the first person I thought of. If anyone in this office stands a chance of getting Kyle Rhodes to voluntarily cooperate, it's you. I read the transcript from Tuesday's motion. From Rhodes's point of view, you're the one person here who has actually argued *for* his release." She grinned. "Hopefully you can now use those persuasive powers to get him to talk."

Or maybe he'll just slam the door in my face.

Probably not the best time to tell her new boss that she'd

kissed the defendant in her first case, then given him the cut direct in court.

"And if that doesn't work?" Rylann asked. "How far do you want me to take this?"

"All the way." Cameron sat forward in her chair, turning serious and appearing every bit the U.S. attorney right then. "When I took over this office after my highly unesteemed predecessor, I made a vow to take down government corruption at all levels. Based on what the FBI has told me, we've got a federal corrections officer who's been exacting his own form of justice against inmates, and his actions have now led to a man's death. He's not getting away with that on my watch." She looked Rylann in the eyes. "If Kyle Rhodes heard that threat, I think we've got enough for an indictment. Let's make that happen."

Seeing the look of determination on her boss's face, Rylann had only one answer to that.

"Consider it done."

Nine

NOT HAVING ANY plans that evening, Rylann stayed at the office until eight and ordered Chinese takeout for dinner when she got home. She changed into jeans and a T-shirt, then settled into the couch to call her parents. They'd retired several years ago and now spent the winters in a two-bedroom townhome they'd bought near Naples, Florida. Over the course of the last few years, Rylann had noticed that her parents' definition of "winter" seemed to be significantly expanding, and thus had a sneaking suspicion she wouldn't see them north of the Mason-Dixon Line anytime before June.

"Well, if isn't the woman of the hour," Helen Pierce said with a note of pride when she answered the phone. "Why didn't you tell me you were working on the Twitter Terrorist case? I've been showing off your photograph to everyone in the neighborhood. The one they got of you in the courtroom, standing next to that Kyle Rhodes."

"It was a last-minute thing," Rylann explained. "My boss needed me to cover for someone else."

"I think he's staring at your chest."

It took Rylann a moment. *Right*, the photograph of her and Kyle. "He's not staring at my chest, Mom."

"Then what's with the look? That's the kind of look a man gives you when he's seen you naked. Or wants to."

Immediately, Rylann thought back to the daring way Kyle had held her eyes the moment that photograph had been taken.

He'd remembered her, all right.

"I didn't notice anything strange about the look," she fibbed.

Helen didn't seem entirely convinced. "Hmm. Good thing your work on that case is done, or I'd probably have to give you some kind of lecture about staying away from boys like that. Motherly duty and all."

Rylann smiled at that. "Kyle Rhodes is hardly a boy, Mom."

"Oh, believe me, I noticed."

Ewww. Rylann was about to change the subject, deliberately failing to mention that her work with Kyle wasn't quite finished, when her mother beat her to the punch.

"So aside from the Twitter Terrorist case, what else do they have you working on?" Helen asked. Before retiring, she'd been a paralegal at a criminal defense firm in Chicago and enjoyed talking shop about Rylann's cases—even if, as she often joked, her daughter played for the "other team."

For much of Rylann's childhood, the traditional gender roles had been reversed in the Pierce household. In fact, her mother had been the primary breadwinner during most of those years. Rylann's father, an HVAC repairman, had injured his back when Rylann was seven years old, and despite treatment and physical therapy, he had never been able to work more than a part-time schedule after that. Thus, her dad had been the parent who would drop her off and pick her up from school, working a few repair jobs in between, and at six o'clock her mother would walk through the door, change out of her business clothes, and join them for dinner—usually entertaining them with stories about the cases she and "her lawyers" were working on.

Even as a young girl, however, Rylann had quickly realized one thing about those stories: she didn't like it when the bad guys won. And from those seeds, her career as an assistant U.S. attorney had sprung.

Rylann spoke with her mother for a few more minutes, until her door buzzer rang. Then she ran downstairs to collect her food, and settled in for the night with her case files, a carton of kung pao chicken, and a glass of a Riesling she'd scored in the post-breakup division of the wine collection she and Jon had owned. Yet another quiet Friday evening, like many others she'd had over the last six months.

And, wow, she'd just come dangerously close to feeling sorry for herself there. Good thing she had work to focus on—that, at least, never changed.

Seated at the kitchen counter, she read through the files. Despite the fact that the Brown case was neither the biggest nor the most glamorous case she had ever handled, she'd already bumped it up to the top of her priority list. First of all, a man had been brutally beaten to death. Not much got the prosecutorial juices flowing more than that. Second, the case was clearly important to the U.S. attorney. And if the case was important to Cameron, there was no way that Rylann, the "new girl," was going to screw it up.

Which meant that she and Kyle Rhodes had some unfinished business to tend to.

ON MONDAY MORNING, Rylann strode into the office charged and ready to take on a certain billionaire heir ex-con.

As soon as she'd settled in at her desk, she looked up the phone number for the law firm representing Kyle. Technically, she was permitted to contact him directly, since the matter she wanted to speak to him about wasn't one for which he had obtained counsel or was under investigation. Nevertheless, she thought it prudent to reach out to his attorneys first as a courtesy.

A courtesy that, unfortunately, was not returned.

"I'll tell you the same thing I told the FBI, Ms. Pierce. You're out of your goddamn mind if you think I'm letting you talk to my client," was the blistering reply from Mark Whitehead, Kyle's lead defense attorney. "Not after the way your office railroaded him five months ago."

"This has nothing to do with Mr. Rhodes's case," Rylann said in her best let's-be-friends voice. "I'd like to speak to him about an ongoing investigation pertaining to an incident that occurred two weeks ago at Metropolitan Correctional Center. While I'd prefer not to get into specifics over the phone, I can assure you that your client isn't under suspicion for any criminal activity in this matter."

Mark scoffed at that. "My client wasn't even at MCC two weeks ago. He'd been released prior to that."

"Even more reason for you to trust me when I say he isn't under suspicion."

"It's still a no. If you want to talk to Kyle Rhodes, go get a subpoena," Mark said.

"With all due respect, we both know that I don't need your permission. I'll contact Mr. Rhodes directly if I have to," Rylann said.

Mark laughed. "Good luck with that. I'm sure the Twitter Terrorist has several things he'd *love* to say to the U.S. Attorney's Office. Although I doubt any of them would be helpful to your investigation."

"We can do this the easy way, Mark, or I can go to the grand jury and drag him in. And if I have to do that, *you* don't get to be there," Rylann pointed out. It was the best card she could play, the fact that witnesses weren't permitted to bring counsel into the grand jury room.

"You're serious about this, aren't you?" Mark sighed. "And I thought Morgan was a pain in the ass. All right, I'll call Rhodes. But I wouldn't get my hopes up if I were you."

Rylann hung up the phone, satisfied to have made at least some progress. She wasn't sure what Kyle's response would be given his history with her office, although she'd fully prepared herself for something along the lines of *Kiss my felonious ass, counselor.*

She smiled to herself at the thought. Let him try to ignore her. She could be quite persistent when she wanted to be.

A few minutes later, Rylann heard a knock at her door and saw a tall, very attractive man with brown hair standing in her doorway—a man she recognized from the press coverage of the Twitter Terrorist case.

The elusive Cade Morgan had finally made his appearance.

"I think I owe you a cup of coffee," he said with a grin.

Rylann gestured to a Starbucks cup already sitting on her desk. "You're off the hook. I'm fully caffeinated."

He walked over to shake her hand. "Cade Morgan. I hear you covered my case on Tuesday."

"No problem. I was happy to help."

"Sorry I didn't drop by earlier to introduce myself," he said. "I was on trial all last week. Just got my jury verdict."

"How did it go?"

"Convicted on all five counts."

"That explains the victorious glow. Congratulations."

"Thanks. I heard you picked up an interesting homicide case yourself," Cade said. "Since I handled the Twitter Terrorist case, Cameron thought I should know that Kyle Rhodes might be one of your witnesses." He leaned back against the bookshelf, looking casually self-assured in his navy pin-striped suit. "I don't know if Cameron warned you, but I wouldn't expect much cooperation from Rhodes. I probably burned that bridge by calling him a terrorist."

Personally, Rylann had always thought that was extreme. But since she generally tried to avoid judging how other AUSAs handled their cases, she went with a more diplomatic answer. "You were obviously very passionate about that case."

"It's fair to say the Twitter Terrorist case was at the top of somebody's agenda. Just not mine."

Rylann looked at him quizzically. "You lost me there."

"Don't get me wrong, I stand behind all charges we filed against Kyle Rhodes," Cade said. "He broke the law and caused a whole mess of trouble. *Worldwide* trouble. No way could we have let that slide with a mere slap on the wrist."

She raised an eyebrow. "But?"

"But this office was a different place five months ago. And I suppose you could say that we were a bit . . . overly vigorous in the way we handled that prosecution." Cade's expression changed to one of annoyance. "My former boss, Silas Briggs, made it clear that he expected nothing less from me. He was always looking for an opportunity to get this office—and

himself—into the public eye, and he figured that the Twitter
Terrorist case was the perfect chance to do that. No one cares
when you pick on a billionaire heir."

"Except the billionaire heir," Rylann noted.

"Well, I wasn't exactly thinking we'd need his help down
the road." Cade flashed her a good-natured grin. "Good
thing that's your problem now and not mine." He pushed away
from the bookshelf and paused in the doorway. "Hey—in all
seriousness, if you need anything, I'm just down the hall. Feel
free to stop by anytime, new girl." He pointed. "And tomorrow, the coffee's on me."

Not bad, Rylann mused appreciatively after Cade left. He
was definitely good-looking in an all-American kind of way.
Perhaps a little on the overly confident side, but this was not
uncommon among AUSAs, especially those in the special
prosecutions division. Regardless, Cade Morgan was off-
limits, and she'd known that before he'd even stepped into her
doorway. Office romances had too much potential to get
messy—and, as a rule, she didn't let things get messy when
it came to work.

Just then, her phone rang.

"Rylann Pierce," she answered.

"It's Mark Whitehead. I talked to my client," he said, not
sounding pleased. "For the record, I'm totally and completely
against this."

"Fair enough. That has been noted for the record." No clue
what he was talking about.

"Mr. Rhodes agreed to meet with you this afternoon, at
his office. *Alone*," Mark said with emphasis. "He was quite
clear on that last point, despite all my attempts to persuade
him otherwise."

That certainly was not the response Rylann had expected.
Judging from the *five* lawyers who'd been present at last Tuesday's motion call—a fact she still found ridiculous—she'd
been under the impression that multimillionaire Kyle Rhodes
would never agree to a meeting with the U.S. Attorney's
Office without counsel present.

Still . . . this development served her interests, as well. She wasn't exactly advertising her prior connection to Kyle, and they could speak more freely without an audience present. "Fine. I can meet Mr. Rhodes later today." She grabbed a pen. "Where is his office located?"

"Well, Ms. Pierce, seeing how my client is unemployed, his current office is his home. Eight hundred North Lake Shore Drive. The penthouse. Mr. Rhodes will be expecting you at four thirty sharp."

Ten

THE PHONE ON Kyle's desk rang, the double ring that indicated the call came from the security desk in the lobby of his building.

"Ms. Pierce is here to see you, Mr. Rhodes," Miles informed him when he answered the phone.

"Thanks, Miles. Send her up."

Kyle hung up the phone and saved the document he'd been working on, thinking that this was indeed an interesting turn of events. If anyone else from the U.S. Attorney's Office had asked to see him, he would've told him or her exactly where to shove that request. Even though they'd held up their end of the deal last Tuesday, they were still at the top of his shit list for the whole "terrorist" business, which meant no favors for federal prosecutors. Period.

Except he'd found this particular request, from the illustrious Rylann Pierce of the amber eyes and sharp tongue, difficult to say no to.

He was . . . curious to know what she wanted.

This story she'd told his lawyers, about some "investigation" into an incident that had occurred at Metropolitan Correctional Center two weeks ago, sounded a little fishy. He'd already been released from MCC by that time, so he wasn't sure what knowledge, if any, he would have about anything that had happened after that. But according to his lawyers, she'd been quite vehement in her desire to meet with him.

And that intrigued him even more.

Last Tuesday, when he'd gotten home from court, he'd done

two things: first, he'd gone on a long run, taking his sweet-ass time and going as far as he'd wanted without having to worry about ankle monitors, U.S. marshals, or SWAT teams storming the beach. Then the second thing he'd done was Google Rylann Pierce.

He'd found her on LinkedIn and saw that she'd clerked with a federal appellate judge in San Francisco before joining the U.S. Attorney's Office. He'd also read press releases from the Northern District of California regarding several high-profile cases she'd prosecuted. From what he could tell, she'd had a successful career in California and then, suddenly, she'd moved back to Chicago.

He had a feeling there was a story there, but whatever it was, Google wasn't saying.

Kyle heard a knock at the door. He got up from the desk and made his way through the penthouse, not realizing he'd been grinning the whole way until he saw his reflection in the foyer mirror.

Chill out, dickhead. She's just some girl you walked home.

Perhaps this was, in fact, all a bizarre coincidence, and she really was there to talk about some case. Or maybe . . . it was something else. Maybe she'd been thinking about him all week, the same way he'd been thinking about her, and just couldn't stay away.

His smile widened. Only one way to find out.

Kyle opened the door and saw her standing on his doorstep, long, dark hair a-flowing and looking like a Hitchcock heroine, with her belted trench coat and high heels, and carrying a briefcase at her side.

"Counselor," he drawled.

"Mr. Rhodes," she said, her voice slightly husky.

That was as far as they'd made it on Tuesday. But this time, there were no reporters, no cameras, and no team of defense attorneys. It was just the two of them now.

Kyle pushed open the door. "Come on in."

"Thank you for meeting with me." She brushed past him, the delicate scent of something floral and feminine trailing after her, and stepped into the foyer.

He shut the door, then turned and looked her over. Nine years ago, she'd been eye-catchingly attractive, but now there was something else, something more polished, sophisticated, and undeniably appealing.

Something a man who'd spent most of the last five months in *prison* would be hard-pressed not to notice.

"It's been a while, Ms. Pierce," he said.

Her lips twitched in a smile. "Actually, it's only been about a week."

He folded his arms across his chest challengingly. "Couldn't stay away?"

She opened her mouth to say something, then appeared to change her mind. "Maybe we should sit down somewhere and talk."

Right. About this mysterious "investigation." He gestured to the open expanse of the loft-style penthouse. "Make yourself at home."

Rylann walked into the living room area, curiously checking out the place. "Looks like you've done well for yourself these past few years." She threw him a sideways look, her eyes dancing with amusement. "Aside from that tiny issue with Twitter."

"Just so I know, how many jokes can I expect about that?"

"It's almost too easy," she said with a laugh. "You once said that someone was going to cause a lot of panic and mayhem if companies didn't start paying more attention to denial of service attacks. How prescient of you."

Kyle stopped. "You actually remember I said that?"

Rylann paused for a moment, then shrugged nonchalantly. "Only because of the Twitter fiasco." Moving on, she took a seat in one of the sleek Italian leather armchairs and set her briefcase on the floor.

Kyle sat on the couch across from her, watching as she slid off her coat, revealing a dark gray suit with a cream silk shirt underneath. "Before you say anything else, maybe we should address the eight-hundred-pound gorilla in the room."

She looked momentarily confused. "Meaning . . . ?"

"About that night." He held her gaze. "I assume you know why I never showed up for our date?"

Her expression softened. "Oh. Yes. I was very sorry to hear about your mother."

"Thank you." Kyle tried to lighten the mood, glad to have that bit of awkwardness out of the way. "It's a shame, you know. Because I was going to be really charming on that date. You wouldn't have stood a chance."

She laughed. "I'm sure you think that."

Kyle stretched his arm along the back of the couch, getting more comfortable. "So. What brings you here tonight, Rylann Pierce?"

She shifted in her chair, then crossed one leg over the other. "Murder, actually."

Kyle blinked, and his grin faded. Whatever he'd been expecting her to say, it wasn't that. "Murder?"

"Yes. An inmate was beaten to death at MCC two weeks ago."

From her expression, he could tell she was serious. And just like that, the whole tone of their conversation changed. "You're really here about a case," he said, not realizing until that moment how much he'd begun to convince himself otherwise.

She cocked her head, as if not following. "Why else would I be here?"

So much for not looking like a dickhead. "Never mind. Tell me what happened at MCC."

She proceeded to do exactly that. Kyle said nothing as Rylann related the circumstances surrounding Darius Brown's death and explained her belief that Quinn, the prison guard, had orchestrated the attack in retaliation.

"We know that Quinn and Brown had a previous altercation," she said, "and that Brown came out of disciplinary segregation and told his friends that Quinn had threatened him."

Hearing that, Kyle got up and began pacing the room.

"We know that you were also in disciplinary segregation

during that time, in the cell next to Brown," she continued.
"I came here to find out whether you heard that threat. Candidly, I'm hoping you did."

She fell quiet then, waiting for his response.

Kyle stopped with his back to her, gazing out the floor-
to-ceiling windows that overlooked the lake. In the distance,
he could see the Ferris wheel at Navy Pier. " 'You're gonna
pay for what you did to my wrist, you piece of shit.' " He
turned around. "Is that the threat you're looking for?"

Rylann exhaled, obviously relieved. "Yes."

Kyle ran his hand over his mouth. This whole situation—
the fact that *he*, a former vice president of a billion dollar
corporation, had direct knowledge regarding the murder of
an inmate—was completely surreal. "I had no idea. Hell, I
didn't even know Brown was dead."

"Did you know him well when you were in prison?" she
asked.

He shook his head. "The only time I ever spoke to the guy
was through our cell bars during those two days we were both
in disciplinary segregation." Still, he felt a mixture of emotions right then—guilt included—and felt the need to clarify
something. "I thought Quinn was just talking trash, trying to
act tough. I had no idea he'd actually follow through with that
threat." He exhaled, trying to wrap his mind around everything she'd told him. "So what happens from here?"

Rylann got up from her chair and walked over. "I present
the matter to the grand jury. And I'd like you to be one of the
witnesses who testifies."

Kyle laughed humorlessly. "Right. The infamous Twitter
Terrorist as a witness for the prosecution. I'm sure that'll go
over great with the grand jury."

"Actually, you're the perfect witness," she said. "If you'd
still been in prison, any defense attorney worth his salt would
try to impeach you, claiming that you were testifying to gain
favor with the U.S. Attorney's Office in hopes of a reduction
in your sentence. But now that you're out, you obviously have
no such motive."

Kyle fixed his eyes on her, suddenly realizing something. "You need me for this case."

After hesitating, Rylann acknowledged this with a nod. "Yes."

He stepped closer to her. "Tell me something: would you have offered me a deal in exchange for my testimony if I'd still been locked up?"

"I probably would have considered offering you a deal, yes."

"Then consider offering me one now."

Rylann gestured to the penthouse. "You're already out. There's nothing I can offer you."

He took yet another step closer. "But that's not true, counselor. There is something I want—very much, in fact." He peered down into her eyes. "An apology from the U.S. Attorney's Office."

Rylann burst out laughing. "An apology? That's a good one." She brushed her hair out of her eyes and flung it back over her shoulders, then pulled back when she saw the look on his face. "Oh my God, you're not joking."

He shook his head slowly. "No, I'm not."

"Kyle, that will never, ever happen," she said in all seriousness.

He shrugged. "If you want me as your witness, that's what it's going to take." Yes, he was being a hard-ass—and as far as he was concerned, he had every right to be. She may have had her sexy skirt suit and her smiles, but tonight she also had an agenda. This little reunion of theirs had nothing to do with any walk home or some instant connection he'd thought he'd once felt with Rylann Pierce a long time ago. Tonight she was there solely for professional reasons, which meant he could be all business, too.

Bottom line, he was a free man now. So if the U.S. Attorney's Office wanted to play ball, it would have to be by his rules.

"I'll give you until tomorrow to think it over," Kyle said. "Otherwise, I bring in the lawyers. And anything else you have to say, you can say to them."

Rylann studied him, not looking particularly intimidated. "Hmm. They warned me you might be a little prickly."

"Well, *they* were right."

"I see that." She walked over to the armchair and grabbed her coat and briefcase. She pulled something out of the outside pocket of the briefcase, then strode back to him, all lawyerly efficient in her heels. "Let me explain how this works, Kyle. You can come down to my office, with your lawyers if you like, and we can discuss your testimony there. That's the easy way. Or I can get a subpoena, drag you in front of the grand jury, and you'll still tell me everything you know. Either way, I get what I want."

Is that right? Kyle shrugged off the threat, not particularly intimidated, either. "You forgot option three. Where I conveniently forget everything I heard Quinn say that night."

He saw the spark of anger in her eyes.

"You wouldn't," she said.

"Are you willing to bet your case on that, counselor?" he asked. "How well do you think you know me? Because five months ago we all saw that I'm plenty capable of doing things I'm not supposed to."

Surprisingly, his words made her pause. She looked around the penthouse, then back at him. "You're right," she acknowledged. "I don't know you, really. We spent all of about thirty minutes together nearly a decade ago. Still, I think the Kyle Rhodes who walked me home and gave me the shirt off his back would do the right thing no matter how pissed he was at my office. So if *that* guy is hanging around this penthouse anywhere, tell him to call me."

Kyle folded his arms across his chest. "Were you this pushy and obstinate nine years ago? Strange how I don't remember that."

She held out her hand, offering her business card. "My number, should you decide on the easy way."

He took the card from her. And despite everything, he found he couldn't resist riling her, just a little. "You really do want to see me again." He raised an eyebrow, his voice sly. "Are you sure this is solely about business, Ms. Pierce?"

She said nothing for a moment, then moved a step nearer to him. They stood close now, their bodies practically touching as she peered up at him. "Call my office, Kyle," she said. "Or I'll subpoena you so fast your head will spin."

Then she stepped back, flashing him a deceptively sweet smile as she headed toward the front door. "Oh—and have a good night."

Eleven

RYLANN CHECKED HER watch as she walked into the lobby
of Metropolitan Correctional Center, the maximum-security
federal prison located in the middle of downtown Chicago. The
five-block walk from her office had taken a little longer than
expected, but she still had a couple minutes to spare.

She'd arranged this meeting, her first with one of the agents
from the Chicago FBI office, after reviewing the Brown files
over the weekend. While the special agent assigned to the
case had done a thorough job in his investigation, he'd unfortunately struck out anytime he'd tried to talk to inmates other
than Brown's closest friends. There was, however, one possible exception: he'd noted that an inmate named Manuel
Gutierrez, who'd been in the cell next to Watts the night
Brown had been beaten to death, had refused to speak to the
FBI but had hinted that he might be more willing to talk
directly to the U.S. Attorney's Office.

Rylann had heard these kinds of demands before—it was
not an infrequent refrain anytime the FBI wanted to interview
an inmate. Convicted felons were like eager-beaver first-year
law students when it came to knowing the ways to get *out* of
prison, including being fully educated on the provisions of
Rule 35, which allowed courts to reduce the prison sentences
of cooperating inmates. And the savvier inmates also knew
that only the U.S. Attorney's Office, not the FBI, had the
authority to seek such a reduction.

Generally, Rylann wasn't the biggest fan of making deals
with inmates under Rule 35. For starters, as she'd indicated

to Kyle the night before, it opened the door for the witness to be subject to possible impeachment on the grounds of bias. Second, as a prosecutor, her job was to put criminals *behind* bars, not provide them with the means to an early release. But she was also a practical person, and it was sometimes critical to the success of a case to have an inmate's testimony. She also understood that, from the inmate's perspective, it could be dangerous to provide information to the authorities. Life in prison for someone seen as a rat could be rough, no doubt about it. Thus, on occasion, Rule 35 was the only incentive she had to get someone behind bars to cooperate.

Consequently, today's mission was to find out what, exactly, Manuel Gutierrez knew about Darius Brown's death. First thing that morning, Rylann had called the FBI agent assigned to the investigation and suggested they pay a visit to Gutierrez. As luck would have it, the agent had been free that afternoon.

"Ms. Pierce?"

Walking toward her was an African American man in his midtwenties with what had to be the most friendly smile— and by far the nicest suit—she'd ever seen on an FBI agent.

He extended his hand. "Special Agent Sam Wilkins at your service. I saw the briefcase and guessed it was you."

"It's a pleasure to meet you, Sam. Please, call me Rylann."

They made small talk as they stopped at the lock boxes so Wilkins could check his firearm. Within minutes Rylann learned that he was relatively new to the FBI, having joined straight out of Yale Law School, and that the Brown matter was the first solo investigation he'd been assigned within the FBI's violent crimes division.

"What made you choose violent crimes?" she asked curiously. Wilkins's style seemed a little less rough and gruff than many of the other FBI agents she'd worked with.

He shrugged. "It's probably better to say that it chose me. When I first started, they paired me up with a senior agent in that division, and one of the first cases we handled was a high-profile murder investigation. Somebody must've liked the job we did, because now Jack and I seem to be first on the list whenever someone finds a dead body."

Wilkins paused as they both showed their badges to the guards before removing their suit jackets to pass through the metal detectors. Having never been to MCC before, Rylann followed his lead as they headed to the elevators that would take them up to the interview rooms.

"By the way, we caught a break," she told him. "That lead with the inmate in disciplinary segregation turned out to be a good one." She briefed Wilkins quickly on the situation involving Kyle Rhodes, and then all discussion about the case ceased as they entered the elevator with several other visitors.

When they stepped off at the eleventh floor, Wilkins led her down a corridor to the interview rooms used by police officers and federal agents. "Do you think he'll call? Kyle Rhodes, I mean."

Rylann thought about that. She'd put the ball in his court—frankly, she had no clue what he'd do with it. "Only time will tell."

TEN MINUTES LATER, they sat in a small interview room across a wooden interrogation table from Manuel Gutierrez.

"What's in it for me if I talk?" the inmate demanded to know. He gestured to the door with his cuffed hands, referring to the prison guard who'd left after escorting him into the room. " 'Cuz there's no way I'm sticking around this place after ratting out one of them. Or I'll be the next guy they're taking out of here in a body bag."

"First tell me what you know, Mr. Gutierrez," Rylann said. "If I decide I need your testimony, then we can talk about next steps."

Gutierrez thought about this for a moment, then leaned in, lowering his voice. "All right. You know that I used to be in the cell next to Watts, right? Before they moved him permanently to no-man's-land for killing Brown, anyway. So the day before Brown got transferred to Watts's cell, I overheard a conversation between Quinn and Watts—a conversation that seems pretty fucking suspicious in light of what happened."

"What did Quinn and Watts say?" Rylann asked.

"I heard Watts ask Quinn, 'How bad do you want me to rough him up, boss?'"

Now *that* had Rylann's attention. "And what was Quinn's response?"

Gutierrez hemmed a little at the next part. "Well, all I heard Quinn say was *'Shh.'* You know, like he didn't want anyone to hear them talking." He looked between Rylann and Wilkins. "But that's still something, right? I mean, you can use that, can't you?"

Rylann mulled this over. Of course, it would've been better if there'd been more to the conversation, but it was nevertheless another piece of the puzzle. "It's helpful. Thank you."

Gutierrez mistook her pause for hesitation. "Listen, everyone knows what happened. Quinn locked Brown in a cell with that racist piece of shit and told Watts to have at him. You ever seen Watts? The guy's over two hundred pounds and all muscle. Brown was five-foot-eight." He held up his handcuffs. "People might think we're the scum of the earth in here, but we still got rights." He pointed, getting a little too close to Rylann's face. "You need to nail that guard to the wall, lady."

Wilkins tensed protectively. "Take it down a notch, buddy," he growled in a low voice.

Rylann put her hand on the table between her and Wilkins, indicating that everything was fine. Without looking away, she held the inmate's gaze.

"That's exactly what I'm trying to do, Mr. Gutierrez."

THAT AFTERNOON, KYLE walked through the front door of DeVine Cellars, the wine store owned by his sister, just in time to see Jordan carrying a heavy box up from the cellar.

He crossed the room in two strides. "Hand it over, Jordo."

She did so, and then pointed to the bar in the center of the store. "Thanks. Just put it over there."

Kyle set the box down and gestured to the cast on her wrist. "You have a shop full of employees working for you. Use them."

Jordan raised an eyebrow as she began unpacking wine bottles. "My, aren't we in a mood today. Something wrong?"

Yes, he was in a mood—a foul one at that—and had been ever since a certain pushy and obstinate assistant U.S. attorney had come back into his life with her sassy subpoena threats and moral judgments. But that wasn't anything he wanted to discuss with his sister. "I'm just tired," he said dismissively. "I didn't sleep well last night." Undoubtedly because said pushy and obstinate assistant U.S. attorney's words had been ringing annoyingly in his head.

The Kyle Rhodes who walked me home and gave me the shirt off his back would do the right thing no matter how pissed he was at my office. So if that guy is hanging around this penthouse anywhere, tell him to call me.

Oh, wasn't she just so . . . righteous. As if he needed to make excuses for the way he'd lived his life for the last nine years. Sure, he had an excuse: he'd been having *fun*. Maybe that was something Rylann Pierce needed to try more often—assuming she had any time for fun in her current forty-two-year career plan or whatever.

"Seriously. What's with the face?" Jordan asked. "You're scaring my cabernets with that scowl."

"I'm just working through some stuff," he said vaguely.

Jordan raised an eyebrow, studying him. "Prison stuff?"

"More like post-prison stuff. Nothing we need to talk about." The last thing he needed his super-perfect twin sister with her super-perfect FBI boyfriend knowing was that he was in another dispute, of sorts, with the U.S. Attorney's Office. He was cranky enough about the situation without Jordan laying into him about it. He'd left prison several weeks ago and was *supposed* to be moving on with his life, yet the vestiges of the place still clung to him. Like bad BO.

He picked up four of the wine bottles Jordan had unpacked. "Where do you want these?"

She pointed. "In the empty bin over there, with the other cabernets." She looked over when Kyle came back to the bar. "So what kind of post-prison stuff?"

Now he was getting suspicious. "What's with the twenty questions?"

"Sue me for trying to open a dialogue here. Geez. I've just

been a little worried about you, since I've heard that it can sometimes be difficult for ex-inmates to reenter normal life."

Kyle shot her a look as he grabbed more wine bottles. "Where, exactly, did you hear that? Siblings of Ex-Cons Anonymous?"

Jordan glared. "Yes, we have weekly meetings at the YMCA," she retorted. Then she waved her hand vaguely. "I don't know, it's just . . . something I saw on TV this past weekend."

Ah. Kyle suddenly had a sneaking suspicion about the cause of his sister's concern. "Jordo . . . by any chance were you watching *The Shawshank Redemption* again?"

"Pfft. *No.*" She saw his knowing expression and caved. "Fine. I was flipping through the channels and it was on TNT. You try turning that movie off." She looked at him matter-of-factly. "It's very compelling."

Kyle fought back a smile. "Sure it is. But I'm not scarred for life or planning to hop on the next bus to Zihuatanejo. MCC is not Shawshank."

"Really?" Jordan asked. "Because I just read in the papers that an inmate was killed there a couple weeks ago. Apparently the FBI's investigating. A guy named Darius Brown— did you know him?"

Next topic. Kyle feigned nonchalance. "I knew him a little." Quickly, he changed the subject before his nosy sister asked any further questions. "So you said you wanted to talk about my business plan?" Jordan was the first person he'd shown it to, figuring he could use the advice of someone with an MBA.

"Yes, I did." She grabbed a towel to wipe the dust from the wine bottles off her hands, then pulled the twenty-page business plan he'd drafted out from underneath the bar.

"And?"

Jordan hesitated. "And I hate to say this, considering you're my brother and all, but I think it's sort of . . . brilliant."

Kyle proudly rocked back on his heels. "Brilliant, huh? Feel free to elaborate."

"Oh, don't get me wrong. There's a good chance you're going to fail spectacularly in this," Jordan told him. "But you've covered the three primary concerns of revenue, cost, and cash flow. You've got a large potential market and a unique service. Whether anyone is going to be interested in that service"—she held out her hands—"tough to say."

That was indeed the half-billion dollar question. "I'm going shopping for office space next week," Kyle said.

"Wow. You're really raring to go."

Yes, he was. "For four months I sat in prison, thinking about all the things I was going to do to get my life back on track as soon as I was out. Now it's time to put those plans in motion." He pointed, remembering something. "But do me a favor—don't tell Dad about this."

"Now there's something I've never heard from you before," Jordan said, rolling her eyes. "He's a very successful businessman, Kyle. He could help you."

"Did you ask for Dad's help when you opened this wine shop?" Kyle asked pointedly.

Jordan leaned against the bar, proudly taking in the store. "Of course not."

Enough said.

A HALF HOUR later, Kyle left the wine shop in good spirits after his conversation with Jordan. But almost immediately, as he crossed the street and walked a half block to his car, the nagging feeling crept back in. And he knew the exact source of that.

This situation with Prosecutrix Pierce had become a serious burr up his ass.

At the end of the day, it shouldn't matter what he did about the Darius Brown case. Rylann had been right; he wouldn't lie under oath. So he was free and clear to be the asshole and make her go get her subpoena. He'd tell the grand jury what he knew, and justice would be served. And he would have the satisfaction of knowing that he'd made the U.S. Attorney's Office—people who had certainly never shown him any courtesies—scramble through a few hoops.

It was a good plan. He *wanted* to be the asshole here.

Why, then, he reached into the pocket of his jacket and pulled out his cell phone and Rylann's business card, he honestly couldn't say.

He dialed her number, got her voicemail, and left a message.

"Sorry, counselor, but I looked all around the penthouse and found only one Kyle Rhodes." He paused. "And he will be at your office tomorrow at two o'clock. Expect lots of prickliness."

Twelve

BY ONE THIRTY the next afternoon, the entire U.S. Attorney's Office was in a stir.

As it turned out, Rylann had not originally been available at two o'clock, but she'd switched her schedule around to accommodate a particularly prickly witness who seemed to believe that he was calling the shots in this situation. After that, she'd told her secretary to add Kyle Rhodes to the visitor's list, and the information had spread like wildfire.

Cade popped into her office right before her meeting, doing a slow clap. "Well done. How did you manage to bring in the Twitter Terrorist?"

"I have my ways," Rylann said mysteriously. Although she wasn't quite sure she knew the answer to that herself. "By the way, I think we can just call him Kyle Rhodes now."

Cade raised a curious eyebrow at that. "Can we now?"

A call from her secretary interrupted them with the news that her visitor had arrived. "That's my cue," Rylann said, standing up from her desk.

Cade walked alongside her on the way back to his office. As they passed by the secretaries' desks and the other AUSA offices, Rylann noticed that everyone's eyes were on her.

"You'd think I'd asked Al Capone to drop by," she muttered under her breath.

"Get used to it. When it comes to Kyle Rhodes, people are curious." Cade saluted as he ducked into his office. "Good luck."

Rylann rounded the corner, slowing her stride as she surveyed the scene in the reception area.

Kyle stood with his profile to her, looking at the photograph of the Chicago skyline. Surprisingly, he appeared to be alone. He'd dressed in business-casual attire, looking professional and confident, with the top button undone on his blue pin-striped shirt and his hands tucked into his pants pockets. Ironically emblazed in bold silver letters on the wall behind him were the words "Office of the United States Attorney."

Rylann had to admit it. She was impressed.

Clearly, there was no love lost between him and her office. Five months ago, they'd gone after him hard—probably a little too hard, from what Cade had told her. Yet now they needed Kyle, and so there he stood: head held high, not trying to hide or shield himself with the team of attorneys most men in his position would have insisted be present.

Kyle turned and saw her, watching with a wary expression as she approached. He'd said some things last night, and so had she—but still, he'd shown up. And as far as Rylann was concerned, that said so much more than a few heated words.

"Looks like we have an audience," he said when she stopped before him.

Rylann looked back and saw that several secretaries and attorneys were staring at them as they "happened" to walk by the reception area.

"No lawyers again?" she asked.

"I don't have anything to hide, Ms. Pierce," he said coolly.

"Actually, I'm glad they're sitting this one out. I couldn't afford to buy all fifty of them coffee, anyway."

Surprise flashed across his face. "We're not staying here?"

Rylann knew that if she brought him back to the conference room, as she'd originally intended, people would be gawking and whispering at him the entire time. And frankly, she thought it was about time that somebody from her office cut Kyle Rhodes a small break. "I figured we could go someplace that's a little less . . . stifling." She lowered her voice. "It's a weird situation, Kyle. I know that. But I'm trying here."

He studied her for a long moment, seeming to debate whether to accept the olive branch she had offered.

"I like your hair better this way," he finally said.

Rylann smiled to herself. Well, that was a start. "Does that mean we have a truce?"

Kyle began walking in the direction of the elevators. "It means I'm thinking about it."

But when he pushed the down button and stole a glance at her, the familiar devilish spark back in his eyes, Rylann knew she was in.

KYLE SAT OPPOSITE Rylann in the booth, checking out the scene around them.

She'd brought him to a diner—the quasi-seedy, retro-but-not-in-a-hip-way kind of diner complete with vinyl booths and plastic menus—that was located under the L tracks a block from her office.

"How did you find this place?" He picked up the menu. "They actually have meat loaf on the menu."

Rylann shed her jacket and placed it on the booth next to her. "One of the other AUSAs told me about it. It's a court-house hangout."

With a loud *pop!* the lights suddenly went out.

Rylann waved her hand dismissively. "Just a fuse. Happens all the time." She set her menu off to the side and looked at him through the dim light filtering in through the windows. "So. I've read your file."

Of course she had. "And what did this file tell you about me?" Kyle asked.

She pulled a legal pad and pen out of her briefcase. "Well, I can tell you one thing it *didn't* tell me: why you were in disciplinary segregation." She clicked her pen and poised it over the legal pad, ready to go. "Perhaps you could explain that?"

Kyle fought back a grin, wondering if she knew how oddly enticing she looked when she went all official on him. "All the times I was in disciplinary segregation, Ms. Pierce, or just the time I was locked up next to Brown?"

She blinked. "How many times were you in disciplinary segregation?"

"Six."

Her eyes widened. "In four months? That's quite an accomplishment."

The lights suddenly flickered back on, and some of the diner's other patrons cheered approvingly.

"There we go," Rylann said with a warm, easy smile. "All part of the ambience."

Hmm.

Kyle remembered that smile. He'd once walked up to a complete stranger in a bar because of one just like it. And had then been thoroughly sassed.

"You were about to tell me about the six times you were in disciplinary segregation?" she prompted him.

He sat back, casually stretching his arm along the booth. "I guess some of the other inmates thought a rich computer geek would be an easy mark. From time to time, I needed to defend myself to correct that misimpression."

Rylann jotted something down on her legal pad. "So you had problems with fighting."

"Actually, I did quite well with the fighting. It was the getting caught part that I had problems with."

Kyle smiled innocently when she threw him a look. He couldn't help it—something about Rylann Pierce and her suit and no-nonsense legal pad made him want to . . . agitate her.

"Any noteworthy fights I should know about?" she asked.

"I once shoved a guy's face in a plate of mashed potatoes."

He was pretty sure he saw her fighting back a smile at that one.

"Tell me what it was like being in prison," she said.

"You're a prosecutor. You must have some idea what it's like," he said.

She acknowledged this with a nod. "I'd like to hear you describe it in your own words."

"Ah. So you know what I'll say when I testify on the subject."

"Precisely."

Kyle thought about where to start with that one. Interesting that Rylann would be the first person to directly ask about his prison experience, instead of dancing around the subject the way his friends and family all had. "Most of the time, it was boring as hell. Same routine every day. Wake up at five A.M., breakfast, wait in your cell for a head count. Leisure time if you passed inspection. Lunch at eleven, another head count, more free time. Into your cell for yet another head count, dinner at five o'clock, free time until nine, and then—you guessed it—another head count. Lights off at ten." He pointed. "Not much to write about that on your legal pad."

"What about the nighttime routine?"

He shrugged. "The nights were long. Cold. Gave a man a lot of time to think." He took a sip of his coffee, figuring there wasn't much else he needed to say about that.

"You mentioned you had some issues with the other inmates. How about the guards?" she asked.

"Other than the fact that they kept tossing me in segregation for defending myself, no."

"Would you say that you resent the fact that they kept putting you in segregation?"

Kyle saw where she was going with this—already thinking ahead to what a defense attorney might bring up on cross-examination. "I have no ax to grind against prison guards, counselor. I understand they were just doing their jobs."

"Good," she said with a nod. "Now tell me about Quinn."

"Quinn's a different story. That guy is one mean son of a bitch." He watched her. "You're actually writing that down?"

"Yes. And feel free to say it exactly like that to the grand jury."

Kyle was glad she'd brought that subject up. She may have been confident about her case, or at least she seemed to be, but he had his doubts. "You really think the grand jury is going to believe what I have to say?"

"Sure," she said with a shrug. "I believe you." When she finished writing, she looked up from her legal pad and saw him staring at her. "What?"

It was nothing, really, that she believed him. Just words. "You've asked a lot of questions about me. Now it's my turn."

"Oh, sorry. But that's not how this works," she said sweetly.

"It is this time, counselor, if you want to keep me sitting in this booth," he replied, just as sweetly.

She shook her head. "You are just as annoyingly cocky as you were nine years ago."

"Yes." Kyle's gaze fell to her lips. "And we both know how that turned out."

Much to his surprise, she actually blushed.

Well, well. Apparently the unflappable Prosecutrix Pierce could be . . . flapped after all.

Interesting.

She recovered quickly. "Fine. What's your question?"

Kyle thought for a moment, wondering where to start. He decided to go right to the heart of the matter. "Why did you leave San Francisco?"

Rylann raised an eyebrow. "How do you know I lived in San Francisco?"

"On a scale of one to ten, how pissed would you be if I said that I hacked into the DOJ's personnel records and did some poking around about you?" He whistled when he saw her look of death. "Okay . . . ixnay on the ex-con humor. Relax, counselor, I Googled you. From what I could tell, you had a good thing going back in California."

He saw a flicker of something unreadable in her eyes.

"I felt like it was time for a change," she said simply.

Yep, definitely a story there.

"Does anyone actually buy that excuse when you say it?" Kyle asked.

"Of course they do. It's the truth."

"But not the whole truth."

She acknowledged this with a slight smile. "Perhaps not." She readied her pen once again. "Now. Back to your testimony."

"All business once again," he teased.

"In this case, yes. If the past is any indication, you and I only get along in about eight-minute stretches and"—she checked her watch—"uh-oh, our time is almost up on this one."

Kyle laughed. She was just so frustratingly, amusingly self-assured. "One last question. Then you can ask me anything you want." He paused and locked eyes with her. "Admit that you liked that kiss."

Her lips parted in surprise. "That wasn't a question."

"Admit it anyway."

As she held his gaze, the corners of her lips turned up in a smile. "I told you then. It wasn't bad."

Then she clicked her pen once again. "Now. Back to your case."

THE REST OF the interview went smoothly enough, as far as Kyle could tell. Rylann spent a good twenty minutes firing questions at him about the night Quinn threatened Brown— whether he'd actually *seen* Quinn talking (yes), whether he was *sure* he'd heard the threat (also yes), whether he was making the whole story up because he was an egomaniac attention hound desperate to be in the limelight again.

He paused with his coffee cup midway to his mouth at that one.

Rylann smiled mischievously. "Just a little prosecutor humor."

There was a brief awkward moment when the check came and they both reached for it at the same time. His fingers softly grazed hers as their eyes met. "Sorry. Instinct."

After she paid the bill, they walked out of the diner and stood momentarily underneath the L tracks.

"I plan to bring the matter to the grand jury next week," Rylann told him, raising her voice to speak over an approaching train. "I'll call you as soon as I have the exact date and time you'll be testifying."

She extended her hand in farewell, and Kyle closed his hand around hers.

"This is a good thing you're doing, Kyle," she said. "Just remember—"

The train roaring directly overhead made it impossible for him to hear her. Kyle gestured to his ear, shaking his head. She stepped close to him and put her hand on his shoulder as she stood up on her toes to speak in his ear.

Her breath was a soft caress on his neck, her voice low in his ear. "—Don't screw it up."

He turned his head so that they were eye to eye, his lips mere inches from hers. He said nothing for a moment, and neither did she, and he became very aware of the catch in her breath, the warmth of her hand on his shoulder.

Kyle felt a sudden urge to pull her closer. He'd teased her in the diner about their kiss, but unless he was wholly off his game after those four months in prison, the vibe he was getting from her right then was very real. If he bent his head just the slightest, he could brush his lips over hers. Find out if she tasted as good as she did in his memory.

"How are we doing on that eight-minute stretch of getting along?" he asked huskily.

Rylann stayed where she was at first, their lips still so close. Then she cocked her head and met his gaze. "Time's up."

She pulled back from him and turned and walked away, the roar of the L train fading as it passed by overhead.

BACK IN THE safety of her office, Rylann shut the door behind her and exhaled.

That had been a little too close for comfort.

As a lawyer, there were certain lines she would never cross, and getting involved with a trial witness was definitely one of them. She and Kyle might exchange a few quips here and there, there may even have been a reference to a nine-year-old kiss, but as long as she needed his testimony in the Brown matter, that was as far as things could go.

She ran her hands through her hair, collecting herself, then took a seat at her desk. Welcoming the distraction of work, she checked her messages, first her voicemail and then she turned to her computer. She had just begun to scroll through her unread e-mails when she saw something that caught her completely by surprise.

A message from Jon.

There was no subject, and she hesitated to click to the message, not wanting its contents to show up on her preview pane.

First, she needed a minute to process this unexpected development.

She checked the calendar on her desk, realizing that in one week it would officially be six months since she'd had any contact with him. By mutual agreement, they had decided not to call or e-mail each other, thinking that would make it easier on both of them to get over the breakup. Yet here he was, changing things up.

Normally very decisive in her actions, Rylann caught herself debating her next move. Part of her was tempted to delete the e-mail without reading it, but that seemed too bitter. And though she certainly had mixed emotions about the fact that Jon had reached out to her, she was pleased to realize that bitterness wasn't one of them. Plus, heaven forbid he was e-mailing to tell her some kind of bad news. In that case, she'd feel horrible if she never replied.

But beyond that, there was a small part of her that was curious. Did he miss her? As practical minded as she liked to think she was, the idea that there might be a man somewhere out there who was pining for her, potentially wracked with guilt and angst over the demise of their relationship, a man who'd spent hours pouring his heart and soul into this sentimental missive sitting unopened in her inbox between an e-mail from a DEA agent she worked with—subject: "Need a subpoena ASAP"—and an e-mail from Rae—subject: "OMG—DID YOU WATCH THE GOODWIFE LAST NIGHT???"—was heady indeed.

So she clicked on the message.

Rylann read the entire e-mail, then sat back in her chair to contemplate its meaning. Given that this was their first correspondence in nearly six months, it would be tempting to read too much into Jon's every word. Luckily, he had been thoughtful enough to spare her from the rigors of that exercise.

After three years of dating, a year of living together, and six months of being apart, he'd written *one* word to her.

HI.

Thirteen

"*HI? THAT'S IT?*"

Rylann grabbed another carrot stick and dipped it into the hummus plate she and Rae had ordered. "Yep. That's all he wrote." She waived the carrot in the air. "What does that even mean? *Hi*."

"It means he's a jackass."

Rae had always possessed a talent for getting to the heart of the matter.

"Is this his way of testing the waters or something?" Rylann asked. "He throws out a *hi* to see if I'll write back?"

"Well, for one thing, it's a sign that he's thinking about you," Rae said.

The bartender returned with their martinis—between the interview with Kyle and Jon's stupid *Hi*, Rylann had called for an emergency post-work happy hour at a bar in between her and Rae's offices.

She chewed her carrot stick, musing over Rae's comment. Then she shook her head. "You know what? I'm not going down this road again. I've already spent plenty of time analyzing and second-guessing every word of my last few conversations with Jon." That had been stage one of her six-month plan to get over the breakup—a stage that had gone *nowhere*.

"Cheers to that." Rae clinked her glass to Rylann's and took a sip of her French martini. "So are you going to write back to him?"

"Sure. How about 'Bye'?"

Rae laughed. "Probably not the response he was hoping

for. But over the last six months, Jon has displayed a shockingly poor ability to read you. I guess we shouldn't be too surprised by this."

"More than six months, since we obviously hadn't been on the same page about our relationship leading up to the Italy thing," Rylann pointed out.

Rae snorted in agreement. "How he ever thought you were going to go for that idea, I have no clue."

Rylann had expressed that very sentiment on several occasions since the breakup, but something about the way Rae said it made her feel as though she needed to clarify something. "Right. Because I would've been a fool at this point in my life to quit my job and follow some guy to Italy who can't commit to marrying me."

Rae set down her glass. "Absolutely. But even beyond that, he should've known you would've never gone with him."

Rylann hedged, not sure she liked the sound of that. "Well, I wouldn't say never."

Rae gave her a get-real look. "Please. *You* go to Italy? You have your plans, remember?" She held up her hands innocently. "Why are you looking at me like that? Come on—you know this about yourself."

"True. But when you say it, it makes me sound so . . . lame." Suddenly concerned, she leaned in, lowering her voice. "I'm not lame, am I?"

"Sweetie, you're not lame."

Rylann grabbed her drink. "Look at this, I drink martinis on workdays—that can't be lame, right? And this wasn't even planned."

Rae smiled. "You know I love you, right?"

Rylann eyed her warily. "That's typically a lead-in people say to give themselves permission to tell you something you don't want to hear."

"Okay, then let's start with the part you *do* want to hear: you are a brilliant trial lawyer, Ry. And part of that comes from your ability to plan ahead—you're always three steps ahead of the other guy, and have figured out the solution to the problem before he even realizes there is one."

Rylann sniffed, partially mollified. "Go on."

"But let's be honest: did any part of you, even for one second, think about chucking it all and getting on that plane with Jon?"

"No," Rylann said matter-of-factly. "Because that would've been crazy. And I don't do crazy. Crazy is for women in their twenties."

"You didn't do it then, either."

"So I'm ahead of the curve." Rylann took a sip of her drink, mulling something over and turning serious for a moment. Rae had been her best friend for years, even when they'd lived two thousand miles apart. She trusted her opinion more than anyone's. "If it had been you, would you have gone to Rome?"

Rae thought this over. "Probably not. I don't do crazy, either."

Rylann threw her hands up in exasperation. "Then why are you riding me about this?"

"I don't know. Maybe because we're both thirty-two and single. It used to be bridal showers and bachelorette parties. Now a week doesn't go by without the mailman bringing me some sort of announcement or invitation with a baby booty on it." She shrugged. "So maybe not doing crazy isn't working so great for either of us."

The words hung in the air between them.

"Well, thanks, Mendoza—now I'm just depressed. Actually, no. The hell with that." Rylann reached across the table and squeezed Rae's hand. "Just because we haven't met Mr. Right doesn't mean we're doing anything wrong. And by the way, you're brilliant and awesome, too. If I were a lesbian, I'd totally settle down with you and make lots of in vitro babies."

Rae smiled, just as Rylann had hoped. She hated to see her friend—normally so upbeat about the dating scene—get down about this. Plus, it unsettled her. Rae was a smart, attractive, successful woman. If she didn't have her pick of the litter, Rylann had no clue what men were looking for.

"Have I told you how glad I am that you moved here?" Rae asked.

"Me, too." And as she said the words, Rylann realized just

how true they were. Sure, she missed San Francisco at times, but even in the couple short weeks Chicago had begun to feel like home again. "So there's something else I wanted to tell you. Not related to Jon."

Rae took a sip of her martini. "It's something good, isn't it? I can tell by the look on your face. Let me guess: work hottie."

"No." Rylann thought about that. "Actually, there is a work hottie. A couple of them, in fact. But that's not it." She lowered her voice. "I can't tell you any details because the matter is still in the investigatory stage, but Kyle Rhodes is a witness in one of my cases. We met for coffee earlier today."

"Get out of here." Rae's expression changed from one of surprise to curiosity. "What kind of case is it? Computer hacking or something?"

"It's an investigation related to the prison," Rylann said vaguely. "He overheard something while he was there."

"Did you two manage to exchange more than three words this time?" Rae asked teasingly.

"We did."

Rae waited expectantly. "And . . . ?"

"And we talked and had coffee." Rylann looked at her pointedly. "Obviously, that's as far as that story can go. He's my witness now."

Rae considered that. "Technically, it's not an ethics violation to be involved with a witness, you know." She held out her hands at the look Rylann gave her. "I'm just saying."

"I think we're way ahead of the game here. And regardless, technical violation or not, it would be a *really* bad idea."

"Yes, it would," Rae said, without hesitation.

"Can you imagine what would happen if this case went to trial and it came out that Kyle and I were involved?"

"Sure I can, I'm a defense attorney. I'll tell you exactly what would happen if that came out at trial—I would light his ass up on the witness stand." Rae set down her martini glass and went into mock cross-examination mode. " 'Mr. Rhodes, is your testimony here today at all impacted by the fact that you're having *sex* with the assistant U.S. attorney handling this case?' "

Rylann tipped her glass in agreement. "Exactly."

" 'Did Ms. Pierce ever talk about your testimony in bed, Mr. Rhodes? Perhaps give you a few pointers, lover to lover, on what you should say on the witness stand?' "

"Right. So you see my—"

" '—You like to please your lovers, don't you, Mr. Rhodes? You'd say anything to help Ms. Pierce win her case, wouldn't you?' "

Seeing that this could take a while, Rylann sat back in her chair and got comfortable.

Rae smiled. "Speaking for a moment as a defense attorney and not as your friend, that would be *so* much fun."

"Well, that kind of fun is not happening in any case I handle," Rylann said. And it wasn't just Kyle's reputation as a witness that she was thinking about. Just as important was her own reputation. She couldn't imagine the embarrassment of sitting in court while a defense attorney grilled one of her witnesses about a sexual relationship with *her*. She was a former clerk; she knew exactly what the judge would think of any lawyer who allowed herself to be put in that situation. Not to mention the stir that would cause around her office.

Bottom line, she was trying to impress her new boss and coworkers, and make a name for herself in the Chicago legal community. And being the dimwit who slept with a witness sure as heck wasn't the way to do it.

"Well." Rae gave Rylann a disappointed look. "That kind of sucks. I mean, not to rub it in or anything, but he's really hot. Like, movie star hot."

This had not escaped Rylann's attention. "I wouldn't want any part of that scene, anyway," she said with a shrug.

"Right. Because the hot guy scene is such a drag."

"I meant Kyle's scene. How many times did I see his name mentioned in Scene and Heard, PageSix, or TMZ.com, gossiping about how he was with some model at a hot new club or restaurant?"

Rae raised an eyebrow. "I don't know, how many times *did* you see that?" Her tone turned sly. "Wait a second . . .

have you been Googling Kyle Rhodes these past nine years, Ms. Pierce?"

Rylann blushed furiously at that. "*No*," she said as Rae began laughing in delight. She shifted uncomfortably, suddenly feeling like a witness in the hot seat. "I may have accidentally, wholly inadvertently, stumbled across his name one or two times"—*or ten*—"when I happened to be perusing a few gossip websites. That's all."

As Rae continued to smile, Rylann shot her a look over her martini glass. "Oh, like you've never looked up a guy you once knew on Facebook or anything."

"So you admit it."

Rylann tossed her hair back dismissively. "I admit nothing except for the fact that the man is now my witness."

"Over ninety percent of federal criminal cases plead out before going to trial, Ry." Rae winked knowingly. "Kyle Rhodes won't be your witness forever."

LATER THAT EVENING, Rylann sat cross-legged on her bed with her laptop open. She'd been dreading this moment since she'd gotten home—trying to come up with some kind of appropriate response to Jon's e-mail.

Finally, she typed, HI YOURSELF.

She immediately deleted it. That sounded too flirty.

This prompted a new question: Did she *want* to sound flirty?

Definitely not—he'd *dumped* her.

So she tried again. GOOD TO HEAR FROM YOU, she began, before deleting that, too. Frankly, it wasn't all that great to hear from him. Particularly since he'd thrown her into a tailspin over the damn *Hi* and now she was up at night, writing and rewriting a response to an e-mail that barely deserved one.

So ignore it. He'll get the hint.

But ignoring it made it seem as if she wasn't ready to face Jon, even via e-mail, and that wasn't the case. She was . . . okay with the breakup.

She perked up as that realization hit her. Suddenly, the

pressure to write the perfect response was gone, and she just went with her gut.

> HEY YOU—HOPE ALL IS WELL IN ROME AND THAT IT'S
> EVERYTHING YOU WERE LOOKING FOR. IF YOU GET A
> CHANCE, DROP ME A LINE IN ANOTHER SIX MONTHS. :)

There. She read it again and was satisfied that she'd struck just the right tone. Friendly enough—she'd even thrown in a smiley face emoticon—but not overly so. Assuming the whole point of Jon's e-mail was to check in and see how she was doing, her reply conveyed the message that he was free and clear to go about his business.

And also that she was going about hers.

Fourteen

KYLE CAREFULLY EASED his car into a tight parking spot, trying hard not to laugh at the sight of Dex, who stood on the sidewalk sporting a visor over a brown mess of seriously ridiculous bed hair.

After shutting off the engine, Kyle grabbed the handle of the gull-wing door of his Mercedes and pushed the door open upward toward the sky.

Dex grinned. "Dude, I don't care how many times I've seen you do that. That car is so fucking cool."

No disagreement there. Kyle pushed the button on his key, locking the car, and pointed to his friend's head. "Any particular explanation for the hair?"

"A hookup that ran late."

"I really hope she didn't see you on the way out. Because I think I see a gaggle of birds nesting in there." Not that it was the first time Kyle had seen Dex looking less than stellar, seeing how they'd shared an apartment their senior year of college and also during the two years thereafter.

"That's funny, man."

"I thought so. How was the hookup?"

"Good enough to last until noon," Dex said with a grin. Then he turned to the matter at hand, proudly gesturing to the bar they stood in front of. "Ready to check out the place?"

"Absolutely," Kyle said.

Eight years ago, after managing a campus bar in Champaign, Dex had moved up to Chicago and opened a sports bar on the north side of the city. Having done well for himself with that venture, he was now opening his second bar, an upscale nightclub called Firelight in the heart of the city's affluent Gold Coast neighborhood.

Once inside, Dex first gave Kyle a tour of the main bar. From the looks of the sable suede lounge chairs and couches, the large curving bar, and the subtle touches of deep red and copper fabric throughout, it appeared that Dex had spared no expense.

Next, Dex led him up some steps that would take them to a VIP lounge. "We open in four weeks. I heard a rumor that the food and dining section of the *Trib* is going to run an article this weekend, calling it the most anticipated bar opening of the season." He pointed. "You'll be there, right?"

"Ten U.S. marshals couldn't keep me away." Kyle looked up at the ceiling and admired the glittering sheets of red and burnt orange wavy glass. "Like fire. Nice touch."

"I worked with the designer for almost a month on that." Dex lifted the visor up to scratch his forehead, then caught Kyle's grin. "Come on. The hair's not that bad."

"Remember Kid 'n Play?"

Before Dex could respond, Kyle's cell phone rang. He pulled the phone out of his pocket and checked to see who was calling.

Rylann Pierce.

How intriguing.

"I should probably take this in private," he told Dex. He stepped out of the VIP room and then answered. "Counselor. To what do I owe this pleasure?"

Rylann spoke above the sounds of car horns and a jack-hammer in the background. "We're all set. Thursday at two o'clock. Just you, me, a court reporter, and a grand jury of twenty-three of your peers."

"Where are you?" Kyle asked. Her voice sounded a little breathless.

"Outside the courthouse, trying to catch a cab. I've got a meeting at the FBI building in twenty minutes."

He could picture her in her trench coat and heels, trusty briefcase at her side, all fired up and ready to throw around a few subpoena threats.

The image was strangely hot.

"Thursday, two o'clock," he confirmed. "Where do I go?"

"Room 511. For confidentiality purposes, there's nothing but a room number outside the door. You should wait in the witness room closest to the door until I come get you," she said. "Although you've refrained from retaining counsel on this matter, I'm obligated to say that you can still choose to bring a lawyer, but he or she would have to wait out in the hall. No one is allowed inside except for the witnesses, the jurors, the court reporter, and me. Think of it like Vegas—what happens in the grand jury room stays in the grand jury room."

Unable to resist, Kyle lowered his voice, teasing her. "I didn't think good-girl prosecutors knew about the types of things that happen in Vegas."

"There are probably a lot of things bad-boy ex-cons don't know about good-girl prosecutors."

Kyle raised an eyebrow. That actually sounded flirtatious.

But then her tone changed, back to all business. "I'll see you Thursday, then. Two o'clock."

"It's a date."

"No, it's a grand jury proceeding," she said firmly.

"You say tomato, I say—"

"Good-bye, Kyle." She hung up on him before he could finish.

Chuckling, Kyle tucked his cell phone into the pocket of his jeans and walked back into the VIP room.

Dex looked him over. "Whoever that was, she sure put a smile on your face."

Kyle waved this off. "Just this project I'm working on."

"Does this 'project' have a name?"

Sure. Rylann Pierce, aka Burr Up My Ass. "It's not what you think. That was someone from the U.S. Attorney's Office. I'm sort of . . . helping them in an investigation."

Understandably, that took Dex by surprise. "Wow. She must be *smoking* hot to have talked you into that." Then he cocked his head. "Hold on . . . is it that assistant U.S. attorney you were in court with the other day? The dark-haired one whose rack you're checking out in that photograph?"

Kyle stood against the onyx bar, waving this off. "We were in the middle of a courtroom—I wasn't checking out her rack. My eyes were on hers the entire time."

"Must be some eyes."

Kyle opened his mouth to protest, then stopped.

Well, actually, yes.

Fifteen

"I HAVE NO further questions, Agent Wilkins."

Rylann looked over her shoulder at the twenty-one people sitting behind her in three-tiered rows. Everyone was still awake, which was always a good sign. "Does the grand jury have any questions for this witness?"

There was a pause. Up front, next to the witness stand, sat the jury foreman and the recording secretary. The foreman shook his head no.

Rylann nodded at Sam. "You may step down, Agent Wilkins. Thank you." She turned and watched him leave the room, stealing another peek at the jurors. She could tell from their expressions that they'd liked him, and they had every reason to. He'd been engaging, professional, and prepared, not once needing to look at his investigative reports while testifying. If the case against Quinn went to trial—which, in reality, was unlikely—she had no doubt that Sam would make an excellent witness.

Her job today, simply, was to tell a story. Granted, because this was a grand jury proceeding and not a trial, she could eliminate many of the details of that story, but through her witnesses she needed to convey the who, what, where, when, why, and how of the crime. This particular story had three acts: Agent Wilkins, Kyle Rhodes, and Manuel Gutierrez. At the conclusion of the witnesses' testimony, she would hand the jury a proposed indictment that laid out the charges against Quinn. Then the rest was in their hands.

Today she would be asking them to indict Quinn on two

counts: second-degree murder and conspiracy to violate the civil rights of a federal prisoner. Since she had no direct proof that Quinn had instigated Watts's attack on Brown, she was asking the grand jury to infer that connection based on circumstantial evidence. It was not a perfect case, but it was one she believed in regardless. And all she needed was sixteen of the twenty-three men and women sitting in that room to believe in it, too.

When the door shut behind Agent Wilkins, Rylann looked over at the jury members. Since there was no judge in the room, the assistant U.S. attorney ran the show. "Why don't we take a ten-minute break before our next witness?"

She waited until the jurors and court reporter left, then she made her way to the witness room across the hall. She paused momentarily at the door, then pushed it open and found Kyle looking out the window at the view of the building most Chicagoans still refused to call anything but the Sears Tower.

"It's showtime," she said.

He turned around, looking strikingly handsome—and conservative—in his dark gray pin-striped suit, blue banker shirt, and gray and blue striped tie. He wore his hair neatly brushed back, the first time she'd ever seen it styled like that, and the color of his shirt brought out the blue of his eyes from across the room.

Rylann felt a little fluttering in her stomach, then quickly brushed it aside. Just a few butterflies of anticipation.

Kyle tucked his hands into his pockets, looking ready and raring to go. "Let's do this."

KYLE FOLLOWED RYLANN through the doorway, his curiosity piqued. He knew virtually nothing about grand jury proceedings, but the confidential nature of the process shrouded it in an aura of mystery. He walked into the room and saw that it was smaller than he'd expected, probably only half the size of a regular courtroom. To his right was a witness stand and a bench, the same kind a judge would normally sit behind. On the opposite side of the room was the table from which, presumably, Rylann would question him, and behind that, three rows of chairs for the jurors, stacked like a movie theater.

Chairs that were noticeably empty.

"Counselor, at some point do you plan to have any actual jurors at this grand jury proceeding?" he drawled.

"Ha, ha. I sent them out for a break. I want the jurors' first image of the infamous Kyle Rhodes to be of you sitting in that stand. I don't care what they've previously heard or read about you—today, you're simply a witness." She gestured to the stand. "Why don't you take a seat?"

Kyle stepped up and took a seat in a well-used swivel chair, banging his knees against a sturdy metal bar bolted to the underside of the podium. "Whoever designed these clearly didn't have tall men in mind," he grumbled.

"Sorry. It's for handcuffs," she said, referring to the bar.

Of course it was. Kyle looked out at the small courtroom. "So this is what I missed out on by pleading guilty."

Rylann approached the witness stand with a reassuring smile. "This is nothing. No cross-examination, no objections—just think of it as you and me having a conversation. The jurors can ask you questions when I'm done, although it's unlikely they'll do so. Assuming I've done my job right, they shouldn't have any questions."

She was awfully cute when she did her lawyer thing. "I like the pep talk, counselor," Kyle said, appreciating the fact that she was trying to make him feel comfortable.

"Thanks. Do you have any questions before we get started?" she asked.

"Just one." His eyes coyly skimmed over today's skirt suit varietal, which was beige. "Do you actually own any pants?"

"Any other questions?" she asked without batting an eye.

They were interrupted when the court reporter walked in, followed by two jurors. Immediately, things got serious again. The trio spotted him in the witness stand, and two of them, including the court reporter, did a double take. Ignoring their looks, Rylann returned to her table and nonchalantly studied her notepad, as if she put notorious billionaire heir ex-con hackers on the stand every day.

Over the course of the next two minutes, the remaining twenty-one jurors trickled in. Kyle was pleased to see that four of them didn't seem to recognize him at all, and three other jurors merely looked at him curiously, as if they couldn't quite place him. The remaining thirteen appeared highly intrigued by his presence.

When all the jurors had returned to their seats, Rylann nodded at the foreman. "You can swear in the witness."

"Raise your right hand," he said to Kyle. "Do you solemnly swear that the testimony you're about to give is the truth, the whole truth, and nothing but the truth?"

"I do."

Rylann locked eyes with him, with a hint of a smile on her lips only he understood.

They had sure come a long way from the cornfields of Champaign-Urbana.

"State your name for the record, please," she began.

And away we go.

"Kyle Rhodes."

KYLE HAD TO say, he was impressed.

She was good.

Of course, he'd guessed that Rylann would be a force to be reckoned with in court, since everything about her screamed Bad-Ass Attorney, but it was another thing to actually see it. Although she never moved once from the table, she commanded the room with her questions, drawing out his testimony in a way that hit all the right notes. She spent the first few minutes asking questions about his background, focusing on his education and work experience, which simultaneously gave Kyle a chance to settle into the witness stand and gave the jurors a chance to see him as someone other than the Twitter Terrorist. She addressed the circumstances of his conviction directly but moved on quickly after that, and then talked with him for a while about prison life.

Not exactly the proudest four months of Kyle's life, nor a subject on which he enjoyed being an expert, but he understood the role he needed to play that afternoon.

She slowed the pace when they got to the night Kyle overheard Quinn's threat, first eliciting testimony from him that set the scene.

"Can you explain what disciplinary segregation is, for those jurors who may not be familiar with the term?" she suggested.

"It's a cell block where they separate inmates from the general population. One inmate per cell, and there are none of the regular prison privileges. Meaning no leisure time, and you eat your meals in your cell."

"Is it quiet?" she asked.

"Very, especially since inmates in segregation aren't supposed to talk to each other. If a man's stomach growled, you could hear it three cells over."

He could tell she liked that answer.

Back and forth they went, grabbing the jurors' attention and reeling them in. They steadily made their way to the climax of their story—Quinn's threat. Kyle could see that the jurors were listening with much interest, practically on the edges of their seats as he repeated the words Quinn had said to Brown that fateful night. The tension and excitement in the room was palpable as Rylann circled back to the threat two times, hitting hard with her questions to emphasize this part of her examination, and then suddenly—

It was over.

She paused for a moment, letting Quinn's threat hang dramatically in the courtroom air. Then she nodded soberly.

"Thank you, Mr. Rhodes. I have no further questions." She turned to the jurors behind her. "Does the grand jury have any questions for this witness?" After a moment of silence, she smiled politely at Kyle. "You may step down, Mr. Rhodes. Thank you."

With a nod, Kyle rose from the swivel chair. Ignoring the curious glances of the jurors, he strode out of the room. When the door shut behind him, he stood alone in the hallway feeling satisfied yet strangely dismissed—like a man who'd barely finished his last pump during a hot one-night stand before being shoved out the door with his shirt and shoes in his hands.

He hadn't expected her to hang around for hours making post-testimonial chitchat, but, *boy*, that was . . . anticlimactic. For one thing, she hadn't even said when they were going to see each other again. Oh, sure, in a few weeks she'd waltz back into his life with her notepad and briefcase and fiery little subpoena threats, and she'd charm and sass and get whatever she wanted, and then wham-bam-thank-you-sir, she'd be on her merry little skirt-suited way again.

This whole grand jury experience had left him feeling very discombobulated.

Kyle made it all the way down to the lobby before he realized he could turn on his cell phone again. He did so, and moments later a text message popped up.

From Rylann, presumably on a break before her next witness.

YOU DID GREAT. I'LL CALL WHEN I KNOW ABOUT THE INDICTMENT.

Kyle stuck his phone back into his suit coat, only later realizing that was the first time in six months he'd left the courthouse with a smile on his face.

LATER THAT EVENING, Rylann walked out that very same door with a similarly pleased expression.

Unlike trial juries, which could take days or even longer in deliberation, a grand jury typically voted quickly. Today, thankfully, had been no exception. Ten minutes after Manuel Gutierrez left the witness stand, the jury foreperson had brought to the chief judge's chambers a true bill in the case that henceforth would officially be known as *United States v. Adam Quinn*.

She had her indictment.

Sixteen

FRIDAY MORNING, RYLANN received her second piece of good news in twenty-four hours.

"My client signed off on the guilty plea," said Greg Boran, an assistant federal defender for the Northern District of Illinois.

Over the course of the last week, Rylann had been negotiating the terms of a plea agreement for Watts. She'd known, as soon as Cameron had handed over the files, that this part of the case would plead out quickly. Watts was already a lifer, and the case against him was a slam dunk. Two men had been locked in a cell together, and one of those men had been beaten to death—not exactly a mystery who the attacker had been. In fact, Watts hadn't even bothered to claim self-defense— disgustingly enough, he seemed almost proud of his actions.

There was just one sticking point she'd been unable to make any headway on. "Any luck getting him to agree to flip on Quinn?"

"Sorry. He says he's got nothing to say about that," Greg said.

"Even if I knock the charge down to voluntary manslaughter?"

"Knocking down the charge won't make any difference in this case—which is precisely why you're so willing to offer it," Greg said. "Watts is already serving two life sentences. Shaving a few years off this conviction would be irrelevant."

"How about the fact that it would be the right thing to do?" Rylann asked. "Your client might want to try that some time."

Greg remained firm. "He's a lifer, Rylann. He's not going to shit where he eats just to throw you a solid. I don't think it'll go over so well with the other guards if he's the guy responsible for sending one of them to prison."

Maybe not. Still, Rylann gave it one last shot. "I can arrange for him to be transferred out of MCC. Move him somewhere where the sun shines on the prison yard all year long. As a matter of fact, I happen to know that there are some lovely institutions in California that would be happy to welcome Mr. Watts as a guest."

Greg chuckled. "I already made the suggestion. But you can move him anywhere you want, and he'll still be known as the inmate who ratted out a guard. Sorry, but if you want to nail Quinn, you're going to have to do it without Watts."

Rylann sighed. Not the response she'd been hoping for, but that wasn't Greg's fault. She had a lot of respect for the attorneys in the Federal Defender's Office—they handled caseloads as heavy as those of the prosecutors they faced off against yet had one of the most thankless jobs in the legal profession. "It was worth a shot. I'll see you in court next week."

BRIGHT AND EARLY the following Monday, Rylann got her first look at another man she'd set her sights on: Adam Quinn, the "mean son of a bitch" prison guard who'd instigated and arranged Watts's brutal attack against Brown.

Quinn had been arrested by the FBI the night before, and they were in court for his initial appearance. When Rylann walked through the courtroom doors, she immediately noticed two things: first, that Quinn looked younger than his twenty-eight years, and second, that he appeared to be extremely nervous.

As well he should.

Before taking a seat at her table, she introduced herself to Quinn's defense attorney. "Rylann Pierce," she said, extending her hand.

"Michael Channing. I'd like a moment of your time after the arraignment, Ms. Pierce," he said tersely.

"Of course. I can even give you two moments," she said with a pleasant smile. She'd been litigating against guys like this her entire career—lawyers who seemingly confused brashness with being tough. Good thing she'd stopped being unnerved by that kind of strategy somewhere around her third trial.

She went over to the prosecution table and set her briefcase off to the side. Shortly thereafter, the clerk called the case, and they were off and running. Because an indictment had already been returned against the defendant, the magistrate judge combined the initial appearance and the arraignment. Quinn, not unexpectedly, entered a plea of not guilty.

At the conclusion of the hearing, Michael Channing made a beeline for Rylann's table. "Second-degree murder? My client never even touched the guy." He peered down at her with a smirk. "I looked you up. You're new here."

"The law in the Seventh Circuit is clear, Mr. Channing. Anyone who aids in the commission of a crime can be found guilty of that crime. I've been here long enough to know that, at least."

"I know what the Seventh Circuit says," he said with a glare. "But this whole thing was just a fight between two inmates gone wrong. Show me what you've got that proves anything other than that."

Rylann could already tell—he was going to be an absolute *joy* to litigate against. "I'm happy to." She unzipped her briefcase, pulled out a file that she'd prepared with all of Special Agent Wilkins's investigation reports, and plunked it into Channing's hands. "Here you go. There's a letter on top outlining my proposed discovery schedule. Exculpatory evidence three weeks before trial, full witness list two weeks prior."

He looked down at the file in surprise, obviously not having expected to walk out with the FBI reports *today.* "Yes, well. I'll . . . be taking a look at these right away."

"One other thing I should mention. For security reasons, Manuel Gutierrez has been transferred out of MCC and moved downstate to Pekin." Given the inmate's concerns about his safety, Rylann had felt that was the safest course of action.

Channing nodded. "I see."

From his blank expression, Rylann guessed that he did not, in fact, see. Most likely, Channing had no clue who Manuel Gutierrez was. Which was precisely why she liked to hit defense attorneys with the FBI reports right away. It sent them a message, right from the get-go, that they had some catching up to do.

Not surprisingly, Channing had no further demands at that hearing.

UNFORTUNATELY, THE SWEET taste of victory did not linger long.

"I'm striking out with the other inmates," Agent Wilkins said over the phone later that afternoon when Rylann was back at the office.

To further bolster her case against Quinn, Rylann had asked Wilkins to talk to some of the inmates at MCC to see if any of them could provide support for their theory about Quinn—that he'd been giving preferential treatment to certain inmates who'd carried out his retaliation. "Are they afraid to talk to you?"

Wilkins snorted. "They're not afraid—they all want *deals*. They know that Gutierrez was taken out of MCC after meeting with us. Apparently, the rumor floating around is that he's playing golf at a minimum-security facility in Miami."

"Of course that's the rumor. One day I have to find this elusive federal prison where everyone runs around free, plays golf, and eats five-course meals."

"Frankly, I don't think most of these guys know anything about any special treatment Quinn was giving Jones and Romano," Wilkins said, referring to the two other inmates they believed had done Quinn's dirty work. "But I wouldn't put it past them to claim otherwise if they think it means they'll get a shortened sentence and an all-expense-paid trip to southern Florida."

"What about going directly to Jones and Romano? Are they willing to talk?" Rylann asked.

"Not a chance. As soon as I mentioned Quinn's name, they both demanded to speak to a lawyer. They know exactly why we want to talk to them—the whole prison is buzzing about Quinn being indicted." Wilkins's tone turned apologetic. "Sorry I couldn't come up with more."

Rylann rocked back in her desk chair. She was disappointed but not surprised. "Like you said, if these guys are so insistent on deals, I couldn't trust anything they said anyway."

"Too bad Manuel Gutierrez didn't know anything. Since he's already agreed to testify, that would've been perfect," Wilkins said. "What about Kyle Rhodes? I take it the same goes for him?"

"Not sure. I've been in court so much recently, I haven't had the chance to circle back to him yet," Rylann said.

"I could do the follow-up interview if you like," Wilkins offered politely. "It's just that you've been the contact person with him thus far . . ."

"Nope, I've got it covered. I'm adding it to my to-do list for the day as we speak." As Rylann reached for a pen, her second phone line rang—and then her cell phone chimed immediately after that with a text message. She quickly checked the caller ID on both while jotting down a note on her daily calendar.

"You sure?" Wilkins said with a chuckle. "You sound awfully busy right now."

Sure, she was a little inundated right then. But since she was the one who'd established the relationship with Kyle Rhodes, it would be odd to suddenly send in the FBI to talk to him. Besides, there was no way that Meth Lab Rylann was going to get a reputation in her new office of not pulling her weight. "I'm positive. It's on the official checklist," she assured him. "Which means—"

Rylann stopped abruptly when she saw what she'd written amid all the distractions.

Do Kyle Rhodes.

Clearly, she and her subconscious needed to have a talk about that one.

Seventeen

KYLE ALMOST HAD a heart attack when he peered down at the Post-it note his sister had given him.

"*This* is your password? Clearly, that's the next thing we need to fix," he said as he logged on to her laptop. Jordan had asked him to stop by her store to see if he could figure out why her Internet connection had suddenly crashed. Based on her password alone, he was already dreading what he might find.

Standing next to the desk, Jordan gave him a quizzical look. "Mom's maiden name and the years Grandma and Grandpa Evers were born. Why would anyone ever think of that combination?"

"Or you could just make the password one-two-three-four," he offered. "Since you're obviously trying to have your identity stolen." He pointed, lecturing. "Listen and learn: you need fourteen characters, minimum. Use random letters, not words. Here's a tip: think of a sentence, and use the first letter in each of those words. Mix it up between upper and lower case. Then pick two numbers that mean something to you—not dates—and stick them somewhere between the letters. Put a punctuation mark at the beginning of the password and then a symbol, like a dollar sign, at the end."

"Yes, sir." Jordan grabbed a pen and another Post-it note. "Um, could you repeat everything that came after mixing up the upper and lower case?"

Kyle took the pen from her. "I'll come up with something

for you." He shooed her off. "Now go away. Sell some wine. I'll call you if I need someone to push an on-off button." He thought of one last thing. "By the way, when's the last time you updated the firmware on your router? Okay, from your blank expression, I'll mark that down as a big 'never.' "

Shortly after she left, his cell phone rang, and Kyle saw that it was Rylann. The two of them had been playing phone tag all afternoon—not that he particularly minded hearing her sexy, throaty voice on his voicemail.

He knew, from the press release the U.S. Attorney's Office had issued last Friday morning, that the grand jury had indicted Adam Quinn. Since then, there'd been some local media interest in the case—a guard instigating the murder of a federal inmate was exactly the kind of juicy public corruption scandal that Chicago journalists loved to report about—but thankfully, none of the witnesses' names had been revealed. He was more than happy to stay out of the spotlight as long as possible on this one.

"It appears congratulations are in order, Ms. Pierce," he said when he answered his phone. "I see you got your indictment. I believe a certain somebody said something about calling me when that happened."

"I've been waiting for a time when I had more than five seconds to talk."

"Oh." Kyle rocked back in the desk chair, liking the sound of that. "I'm flattered."

"Because I also need a favor from you."

Of course she did. "You know, counselor, I think that card you keep playing—the one that says, 'Redeemable for old times' sake'—has officially expired."

"Uh-oh, I better check." There was a pause on the other end of the line. "Nope, May 2012. We're still good."

He fought back a grin at that one. "What do you need?"

"I have a few follow-up questions related to Quinn," Rylann said. "It should only take twenty minutes. Thirty, tops. Is this a good time?"

As if on cue, Jordan stuck her head into her office. Seeing

him on the phone, she pointed to her computer and whispered. "Is it fixed?"

Kyle shook his head. *No. Go away.*

He waited until Jordan left before answering Rylann. "Actually, I'm in the middle of something at my sister's wine shop. Can I call you back?"

She hesitated. "How long do you think it'll be?"

"Maybe a half hour."

"I have plans later tonight, so I was going to leave work after I finished talking to you. You were the last item on my checklist," she said. "Maybe we can talk tomorrow instead?"

"Unfortunately, I'm going out of town tomorrow morning and will be gone all week," he told her. He was flying to Seattle, San Diego, and then to New York to talk to three potential candidates for a senior-level position in his start-up company. Given the whole Twitter debacle, it had taken some convincing even to get these guys to agree to meet with him.

"This was something I'd been hoping to wrap up in the next few days . . ." she mused out loud. "How about if I call you in a little while, after I get home? I live in Roscoe Village, so it should be about thirty minutes. Does that work?"

"Roscoe Village is right by my sister's store. DeVine Cellars, on Belmont. Why don't you just stop by here on your way home and we can talk in person?"

The words flew out of Kyle's mouth before he could even think about them.

Apparently, Rylann was just as surprised by the offer as he was. "I, um . . . hadn't considered that possibility."

Neither had he, but the more he thought about it, the faster he was warming to it. If for no other reason, he was curious to check out today's skirt suit selection. "Well, if you want to talk to me this week, counselor, I'd start considering it. That's the only time I'm available for pesky assistant U.S. attorneys."

"*If* I were to agree to this, it would be solely because—as it so happens—I've been wanting to check out your sister's shop for a while now," she said. "I hear she's got the best wine selection in the city."

Kyle grinned. "You keep telling yourself that, counselor. Maybe in thirty minutes, when you get here, you'll actually believe it."

A DEFIANT THIRTY-SEVEN minutes later, when Rylann walked into DeVine Cellars and felt the cool air of the shop hit her, she momentarily felt as if she were back in San Francisco. There had been a store just like this only a block from her old apartment that she'd frequented often—cozy yet sophisticated, highboy tables scatted throughout, and bin after bin filled with wine bottles.

Rylann scanned the store and saw customers at two of the tables but no sign of Kyle. She walked over to an empty table tucked into a corner against the wine bins, hung the strap of her briefcase on the back of one of the chairs, and took a seat.

She'd just begun to read the chalkboard over the main bar, which listed the wines the store had available by the glass, when she heard a friendly voice to her right.

"Looking for anything in particular?"

A slender, very pretty blond woman with blue eyes smiled as she approached the table. Even if Rylann hadn't recognized Jordan Rhodes from the photos that had been in the media over the years, she would have known instantly that she was Kyle's sister. Though nearly a foot shorter than Kyle, and with hair that was several shades lighter, those blue eyes gave it away.

Before Rylann could say anything, Jordan cocked her head with a look of recognition. "I know you. You're the prosecutor who handled the motion to reduce my brother's prison sentence."

Rylann assumed Jordan had been in court that morning to support Kyle. Or maybe she'd seen the photo of the two of them that had done the media circuit. "You have a good memory. Actually, I'm meeting Kyle here tonight. Is he around?"

For whatever reason, Jordan appeared shocked by the question.

"You're meeting my brother *here*?" she asked. "Are you sure about that?"

"Pretty sure. It was his suggestion, actually."

Jordan stared at her. "Are we talking about the same Kyle Rhodes? Tall; freakishly lustrous, shampoo-commercial hair; has this weird thing about giving people nicknames?"

"I heard that, Jordo." Kyle came around the wine bins, wearing jeans and a navy crewneck sweater. As he approached, Rylann noticed that he hadn't shaved that day and that the scruff along his strong, angular jaw made him look very . . . beddable.

Witness, she reminded herself.

He stopped at Rylann's table. "I see that you've had the non-pleasure of meeting my sister." He gestured, making the introduction. "Jordo, this is Rylann Pierce."

Jordan raised an eyebrow pointedly at Kyle.

He glared.

An entire dialogue seemed to pass between them.

Then Jordan extended her hand warmly. "It's a pleasure to meet you, Rylann. Please let me know if there's anything I can get you." She pointed to the chalkboard. "I've got a great cabernet open tonight."

"I see that. Actually, I think all the Kuleto Estate cabs are great," Rylann said. "The India Ink is probably in my top five wines."

Jordan pulled back, impressed. "You speak wine, I see." She nodded approvingly at Kyle. "I like her already."

"Jordo . . ." he said warningly.

"What? That was a compliment." She turned back to Rylann. "Question: you're not secretly a money-grubbing skank, are you?"

Kyle looked pained. "My God, Jordan."

"What? It's a fair question given your past predilections."

Rylann smiled at the dynamic between the two of them. "Your brother is safe with me. We're not together, we're just . . ." She paused, looking at Kyle and trying to decide how best to describe their situation, since she had no clue whether he'd mentioned to his family that he was working with the U.S. Attorney's Office. ". . . old friends," she finished.

Jordan raised a skeptical eyebrow at Kyle. "Old friends with the U.S. Attorney's Office? Sure."

"The wine, Jordo?" he said pointedly.

She flashed them both a grin. "Coming right up," she sang cheerfully as she walked away.

Kyle took a seat in the chair next to Rylann. "Sorry about that. For years, my sister has labored under the impression that she's funny. My father and I have humored her in this."

Rylann waved this off. "No apology necessary. She's just protective of you. That's what siblings do—at least, I assume it is."

"No brothers or sisters for you?" Kyle asked.

Rylann shook her head. "My parents had me when they were older. I asked for a sister every birthday until I was thirteen, but it wasn't in the cards." She shrugged. "But at least I have Rae."

"When did you two meet?"

"College. We were in the same sorority pledge class. Rae is . . ." Rylann cocked her head, trying to remember. "What's that phrase men always use when describing their best friend? The thing about the hooker and the hotel room."

"If I ever woke up with a dead hooker in my hotel room, he'd be the first person I'd call. A truer test of male friendship there could not be."

Rylann smiled. "That's cute. And a little scary, actually, that all you men have planned ahead for such an occasion." She waved her hand. "Well, there you go. If I ever woke up with a dead hooker in my hotel room, Rae would be the first person I'd call."

Kyle rested his arms on the table and leaned in closer. "Counselor, you're so by the book, the first person you'd call if you woke up next to a dead hooker would be the FBI."

"Actually, I'd call the cops. Most homicides aren't federal crimes, so the FBI wouldn't have jurisdiction."

Kyle laughed. He reached out and tucked back a lock of hair that had fallen into her eyes. "You really are a law geek."

At the same moment, they both realized what he was doing. They froze, eyes locked, his hand practically cupping the side of her cheek.

Then they heard someone clearing her throat.

Rylann and Kyle turned and saw Jordan standing at their table.

"Wine, anyone?" With her blue eyes dancing, she set two glasses in front of them. "I'll leave you two to yourselves now."

Rylann watched as Jordan strolled off. "I think you're going to have some explaining to do after I leave," she whispered to Kyle.

"Oh, without a doubt, she's going to be all up in my business over this."

Rylann laughed. Then she gave her glass a swirl, opening up the aromas of the wine and checking its hue. It gave her a convenient excuse to look away from Kyle.

The scruff was *killing* her.

Time to get down to business. "So about this case . . ."

TRY AS SHE might to hide it, Kyle hadn't missed Rylann's reaction when he'd touched her.

She was in lawyer mode again, naturally, asking him about Quinn and various things he'd noticed at MCC. But he wasn't a fool—moments ago, he'd seen the flare of heat in those gorgeous amber eyes. The spark he'd felt between them the night they'd met was still there, no doubt, but she was either fighting it or playing hard to get.

So he played along, answering all her questions like a good little ex-con. Whether he'd ever seen Quinn showing any favoritism to certain inmates, whether he'd heard rumors about any such favoritism, and if he had any idea who, out of all the inmates, had been most tapped into the gossip and thus might know more than he did.

Somewhere along the way, he found himself getting a little . . . distracted. Maybe it was the way her hair spilled over her shoulder as she leaned forward to jot something down on her legal pad. Or how her cheeks had picked up a rosy flush as she continued taking sips of her wine. Or possibly it was the lovely, slender curve of her neck as she rested her head on her hand while listening to him.

Mostly, though, it was just the direct way she held his gaze and listened to him, as if they were the only two people in the room.

"I get the impression I wasn't much help to you tonight," he said when she appeared to be wrapping up with her questions.

Rylann swirled her glass on the table. "It was a long shot. Agent Wilkins and I have been striking out all week with this."

When she took another sip of wine—her glass almost empty—Kyle knew that the interview portion of this evening had come to an end. Which meant that it was time for him to take things up a notch.

He gestured to her wineglass, starting with a softball question to warm her up. "So is wine something you got into when you lived in San Francisco?"

She nodded. "I knew nothing about it when I first moved there from Champaign. But most of the people I hung around with drank wine, so I slowly began drinking it more often, figuring out what I like. And what I don't like."

Now time for a not-so-soft question. "You never did tell me the whole truth about why you left San Francisco."

She glanced at him sideways. "Why are you so interested in that?"

"You know so much about me, it seems only fair." Kyle decided to go for broke. "Did it have something to do with a guy?"

For a moment she seemed to debate whether to answer this. "Yes."

"Is he still in the picture?"

"No."

He'd be lying if he said he wasn't glad to hear that. "Not very talkative about this subject, are you?"

"Maybe instead we could talk about your breakup with Daniela."

Kyle rested his arm on the table, leaning closer to her and speaking in a lower voice. "And maybe, just once, you could restrain yourself from turning one of our conversations into a verbal tennis match."

Her eyes held his for a moment, as if she were considering this, then she looked away and gave her wineglass another swirl. "My ex-boyfriend and I broke up after he decided he wanted to move to Rome. With or without me."

"Sounds like your ex-boyfriend is a douchebag."

Rylann smiled at that. Then, quite deliberately, she shifted away from that topic by checking her watch. "Well, look at that. I think you and I finally managed to break our eight-minute record of getting along." She took her last sip and then set her glass on the table. "Speaking of time, I really should get going."

"That's right, you mentioned earlier that you have plans tonight. Hot date?" Kyle asked.

Real subtle, asshole.

"I'm just going to the movies with Rae," she said. "We're seeing *The Hunger Games* at eight thirty."

Kyle checked his watch. "Eight thirty? You still have time." He looked straight into her eyes, deciding to go for broke. "Stay for a little longer, Rylann." His voice turned huskier. "We'll have another glass of wine and catch up. That's what old friends do, isn't it?"

She studied him for a long moment.

Too long.

"I don't think that's a good idea," she finally said. "I wouldn't want people to get the wrong idea about our situation."

Kyle looked around the wine store—there was only one other table of customers, and they weren't paying any attention to them. So by "people," she obviously meant him.

"The situation?" he asked.

"You know, the whole lawyer–witness thing." Her tone was casual, but her eyes held his quite directly. "I wouldn't want anyone to think there was something going on here. Because that couldn't happen, obviously."

Right. That situation.

Kyle took a sip of his wine as the meaning of her words hit him.

It didn't mean a thing, he reminded himself. She was just one girl.

"Of course." He threw her an easygoing grin. "Actually, I was just trying to avoid having to get back to the whole mess of network connection problems waiting for me in Jordan's office."

"Oh. Sorry I couldn't help you out with that." Rylann stood up and threw the strap of her briefcase over her shoulder. "So . . . I'll be in touch if there's any development in the Quinn case."

Sure she would. No clue how long that might be. "You know how to find me, counselor."

"Right." She smiled in farewell. "Thanks again for meeting with me. I promise to stay out of your freakishly lustrous, shampoo-commercial hair. At least for a while."

After she left the wine shop, Kyle sat at the table, playing distractedly with his glass.

"She didn't want to stay?"

Kyle looked up and saw Jordan standing at the table. For once, shockingly, she didn't appear ready to harass or needle him.

"She had plans with a friend," he said with a shrug.

"You've never introduced me to a woman before."

Kyle shook his head. "It's not like that, Jordo," he said. "Rylann is just—"

"—an old friend." With a soft smile, she reached out and ruffled his hair. "Got it."

Eighteen

AS IT TURNED out, Rylann wasn't quite as good as she'd thought she was.

Over the last five years she'd prosecuted cases, she'd become quite skilled at reading defendants and their lawyers at the initial court appearance. Given Quinn's obvious nervousness, she'd originally predicted that his lawyer would be calling her within two weeks to negotiate a plea agreement.

Instead, it took him two weeks and three days to make that call.

"I've read the FBI reports," Michael Channing led in shortly after Rylann answered the phone. There was a touch less bravado in his voice in comparison to the last time they'd spoken at Quinn's arraignment. "I'd like to talk about a plea bargain. In person. My client has something he wants to say."

"How about tomorrow?" Rylann asked. "I'm in court in the morning but can make myself available later on. Say, two o'clock?"

"Two thirty," Channing said brusquely.

Clearly, it was going to be one of *those* kinds of discussions.

THE FOLLOWING AFTERNOON, Rylann sat across the table from both Quinn, who looked uncomfortable in his navy suit, and his lawyer, who looked put out and cantankerous, per usual. She'd reserved one of the conference rooms for this meeting—no need for them to see the mountain of files on her desk. Today she wanted to convey the impression that this case was her top, and only, priority.

"You said you wanted to talk?" Rylann began.

Channing gave his client a go-ahead look. "It's okay. Anything you say here is inadmissible at trial if we don't come to an agreement on a plea."

Quinn glanced mistrustfully at Rylann, appearing to want confirmation of this.

"He's correct," she said. "Unless you were to take the stand at trial and perjure yourself. Which I strongly recommend against doing."

Quinn ran his hand over his mouth, then rested his hands on the table. "You've got this whole thing with Darius Brown wrong, Ms. Pierce. It's not what you think."

Rylann's face remained impassive. "How so?"

"I never told Watts to kill Brown," he said emphatically. "I only told him to rough the guy up, that's all. You know, teach him a lesson."

"That was some lesson."

"Look, Brown attacked me first. You can't have that in prison. You get too much of that and the inmates will be running the damn asylum." Quinn attempted a smile, then it faded when he saw that the serious expression on Rylann's face remained unchanged.

His tone became more angry, a quick flash of temper. "You sit there, looking so smug," he said to her. "But who do you think watches these animals after you get your convictions? You see them at trial for—what?—a couple days, maybe a week, and then you pass the buck on. I have to deal with them for years. You and your whole office should be thanking me for doing my job."

"Doing your job doesn't include killing an inmate, Mr. Quinn."

"I told you, that wasn't supposed to happen," he said, getting louder.

There was a pause as the two men exchanged a look, then Channing spoke. "We'll agree to involuntary manslaughter. And you also agree to drop the civil rights charge."

"Not going to happen," Rylann said matter-of-factly. "You deliberately put Brown in harm's way," she told Quinn. "Voluntary manslaughter, and the civil rights charge stands."

"No fucking way," Quinn said to Channing. "I'll take my chances at trial."

"You go to trial, and you're looking at a murder-two conviction," Rylann said.

"Or he might walk away free," Channing said. "All you can actually prove is that my client arranged to put Brown in a cell with Watts. Whether he did that out of payback and colluded with Watts to attack Brown is based entirely on speculation."

"Not true. I've got two witnesses who can establish both retaliatory motive and that Quinn and Watts were working together."

"Witnesses who are both convicted felons," Channing said. "One of whom is undoubtedly hoping to score a sweet deal with you in exchange for his testimony, and the other of whom is Kyle Rhodes." He laughed humorlessly. "Do you really think the jury is going to believe anything the Twitter Terrorist says?"

"Absolutely," Rylann said without hesitation. "Let me tell you what the jury will think when I put Kyle Rhodes on the stand. They'll see a witness with no motive or agenda—someone who's testifying solely because it's the right thing to do. Sure, he made a mistake, but he also had the guts to own up to that by pleading guilty and accepting full responsibility for his crimes. Frankly, Mr. Channing, if your client is half the man Kyle Rhodes is, he'll do the same."

Quinn jumped back in. "Oh, so the Twitter Terrorist is some hero, and I'm the fucking scum of the earth." He pointed to the case file in front of Rylann. "Does your little file tell you what Darius Brown did before the FBI locked him up at MCC? He robbed a bank with two of his buddies and pistol-whipped one of the tellers. Trust me, your 'victim' wasn't exactly a saint."

"And Darius Brown went to prison for his actions," Rylann said. "Just like you will go to prison for yours."

She saw him open his mouth and beat him to the punch. "Let's talk straight, Mr. Quinn. This isn't the first time you've done this. On two other occasions you orchestrated attacks on an inmate, but this time you picked the wrong guy to carry out your dirty work. Watts beat Brown to death with a padlock attached to a belt, and *you* made the whole thing happen." She turned to Channing, repeating her earlier terms. "Voluntary manslaughter, and the civil rights charge stands. That is the best, and only, deal you will get from me."

The words hung in the air between them.

"This is not what we'd hoped for, Ms. Pierce," Channing said coolly.

"Understood." Rylann stood up from the table and gathered her file. "You can let me know your decision after you and Mr. Quinn have had the opportunity to talk. If you're not interested in my terms, then we'll prepare for trial. I assume you know your way out?"

She made it all the way to the reception area before she heard them call her name. She turned and saw Quinn and Channing walking in her direction, en route to the elevators. Quinn strode past her without a second glance, and Channing barely slowed his pace as he addressed her.

"E-mail me the agreement as soon as it's ready," he said. "I'll call the clerk and have him put us on the docket for a change of plea."

And that was that.

Rylann watched Quinn and Channing go, thinking that it was almost a shame they'd given in.

She would have rather enjoyed kicking both their asses at trial.

THE REST OF the week flew by, a flurry of motion calls, witness interviews, and meetings with various FBI, ATF, and DEA agents. Before Rylann knew it, on Friday morning she was in court for the entry of Quinn's guilty plea.

Afterward, she walked out of the courtroom feeling good about the resolution of the case—and even better twenty minutes later in her office, when Cameron stopped by to congratulate her.

"I just saw the press release Paul is putting together regarding Adam Quinn's guilty plea," Cameron said, referring to Paul Thompkins, the office's media representative. "Well done. The official word from the U.S. Attorney's Office is that this case demonstrates that we will vigorously prosecute law enforcement officials who abuse the trust individuals—including inmates—place in them." She smiled. "And we have you to thank for that."

Rylann waved off the praise. "Agent Wilkins deserves the credit as well. And for what it's worth, Kyle Rhodes really stepped up to the plate."

"The Twitter Terrorist comes through for us. Who would've thought?" Cameron asked. "I heard from Cade that Quinn and his lawyer were both jerks during the plea negotiations."

Rylann had talked to Cade about the case during one of their afternoon Starbucks runs. He was quickly becoming her go-to guy in the office, which was nice—it was good to have a friend she could trust in the special prosecutions group.

"You should've seen how sanctimonious Quinn was," she told Cameron. "It's fortunate we caught him now. If it hadn't been for the tip from that undercover FBI agent, this might've gone on for years."

"I suspect Quinn's tune will change quickly now that he'll be on the other side of those prison bars," Cameron said.

"Very true."

A few minutes later, after Cameron had left, Rylann called Rae.

"Are you free tonight?" she asked Rae. "Drinks are on me—I feel like celebrating."

Rae sounded excited. "Ooh, let's make a night of it. What are we celebrating?"

"The end of a very long workweek."

Rae laughed. "I hear that. Since you mentioned it, I was just reading in the *Trib* about this new bar, Firelight, that's opening tonight. Supposedly, it's *the* place to be this weekend. Want to check it out?"

Rylann thought about that. "Opening night at a hot new club? Think we'll get in?"

"If we look good enough, we will."

Rylann laughed. "I like your confidence, Mendoza. I'll cab over to your apartment at nine o'clock to pick you up."

Nineteen

KYLE STOOD AT the black onyx bar in the corner of the room, surrounded by a group of his friends. Firelight was packed to the gills, with everyone dressed in their Friday finest. By all accounts, the nightclub's opening appeared to be a huge success, and for Dex's sake, Kyle was thrilled.

Too bad he, personally, wasn't quite feeling it.

Maybe there *was* something to this whole inmate adjustment process Jordan had been babbling about. Because all around him, people were laughing, drinking, partying, and generally having the time of their lives. Even better, there were beautiful women everywhere, many of whom had been trying to catch his eye all night. Yet something was off.

Kyle excused himself from the other guys, saying he wanted to walk around and check out the crowd. He found Dex just outside the door, standing at the balcony railing and proudly looking down at the packed crowd in the main bar below.

Kyle joined his friend at the railing—no matter what his issues were, he sure as hell wouldn't let them spoil this moment for Dex. "How's it feel?"

"I won't lie. It feels good—real good," Dex said. "Ten years ago, I was bartending in a college bar in the middle of central Illinois. Now I have this."

"You earned it." Better than anyone, Kyle knew how hard Dex had worked to open the nightclub.

"Yes, I did," Dex said, his eyes traveling over the crowd. Then he paused at something he saw and looked over at Kyle with a sly grin. "Hmm. I think I might've found the cure for that emo mood you've been in these past few weeks."

"Emo?" Kyle laughed at the thought. "Screw you. I'm fine."

"If you say so. Still, you might want to check out the main bar. Red dress, two o'clock."

Kyle's eyes scanned the crowd half-interestedly, expecting to see some random hot, provocatively dressed girl. But when he finally located the red dress and, more important, the woman wearing it, he paused and just had to . . . stare.

Apparently, Prosecutrix Pierce had something other than skirt suits in her closet, after all.

Her hair fell over her shoulders in gorgeous raven waves, hitting right at the enticing V neckline of the sleeveless red dress she wore. Since she was partially blocked by the bar, Kyle couldn't see anything below her waist, but his imagination was running wild at the thought of what the rest of her looked like.

"Oh, look who suddenly perked up now that a certain assistant U.S. attorney has made her appearance," Dex said with a chuckle.

Kyle feigned nonchalance. "So she's got a hot dress. Big deal."

"Right. FYI, I'd lose the shit-eating grin before you go talk to her. And try not to stare at her rack this time."

"Who said I was going to talk to her?" Kyle grumbled. With their lawyer-witness "situation," it was probably better if he and Rylann stayed on opposite sides of the bar. Especially seeing how he was quite positive that getting any closer to her in that dress would classify as cruel and unusual punishment.

"If you don't talk to her, somebody else sure will." Dex pointed. "In fact, I think you've got competition already. "Five o'clock."

Kyle whipped around, peering down at the scene below, and saw a guy with a white button-down shirt on the opposite end of the bar sipping his drink and staring at Rylann with obvious appreciation. The sleeves of the guy's shirt were rolled up, revealing a tattoo with some sort of Celtic design on his forearm. Ooh . . . because that made him so tough.

Try having a prison record, dickhead.

As Kyle stood there watching Rylann, he suddenly realized exactly why he'd been in a funk for the last three weeks.

Because for the first time in a long time, he wanted something he couldn't have.

But there was one other thing he knew. No man—dickhead or otherwise—was making moves on Rylann Pierce that night. She may have had her rules, but he'd be damned if any other guy was going to flirt with her while *he* was watching.

And he knew just the man who could help him with that.

"Dex, old buddy, I need to ask you for a favor."

ONCE AGAIN, RYLANN tried to catch the eye of the female bartender working Firelight's main bar.

"One of the few times I've ever wished for a penis," she said to Rae when the bartender stepped up to take the order of yet another *male* customer. They'd been waiting to be served for over twenty minutes. She'd even worn the red magic boob dress tonight, but unfortunately its mojo offered no help in this particular situation.

"You haven't had sex in six months," Rae said. "If I were you, I'd be wishing for penises every night."

Rylann laughed. "Good, I think she's finally coming this way." She watched as the bartender sailed right past her. "And . . . no." She suddenly remembered something. "Hey, how did your date go on Tuesday?"

Rae rolled her eyes. "I think I'm giving up on Match," she said, referring to a string of bad dates she'd arranged via Match.com. "These guys sound so promising online, but then you meet them and they're entirely different people. This last guy started off the evening by being fifteen minutes late. Then he finally shows up at the restaurant carrying a bicycle helmet, and when he sits down at the table, I notice that he's sweating profusely and he *smells*."

Rylann made a face. "That's one way to kill the ambience. So what did you do?"

"I stayed for one drink, paid the bill, and politely said that I didn't think we had a connection," Rae said matter-of-factly.

"Look at you," Rylann said, impressed. "Very suave and direct. You're a pro at this."

"Great," Rae said dryly. "That's exactly what I want to be a pro at: bad first dates. I read somewhere that you can tell within five minutes whether you're going to click with a person. Personally, I think I know even faster than that." She nudged Rylann. "Speaking of which, somebody's totally checking you out. The guy with the white shirt, across the bar. Tattoo on his forearm—mmm, *nice*."

Rylann casually checked out the guy while pretending to look at the bartender. He was cute. More than cute, actually. But much to her annoyance, a certain pair of devilish blue eyes kept popping into her head, distracting her.

"He's grabbing his drink," Rae whispered. "I think he might be heading this way. Don't worry—I'll make myself scarce."

Granted, it had been a long time since she'd done this, but if memory served, Rylann was supposed to be feeling jitters of excitement right about that very moment. Then again, she was thirty-two now—maybe the butterflies in her stomach were taking a more cerebral, mature approach to the dating game and waiting to see how things developed.

A male voice spoke from behind her and Rae.

"Ladies, it seems that I owe you an apology."

Rylann turned and saw a man, wearing a suit, who was in his early- to midthirties and had wavy sandy-brown hair.

He smiled in introduction at both her and Rae. "Gavin Dexter—call me Dex. I own the place. It's come to my attention that you've been waiting awhile for your drinks. To make up for that, I'd like to invite both of you to the VIP lounge. I even took the liberty of reserving a table for you."

Rae looked at her with a raised eyebrow, and then turned back to Dex. "That sounds great. Thank you."

He gestured toward a staircase. "Perfect. Follow me."

When he turned his back, Rae leaned in toward Rylann and chuckled under her breath. "We must look even better than I thought tonight."

They followed Dex up the stairs and past a bouncer who guarded the door of the VIP room. Once inside, Dex led them through the crowd to a private, sable suede booth in the back of the room that was enclosed by a red velvet curtain on three sides.

After Rylann and Rae settled into the booth, Dex held out his hands magnanimously. "How about some champagne to start? Anything you ladies want. Your tab for the evening has been taken care of."

Rylann looked at him quizzically. She was flattered, but this was getting a little odd. "By who?"

A familiar teasing voice answered her.

"Did anyone ever tell you that you ask too many questions, counselor?"

Rylann looked to her right and saw Kyle walking over, looking unbelievably handsome in his gray suit and tieless black shirt with the top button undone. And just like the night she'd met him, she felt it—instant butterflies.

So much for taking the cerebral approach.

"It's an occupational hazard," she told him.

"So I've seen firsthand." Without missing a beat, Kyle made the introductions. "Dex, this is Rylann Pierce and Rae . . ." he paused, prompting her for her last name.

"Mendoza," she said.

Dex smiled at Rae, then turned to Rylann with a curious expression. "Oh, *Ry*-linn," he said, pronouncing her name. "I'd been saying it wrong after I saw the picture of you and Kyle in the paper." He cocked his head. "Not a very common name, is it?"

"It's Irish. I was named after my grandfather," she explained. As the story was told, her mother had been very insistent upon the name, and her father, who had no particular allegiance to his Welsh heritage, had gone along with it.

Still, Dex looked intrigued. "By any chance did you go to Illinois law school?"

Rylann pointed to Rae. "We both did. Why?"

Dex rocked back on his heels and laughed. "Holy shit, I should've caught that earlier. You're the chicken wings girl."

It took Rylann a second, then she remembered her conversation with Kyle the night they'd met.

I don't mind hot and spicy. Actually find that appealing in a girl. And chicken wings.

With a laugh, she looked at Kyle. "You told him that story?"

Dex slapped Kyle's back. "Sure he did. I was working at the Clybourne that night, and Kyle here was grinning like a fool when he got back after walking you home. Hell, I half-expected him to burst into a song and dance number."

Kyle cleared his throat, shifting awkwardly. "I . . . think that's a bit of an exaggeration." He grabbed Dex's shoulder and squeezed hard. "Don't you have somewhere you need to be, buddy? Full club, busy night—really, we'd hate to keep you."

Rae waved a finger at them. "Hold on, *someone* better tell me the chicken wings story."

Dex looked at Kyle, who looked at Rylann.

She said nothing for a moment. Then she slid over in the booth, making room next to her. "That was one of your gems—might as well be you," she said to Kyle.

He looked surprised by the invitation, then his eyes turned a warm, deep blue. Without a word, he took a seat in the booth next to her. In the background, Rylann heard Rae and Dex begin chatting about the drink menu. But as she held Kyle's gaze, all other voices faded away.

"Oh, *now* you want to be nice," he said in a teasing voice.

Rylann smiled, her answer the same as it had been nine years ago. "I'm considering it."

IF THE CIRCUMSTANCES had been different—and there'd been no "situation" between them—Kyle would've said he was on the best first date of his life.

He had a smart, funny, gorgeous woman next to him, and they'd been talking, just the two of them, for over an hour. Rae had disappeared to talk to some guy at the bar, and since then Rylann had been cracking him up with stories about a few very memorable cases she'd prosecuted—including one, from her first year on the job, about some genius who'd stuck a hair dryer in his jacket and pretended it was a gun, then tried to rob a bank with the power cord dangling between his legs.

The drinks were flowing, and the ambience was perfect— soft candlelight on the table between them, the velvet curtain secluding them on three sides. They were sitting close to each other in the booth, which gave Kyle the perfect vantage point to stare at . . . well, everything. Her full, lush mouth as she told her courtroom stories and sipped her wine. Her long, slender legs that were crossed in his direction. The creamy skin of her shoulders, with an adorable scattering of freckles he wanted to trace his tongue over. And that V neckline . . . hell, that *was* cruel and unusual punishment. Being a good nine inches taller than Rylann, he could see a lot from where he was sitting, and all he could think about was pulling down the straps of her dress and getting his mouth on those luscious breasts.

And . . . apparently, from the way she'd paused expectantly, she'd just asked him a question.

Oops.

Kyle quickly covered, pointing to his ear. "Sorry. I couldn't hear you with all the noise from the bar."

"Oh." Rylann scooted in a little closer, so that her thigh brushed against his.

Kill me now.

"I just asked what plans *you* have, now that you're no longer working for Rhodes Corporation," she said. "I feel like I've been talking this entire time."

He tried to focus. Christ, she smelled good—some light, citrusy perfume, or maybe it was her shampoo. He wanted to bury his face in that incredible dark hair to find out.

Get it together, asshole. Remember the "situation."

"I've got some things in the hopper," he said vaguely in response to her question. He wasn't ready to share details about his start-up company yet—not until things were more certain.

She raised an eyebrow. "*Legal* things, I hope?"

Cute. "Yes, *legal* things, counselor," he said. "Trust me, if I never see the inside of a courtroom again, it'll be too soon." Then he remembered. "Except for the Quinn case, obviously."

"Right." Rylann looked down at her wineglass, as if thinking something over. Then she looked up at him sideways, with a gaze that seemed a bit more . . . interested. "Why did you send Dex out to get me and Rae?"

The moment of truth.

Kyle knew he could follow their standard code of conduct and answer her with some dry quip, or joke, or sarcastic comment. But something about the ambience and the way she looked—and, more important, the way she was looking at *him* right then—made him want to forego the usual games. So instead, he held her gaze directly. "Because nine years ago, I walked up to the most beautiful girl in the bar, and tonight she's still the only person I want to talk to."

Her eyes widened at his words, and he waited for her to say something, anything, that would let him know that she wasn't the only one feeling this way tonight. But instead, she turned back to her wineglass and toyed with the stem.

"There is something we should probably talk about," she said. "I was in court today."

Court. Kyle pulled back and shook his head in disbelief. Here he was, putting himself out there, and still all she wanted to talk about was work. "Really," he said dryly.

"It was actually a fairly routine matter," she continued. "But since you've been involved in the case, I thought you might be interested in knowing that Quinn pled guilty this morning. To voluntary manslaughter and conspiracy to violate a prisoner's civil rights."

Kyle went still. "What does that mean?"

Her eyes sparkled coyly. "Voluntary manslaughter? It's a type of homicide where there's no prior intent to kil—"

He put his hand over her mouth, cutting off the sass right quick. "What does it mean?" he repeated in a low voice. When he took his hand away, he saw the edges of her lips curving up in a smile.

"It means you're no longer my witness. There'll be a sentencing hearing, but for all intents and purposes, the case is over."

That was all Kyle needed to hear.

He threaded his fingers through her hair and gently cupped her neck. No more games. "You didn't have to tell me that tonight."

She held his gaze unwaveringly. "No, I didn't."

An admission that spoke volumes. Kyle ran his thumb possessively along her lower lip, his voice a soft growl.

"Let's get out of here."

Twenty

RYLANN KNEW, FROM the look in Kyle's eyes, exactly what would happen if she left the bar with him. His hot, smoky-blue gaze made it perfectly clear.

Sitting in that booth, she could think of a hundred reasons to say no to him. And only one reason to say yes.

Because, simply, she wanted to.

She *always* did the right thing. And from a rational perspective, doing the right thing would mean getting up and walking away from Kyle and the wicked promise of his words. But he was sinfully attractive, intelligent, and witty, and it had been a long time since she had done anything that felt this . . . breathtakingly exciting. If ever.

"I need to say good-bye to Rae," she told Kyle.

And here she'd thought the look in his eyes had been hot before.

He brought her hand to his mouth and brushed his lips over her fingers. "Meet me at the bottom of the staircase. I'll tell Dex I'm leaving."

After he slid out of the booth and walked away, Rylann took a deep breath, needing a moment to steady herself. This *so* was not something she normally did—left bars with playboy billionaire heir ex-cons. Still, although it felt a little wild, it also felt good. And for tonight, that was enough.

She grabbed her purse, climbed out of the booth, and walked over to the bar to talk to Rae.

"My God, it's about time," Rae said after Rylann explained

who she was leaving with. "For a while there, I thought it was going to take another nine years."

"You're okay catching a cab?" Rylann asked.

"Of course. Go." Rae threw her a knowing grin. "Have fun."

Well, yes . . . that was the plan. Then Rylann corrected that thought, smiling secretly to herself as she left the VIP room. Nope, no plans tonight. Until sunrise, she was officially winging it. Being spontaneous. Crazy, even.

Assuming she didn't have a panic attack in about two seconds at the thought.

She descended the staircase that led to the bar's main level and saw Kyle standing at the bottom, waiting for her. His eyes never left hers as she approached, and when she got to the last step, he held out his hand.

"Ready?" he asked. Despite the heat in his gaze, the devilish grin at the corners of his mouth was comfortingly familiar. Once upon a time, this man had made her heart skip with just a kiss—now it was time to finally see what other tricks he had up his sleeve.

Rylann slid her hand into his. "Yes."

The crowd in the main level of the club was thick, and the driving beat of a fast, techno-pop song pumped through the speakers as Kyle led her through the mass of bodies. About halfway to the door, he began tracing slow circles over her fingers with his thumb. A warm flush spread over her body—such a simple touch, but one that turned her on nevertheless. So much so that she barely felt the cool breeze of the nighttime air when they stepped through the nightclub's doors.

"We can catch a cab at the corner," Kyle said in a thick voice.

Walking briskly, he led her toward the nearest intersection. They passed an alley about fifty feet before the corner, and without any warning, he gripped her hand tighter and pulled her in. Rylann knew exactly what was coming, and—God, *yes*—she was ready for it, so she wrapped her arms around his neck just as he pushed her against the brick wall, and his mouth came down hungrily on hers.

His lips parted hers demandingly, his long, muscular body

pinning hers against the wall. His tongue claimed hers in hot, possessive sweeps as he held her chin firmly and took her mouth, again and again, until she was breathless.

"I've been wanting to do that since the moment you walked into the courtroom that morning," he said, breathing heavily, when he finally pulled back. Then he took her hand in his again, quickly led her out of the alley, and flagged down a cab at the street corner.

When the taxi pulled to a stop in front of them, Kyle opened the door, and they both climbed in. He gave the driver the address of his penthouse, and since that was closer than Rylann's apartment, she didn't argue. A short five minutes later, they arrived at Kyle's building, the taxi barely coming to a stop before he shoved a twenty-dollar bill at the driver and stepped out. He held out his hand, helping Rylann out of the cab, and then ushered her through the revolving doors.

Kyle nodded at the doorman and took her to the elevators. As soon as they stepped inside—alone—and the doors shut behind them, he backed her up against the wall and kissed her again, hot and hard. A few moments later, Rylann heard the ding of the elevator, and then she and Kyle were stumbling out, making their way to his front door. She threaded her fingers through his hair as he worked the lock with one hand, then with a groan he wrapped his arm around her waist and pushed the door open.

After slamming the door behind them, Kyle took her purse and tossed it to the floor. His keys followed, then he wrapped his arms around her waist, once again claiming her mouth as he led her through the penthouse.

When they finally came up for air, Rylann saw they were in the doorway of his bedroom. The décor was modern and masculine, but not overly so. Two light suede armchairs sat in one corner, flanking a heavy mahogany end table. A huge plasma television was mounted on the wall in front of the chairs, and on the opposite end of the room was a king-sized bed covered with several oversized pillows.

Kyle pressed her against the door, drawing her attention back to him, and swept his tongue over hers. When she moaned and arched instinctively against him, he pulled back, his eyes dark and smoky. "You're sure this is what you want?"

She tangled her fingers in his hair. "I'm sure."

"Good." He took her hands and led her into the bedroom with a daring glint in his eyes. "Then show me." He walked to one of the armchairs, released her hands, and took a seat. He waited expectantly, looking every bit the multimillionaire used to being in charge. "Start with the dress."

Oh, really? Rylann cocked her head. "You take it off me if you want to see what's underneath."

He shook his head slowly. "Sorry, counselor, but this isn't the grand jury room. I'm making the rules tonight."

Thank God she still had her dress on; otherwise, Smug Dimples would've seen her nipples go instantly hard right then.

Playing it cool, she stepped between his legs, then reached back and unzipped her dress. While holding his gaze, she slipped one strap over her shoulder, then the other. Then, ever so slowly, she slid the fabric over the cups of her strapless bra, past her stomach, and over her hips and let it fall to the floor at her feet.

Kyle's eyes burned a path over every inch of her, taking in her ivory silk bra and matching panties. "You are so fucking beautiful, Rylann." His gaze fell to her bra. "Now let me see those breasts you've been teasing me with all night."

"If you insist." With a slight smile, she reached back and unhooked the clasp of her bra. She eased the cups off her breasts, and then dropped the bra onto the floor, next to her dress.

Kyle said nothing for a moment, just looking at her. Then he beckoned with his hand. "Come here."

She shook her head. "I'm not finished yet."

"Come here anyway."

She kicked off her heels and straddled his lap, settling his thick erection between her legs.

His jaw twitched as he gazed at her through hooded eyes. "Kiss me."

Feeling slightly scandalous—but also very sexy—being

nearly naked while he was still fully dressed, Rylann leaned forward and took her time, nibbling his lower lip with her teeth before lightly brushing her tongue along his. When he tried to deepen the kiss, she pulled back and teased him with her lips, hearing a low rumble in his chest.

"Good-girl prosecutors shouldn't tease a man who's been in prison," he warned in a low voice.

She leaned forward to whisper in his ear. "I thought we'd already established that I'm not going to be a good girl tonight."

She smiled slyly when she felt his erection twitch between her legs—then bit back a gasp when his hands slid to her breasts.

"Let's find out what bad-girl prosecutors like, then." He brushed his thumbs across her taut, sensitive nipples in a slow, maddening pace. She closed her eyes and exhaled unsteadily, then moaned moments later when his mouth replaced his hands.

"Kyle . . ." She tangled her fingers in his hair, arching back as his tongue licked one nipple and then the other, turning them into stiff, aching peaks.

"I'm going to make you feel so damn good tonight, baby," he murmured. As if to prove just that, he teased her breasts with his lips, teeth, and tongue until she began rocking gently in his lap, needing more.

"Hold on to me," he whispered.

She wrapped her hands around the back of his neck and held on tight as he got up from the chair and carried her to the bed. He set her on top of the covers, gazing down at her with a scorching-hot look as he began to undress, first his jacket and shirt, then all the rest.

Over the years, Rylann had secretly harbored a few thoughts about what Kyle Rhodes might look like naked, based mostly on the brief feel of his toned body against hers when they'd kissed all those years ago.

None of her fantasies came close to the real thing.

As he stood naked before her, she unabashedly took in every hard, chiseled inch—the firm chest, tight abs, lean hips, and strong, muscular thighs—and came to one inescapable conclusion.

Prison did a body *good*.

Her eyes traveled down to his erection, big and hard and ready to go. With a knowing grin, Kyle moved over her on the bed and hooked his fingers around the waist of her panties. He pulled them down, slid them off her legs, and then sat back and looked at her.

"Perfect," he said huskily.

He lowered himself onto his forearms and kissed her, his hand moving between her thighs. Rylann trembled as his hand went higher to part the soft folds between her legs, spreading her open. He expertly teased her with his forefinger, making her gasp against his mouth, before sliding a finger into her.

"You're so wet." He added a finger and began moving them in a smooth, torturous pace. "That's going to be my cock in a minute."

"Kyle." She pressed instinctively against his hand as he made her body burn.

"Touch me, Rylann," he said, nuzzling her neck.

He rolled onto his side and she followed, all too happy to oblige that particular request. She slid her hands over his chest, down his stomach, then heard the catch in his breath as she continued downward.

He closed his eyes and moaned when she wrapped her hand around his shaft. "God, yes . . ."

He was hard and throbbing as she smoothed her thumb over the head, then she began stroking him in the same smooth, slow pace he'd used on her. She leaned forward and kissed him, her nipples brushing against his chest as their tongues tangled. She stroked and teased, hearing his breath turn more and more ragged.

Suddenly, he rolled her onto her back and pinned her hands against the bed. "I need to fuck you," he rasped. "Now."

Hot flames licked at her body. "Please tell me you have something."

In answer, he reached over and yanked open a drawer on his nightstand. He ripped open the wrapper and rolled the condom on, then moved between her legs.

He settled the tip of his erection right at her warm, wet

entrance and spread her legs wider with his knee. Then he slowly entered her, filling her completely, until he was fully buried inside.

"Christ, you are so damn sweet," he groaned. He clenched his jaw as he began to move. "I'm going to be inside you all night," he said in a guttural voice. He pinned her with his gaze as he took her in smooth, deep strokes. "Just like this."

"Yes," she breathed as she arched to meet him. Together, they found their rhythm, and right as she was getting close, Kyle sat back on his knees and teased her with short, shallow thrusts.

"I want to see you when you come," he said, reaching down and stroking her between her legs. Rylann cried out and exploded as he continued to thrust, now hard and deep, riding her through her climax. He pulled her up to straddle him, and she held his face and kissed him as he cupped her bottom and guided her up and down on his shaft. He was so hard in her, and the friction between their bodies was so intense, that suddenly, she felt another orgasm building.

She gasped against his mouth, her legs shaking. His hands were firm, pressing her against him in just the right way, and she knew that *he* knew exactly what he was doing. She whimpered when the second climax hit her, and then he picked up the pace, their bodies moving together, until he gripped her hips and growled as he exploded deep inside her.

They stayed entwined like that for several moments, both panting, until Rylann finally slid her body off of his. They fell back onto the bed, and Kyle braced himself over her, his hair falling across his forehead and his cheeks flushed as he peered down at her.

There was a proud spark in his eyes. "So?"

She smiled. "Okay. Maybe a little bit better than 'not bad' this time."

"You know, you really are a burr up my ass."

Rylann laughed hard at that, reaching up to cup his face. "Why, Kyle Rhodes. You say the sweetest things."

Twenty-one

WHEN RYLANN WOKE up and felt the warm, hard body next to her, for a split second she thought she was back in San Francisco with Jon.

But as her eyes fluttered open and she took in the scene—shades pulled down over floor-to-ceiling windows; plush, taupe covers and oversized pillows on the bed; enormous plasma television on the wall—she suddenly remembered.

Kyle.

As the soft morning light filtered in through the shades, the reality of the situation hit her.

She'd slept with an ex-con.

And not just any ex-con—she'd slept with the Twitter Terrorist, one of the most famous convicted felons to be prosecuted in recent years by the very office she worked for. A man who, just one day ago, had been her witness.

I'm not going to be a good girl tonight.

Safe to say she'd accomplished *that* goal.

She lay there in Kyle's bed, not feeling guilty, just perhaps a bit . . . out of sorts. Meth Lab Rylann didn't mix business with pleasure. She didn't do office romances, she didn't sleep with ex-witnesses, and she sure as hell didn't have sex with ex-cons. Three times.

Quickly, she scrolled through her memories of the night before.

Those were some damn steamy memories.

A very clear, erotic image popped into her head of her straddling Kyle during round two, her hands running over the hard muscles of his chest as he murmured her name while she rode him. Then another one, of the two of them in his steam shower, the multiple jets beating a sensual massage against her skin as Kyle kneeled before her, pressing her against the warm marble and teasing her with his mouth as her moans echoed through his gigantic bathroom.

Rylann paused suddenly, remembering that one.

Oh crap, the *shower*.

Her hand flew to the mess of unruly curls tangled around her head and shoulders.

Lovely.

Time to make her getaway.

She peeked over her shoulder at Kyle, who slept facing her, with one arm tucked under his pillow. Seeing the rugged stubble along his jaw and the slight upturn of his lips, she had to fight the urge to snuggle against him, run her hands over his amazing body, and wake him up for round four. Unfortunately, such actions were directly contrary to her plans to: (a) make sure the sexcapades, though spectacular, remained a one-night deal, and (b) get the hell out of Dodge before Kyle noticed that she'd mysteriously sprung a Chia Pet from her head.

Slowly, she eased out of the bed, fully naked. She found her panties on the floor by the foot of the bed and quietly slid them on. Then she tiptoed across the room to the armchair, where she'd done her striptease for Kyle the night before— very fun and naughty, but there was no time to linger over more steamy memories—and found her bra, shoes, and dress. With her back to the bed, she hurriedly put on her bra, then realized the zipper of her dress would make too much noise and might wake Kyle up. Deciding to put the dress and her heels on in the living room, she bent over to pick them up and—

"Very nice."

Rylann stood up, clutching her dress against her chest, and looked over her shoulder.

Kyle lay in bed, propped up on one elbow while watching her with an amused expression. "Fleeing the scene of the crime, counselor?"

This man could read her like a damn book sometimes.

"No," she said defensively. At least not for the reasons he likely assumed. She had no problems with the sex—all three scorching rounds of it. It was the *ex-con* part that had her somewhat agitated. "I just have this . . . thing I need to go to."

He glanced at the clock on his nightstand. "At seven thirty on a Saturday morning?"

"It's an early-morning thing. And I have to go home and shower first, obviously."

"Of course. Here's a tip, counselor: plan your getaway excuses the night before."

Right. She'd forgotten that she was dealing with a pro. "I'll keep that in mind for next time." Since there was no need to sneak around anymore, she stepped into her shoes and was about to put on her dress when she noticed the way Kyle was staring at her in her underwear and high heels.

His eyes went all warm and dark, taking in the sight. "Maybe you really should stay a little bit longer."

The lure of those blue bedroom eyes was tempting.

Then his gaze shifted to the wild bush sprouting from her head. "Wow. Did I do that to your hair?" He looked oddly pleased at the thought.

Rylann made a mental note to throw a flat iron in her purse the next time she had sex in the shower with a billionaire ex-con. Not that there was going to be a next time. "Not all of us are lucky enough to have freakishly perfect, shampoo-commercial hair. This is what happens when I get wet."

His expression turned wicked. "I know exactly what happens when you get wet, counselor."

Yep, she'd walked right into that one.

"Usually there's a lot of moaning and heavy breathing," he continued. "Although my favorite part is the way you say my name—"

"Kyle," she interrupted, glaring at him.

"Nope, not like that. A bit more fiery and enthusiastic." He patted the bed next to him. "Let's work on it until we get it perfect."

"I'm going now," Rylann said.

"Are you? Because I see you fighting back a smile there."

Well, maybe she was. But she was still going. "Since you mentioned the hair—do you have a rubber band anywhere?" It was bad enough she had to do the walk of shame through his lobby wearing the red dress. No way was she letting anyone see the full extent of how mussed she was after one night with Kyle Rhodes.

"I'll find something," Kyle said.

He threw back the covers, giving her the perfect view of his delectable body, erect penis and all—seriously, did that thing *ever* go down?—and strode around the bed. He grabbed his gray boxer briefs off the floor and pulled them on. "I saw you peeking."

Busted. "I was just noticing that you have really impressive . . . thighs."

"I run a lot."

Rylann could picture him, all sweaty and slick, peeling off his clothes when he got back to the penthouse after a jog.

Hmm.

"Counselor, if you want to leave, I wouldn't look at me like that when you're standing in my bedroom in your underwear and heels."

She blinked. Right—the getaway. "Sorry. The rubber band?"

While Kyle went to look in the bathroom, Rylann slipped on her dress and left the bedroom. In the hallway, she found her purse—a small clutch that held her cell phone, keys, and, thankfully, mints. She popped one in her mouth and stole a look in a large framed mirror in the foyer.

Great. Crazy hair *and* no makeup.

"Try this." Kyle came up behind her in the mirror and held out his hand.

Rylann looked down and saw a black hair band in his palm. "Something one of the models left behind?"

He threw her a look. "No, it's mine. The freakishly lustrous, shampoo-commercial hair is a pain in the ass if I don't pull it back while running."

With a smile, Rylann took the band and began combing her fingers through her hair. "I can't picture you with a ponytail."

"It's not a ponytail. I just pull back the sides and top."

"Ah. Like a partial updo."

"Remember the thing I said last night? About being a burr up my ass?"

Indeed, she did. He'd said it right after giving her two of the best orgasms of her life. And then had followed it up with two more.

Pushing the memories from her mind, she pulled back to inspect her hair, which she'd wrangled into a bumpy, messy ponytail. "Probably not as fancy as your updos, but it'll have to do."

Then she met Kyle's gaze in the mirror. "Last night was great."

His expression was uncharacteristically unreadable. "That's supposed to be my line."

And she had no doubt he'd said it plenty of times. But that was neither here nor there. She managed a coy smile. "You should feel free to say it, too," she joked.

He turned her around, lowered his head, and softly kissed her lips. "Last night was great."

Since there was nothing more to say, Rylann stepped back and headed toward the front door. She noticed now that he'd thrown on a pair of jeans after looking for the hair band, and she realized that this would probably be her last image of Kyle Rhodes—sexy, bare chested, and barefoot in his jeans, standing in his foyer as they said good-bye.

She turned and grabbed the handle, about to open the door, when he stopped her.

"Rylann—wait."

Her heart skipped a beat as he crossed the foyer with a serious look in his eyes, reaching his arm out to—

—pull up the zipper of her dress.

"I just noticed that," he said.

"Right. Thanks." She unlocked the door and opened it. "So we'll . . . talk."

"You know where to find me, counselor."

Then Rylann stepped out into the hallway and walked to the elevators. As she pushed the down button, she heard the soft click of the lock behind her.

Twenty-two

"AND THEN YOU just left?"

Rylann shrugged at Rae's question. "What else was I supposed to do?"

They'd scored an outdoor table at Kitsch'n, a popular neighborhood brunch place a few blocks from her apartment. Naturally, she'd called Rae that afternoon for the post-sexcapades debriefing.

Rylann drizzled syrup over her coconut-crusted French toast, continuing on as Rae took a sip of her mimosa. "It's not like we were going to run out for coffee and pancakes. Last night was fun, but that's all it was."

Rae raised an eyebrow. "How much fun?"

Rylann grinned mischievously. "Three rounds of fun. Including one in the shower." She cheekily took a bite of her French toast, saying nothing further.

Rae laughed. "Wow. Clearly, I need to find myself an ex-con. Since prison is probably the only place in this city I haven't looked for Mr. Right yet," she added dryly.

"What about the guy at the bar last night?" Rylann asked. "You were talking to him for a while."

Rae sighed. "He was nice, I don't know . . ." She shrugged, discouraged. "I keep waiting for this magic moment where I meet a guy and just *know*. But maybe that's not what my story's going to be." She looked at Rylann and waved this off. "Ignore me. I don't want to talk about my nonexistent love life today."

"Are you sure?" Rylann asked. Actually, she had an idea

on that front—she'd been trying to come up with a sneaky way to introduce Rae to a certain single, good-looking, all-American male prosecutor at the U.S. Attorney's Office—but she didn't have the details worked out yet. She needed to tread cautiously on that front, since Rae hated setups.

"Very sure." Rae said emphatically. "Let's get back to the part where you hightailed it out of the multimillion-dollar penthouse of the gorgeous billionaire heir who obviously has the hots for you big-time. You bitch." She smiled. "Whoops. Did I just say that out loud?"

Rylann pooh-poohed this with a wave of her own. "That gorgeous billionaire heir is doing just fine. Trust me, Kyle Rhodes is not pining away in his penthouse for me. The guy goes through women faster than I go through legal pads."

"Yeah, but you heard what his friend Dex said. About how Kyle was grinning like a fool after walking you home the night you met."

Rylann paused at that. That *was* a really cute story. But still. "That was nine years ago, Rae. A lot has happened since then. He's not some unknown, charmingly irritating grad student in a flannel shirt and work boots anymore." She looked around, lowering her voice. "He's the Twitter Terrorist. And I'm an assistant U.S. attorney. There's only so far this can go. My office prosecuted Kyle just six months ago. Called him a 'cyber-menace to society.' Do you know how awkward it would be at work if anyone found out that he and I were sleeping together?"

"It would be weird. No doubt," Rae said in complete agreement.

"Exactly. And I don't want things to be weird. I've got plans for that office—like kicking butt and making a name for myself. And that name is not going to be 'That New Girl Who Boned the Twitter Terrorist.'"

"Uh-oh." Rae grimaced. "Then I hate to be the one to break this to you . . . but you and Kyle are in this morning's Scene and Heard column."

Rylann's heart stopped. "What? *No.*"

"Not your name," Rae said quickly. She took out her

iPhone and pulled up the gossip column online. "I'd been waiting to mention this, thinking you were going to get a kick out of it. Guess I called that one wrong." She began reading out loud. " 'Kyle Rhodes, Chicago's Twitter Terrorist and son of billionaire businessman Grey Rhodes, made his return to the social scene at the much-anticipated opening of Gold Coast hot spot Firelight, where he was spotted cozying up to an unknown brunette bombshell wearing a knockout red dress. Sources say the couple shared several drinks and appeared to have eyes only for each other as they left the nightclub together . . .' "

Stunned, Rylann said nothing for a moment.

She cursed the red magic boob dress.

"On the bright side, they did call you a brunette bombshell," Rae said.

And under different circumstances, Rylann would've preened shamelessly for at least two or three minutes over that, but right now she was too busy panicking. Back in March, there'd been that picture of her and Kyle in court, the one that had been blasted all over the media. If anyone connected the dots between that and the "brunette bombshell" he'd been seen with last night . . .

Not good.

"They don't have any photographs of Kyle and me at the club, do they?" she asked anxiously.

"Just another one of him staring at your boobs." Rae put down her phone, seeing Rylann's face. "I'm kidding. Take a deep breath, Ry. You're fine. No one will know this is you. It's a big city, with lots of brunettes."

"Right." Rylann exhaled, slowly climbing down off the ledge and thinking how close she'd come to carelessly blowing her cover.

Too close.

ON HER WAY home from the restaurant, Rylann's cell phone rang. For a moment, as she dug around in her purse to find it, she wondered if it would be Kyle, calling her about the Scene and Heard column. She could practically hear his low, teasing voice already. *Just calling to check up on my favorite brunette bombshell, counselor. Thought I'd see if you'd be up for round four tonight.*

Rylann finally found her phone.

Oh. Just her mother.

"Mom . . . hi," she answered.

"Looks like I was right to warn you about that Kyle Rhodes."

Rylann stopped at a four-way intersection, immediately on high alert. How could her mother, down in Florida, possibly know anything? So she played it cool. "Not sure what you mean, Mom."

"I was just reading the *Trib* online," Helen said. "The Twitter Terrorist made the Scene and Heard column again."

"You read Scene and Heard?" Rylann asked.

"Sure. How else am I supposed to keep up with all the local gossip while we're down here for the winter?"

And by *winter*, she meant early May. "I haven't seen this morning's column," Rylann said. And technically, that was true—she'd only *heard* it. "I was busy this morning, then went to lunch with Rae . . . just walking home now."

"Apparently, he was spotted at some hot new nightclub. Leaving with a mysterious brunette bombshell in a red dress. Probably some skank he met that night."

Then her mother changed the subject, cheerfully moving on. "Anyway, what's new with you, sweetie? Did you do anything exciting last night?"

Yes. Kyle Rhodes. "Um, nothing special. Rae and I went out for a few drinks." Rylann figured it was best to gloss over the rest of the details, seeing how her mother had just called her a *skank*. "Out of curiosity, what's with all the animosity toward Kyle Rhodes? You don't even know him."

"I told you. I didn't like the way he was looking at you in that photo," she said. "Who looks at a woman, a perfect stranger, like that in a *courtroom* of all places? My firm used to represent men like him all the time. Wealthy, charming, think they own the world and can get away with anything."

"It's not like he killed anyone, Mom. He shut down Twitter," Rylann said. She knew she sounded a bit defensive, but her mother's words bothered her. She'd seen firsthand the real Kyle Rhodes—the guy who, despite everything, had voluntarily helped her in the Quinn case. Yes, he had his flaws, but there were good parts, too. And not just the naked parts.

Quickly, she changed the subject, not wanting to talk any more about Kyle Rhodes, the Scene and Heard column, or anything else related to last night. The message had been received, loud and clear: going home with Kyle had been crazy. And Meth Lab Rylann didn't do crazy.

Starting now.

Shortly after arriving home, she hung up with her mother and dropped her purse on the floor in her bedroom. Stuffed to the gills with coconut-crusted French toast and thoroughly exhausted after her night of debauchery with Kyle, she kicked off her shoes and crawled into bed for a nap.

Over three hours later, Rylann woke to the sound of her cell phone ringing. She sat up in bed, foggy-headed with sleep and disoriented by the fact that it had begun to get dark outside. She leaned over and reached for her purse, grumbling to herself as she rooted around for her cell phone. Somebody had better be dead—and she meant that literally. If there wasn't an FBI, a DEA, a Secret Service, or an ATF agent on the other end of the line with a major case-related crisis, heads were going to roll.

She pulled the phone out of her purse and saw "Blocked" on the screen.

"Rylann Pierce."

A familiar male voice spoke.

"I can't believe how good it is to hear your voice again."

Rylann rolled back on the bed, unable to conceal her surprise.

"Jon."

Twenty-three

RYLANN LOOKED OVER at the clock on her nightstand and did the math. Rome was seven hours ahead of Chicago. "It's after two o'clock in the morning for you."

"So it is," Jon said cheerfully. "I just left a friend's party. There's a woman in the Rome office, also an expat, who introduced me to some locals. We were celebrating . . . well, come to think of it, I have no clue what we were celebrating. It's a fun group."

"I'm sure it—"

He kept right on talking. "One of the guys has a brother who owns a vineyard in Tuscany where we hang out on weekends. You'd love it, babe. The main house is gorgeous. It's this eighteenth-century villa that's been renovated and is set right into these green, rolling hills. *Molto bello*."

Rylann blinked.

Oh, boy.

Putting aside the fact that Jon was babbling and suddenly breaking out the Italian, she'd caught the "babe" he'd slipped in there. As she knew well from the three years they'd dated, that could mean only one thing.

She'd just been internationally drunk-dialed.

"It sounds like Italy has turned out to be everything you'd hoped it would," she said, still trying to shake the sleep from her head. This conversation had suddenly become very surreal.

"Not everything." He sighed dramatically. "The party was at an apartment not far from the Piazza Navona. I left before the others and just started walking. Before I knew it, I was standing at the Bernini fountain, looking at the trattoria with the yellow awning that we loved so much when we came here together. Do you remember?"

Yes, she did. After a two-day sightseeing whirlwind that had included the Roman Forum, the Vatican, the Spanish Steps, and the Coliseum, they'd decided to take a break. The following day they'd slept in, found a restaurant for lunch, and sat at an outdoor table for hours while talking, people watching, eating good food, and drinking wine. Afterward they'd gone back to the hotel and made love. "I remember. Although that seems like a long time ago now."

"Yeah. A lot of things seem like they were a long time ago." He changed the subject. "So? How have you been?"

First an e-mail, now he was drunk dialing her. No clue what was going on with her ex these days, but it was probably time she figured it out. "Jon. No offense but . . . what are you doing? Are we really going to have this conversation at two o'clock in the morning?"

"*We* are not having this conversation at two o'clock in the morning. It's only seven P.M. for you," he said cutely.

Rylann thought it was best not to mince words. If for no other reason, the economically frugal government-salaried lawyer in her was very conscious of the fact that this call was costing him a pretty Euro per minute. "Why are you calling?"

"Can't a man say hi to an old friend without it being a federal offense?"

She assumed the pun was intended. "I got the e-mail, remember? We've already done the 'Hi' thing."

"I just wanted to see how you're doing, Ry. From your response you seemed okay, but who can tell anything over e-mail?"

Rylann ran one hand through her hair. Perhaps, because she and Jon had agreed not to talk after the breakup, it was inevitable that this conversation would occur at some point. People liked to have closure. "I'm doing well. I think Chicago is going to be a good fit for me."

"I've kept in touch with Keith, Kellie, Dan, and Claire," Jon said. "They tell me that they've only traded a couple e-mails with you since you left San Francisco. When I heard that, I got a little worried."

Ah, now she had a better sense of what was going on here. She'd gotten so swept up in her new life in Chicago that she'd pushed aside, perhaps too quickly, her old one. This had not been entirely unintentional. Keith, Kellie, Dan, and Claire had been their "couple" friends, and after she and Jon had broken up, the whole dynamic had been thrown out of whack. Sure, she'd given it the college try, she'd even met the girls for drinks a few times during the four months she'd still lived in San Francisco after the breakup. But mostly, Kellie and Claire kept asking if she'd talked to Jon after he'd left for Rome—a subject she hadn't been keen to revisit umpteen times. Especially since the answer had been *no*.

"I've been busy with work, that's all," Rylann said. "But you're right—I should give them a call."

"They're worried that you're sitting in Chicago, wallowing in misery." Jon chuckled. "They even have these romantic notions that you've been pining away, thinking about me. So I can e-mail them and say that you're officially a-okay?"

His tone was light and jesting, but Rylann wondered if she heard an unspoken question there. "I'm fine. Truly."

"They'll be relieved to hear that. You remember how nosy those guys can get." His tone remained casual. "And of course the next thing they'll ask is whether you're seeing anyone. So the answer to that would be . . . ?"

"That they should probably stop asking questions while they're ahead."

"Of course."

There was a long pause on the other end.

Jon's voice turned serious, and suddenly, the whole conversation changed.

"And what if they said that they miss you?" he asked quietly.

There it was.

Rylann took a moment to answer, wanting to see what

effect, if any, the words had on her. She felt nostalgic and perhaps even a little sad. Her tone was gentle. "I'd say that they are obviously having this very sentimental, Italian moment with the Bernini fountain and the wine, but that they will undoubtedly wake up in the morning and regret this call."

"That was a really good day for us, Ry."

She assumed he was still looking at the trattoria with the yellow awning. "It was. But that day is over, Jon."

"I don't know . . ."

"We can't do this," Rylann interrupted. "I want you to be happy, I really do. But talking makes things too confusing. I think it's better for both of us to just . . . move on." She paused, finding this harder than she'd expected. But still, it was the right thing to do. "Good-bye, Jon."

She hung up the phone and exhaled deeply. Then she turned her cell phone off and stared at it for a long moment.

Beyond a doubt, one of the strangest weekends she'd ever had.

Twenty-four

BRIGHT AND EARLY Monday morning, Kyle stood in his new office space, surveying the final touches of the renovation.

"It looks good," he told the contractor, Bill, who stood by his side.

"Of course it looks good," Bill said, looking satisfied. "I did it."

The contractor had come highly recommended by the designer who'd remodeled Dex's bar, Firelight. He'd cost a fortune, but Kyle wasn't looking to do things on the cheap. From the moment his future clients—and hopefully there would be some—stepped through the doors of Rhodes Network Consulting LLC, he wanted them to know they were in the hands of professionals.

Most of the changes Kyle had made to the space had been cosmetic. He'd gotten rid of the industrial gray carpeting and restored the maple hardwood floors underneath. Also gone were the dark paint and heavy oak furniture the former tenant had favored. In its place, he'd brought in low-rise white couches and chairs, and tables and desks made of glass and light-colored marble. The overall effect was an office that looked clean, modern, and sophisticated.

After giving the reception area and conference room a thorough once-over, Kyle moved next to his own personal office. This was where the biggest structural changes had been made. The contractor's team had knocked down a wall that had previously separated two smaller offices and redesigned the space as one large corner office with floor-to-ceiling windows on two sides. Perhaps it was a touch excessive, but after spending four months in prison, Kyle found he still had a distaste for small, confined rooms.

Besides, he thought as he stood in the center of the room, *this felt like a CEO's office.* His *office.*

"The place is ready," Bill said. "Now you just need people to fill it."

"That's the next step," Kyle said. The office included a reception area, four cubicle workstations with significant room to expand, two additional private offices, and a secretarial station outside of Kyle's own office.

"You got a plan?" Bill asked with a grin. "To be honest, I'm kind of curious to see how this works out for you."

Kyle's gaze fell to the sleek, bold, Italian-made aluminum-and-tempered-glass executive desk in the center of his office. It was the desk of a man who wanted to make a statement. "You're not the only one, Bill."

ON TUESDAY MORNING, Kyle gassed up the Mercedes and hit the road. Because it was only seven A.M., traffic was relatively light by Chicago standards, and it took him thirty minutes to reach the city limits. Then he merged onto I-57 and settled in for a two-hour drive.

He was heading south, to Champaign-Urbana. It was the perfect morning to be on the road: the sun was shining, the sky was blue, and the temperature hovered right below seventy degrees. He cracked open the window, breathed in the fresh air, and turned on the radio. It felt good to get away from the hustle and bustle of the city, even if only for a day. It was just him, the open road, a fast car, and good music.

None of which, unfortunately, distracted him from thinking about Rylann.

He'd been busy with work these past couple days, yet he still hadn't been able to get her out of his mind. He'd be riding the elevator up to his penthouse, or going for an early morning run, or taking a shower, and suddenly—*bam*—there she was.

Actually, he thought about her a lot when he was in the shower.

The images of her, wet and naked as the jets beat down around them, would probably be burned in his brain forever. Right next to the memory of her ever-so-fine ass as she practically sprinted out of his penthouse on Saturday morning.

By all accounts, it had been the perfect hookup. Amazing sex, no strings attached. He should have been satisfied. Relieved, in fact, since no-strings-attached sex was exactly what he was looking for at this point in his life. And now he could close the book on this unusual story that had begun between him and Rylann Pierce nine years ago.

Yet the story still felt . . . incomplete.

Kyle shook his head, seriously tempted to bang it against the steering wheel a few times, since he obviously needed to snap the fuck out of whatever haze he'd been living in these past couple days. A man who was a committed bachelor did not complain when a smart and sexy woman blew his mind with three rounds of incredible sex and then left without any expectations in the morning. Probably, that was something *no* man of sound mind and body should complain about. It went against the Man Code of Conduct—like failing to leave a buffer urinal when taking a leak next to another dude in a public restroom.

That settled, Kyle turned his focus to work and contemplated the significance of today's journey. Specifically, that this would be the first time he'd returned to Champaign since the day his mother died. He hadn't intentionally avoided the place; things had just worked out that way. For several months after her accident, he'd been overseeing matters for his father and simply hadn't had the chance. Things had been so busy, in fact, that Dex had even packed up Kyle's things and driven his car up to Chicago.

Eventually, the situation with his father had improved, but by that point Kyle had begun blazing a trail up the corporate ladder at Rhodes Corporation. Shortly thereafter, Dex had moved to Chicago to open his first bar in Wrigleyville, and the two of them, and the rest of their guy friends, fell into a lifestyle of working hard during the week and having a good

time on the weekends—clubs, women, beach volleyball, and
boat parties on the lake during the summer months, football
in Lincoln Park and pickup basketball games at East Bank
Club when the weather turned cooler.

Not a bad life. Far from it. Although perhaps a life that had
begun to feel a bit superficial as Kyle had settled into his
thirties.

And now here he was. Thirty-three years old with a prison
record—but also with a chance to make a fresh start. Rhodes
Network Consulting LLC was his opportunity to show everyone what he was capable of *other* than being the Twitter Terrorist. He'd had a great career at Rhodes Corporation, while
it had lasted, and he had no regrets about working for his
father. But now it was time to take the plunge and build something he could call his own.

And pray like hell that he didn't fall flat on his face while
doing it.

As part of his business strategy, Kyle had e-mailed Professor Roc Sharma, his former PhD advisor and the head of
UIUC's Department of Computer Sciences, and had asked if
they could meet. Sharma had indicated that he was available
today, but he hadn't said much more.

After Kyle had dropped out of the PhD program following
his mother's car accident, Sharma had been understanding
and sympathetic. They'd exchanged e-mails periodically over
the years and had remained on friendly terms. They had not,
however, had any communication since he'd been convicted
in federal court on several counts of cyber-crime.

Safe to say that was a big no-no in the eyes of the Department of Computer Sciences.

Kyle had no idea what to expect when he walked into his
former mentor's office. He was encouraged, at least, by the
fact that Sharma had taken the time to respond. Then again,
the professor had always been known for his long-winded
lectures—perhaps he simply couldn't resist the opportunity
to deliver one personally to the Twitter Terrorist.

Thus, with no small amount of uncertainty, Kyle turned
off the highway and drove to the northeast side of campus.

The Department of Computer Sciences was in Urbana, an impressive minicampus befitting its status as one of the top computer science programs in the country.

He parked at the main building on Goodwin Avenue and climbed out of the Mercedes. Before him stood an impressive, ultramodern 225,000-square-foot structure made of glass, copper, and steel. The computer science building had won awards from both the Illinois Engineering Council and the American Institute of Architects for its skillful use of natural light, open spaces, red iron interior, and internal terraces—all of which had been made possible by a $65 million grant from the man whose name had been etched proudly over the main entrance.

GREY RHODES CENTER
FOR COMPUTER SCIENCE

Kyle walked through those doors, passing directly underneath the words. Inside, he knew exactly where he was going; he'd spent many an hour in this building during his six years of undergrad and graduate school. Sharma's office was on the third floor, along with the rest of the faculty offices.

Because it was the last week before finals, the building was hopping. He walked up the main staircase, an open structure made of glass, steel, and brick. Students passed him in the opposite direction, and he wondered how long it would take before someone recognized him.

All of about ten seconds.

A student, about twenty years old and dressed in jeans and a T-shirt that read "I'm not anti-social, I'm just not user-friendly," was the first to ID him. Spotting Kyle while heading down the stairs, he stopped dead in his tracks on the landing.

"Oh my God, it's you," he whispered in a reverent tone. He grabbed the shirt of the student behind him. *"Look."*

The second guy peered down at Kyle, and his face broke out in a grin. "Ho-ly shit. The Twitter Terrorist, in the flesh."

Kyle gave them a curt nod. "Hello." He passed them on the stairs and kept on going.

"Hey, wait!"

The two students did an about-face and followed him. Kyle could already hear the murmurs starting as more and more people noticed him.

Great.

His two "fans" caught up with him, flanking him on each side. "Dude, we studied you in my Computer Security II class," the second guy said enthusiastically.

"Your attack on Twitter was insane," the T-shirt guy chimed in. "They said it was the most sophisticated hijacking they'd ever experienced. Even the FBI couldn't stop it."

"So what's your secret?" the second student asked. "Smurf attack? Ping of death? SYN flood?"

"Lots of single-malt Scotch," Kyle said dryly.

The T-shirt guy laughed. "So cool. You are a *legend*."

Time to set the record straight. Kyle turned around at the top of the stairs and faced them. "Okay, kids—listen up. Cyber-crime isn't cool, it's stupid. And you know what else isn't cool? Being convicted by the U.S. Attorney's Office and going to *prison*. Trust me, that will come back to bite you in the ass in ways you can't even fathom."

The two students looked at each other. "Dude, you sound like one of those lame public service announcements," the second student said.

"Except for the 'ass' part," the T-shirt guy said. "You're probably not supposed to swear around youths. We're very impressionable."

"You're over eighteen," Kyle said. "That means you're not youths in the eyes of the law." He looked them over. "I'd say you'd both last about a week behind bars. Three days if they stuck you in maximum security." He rubbed his jaw, pretending to think. "And how do you feel about showering with twenty muscle-bound and tattooed guys, most of whom are gang members, murderers, and drug dealers?"

The T-shirt guy swallowed. "Do they at least give you shower shoes?"

Kyle glared.

"Just a joke," the student said with a nervous laugh. "Hacking is bad. Prison is bad. Got it." Then he looked around and lowered his voice to a conspiratorial whisper. "Ping of death, right? Come on—it'll be our little secret."

"Just keep it clean," Kyle grumbled under his breath, turning and leaving them both on the landing.

Sharma's office was located in the southeast corner of the building, an office Kyle had visited several times during his tenure as a grad student. He slowed as he approached the door, steeling himself for a setdown.

He knocked on Sharma's open door and saw the professor seated at his desk, on the phone. Now in his late fifties, there was gray in Sharma's black hair, which had crept in over the last nine years, but everything else was the same—collared shirt and sweater vest, neatly organized desk, Vivaldi playing softly from the speakers on the shelves behind him.

He hung up the phone and peered at Kyle through wire-rimmed glasses. "That's the second call from a faculty member I've received in the last two minutes, asking if I'm aware that the Twitter Terrorist is in the building."

"What did you tell them?"

Sharma stood up and walked over. "That I was thinking about hiring you as an adjunct professor. To teach a course in ethics." The corners of his mouth twitched as he stuck out his hand. "Good to see you again, Kyle."

"You, too, Professor." Kyle silently exhaled.

Sharma gestured to his desk. "Have a seat. I followed the news reports about your case, obviously. I always said you would be as big as your father someday—although I'd envisioned you'd take a different path."

Kyle took a seat in one of the chairs in front of Sharma's desk. "It was a mistake," he said simply.

"Oh, you think?"

When Sharma said nothing further, Kyle cocked his head questioningly. "That can't be it. I sat in four of your classes, Professor. Where's the rest of the lecture?"

"You get the abridged version, since you're no longer a student. Except I would also add that whatever you plan to do next with your talent, I hope that it's something *legal*. People don't always get second chances."

"Perfectly legal," Kyle assured him. "I'm starting my own consulting business, actually."

Sharma appeared intrigued. "What kind of consulting?"

"Network security. Fortune 500 companies. I'll go in, assess clients' security weaknesses, and develop the tools they need to prevent both internal and external threats."

"In other words, you'll teach them how to protect themselves from people like you," Sharma said.

"I certainly plan to capitalize on the notoriety of my conviction, yes," Kyle acknowledged.

"The Twitter Terrorist uses his powers for good instead of evil."

"Something like that."

Sharma looked at him cautiously. "And how can *I* help you with this?"

Kyle leaned in, eager to get down to business. "It's simple, Professor. I just need the names of your two best hackers."

With a laugh, he held up his hands when he saw Sharma's expression.

"I swear—*totally* legal."

AFTER REASSURING SHARMA, again, that his intentions were honorable, Kyle got the names of the two students the professor felt best met his qualifications. Then Sharma went one step further and e-mailed the students, asking if they were interested in learning more about a "unique opportunity."

"The rest is up to you," Sharma said, shaking Kyle's hand in the doorway of his office. "Good luck with everything. And next time, don't make it nine years before you come back around."

And just like that, Rylann popped into Kyle's head. Again. Only this time, it wasn't naughty naked shower images— instead, he thought about the way her amber eyes lit up when she teased him.

It wasn't just the sex, he knew. It was the quips and jokes, too, and the way talking to her for fifteen minutes captivated him more than an entire night spent with most of the women he'd dated over the last nine years. He simply liked . . . being around her.

Christ. Somebody obviously needed to check the pockets of the orange jumpsuit he'd left behind at MCC. For his *balls*.

"Thank you, Professor. For everything," Kyle said, refocusing on work and the matters at hand.

Two hours later, he waited in a small, empty classroom, standing by the windows and looking out at the campus as he waited for the first candidate to arrive. He turned around when he heard the door open.

A man in his early twenties with curly red hair, wearing khaki pants and a button-down shirt, walked into the room. He saw Kyle and stopped. "Okay . . . not exactly what I'd been expecting."

Kyle walked over and introduced himself. "Kyle Rhodes."

"Gil Newport."

Kyle gestured to the table by the window. "Please, have a seat." He figured they could skip the preliminaries. "I assume you know who I am?"

Gil glanced around the room—what he was looking for was anyone's guess. "You may assume that, yes," he said cautiously.

"I asked Professor Sharma to put me in contact with you because I'm putting together a team of specialists for a business venture."

"What kind of business venture?" Gil asked suspiciously.

"Security consulting."

"Of course." Gil did air quotes. "*Consulting.* Got it."

"No air quotes. Actual, real consulting." Kyle couldn't tell whether Gil seemed more or less interested upon hearing this. "Professor Sharma says that you'll finish your master's degree this semester and that your thesis focused on intrusion detection and verification of secure systems and protocols."

Gil raised an eyebrow, looking almost comically sly. "You seem to know a lot about me, Mr. Rhodes."

Kyle tried to fight back a smile. "I hate to disappoint you, Gil, but this is one hundred percent legit. I'm starting a network security consulting business, and I have a position available for someone with your skills. If you're interested, I'd be happy to tell you more."

Gil paused. "You really are serious." He looked Kyle over. "No offense, but you're kind of a wild card. And I'm already entertaining six job offers—six very lucrative job offers."

Kyle dismissed this with a wave. "*If* I decide you're qualified, I can pay you more." He'd known going in to this venture that he might have to pay top dollar for quality talent given his checkered past.

"You don't even know what salaries the other companies offered me," Gil said.

"I still know I can pay more," Kyle said. "*If* you're worth it."

Gil looked almost offended by that. "Oh, I'm worth it."

Kyle held his gaze, throwing down the gauntlet. "So show me."

AN HOUR LATER, Kyle was waiting on the second of Sharma's suggested candidates—a twenty-one-year-old graduating senior named Troy Leopold, whom Sharma had described as "brilliant, with an inquisitive mind."

Right on time, a guy in his early twenties with spiky jet-black hair and wearing leather studded bracelets, ripped jeans, and black eyeliner walked in. He didn't seem fazed in the slightest when he walked over and introduced himself to Kyle. "Troy Leopold. Excuse my casual appearance—if I'd known I was going to have an interview today, I would have worn my polo shirt and khakis."

Kyle grinned, immediately liking him. "I'll try to overlook it."

They took a seat at the table, and Troy dove right in. "I think I should be straight with you. Whatever this interview is, it's very cool that Professor Sharma suggested my name. But . . ." He paused, as if worried he might say something offensive.

Kyle chuckled. "Trust me, Troy, whatever it is, I've heard it all before."

Troy gestured to Kyle's tailored pants and shirt—standard business-casual attire. "I don't exactly see myself in the corporate world. You know, working for the man."

Kyle blinked. Nine years ago, he'd been in Troy's position—except instead of leather studded bracelets and guy-liner, he'd worn flannel shirts and construction boots. Now he was *the man*.

"Wow. I'm suddenly having one of those moments when I realize that I've turned into my father." Kyle clapped his hands together, moving on. "How about this—before you make any decisions, maybe you'd at least like to know what you'd be doing for Rhodes Network Consulting. If I were to hire you."

Troy nodded politely, clearly humoring him. "Fine. Hypothetically speaking, what would I be doing for Rhodes Network Consulting?"

"Well, other members of the team, including myself, will be creating secure operating systems for our clients. Obviously, the only way to confirm that those systems are airtight is to have another member of the team test them for vulnerabilities."

Troy's expression reflected his surprise. "You want to hire a hacker?"

"I was thinking we'd call the position 'security analyst,' but in essence, yes—you would be a professional hacker."

Seeing the gleam of interest in Troy's eyes, Kyle continued on. "Professor Sharma says you're brilliant and ambitious." He leaned forward in his chair, speaking earnestly. "Nine years ago, I was given the opportunity to learn from the best in the industry. It wasn't the path I'd seen myself taking at the time, but one I have no regrets about following. Today I'm here, giving you the same chance. Maybe it's not for you—but speaking from personal experience, you won't know that until you try."

Troy spoke cautiously, thinking this through. "And what if it turns out not to be for me?"

Kyle shrugged. "Give me a six-month commitment. If it's not working out, you can walk away after that. No hard feelings. We both know I can find plenty computer geeks out there who would be thrilled to have this job." He went in for the kill, knowing exactly the last button to push. "After all, those are *my* systems you'd be trying to hack into. A chance to beat the Twitter Terrorist at his own game."

Troy said nothing for a long moment, then his lips curved up in a slight smile. "Can I dress like this at the office?"

"Troy, three months ago I was wearing an orange prison jumpsuit and gym shoes without laces. I think it's safe to say we won't be putting on too many airs at Rhodes Network Consulting. Just don't scratch up my keyboards with those spiked bracelets."

Troy smiled at that. "Deal."

LATE THAT AFTERNOON, Kyle was once again staring at cornfield after cornfield on I-57, heading back to Chicago.

The day had been a success.

He wasn't ready to throw out his shingle quite yet—he may have been good, but he needed more than two smart guys with computer science degrees and zero practical experience on his team. He still wanted to hire at least one person with several years in the field for a management position—the guy in Seattle he'd made an offer to had turned him down—and an administrative assistant, too. Also, he needed to implement phases one and two of his marketing strategy. He had a comfortable amount of start-up capital and was prepared to get more by selling the penthouse if need be, but that wasn't going to last forever.

Tonight, however, he simply wanted to enjoy his accomplishments, especially since it had been a long time since he'd felt this excited and pumped up about work. For years he'd thought about striking out on his own, of stepping out of his father's shadow, and finally that was about to happen.

The sun had just begun to set as Kyle approached the city, the impressive Chicago skyline welcoming him home. He was in a celebratory mood, and thought about dropping by Firelight to knock back a few victory cocktails with Dex. Going as far back as grad school, that had always been his default—hanging out at Dex's bar—whenever he'd been in the mood to kick back and unwind.

Interesting, then, that his car stayed on Lake Shore Drive

and drove past the exit that would have taken him to Firelight.

He had a rough idea where he was going, since Rylann had previously mentioned that she lived in Roscoe Village. At the stoplight at Belmont Avenue, he pulled out his cell phone and scrolled through his contacts. The beauty of text messaging, he realized, was in its simplicity. He didn't have to try to explain things, nor did he have to attempt to parse through all the banter in an attempt to figure out what *she* might be thinking. Instead, he could keep things short and sweet.

I'D LIKE TO SEE YOU.

He hit send.

To kill time while he waited for her response, he drove in the direction of his sister's wine shop, figuring he could always drop in and harass Jordan about something.

This time, however, she beat him to the punch.

"So who's the brunette bombshell?" Jordan asked as soon as he walked into the shop and took a seat at the main bar.

Damn. He'd forgotten about the stupid Scene and Heard column. Kyle helped himself to a cracker and some Brie cheese sitting on the bar. "I'm going to say . . . Angelina Jolie. Actually, no—Megan Fox."

"Megan Fox is, like, twenty-five."

"And this is a problem why, exactly?"

Jordan slapped his hand as he reached for more crackers. "Those are for customers." She put her hand on her hip. "You know, after reading the Scene and Heard column, I'd kind of hoped it was Rylann they were talking about. And that maybe, just maybe, my ne'er-do-well twin had decided to stop playing around and finally pursue a woman of quality."

He stole another cracker. "Now, that would be something."

She shook her head. "Why do I bother? You know, one day you're going to wake up and . . ."

Kyle's cell phone buzzed, and he tuned out the rest of Jordan's lecture—he could probably repeat the whole thing word for word by now—as he checked the incoming message. It was from Rylann, her response as short and sweet as his original text.

3418 CORNELIA, #3.

He had her address.

With a smile, he looked up and interrupted his sister. "That's great, Jordo. Hey, by any chance do you have any bottles of that India Ink cabernet lying around?"

She stopped midrant and stared at him. "I'm sure I do. Why, what made you think of that?" Then her face broke into a wide grin. "Wait a second . . . that was the wine Rylann talked about when she was here. She said it was one of her favorites."

"Did she? Funny coincidence."

Jordan put her hand over her heart. "Oh my God, you're trying to impress her. That is so *cute*."

"Don't be ridiculous," Kyle scoffed. "I just thought, since I've heard such good things about the wine, that I would give it a shot."

Jordan gave him a look, cutting through all the bullshit. "Kyle. She's going to love it."

Okay, whatever. Maybe he was trying to impress Rylann *a little*. "You don't think it's too much? Like I'm trying too hard?"

Jordan put her hand over her heart again. "Oh. It's like watching Bambi take his first steps."

"Jordo . . ." he growled warningly.

With a smile, she put her hand on his shoulder and squeezed affectionately. "It's perfect. Trust me."

Twenty-five

RYLANN'S EYES DID a quick sweep over her apartment as she walked to the front door. Definitely not a penthouse, but it was cute and cozy and, thankfully, clean. Not that Kyle was staying long, she reminded herself. Friday night had been a one-time thing—with the drinks and the romantic lighting in the club and the way he'd been looking at her when he'd said that line about the most beautiful girl in the bar, she'd just sort of let herself be swept up in the moment. But now it was time to face reality.

With that in mind, she threw open the front door. Kyle stood there—more dressed up than she'd expected and looking strikingly attractive in his tailored gray pants and crisp blue shirt.

With an appreciative gleam in his eyes, he took in her cream peasant top and jeans. "So you do own pants."

Rylann opened her mouth, ready to give him the speech about not complicating things, no matter how great the sexcapades had been—when he held up his hand, cutting her off at the pass.

"Before you get rolling with the lecture, or start heading for the hills again, you should know that this is a no-strings-attached visit. I have something for you." He held up a silver wine gift bag that flashed with so many sparkles and sequins it nearly blinded her.

Rylann pulled back in surprise. "Oh. Wow." She hadn't been expecting him to come bearing *gifts*. Especially one so bedazzled.

He shifted uncomfortably in the doorway. "The bag didn't look quite as shiny in the store."

Whatever this was, he looked adorably nervous about it. Rylann held out her hand. "Let me see." Intrigued, she took the bag from him, pulled out the wine bottle, and read the label. *India Ink.*

"It's one of my favorites. You remembered that," she said, staring at the label. "Thank you."

He made a big show of trying to look nonchalant. "It's no big deal. Jordan had a couple bottles sitting out, so I grabbed one."

Rylann leaned against the doorway. "Please don't take this the wrong way, Kyle, because I really love the wine. But what's the catch?"

"No catch." He shrugged. "I don't know, I just thought we could . . . hang out and talk."

He looked as shocked by the suggestion as she was.

"Talk?" Rylann stared at him. "Are you feeling okay? You're being very . . . not you."

"What's that supposed to mean?" he asked indignantly. "That I can't hang out with a girl without sex being on the table?"

Good question. "I don't know. *Have* you ever hung out with a girl without sex being on the table?"

He immediately scoffed at that. "Of course."

"Not including high school."

His busted look said it all.

Rylann smiled. "You might want to plead the Fifth to avoid self-incrimination."

Kyle looked up at the ceiling, shaking his head. "I swear— no more law geeks. Ever. From now on, I'm sticking with simple, easygoing girls whose goals in life do *not* seemingly include driving me insane." He folded his arms across his chest. "Look, here's the deal: today was a good day for me. And strangely enough, you, Rylann Pierce, are the first person I wanted to tell about it." He held out his hands in exasperation. "Do with that what you will."

Later, Rylann could tell herself that she'd simply been sucked in by the wine-bottle gesture and how cute Kyle was when he got worked up and pissed off at her like this. But if she was being honest with herself, she'd have to admit that the fact that he'd wanted to tell *her* about his day had kind of melted her rational, pragmatic, noncrazy heart a teeny, tiny little bit.

So without saying a word, she took a step back, making room for him to come inside. With a victorious grin, Kyle followed her, standing close as she shut the door behind him.

Rylann pointed. "Remember—hands to yourself."

"Of course, counselor." He winked. "Unless you say otherwise."

SINCE THE TEMPERATURE was in the low seventies and the night sky was clear, Rylann suggested sitting outside on the deck located off the back of her third-story apartment. She set the open bottle of India Ink between them, on top of the wooden bistro table she had purchased the previous weekend. She'd also picked up a few planters and some flowers, transforming the deck into an urban minigarden.

"I like it out here," Kyle said, sitting back in his chair with his glass of wine. "That's the one downside of my apartment— no outdoor living space. Trust me, you notice that quickly when serving home detention for two straight weeks."

"I've seen the penthouse, Dimples. I'm not exactly crying a river."

"More tough love from Prosecutrix Pierce," he said. "Shocking."

Rylann laughed. " 'Prosecutrix Pierce'? Is that what you call me?"

"I find it has a certain authoritative ring that suits you." Kyle caught her checking him out. "What?"

She gestured to his shirt and pants. "What's with the business-casual attire? I'm on pins and needles, waiting to hear about this good day you've been having."

"I had two job interviews earlier today."

Rylann raised her glass to his, thrilled for him. "Congratulations. That's really great, Kyle. How do you think the interviews went?"

"Very well. I hired both guys."

Rylann cocked her head, confused. "Wait—*you* hired them?"

He took another sip of his wine, looking pleased with himself. "Weren't expecting that, were you?"

"No. But now I'm really intrigued." Rylann studied him curiously. "What are you up to?"

So he told her. As they sat there drinking wine, Kyle told her all about the consulting business he planned to start. Granted, she understood about half of what he was saying, the other half being coded in computer-speak and tech terms, but it didn't matter. He was clearly passionate about the subject and extremely driven, and that made the entire conversation absolutely fascinating.

It occurred to Rylann that because they'd focused so much these past several weeks on Kyle being an ex-con and her witness, this part of him had been overshadowed. Now, suddenly, she was seeing *him*, this computer genius turned multimillionaire corporate executive who planned to take the tech world by storm.

And she had no doubt that he would do exactly that.

When he finished, Rylann poured them both a second glass of wine, feeling the warm, relaxed glow of the cabernet. "Okay, I admit it. I'm impressed."

He clutched his heart, feigning shock. "Hold on. Was that an actual compliment?"

"Please don't ruin the nice moment. It's so rare that we actually have one."

With a smile, Kyle leaned back in his chair. "You know, that's the second time you've said that I impress you. You also told me that nine years ago, when I mentioned that I'd sat for my PhD exam." He tucked his arms behind his head. "So much for never stroking my ego."

Rylann looked at him, surprised. So it wasn't just her who recalled many of the details of their first meeting. "You still remember I said that after all these years?"

"I remember pretty much everything about that night." He

reached forward and grabbed his glass. "Tough weekend to forget," he said simply. He took a sip, then looked at her.

Since most of her time with Kyle was spent teasing or trading quips, Rylann took advantage of this small opening into real, true emotion and asked something she'd been wondering about ever since they'd reconnected. "Is it weird for you to be around me?" She swirled her glass hesitantly. "Do I remind you of all the bad things that happened that weekend?"

"No." His tone turned quieter, and his eyes were uncharacteristically serious as they held hers. "Being around you reminds me of the one good thing that happened that weekend."

Rylann felt a tightening in her chest.

Run.

There was a part of her that certainly thought she should do just that. Outside her apartment door, she and Kyle didn't make any sense—he was a famous ex-con, and she was a federal prosecutor.

Tonight, however, inside her apartment . . . it was just the two of them.

So she got up from her chair and walked over.

Silently, she climbed onto his lap, her legs straddling his waist. Heat instantly flared in his eyes.

She lowered her head. "Just remember your promise. Hands to yourself." Then she tangled her fingers in his hair and kissed him.

For a long moment their lips and tongues played and teased, like teenagers kissing under the stars. Slowly, Kyle pulled back and brushed a finger along her cheek. "You were not supposed to walk into the courtroom that morning, Rylann Pierce." His eyes met hers. "I want to be completely honest here. I like you. Probably a lot more than I should. But after everything that happened with Daniela, I was planning on staying the hell away from relationships for a long, long time."

He waited expectantly, his body more tense than it had been just moments ago, as if steeling himself—whether for an argument, an interrogation, or simply a talk about *feelings* was tough to say.

Instead, Rylann slid her hands up his chest. "I bet that part of the Kyle Rhodes no-strings-attached speech doesn't always go over so well with the women you date."

He threaded his fingers through her hair, his eyes searching hers. "Does that mean you don't care?"

"Are you asking me if I'm looking for something serious here?"

He nodded. "Yes. And that is definitely not part of the usual Kyle Rhodes speech."

Rylann toyed with one of the buttons on his shirt, trying to decide how best to answer his question. She liked Kyle— probably more than *she* should—but she had genuine concerns about how any sort of long-term relationship between them could work. For both their sakes, things would probably be a lot simpler if they kept it casual.

"Given your history with my office, being in a relationship with you . . . would be difficult," she said. "Prosecutors don't typically date ex-cons. Especially not a prosecutor who's trying to make a good impression at her new office."

She expected Kyle to make a joke, most likely something about good-girl prosecutors, but instead, his expression remained serious.

"So where does that leave us?" he asked.

"Honestly? I have no clue."

He thought about that for a moment, then slid his hand up her back and pulled her closer. "But you're supposed to be the girl with the plan."

"Funny enough, I always seem to forget that around you," Rylann whispered, closing her eyes as he began kissing her neck. Truly, the man had the most wickedly talented mouth. "No more Scene and Heard," she said, inhaling unsteadily and struggling to stay focused as his lips brushed against her earlobe. She needed to set some ground rules. "We have to be more careful. What happens in the apartment stays in the apartment."

"Got it, counselor," he murmured softly. "Now shut up and kiss me."

Before she had a chance to argue, Kyle's hand moved to her neck as he caught her mouth with his. His lips parted hers as he seductively explored her mouth while sliding his hands under her shirt to caress the bare skin of her lower back.

That reminded Rylann of something. She pulled back and peered down at him. "Hey. What happened to 'no hands'?"

"Oh, sorry, that's not how this works," he said with a grin, teasingly repeating the lecture she'd given him at the diner.

She raised an eyebrow. "You'd break your promise?"

His hands slid around front, moving over the thin satin of her bra. "You know you want me to break that promise as much as I do." When her nipples tightened in response to his touch, a satisfied look flashed in his eyes.

Rylann still said nothing.

Kyle paused with his hands cupping her breasts. "You're serious?"

She nodded, fighting back a smile when he sighed dramatically and removed his hands from her chest.

"Now . . . where were we?" she asked coyly. "I think somewhere right about here." When she brushed her lips over his, he was ready for her, taking her mouth in a bold, searing kiss that left her body hot everywhere. As his tongue swept around hers, she sighed softly and pressed her chest against his. She felt his hand at her cheek as he tried to take control once more, then smiled when he swore under his breath and gripped the wooden arm of the chair instead.

"I think I like this," Rylann said when she pulled back.

His eyes burned into hers. "Ask me to touch you. Trust me, I'll do all sorts of things you like even more than this."

"Hmm. I'll take your recommendation under advisement." But for now, she was having too much fun being in the driver's seat. She unbuttoned his shirt, taking her time as she worked her way down. She pushed it open and slid her hands across his chest, exploring the hard, defined planes of his muscles. "Did you lift weights a lot in prison?"

"Every day."

She suddenly caught herself wondering whether she was the first person Kyle had been with after his release, then decided she really didn't want to know the answer to that. The idea of him with someone else, with another woman who'd touched him just like this, made her far more jealous than she wanted to admit.

Careful, Pierce.

She pushed the thoughts aside—what mattered now was that he was here tonight. And she planned to enjoy every lean, hard inch of him.

She leaned forward and kissed his neck, hearing the deep rumble of pleasure in his chest. She could feel his thick erection between her legs, and ever so slowly she began rocking against him.

"You're killing me here, Rylann," he said in a raspy voice.

Exactly her plan. But not here, out on her balcony, in this chair that was far too confining. "Come with me." She stood up and took him by the hand, leading him through the screen door and into her bedroom. She sat on the edge of the bed and was about to tell him to join her when he stepped between her legs and swooped down to take her mouth in a scorching-hot kiss. With his hands braced on the bed on either side of her, she fell back onto her elbows and gasped when he rubbed his hard shaft between her legs.

"You never said no mouths," he said slyly. "Why don't you take off those jeans and spread your legs so I can lick you until you scream?"

She moaned when his erection rubbed against just the right spot. "That's cheating."

With a chuckle, he stood up and pulled off his shirt. All of the rest of his clothes quickly followed, then he climbed onto her bed and stretched out, fully naked and erect. He folded his hands behind his head and watched her. "What do you plan to do with me now?"

A challenge. Rylann pushed off her elbows and stood up, undressing down to her bra and panties. Then she climbed back onto the bed and straddled him once again. "I have a few ideas." While holding his gaze, she licked her lips.

His eyes instantly turned a deep, smoldering blue. "Counselor . . . I really like where you're going with this."

KYLE FELT THE heat coiling in his abdomen as Rylann shifted lower and settled between his legs. *Christ*, he wanted this—she'd been driving him crazy with her no-hands rule ever since she'd first kissed him.

And when she licked his inner thigh, he knew the madness was far from over.

Propped up on pillows, his hands behind his head, since he'd promised he wouldn't touch her, he watched as her long raven hair fell forward, blocking his view of her. "Move your hair out of the way," he said huskily. "I want to watch when you take me in your mouth."

Her look was coy as she sat up and brushed her hair behind her shoulders. Then she reached back, unhooked her bra, and tossed it on the floor.

Kyle gazed at her, aching to feel those rosy-tipped breasts in his hands, to run his tongue over her tight, peaked nipples. "Rylann. Come here."

She shook her head no. Instead, she wrapped her hand around his cock and slowly stroked him, up and down. "So smooth," she said. She shifted her body and licked the head while holding his gaze.

Fuck. He was throbbing already, and she'd barely started. "Deeper, baby," he said in a guttural voice. "Wrap those saucy lips around me."

She slid the head between her lips and sucked lightly, then, inch by delicious inch, took him farther into her warm, luscious mouth.

His eyes nearly rolled back in his head. "Just like that, Rylann," he moaned. He wanted to tangle his fingers in her hair, to palm her head and guide her up and down. But all he could do was watch as she subjected him to the sweetest torture imaginable, licking, sucking, and stroking him with her mouth and hands until he was rocking his hips, thrusting gently into her mouth and dangerously close to exploding.

"Come up here," he said in a gravelly voice.

She released him, trailing her mouth along his skin all the way up and brushing her breasts against his chest. "Did you bring a condom?"

Three of them, actually. But he wasn't ready for that yet. His gaze fell to her panties. "Take those off and straddle me."

"Somebody's getting bossy again."

Yes, *somebody* was. Because *somebody* was determined to break her no-hands ban before it killed him. When she was straddling him once again, he propped up on his elbows and crooked his finger, beckoning her. "I need one of those breasts in my mouth."

"Very bossy," she said. But she did it anyway, gasping when he circled his tongue around her nipple, teasing it into a stiff, hard peak. Instinctively, she began sliding against him, his cock nestled right across her warm, wet core. He was so close to being inside her, but he wanted control—wanted all of her. She moaned again as he rolled her other nipple in his mouth and thrust against her.

"I want you inside me," she said breathlessly.

"Ask me to touch you."

He would've smiled when she groaned in frustration if he hadn't been so near to the edge himself. He used his legs to spread her open as he rocked his hips against her.

Her body trembled as she finally caved. "Touch me, Kyle. Now," she begged.

Thank fucking God.

Kyle slid his hands over the silky skin of her back, tangling them in her long hair as his mouth took hers possessively. "Flip over. On your stomach."

Her eyes flashed at his words, and she slid off him and lay on the bed, watching as he reached around on the floor and found his pants. He took a condom out of his wallet, tore open the wrapper, and rolled it on. "You should probably start keeping these here," he told her. "I plan to be inside you a lot when we're in this apartment."

Then he climbed between her legs and gently lifted her hips. "Up on your knees," he said huskily. He nudged his cock into the wet entrance between her legs, sliding in and out while her tight, slick passage stretched to fit him, squeezing him every inch along the way. "I want to take you hard," he said in a thick voice.

"*Yes,*" she groaned, her hands clutching the blanket.

He gripped her hips and began to move, first in smooth, steady strokes, and then taking her faster, deeper, wanting to claim her and make her his. When he was inside her like this, there were no rules, no complications; neither her job nor his past existed, there was nothing else except the two of them; and this moment, when everything felt so right and so fucking *good*.

"Kyle," she said urgently.

"I've got you." He reached down between her legs and began to tease her. She braced herself on her forearms and thrust back against him, crying out when her orgasm hit her. Wave after wave gripped his cock as he gripped her hips and thrust deep into her, again and again, until he exploded, the force of his orgasm so strong he had to slow down and hold her tightly to him, his jaw clenched as he groaned and finally shuddered to a stop.

Panting, they collapsed on the bed, a thin sheen of sweat covering their bodies.

"Better than . . . not bad?" he asked, out of breath.

Her voice was muffled, her face buried in the blanket as she lay motionless and seemingly utterly spent. "Hell, yes."

With a grin, he rested his forehead against her back.

About time.

Twenty-six

THREE DAYS LATER, Rylann met Rae at the Starbucks across the street from the Federal Building for a midafternoon break. She was on a supersecret stealth mission—Operation Setup—and, deriving inspiration from the FBI agents with whom she often worked, she'd crafted the perfect cover story: she'd claimed that she wanted to get Rae's advice about the situation with Kyle. In truth, however, she had a whole sneak attack worked out—which was necessary, because if Rae caught one whiff of Operation Setup, she'd be out the door in two seconds flat.

The beauty of this situation was that even if Rylann's mission failed, no one would ever be the wiser. Having worked with Cade for a month and a half, she knew his routine: barring a court appearance or meetings, he went to Starbucks at three o'clock sharp every day. Which meant—as Rylann checked her watch—that he would be arriving in approximately eleven minutes.

She and Rae sat at a table within view of the counter, where Cade would see them. Naturally, he would come over to say hi, at which point she would "casually" introduce him to Rae. The rest was up to them.

While they enjoyed their drinks, Rylann caught Rae up on the latest developments with Kyle—being careful, of course, to keep her voice low whenever saying his name.

"So Tuesday was the last time you saw him?" Rae asked.

"Well, technically it was Wednesday morning," Rylann noted with a smile. Since then, Kyle had been out of town, meeting in Silicon Valley with a young executive at a software company whom he wanted to recruit for his security consulting business.

Rae studied her. "You're doing the glowing thing again."

Rylann pointed to her latte. "It's the caffeine. Stimulates blood circulation."

"You like him."

Rylann shrugged. "We have fun together. I'm not ready to call it anything more than that yet." She saw Rae's look. "What?"

"I just don't want you to get hurt, that's all."

Rylann scoffed as she picked up her latte. "Why don't people ever say that to men when they want to keep things casual? Women can't have fun, too?"

"Of course they can. But here's a general rule of thumb: if you're still grinning like the friggin' Cheshire Cat three days after seeing the guy, things have moved a hair beyond *fun*."

Ha, ha. "I've got this, Rae. He and I have talked—we both know the deal. He doesn't want to get serious with anyone, and . . . I don't want to get serious with him."

"All right. If you say so," Rae said, not seeming entirely convinced. "So when are you and Smug Dimples seeing each other again?"

Rylann hemmed and hawed a bit. "Um . . . tonight, actually."

Rae raised an eyebrow. "Two dates in one week."

Rylann shook her head. "Not a date. He's going to the Bulls game with his sister's boyfriend and asked if he could drop by afterward. It's just a hookup."

"A prearranged hookup."

"Exactly," Rylann said.

"In other words, a *date*."

"If we ever step outside the nine hundred square feet of my apartment"—which was not likely—"then I'll call it a date." Rylann checked her watch. 2:59. Which meant that Target B was about to leave his office and would soon be en route to the rendezvous point with Target A. Within minutes, Operation Setup would be fully under way.

Until the whole sneak attack went up in flames.

Rae saw Rylann check her watch, and did the same. "I should probably get going. I've got a pile of document requests waiting for me back at the office." She stood up from the table.

"Wait." Rylann tried to think quickly, needing to stall just a minute or two longer. "Maybe you were right. Maybe it's not a good idea for me to see you-know-who tonight."

Rae waved this off. "You sound like you've got the situation under control."

"Still, perhaps we should fully vet the pros and cons."

Rae ticked off her fingers, running through her list. "You're having sex. Great sex. With a man who brings you expensive wine. Pro, pro, pro." She held up three fingers. "Yep, I'm good with the situation."

Well, when she put it that way . . . Rylann quickly changed tactics, not yet ready to concede failure on Operation Setup. "But we haven't talked about what's going on with you."

"Because, depressingly, there is nothing going on with me."

"Then let's talk about that."

Rae looked her over suspiciously. "Why are you suddenly so insistent that I stay? We talk all the time." She cocked her head. "And come to think of it, why have you been checking your watch this whole time? It's like you're waiting for somebody." Her eyes went wide, then she gasped and pointed her finger. "*No.* Do *not* tell me this is a setup."

"Calm down, it's not a setup." Rylann hedged a little on that. "I'd call it more a meet and greet. Just a guy I work with; it'll be totally casual. He doesn't even know you're—"

"Uh-uh. No way." Rae grabbed her purse and drink off the table. "You know I hate these kinds of things. They're so artificial and forced."

"Come on. After all the matchmaking schemes you've put me through since college, you owe me."

"That's probably true. But still, I'm out of here." Rae took a step back from the table.

As if in slow motion, Rylann saw what was about to happen. "Rae, look—"

"Nice try, Pierce. But you're going to have to try a little

harder to get the jump on me." With a satisfied grin, she whirled around and—

—ran smack into the chest of one designer-suit-wearing Special Agent Sam Wilkins.

A chest now drenched in iced cappuccino.

"Oh my gosh, I am *so* sorry," Rae blurted out.

He sighed. "It would have to be one of the Varvatos suits." Then he peered down at Rae, seeing her face for the first time. "Oh. Hello."

Rae's gaze lingered several seconds, seemingly mesmerized by his dazzling smile. She held up the soggy napkin from her drink. "Napkin?"

He took the napkin from her. "Assault with a loaded cappuccino. That's a new one."

Just in time, Rae recovered her wits. "Purely self-defense. You sidled up on me without warning."

"Those would be my stealth moves." He held out his hand. "Special Agent Sam Wilkins."

"Rae Ellen Mendoza."

Back at the table, Rylann watched this interaction with interest. Rae *Ellen*? This was getting serious. She waved cheerfully at Wilkins. "Good to see you again, Sam."

Rae shot her a look. "You two know each other?"

"Sure do." Wilkins blotted the coffee on his suit with the wet napkin. "We work together."

"How interesting," Rae said. "And you just happened to be in the area?"

"Actually, yes," Wilkins said. "I was in front of the grand jury this afternoon for three hours and needed some caffeine before heading back to the FBI office. Saw Rylann and thought I'd come over to say hi."

"Oh." Rae pointed to his wet suit, making an apologetic face. "Sorry you have to go back to the office like that."

"Since I'm by far the best-dressed agent in the office, you're really putting my reputation on the line here. Luckily, I know how you can make it up to me." Wilkins reached into the inner pocket of his blazer, exposing a glimpse of his gun harness. He pulled out his business card and handed it to Rae.

"That's my info. Call me—so I know where to send my dry cleaning bill," he added with an amused sparkle in his light brown eyes.

Rae looked at the card, then back at Sam. "I'll think about it."

"You do that." He handed her back the soggy napkin. "Because if you don't call, Rae Ellen Mendoza, you're going to ruin a really good meet-cute story."

She smiled. "Since when do FBI agents know about meet-cutes?"

Wilkins winked as he turned to leave. "I think you'll find that I'm not the average FBI agent." He raised his hand in good-bye. "See you later, Rylann."

And just as quickly as he appeared, he was gone.

"Well. That was fun." Rylann picked up her latte and stood up from the table. Clearly, her business here was done.

Rae was silent as the two of them walked out of the Star-bucks together. When they stepped outside, she finally caved. "All right. Tell me."

"Yale Law School, joined the FBI last year. He works in the violent crimes division and specializes in homicide cases."

Rae digested all that. "He's a little young. But that smile is deadly." She shot Rylann a coy look. "That was actually pretty smooth."

The true tactical details of Operation Setup would go with Rylann to her grave. "Of course it was. You're not the only one who's a matchmaking evil genius."

"I meant Agent Wilkins was pretty smooth."

"So he passed the five-minute test?"

"We'll see." But Rae's Cheshire Cat–like grin said it all as she walked away, heading in the direction of her office.

Rylann stood on the sidewalk, watching her friend go.

And all was right with the world.

"Rylann—hey."

She looked over and saw Cade Morgan approaching.

He gestured behind him. "I just ran into Sam Wilkins, covered in cappuccino. He said something about a meet-cute?

No clue what that means." He stopped next to her in front of the Starbucks. "So what did I miss?"

Rylann smiled. *Poor Cade.* So close and yet so far. Maybe next time.

TO ENTERTAIN CLIENTS, Rhodes Network Consulting LLC—aka Kyle—had purchased a premium theater box at the United Center. The box included four private seats with perfect views just twenty-eight rows above the floor, in-seat wait service, and a reserved table at the stadium's exclusive lounge and bar.

Of course, since Rhodes Network Consulting LLC currently had no clients, the box hadn't seen a lot of action as of late. Thus, after Jordan had essentially decreed that he and Nick have a guy's night out to "bond," Kyle had offered up the seats and told Nick to feel free to bring along a friend. He'd also asked Dex to join them—the more the merrier, he'd figured.

Perhaps not always the best words to live by.

Kyle warily eyed the two FBI agents—yes, now there were two; apparently they multiplied like wet gremlins—as they pushed open the red privacy curtain and entered the theater box.

"How nice," he said to Nick. "You brought the guy who nearly snapped my ankle off putting on a monitoring device."

Nick turned to the tall guy with dark hair and dark eyes next to him. "I totally forgot about that."

The other agent—Special Agent Jack Pallas, if memory served—looked just as surprised. "You only said you had an extra ticket," he said to Nick. "You didn't say who else would be here."

Nick looked between Jack and Kyle. "This is a little awkward."

The waitress stepped into the box, having seen the two agents arrive. "Can I get anyone something to drink?"

Four hands shot up. "A beer."

After the waitress left, Nick and Jack took the two seats in the back row, directly behind Kyle and Dex.

"In my defense," Jack said to Kyle, "you were flirting with my girlfriend at the time. And you called me Wolverine."

Kyle smiled to himself, having forgotten that part of the story. On the night he'd been released from prison, the U.S. attorney, Cameron Lynde, along with Agent Pallas, had met with him to explain that she'd arranged for him to serve out the remainder of his sentence on supervised release—all part of Jordan's deal with the FBI and U.S. Attorney's Office, although Kyle hadn't known that at the time.

Seeing as how the U.S. attorney had been the first woman other than Jordan Kyle had seen in four months, and not having realized that she and Pallas were involved, he may have thrown one or two perfectly harmless, mildly flirtatious comments in her direction.

"Maybe you boys could call it even?" Nick suggested, looking between Kyle and Jack.

With a shrug, Jack turned to Kyle. "Not like I have much choice in the matter." He nodded in Nick's direction. "McCall here was just promoted to special agent in charge. I don't want to get shipped off to Peoria on some two-year grunt-work assignment because I screwed things up with the boss's future brother-in-law."

Kyle shot Nick a horrified look. "Brother-in-law?"

From the seat next to him, Dex slapped Kyle on the shoulder. "See? And you were worried we wouldn't have things to talk about."

FORTUNATELY, ALL NEED for nuanced conversation fell by the wayside once the game started. As part of his promise to Jordan to make an "effort," Kyle had specifically chosen a Bulls–Knicks game, since Nick was from New York and apparently a huge fan.

And so the lines were drawn. Team rivalry prevailed, replacing the former divide between ex-con and FBI agent, and the trash talk began to fly. They were men, after all—rare was the issue that could not be at least temporarily set aside within the confines of a sports arena.

Just before halftime, however, they hit their first glitch during a time-out.

"So what's going on with you and Rylann these days?" Dex asked casually.

Kyle froze with his beer halfway to his mouth.

Such a *stupid* way to get caught.

He'd been out of town since Wednesday and hadn't had the opportunity to fill Dex in on the clandestine nature of his goings-on with Prosecutrix Pierce. Nor had he had any idea that Nick would bring Rylann's boss's boyfriend to the game.

Still, he'd be damned if their cover would be blown on his watch. He'd promised Rylann that he would keep their relationshi—er, hot, no-strings-attached fling—a secret, and he intended to keep that promise. Because if *she* thought that her boss thought something was up, she would undoubtedly put the kibosh on all future rendezvous.

And he wasn't ready to give up Rylann quite yet.

So he stretched out in his chair, playing it casual. "Nothing's going on, unfortunately. She shot me down that night at the club. Something about not mixing business with pleasure."

Dex frowned, understandably confused, since Kyle had told him he was going to Rylann's that night, and opened his mouth to say something.

Kyle subtly shook his head.

Dex paused for a split second, then his eyes flickered over to Jack and Nick, seeming to catch on that something was up. So he, too, played it casual. "That sucks. I thought you were in there that night."

"You weren't the only one," Kyle said with a chuckle. "Just wasn't meant to be, I guess."

"You're talking about Rylann Pierce?"

The question came from Jack. Kyle looked over his shoulder and saw the FBI agent studying him curiously.

"Good guess," Kyle said, maintaining a look of nonchalance.

Jack shrugged. "Not really. Unusual name. Plus, I know you worked with her. My partner is Sam Wilkins—he mentioned that Rylann had interviewed you as part of the Quinn investigation."

Damn FBI agents and assistant U.S. attorneys. Apparently, they were thick as thieves when it came to knowing everyone else's business. "Oh. Right."

Jack took a sip of his beer. "When you were working with Rylann, did she ever tell you the meth lab story?"

Kyle studied the agent, thinking he suddenly seemed awfully chatty. He also noticed that Nick was watching both of them closely. "Not that I recall."

"It's a good one. Made its way around all the FBI offices," Jack said. "Apparently, a few years ago, your friend Rylann worked on a big drug case in San Francisco—an organized crime group that was running an underground meth lab in the middle of this overgrown wooded area. Anyway, she tells the agents working the investigation that she wants to see the lab in person. But on the day they're set to go out to the lab, she's running late because of court or something, and she shows up to meet them wearing a skirt suit and heels."

Kyle smiled at that part. Of course she did.

"So these two agents, who were likely being smug and cocky about the situation, decide not to tell Rylann the exact setup of this meth lab," Jack continued. "Then they drive her out to the middle of the forest and take her to this three-foot-wide hole in the ground that's covered by a metal door—kind of like a submarine hatch. And when they open the door, there's nothing but a ladder that goes fifteen feet underground."

"Sounds like something out of *Lost*," Dex said.

"Exactly." Jack cocked his head and looked at Kyle. "Hey, has anyone ever told you—"

"Only people who need to get *lives*, since the show ended two years ago," Kyle growled. He rolled his hand, gesturing impatiently. "Let's get back to this underground hatch." He could picture Rylann, in one of her skirt suits and heels, standing in the forest with two dickhead FBI agents who were trying to rattle her.

Jack went on with the story. "So Rylann and these two agents are standing over the hatch, and she points to the hole in the ground and asks, 'Is that where we're going?' And they say yes, and of course they're looking at her in her suit and heels and thinking she's going to balk at the whole thing. But instead, she takes off her shoes and tucks them into the back of her skirt like it's nothing, and says, 'How about if I go first? That way you boys aren't tempted to look up my skirt.' And then down the ladder she went."

Kyle laughed hard at that. Man, this girl impressed the hell out of him sometimes.

Actually, all the time.

"You were right. That *is* a good story." Mindful of the role he still needed to play, he shook his head with mock regret. "Too bad it didn't work out. She and I could've had a lot of fun."

"Maybe, maybe not," Jack said dismissively. "I heard a rumor that she and Cade Morgan are getting close. Really close, if you know what I mean."

Morgan.

His nemesis.

Kyle gripped the arm of his seat so tightly he was surprised it didn't break off in his hand. "Good for Morgan," he managed coolly.

Just then, the halftime buzzer rang.

Nick stood up. "The scoreboard doesn't lie, sports fans," he said, gloating over the fact that the Knicks were up by eight. "Which means, if I remember correctly, that one of you boys owes me a drink." He clasped Kyle's shoulder. "I'll let you have the honor, Sawyer. Come join me at the bar."

AS SOON AS Kyle and Nick got to the bar in the stadium's private lounge, the FBI agent's expression turned more serious. "You do realize that you're being interrogated, don't you?"

"Thanks, I'm aware of that," Kyle said dryly. And he didn't like it one bit.

"Pallas softens you up with the meth lab story, then hits

you with the comment about Morgan to see your reaction. One of the oldest tricks in the book." Nick gestured to the bartender. "Two Maker's Marks, neat."

"I think your friend Jack needs to mind his own business."

"Jack's a good guy. And he's a fantastic agent," Nick said. "But his number-one priority is, and will always be, to protect the U.S. attorney. And if he thinks there's something Cameron would want to know about—like the fact that one of her top prosecutors is fooling around with the Twitter Terrorist—he's going to be on top of it."

He nodded when the bartender slid the two whiskeys in front of them and handed one to Kyle. "Here. You look like you need it."

Kyle took the glass from him. "Is what Pallas said true? Are there rumors going around about Rylann and Morgan?"

"Just office gossip. I wouldn't get too worked up about it."

A little late for that.

The idea that Rylann might be "getting close" to Cade Morgan, whatever that meant, struck a nerve with Kyle. "Let me ask you something. If you thought some guy was moving in on my sister, how worked up would you be?"

Nick took a sip of his whiskey. "I may or may not have once tossed a guy out of her store for flirting with her." He shrugged. "Total douchebag. Wore a scarf indoors." He studied Kyle curiously. "I didn't realize you and Rylann were getting that serious."

"We're not."

"Then it really shouldn't matter what she's doing with Morgan, should it?"

Kyle shifted uncomfortably, not ready to answer that question. "What is this, another interrogation?"

"Sorry. Habit." A silence fell between them until Nick cleared his throat. "Look, Kyle, I know we got off on the wrong foot. But I'll tell you the same thing I told your father the day I met him: your sister means everything to me. And family is very important where I come from. So with that in mind . . ." He held out his hand. "I would really like it if you and I could put the past aside and move forward."

Kyle paused for a moment, then clasped the other guy's hand. "Jordan gave you the speech about bonding, too, huh?"

Nick grinned. "I'm under strict orders to make an 'effort.' And then I'm supposed to dig up whatever dirt I can about you and Rylann. Probably, I'll just tell her how you beamed like a headlight when you heard the meth lab story."

"Wonderful. Now I've got *two* of you all up in my business," Kyle said dryly.

Nick slapped him across the shoulders, seeming to thoroughly enjoy this. "Get used to it, Sawyer. That's what family is for."

Twenty-seven

RYLANN OPENED HER door to find Kyle standing in the hallway, looking prickly once again.

"I heard an interesting rumor tonight." He brushed past her and entered the apartment.

Rylann shut the door behind him, not sure what *that* meant. "Well. It's good to see you, too."

Standing in the middle of her living room with a no-nonsense expression, Kyle folded his arms across his chest. His question took Rylann completely by surprise.

"Is there something going on between you and Cade Morgan?"

Rylann cocked her head in confusion, wondering where he'd ever gotten such an idea. "No. Why?"

"Jack Pallas said he heard that you and Morgan were getting very close."

Rylann paused. "I think the better question is why you and Jack Pallas were talking about Cade and me in the first place."

"Nick brought him to the Bulls game. He started fishing for information about us after Dex asked about you." Kyle must've seen the look of panic in her eyes. "Don't worry, I covered. No one knows you're sleeping with the Twitter Terrorist." He amended that. "Well, Nick knows. Jordan talked to him about us."

Rylann exhaled slowly. For something that was supposed to be simple and fun, this was suddenly getting very complicated. "Nick McCall is the special agent in charge of the Chicago FBI office. He works with my boss, Cameron, all the time."

"He won't say anything. We're bonding now."

At least one of them was comfortable with the situation. "Great. The future of my career is dependant on some 'moment' you and Nick had at a basketball game."

His eyes pierced hers. "We haven't finished our discussion about what's going on between you and Cade Morgan."

"Because there's *nothing* going on between me and Cade," Rylann said emphatically. "Do you really think I'd be with you if there was?"

His jaw twitched. "No offense, counselor, but this wouldn't be my first blindside."

As soon as the words registered, Rylann felt like a complete jerk. She'd momentarily forgotten that Kyle's last girlfriend had cheated on him, in just about the worst way possible. They'd never talked about Daniela—Kyle didn't seem to be particularly forthcoming about the subject, and Rylann could certainly understand why. But seeing his girlfriend with another guy, something that had ultimately put him in prison, had undoubtedly left him with a few emotional scars.

With that in mind, she walked over to him. She couldn't undo what Daniela had done, but she could assure Kyle that nothing like that would ever happen as long as he was with her. So she uncrossed his arms, wanting nothing between them, and stepped closer. She peered up and looked straight into his eyes. "There's nothing going on with Cade. We work together, and we're friends, but that's it."

He made no move to pull her closer. Instead, he cocked his head, his tone quiet. "You're friends with the guy who called me a terrorist?"

Oh . . . crap. When Rylann saw the flicker of hurt in Kyle's eyes, she knew that had been the wrong thing to say.

Obviously, she understood why he would have a problem with her being friends with Cade. Of course, he didn't know the whole story, that the former U.S. attorney had wanted to send a message to the press and specifically told Cade to go after Kyle hard. But even if that hadn't happened, Cade still would've prosecuted Kyle—and been tough in doing so—because that was his job. Just like it was *her* job.

She wasn't sure what all she could say in these circumstances except for the truth. "Well . . . yes." She sighed. "And here I thought things were complicated before."

"Does that mean you're having second thoughts about . . . whatever this is between us?" When she didn't answer at first, Kyle cupped her chin, making her look at him. "Do you want me to leave?"

Rylann thought about that, then shook her head. "No," she said softly.

His face remained uncertain, as if he needed more convincing. "Are you sure?"

She nodded. "I'm sure." She reached up, winding her arms around his neck. Though she didn't have all the answers, there was one thing she knew for certain—that she wasn't ready to say good-bye to Kyle yet. "See, I've been having this problem the last couple nights. My pillows smell like whatever shampoo you use in your freakishly lustrous hair, and now I can't go to sleep without thinking about you."

Kyle slid his hands up her back, pulling her closer. "Maybe you should wash your pillows. Get rid of all traces of me."

"Or I could just invite you to spend the night again." She stood up on her toes, brushing her lips against his. "Since we never seem to do much sleeping, anyway."

When their mouths met, everything else seemed to fall by the wayside. Perhaps brought on by their near fight, the kiss quickly turned hot and impatient. Kyle gripped her hips and guided her backward, trapping her against the front door. Rylann tugged his T-shirt over his head and then ran her hands over the solid muscles of his chest as their mouths came back together. She moaned his name, needing to feel all of him against her, wanting to be as close to him as possible right then and there.

Apparently driven by the same need, Kyle yanked her T-shirt off, then hooked his hands into the waistband of her yoga pants and panties and hastily pushed them down her hips. Eager to hurry up the process, Rylann helped him out, kicking her clothes aside as he made fast work of the button and zipper on the fly of his jeans.

As their tongues clashed and fought, she pushed his jeans down, and a thrill of excitement coursed through her when his heavy, hard shaft brushed up against her stomach. He reached into his back pocket, pulled out his wallet, and found a condom.

"Hurry," she panted urgently, watching as he ripped open the wrapper and rolled the condom on.

He slid his hands under her bottom and lifted her up against the wall, positioning himself right between her legs, where she was wet and ready for him. He gazed down at her heatedly, his hair falling into his eyes. "As long as we're doing this, for however long it lasts, there's no one else. Got it?"

She tightened her arms around his neck. "There's no one else I want."

Seeming to be satisfied with that answer, he thrust hard and deep, entering her in one stroke. Rylann threw her head back against the door and moaned. "Oh God, it's so good."

Kyle held her firmly against the wall and began moving inside her, his voice deep and husky. "It's perfect."

LATER THAT EVENING, Kyle sat alone in Rylann's living room, toying absentmindedly with his glass of wine while he waited. Apparently, she was the "duty assistant" that night, which—judging from the emergency page she'd received from an FBI team wanting a search warrant—was something like being a doctor on call.

They'd been curled up on the couch together, pretending to watch a movie but mostly just making out like a couple of sixteen-year-olds, when her pager went off. She'd checked it, apologized with a quick kiss, then had headed into her bedroom to return the call in private.

The normalcy of the moment, the everydayness of it, had made Kyle realize that *this* was how things could be between them. Cozy weekend nights together, a good bottle of wine, hitting pause on the TiVo remote while one of them had to sneak off for a work call. A far cry from his "play hard" days spent wining and dining the girl of the week.

But as he sat there on Rylann's couch, listening to the murmur of her voice from the bedroom and waiting for her to join him again, he knew there was no place he'd rather be.

Yep, it was official.

He was falling for her.

Panic set in upon that realization, and in his mind's eye he saw himself pulling a Road Runner and bolting lightning-quick, cartoon-style, out of the apartment. She'd come out of the bedroom after finishing her call and would find no trace of him except a half-empty wineglass and the gaping hole of a man running top-speed through her front door.

Or he could go with option two.

Stay and do whatever it took to convince a certain stubborn, sassy assistant U.S. attorney that this was more than a hot, casual fling.

Undoubtedly, that was a risky proposition. He wasn't even one hundred percent certain that *he* was ready for a commitment, and more important, he had no clue how—or if—he fit into Rylann's world. She loved her job; anyone could see that. Even when the phone rang at ten P.M. on a Friday night and interrupted a mighty fine make-out session, she'd had a gleam in her eye that said some thug out there was about to be served up a steaming-hot plate of Prosecutrix Pierce whoop-ass.

He heard her cell phone ring again, then a short moment later she came out of the bedroom.

"Sorry," she said with an apologetic smile. She set the pager on the coffee table, then picked up her wineglass and curled up on the couch. "I left a message for the emergency judge and had to wait for the clerk to call me back."

"Did you get your search warrant?"

"We did."

"What kind of case?"

She took a sip of her wine. "Terrorism. The FBI got a last-minute tip about a guy being deported tomorrow at six A.M. who they believe is connected to a radical fundamentalist group operating in Chechnya. They want to search his apartment and personal effects, but he's refusing consent."

Of course that's what it was. Because *everyone* took calls

from the FBI and helped take down radical terrorists at ten P.M. on a Friday while wearing yoga pants and casually sipping a glass of wine.

"You amaze me, Rylann," he said, in all sincerity.

And that's when he made up his mind.

She could set all the rules she wanted—but this was one matchup against a federal prosecutor he intended to win.

Twenty-eight

WHEN THE WEEKEND was over, duty called once again.

On Sunday evening, after a four-and-a-half-hour flight, Kyle handed his overnight bag to the valet and walked up to the front desk of the Ritz-Carlton San Francisco.

"I'll be in your former neck of the woods," he'd told Rylann on Saturday morning as they'd stood in her doorway saying good-bye.

"You're going to San Francisco?" she'd asked. "What for?"

"You'll know soon enough."

She'd looked him over with a curious expression. "What are you up to now?"

Despite all her valiant efforts, Kyle had refused to give anything up under cross-examination. He had a lot riding on this trip, since the next twenty-four hours would drastically impact the launch of Rhodes Network Consulting. Either his actions would go down as one of the cleverest ideas in marketing history, or he was about to make a complete ass out of himself.

Only time would tell.

The front desk clerk smiled as Kyle approached. "Welcome to the Ritz-Carlton. How can I help you?"

"I have a reservation, under Kyle Rhodes."

The clerk glanced up from the keyboard, her sudden recognition evident, then went back to typing. "I see we have you booked in one of our Club Level suites, staying with us for one night."

"Could you arrange for me to have a late checkout tomorrow?" he asked. "I have a morning meeting that might run long." Or maybe not. At this point, he gave it 80/20 odds he didn't even make it past the front door.

"Certainly, Mr. Rhodes."

Just then, Kyle's cell phone vibrated. He checked and saw he had a new text message from Rylann.

KNOCK 'EM DEAD, DIMPLES. WHATEVER THE HECK IT IS YOU'RE UP TO.

"Is there anything else I can do for you this evening?" the front desk clerk asked.

With a smile, Kyle tucked his phone back into his jacket. "Nope. I think I've got everything I need."

SHORTLY BEFORE TEN the following morning, Kyle climbed into a taxi outside the hotel.

"Seven ninety-five Folsom Street," he told the driver. When the taxi pulled to a stop a few minutes later, Kyle peered through the window and checked out the modern, six-story office building before him. After paying the driver, he stepped out of the car and adjusted his tie.

Time to face the music.

Portfolio in hand, he pushed through the double doors and took the elevator up to the sixth floor. He watched as the floor indicator counted upward at what seemed to be an excruciatingly slow pace, finally springing open to reveal a simple, minimalist-style reception area.

A receptionist sat behind a white and gray marble desk, her eyes going wide as saucers as soon as Kyle stepped out of the elevator. The wall behind her was devoid of any artwork, bearing only the company's all-too-familiar name in lowercase letters:

twitter

"You actually showed up," she said incredulously. "We've been betting for a week whether you would keep the appointment. A lot of people thought this was some kind of joke."

Kyle had spent hours on the phone with the company's lawyers just to get the appointment—no way would he have backed out after going through that torture. "I take it I don't need to introduce myself?" he asked.

"That would be a definite *no*. You're quite recognizable around this place." The receptionist picked up the phone and pushed a button. "Kyle Rhodes is here to see you." She listened for a moment, and then looked up at Kyle, still speaking into the phone. "You and me both." She hung up and gestured to a waiting area. "Mr. Donello will be with you shortly. You can have a seat if you like."

Kyle eyed the brown suede couch with two blue throw pillows cross-stitched with the words "Home Tweet Home."

"I think I'll stand," he told the receptionist. He half-expected Donello to make him wait all morning, and then blow him off anyway, but the receptionist's phone rang just a few minutes later. After speaking in a hushed voice, she hung up the phone and stood up. "Mr. Donello is ready for you. Follow me."

She led him past the reception desk, through a set of frosted glass doors, and then into the main office area. Virtually everything was painted white except for the light maple hardwood floors. The office contained several rows of cubicles, with each row divided into four workstations.

And every person, at every single one of those workstations, had stood up to watch as he walked by.

They stared silently with a mixture of expressions on their faces, most of which Kyle would not describe as particularly friendly. When they reached the large corner office at the end of the hallway, the receptionist half-smiled. "Good luck."

Kyle stepped into the office and saw Rick Donello, CEO of Twitter, sitting at his desk. He was a relatively young man, in his midthirties, with glasses, thinning hair, and a look in his unsmiling eyes that fell somewhere between disbelief and disdain.

"I'll say this: you've got balls the size of watermelons, Rhodes." He gestured for Kyle to have a seat, then nodded at the receptionist, who closed the door after she left.

Once it was just the two of them, Donello got right down to business. "You have sixty seconds to tell me why I should do anything other than toss you out on your ear."

Fine with him. Kyle was perfectly happy to skip over all the bullshit. "As half the world saw seven months ago, you have cracks in your network that I could drive a truck through. My company can help you with that."

Donello laughed humorlessly. "I'm not an idiot, Rhodes. We updated everything after you hijacked us. I doubt you'd find us so easy to hack into now."

"How much of the revenue from your seven hundred advertisers are you willing to bet on that?"

Donello's gaze was steely. "You've got forty seconds left, so finish whatever it is you've come to say. If nothing else, it'll give me something laughable to tweet about later."

Kyle sat forward in his chair. "I've read all the interviews, Donello. When you took over the company a year ago, you pledged to focus on Twitter as a business by turning what has become a massive communication network into a major advertising platform. You've emphasized the need for reliability—yet I managed to shut you down for forty-eight hours from a single computer while half-drunk on Scotch."

Donello rested his arms on his desk. "So your proposal is that I hire you, the guy who made us look like clueless dickheads seven months ago, and pay your company some outrageous consulting fee to come in here and fix our security problems? That's what you're suggesting?"

"Yes." Kyle held his gaze. "Except I'll do it for free."

Donello paused at that. "For free."

"I'll build a goddamn cyber-fortress around this place—and it won't cost you a penny. I figure I owe you that, at least."

Donello studied him and then leaned back in his chair. He spoke slowly, musing aloud. "You want the publicity that will come with this."

The corners of Kyle's mouth turned up in a smile. His sixty seconds were up, yet there he still sat. "Yes. And so do you."

TWO HOURS LATER, the CEO of Rhodes Network Consulting LLC walked out of that modern, six-story office building having landed the company's first client.

True, the client wasn't paying him, but Kyle was a happy man nevertheless. As he'd hoped, at the end of the day Donello had acted like the businessman he was and seized on the unique opportunity Kyle had offered: better security and a ton of free publicity that would highlight that fact. They'd even worked out the wording of a joint press release that would be sent to the media at eight A.M. Eastern time the following morning.

Now it was time for Kyle to implement the second phase of his marketing strategy. After his arrest and conviction, and then again after his release from prison, he'd been bombarded by interview requests from virtually every media outlet—yet he'd never answered so much as a single question.

But he'd held on to the contact information for one particular person who'd asked for an interview for just this occasion.

Standing on the sidewalk in front of Twitter's headquarters, Kyle dialed the cell phone number of David Isaac, correspondent from *Time* magazine. After getting the reporter's voicemail, he left a message.

"David, it's Kyle Rhodes. There's going to be a press release tomorrow morning—you'll know it when you hear it. If you can get me the cover, I'll give you an exclusive. The whole sordid story, directly from the mouth of the Twitter Terrorist. Trust me, you won't want to miss the part about the cactus in Tijuana."

Twenty-nine

FOR THE SECOND time since Rylann had starting working in Chicago, the U.S. Attorney's Office was abuzz over Kyle Rhodes.

She had, of course, heard the story that had set the Internet on fire earlier that Tuesday morning: that the Twitter Terrorist and Twitter had kissed and made up. She'd been in her kitchen, eating Rice Krispies and catching up on the news on her iPad, when she'd read about the press release. She'd laughed out loud, then had immediately texted Kyle:

SO THAT'S WHAT YOU'VE BEEN UP TO.

She hadn't expected a response given how busy she assumed he was, but to her surprise she'd received a message back within minutes.

NO CLUE WHAT YOU'RE TALKING ABOUT, COUNSELOR. I'LL CALL WHEN I GET BACK TONIGHT.

Sitting at her desk, Rylann looked up when she heard a knock at her office door and saw Cade standing in her doorway with a wry expression.

"I've received over two dozen phone calls from the press today, asking what I think about the fact that the Twitter Terrorist is starting his own network security company." He shook his head. "Just when I thought we'd finally seen the end of that guy."

He said the words offhandedly, just a casual remark, but Rylann nevertheless felt . . . sneaky. A little guilty, even. While she generally believed that a person's personal life wasn't anyone's business but her own, she also didn't like deceiving people. After working with Cade for nearly two months, she considered him a friend—they went on Starbucks runs together, they talked case strategy, and she'd even tried to set him up with Rae. But now here she was, about to lie to the guy.

You're not lying. You're just avoiding the truth.

Apparently, her subconscious had a lot easier time splitting hairs than she did.

Then maybe it's time to say adios to Kyle.

Apparently, her subconscious was also a waffling, capricious bitch.

Rylann threw on a smile for Cade's benefit, pushing aside the self-reflection and inner turmoil for a time when her lover's nemesis wasn't standing in the doorway.

"Wow, two dozen calls," she said. "I bet that was fun to wade through."

"A real hoot. Rhodes is like a boomerang around here—he keeps coming back again and again." He grinned. "I bet you're glad you don't have to deal with him anymore."

Right. She wondered if Cade would consider seven rounds of hot and steamy sex within the definition of "deal with."

"Actually, I didn't mind working with Kyle," she said. "He's not a bad guy, you know."

Cade rolled his eyes. "Don't tell me you've gone starry-eyed, too. What is it about this guy? The half-billion dollars? The hair? Do you know that I used to get death threats from crazed, angry women calling me the Antichrist and demanding Rhodes's immediate release from prison?" He held up his hand. "Swear to God."

"Now, that's definitely something the Antichrist wouldn't do."

Cade laughed. "Have your little crush, Pierce, but I think you're SOL on that front. According to Scene and Heard, the Twitter Terrorist has been getting busy with some brunette bombshell."

It took all of Rylann's de minimis acting abilities to keep a straight face with that one. "Right. I heard that, too."

From that point on, her day—which had started out great after hearing the fantastic news about Kyle and Twitter—went from awkward to worse. She appeared in court for a motion to suppress in a credit card fraud case, a motion she'd felt fairly confident about going in. Although the Secret Service had handled most of the investigation, the initial search of the defendant's premises had been conducted by two Chicago police officers who'd responded to a domestic abuse call made by the defendant's wife. After the cops arrived—and of course after getting consent from the wife—they did a sweep of the house, opened the bedroom closet, and found over a thousand credit cards in different names.

Or at least, that's what Rylann *thought* had been the situation.

On the witness stand, however, the cops completely caved, admitting that—oops—maybe the wife had "technically" revoked consent when they went into the bedroom, but since they were already in the house, they'd just finished the search anyway.

And so Rylann had sat there at the prosecution table, unable to do anything except watch as her case went up in flames when the judge, not surprisingly, granted the defendant's motion to suppress all one thousand credit cards found on the premises.

Not good.

After that, she'd spent the rest of the day listening to the pissed-off rantings of the two Secret Service agents who had taken over the investigation from the Chicago police, scrambling to see if there was any evidence left that would allow her to somehow save the case, and, ultimately, feeling the beginnings of a migraine coming on. By the time she left work at six thirty, her head was throbbing, she felt nauseous, and even the hazy, pre-sunset light outside made her eyes hurt.

When she got home, she immediately changed into sweatpants and a T-shirt, left off all the lights, took two Tylenol, and then lay down on the couch, praying for sleep.

An hour later, she was woken by the sound of her cell phone. She sat up and instantly groaned, feeling as though somebody were driving a jackhammer into her forehead. She reached over to the coffee table and saw it was Kyle calling.

"It's the man of the hour," she answered, trying to muster up an enthusiastic tone before falling back onto the couch with her hand over her eyes. "Oh God, that hurts," she whimpered.

"What hurts?" Kyle asked, sounding concerned.

"The invisible man pounding spikes into my head."

"That doesn't sound good. Maybe you should take out an invisible Taser gun and zap the son of a bitch."

Rylann laughed, then groaned again. "No making me laugh—it hurts too much. I have a migraine," she explained.

"Yes, I figured it was something like that. I'm on my way to Firelight to meet Dex. We're having a few cocktails to celebrate my new partnership with Twitter. Can I bring you anything?"

Awww. "That's sweet. But I'm okay. Just had a supremely crappy day at work, that's all. You go whoop it up with Dex. You earned it. The thing with Twitter was genius."

"You're impressed again," he said, sounding quite pleased with himself. "That's three times you've stroked my ego now, counselor."

"Imagine me saying something really sassy and quippy back to that," Rylann told him. "But right now, it hurts too much to think. I'm officially de-quipped."

TWENTY MINUTES LATER, there was a knock at her front door.

When Rylann opened it and saw Kyle standing there, she immediately pointed. "Go. You should be celebrating."

Ignoring her, he stepped inside. "Dex can wait a few minutes to whoop it up. He's at the bar every night. It's not like he's there just to meet me." He shut the door behind him and looked her over. "So you're de-quipped, huh? I didn't think that was even possible."

"Well, that's because you . . ." Rylann struggled to pull at least one semidecent retort out of the pounding fog that was her brain . . . but came up dry as a bone. She sank exhaustedly against the back of the couch. "I've got nothing. Get in your zingers, go wild with the sarcasm—I'm totally, completely defenseless."

With a smile curling at the edges of his lips, Kyle held up a Starbucks cup. "Drink this. My mother used to get migraines. I remember her saying something about caffeine helping."

"Sweet Jesus, you are a god," Rylann said, taking the cup gratefully. She'd had luck with caffeine before but hadn't had the energy to stop at a Starbucks on her way home from work.

"Very true." Kyle took her by the hand and led her to the couch. "Now sit and drink while I work my magic." He took a seat behind her and began massaging her neck.

"Do you want to tell me about your supremely crappy day?" he asked softly as his incredible fingers worked on the knots in her neck and shoulders.

"I lost a motion to suppress that tanked my whole case." She took another sip of her coffee. "Tell me what happened with Twitter. I can only imagine the looks on everyone's faces when you walked in."

Maybe it was the caffeine kicking in, or the massage, or simply Kyle's rich, lulling voice as he told her the story, but slowly, Rylann began to feel a smidge better. She still had her migraine, but now it felt as though the invisible man were merely pounding her head with a dull, blunt object instead of spikes.

When she'd drunk about half of the coffee, Kyle shifted on the couch, leaning back with his legs outstretched. "Lie down. Put your head in my lap." He saw her raised eyebrow. "Mind out of the gutter, counselor. This isn't a sexual thing."

Rylann set the Starbucks cup on the coffee table while he grabbed one of the throw pillows and put it over his lap. She started to lie down on her side, when he stopped her.

"No, on your back."

She turned around, snuggled comfortably between his legs, and rested the back of her head against the pillow.

"Close your eyes," he whispered.

She did, then felt his fingers brush lightly against her forehead. When he began massaging her throbbing temples, her body melted into a liquid puddle and she actually moaned out loud.

"Oh God . . . that feels so good," she breathed. "Please don't stop. Ever."

"I can do this all night, baby," he said with a soft chuckle. "I told you—I've got you."

LATER THAT NIGHT, Rylann woke up on the couch, curled comfortably against a warm, hard body, and realized that she must have fallen asleep while Kyle was massaging her head.

He'd shifted their positions while she slept, stretching out on the couch next to her, with her head on his chest. He'd also grabbed the chenille throw blanket off the back of the couch and tucked it all around her, just up to her shoulders.

A girl could fall big-time for a guy who'd do something like that.

She lifted her head to peek at him through the darkness, the moonlight casting shadows across the strong planes of his face. Her movement must have woken him, because he stirred, inhaled deeply, then blinked in amusement when he opened his eyes and saw that she was watching him.

"How's your headache?" he said in a deep, gravelly voice.

"Better." Fortunately, it had mostly dissipated into a faint ache while she'd slept. "You should've woken me up," she said softly. "You had such an awesome day—you should be partying right now with Dex."

"I can go out with Dex anytime." He reached up and ran a finger along the side of her face. His voice was a low murmur, barely more than a whisper. "I want to be here, Rylann. You know that, right?"

She knew he wasn't only talking about tonight. "I know." And she knew one other thing beyond any doubt. "I'm glad you're here. I'm getting very used to having you around, Dimples."

"Good. Because I'm taking you out tomorrow. On a real date."

Such a simple request, and yet not so simple at all. "Kyle, I don't—"

He cut her off. "Don't worry. I can make sure no one finds out." He held her gaze in the moonlight, seemingly unwilling to take no for an answer. "Say yes, Rylann."

Maybe it was the fact that the headache had weakened her defenses. Or maybe it was just him.

Either way, with a sleepy smile, she laid her head back down on his chest. "Yes."

Thirty

RYLANN SPENT MOST of the following day reviewing the ATF investigation reports in a new case she'd just picked up—eleven guys in a suburb selling illegal firearms out of a warehouse, yes, yes, very bad stuff—while secretly trying not to wonder where Kyle planned to take her that evening. He'd been very mysterious about his plans, which seemed to be his modus operandi, the only hint being when he'd asked if she could leave work at four thirty.

"Ooh . . . I bet he's whisking you off on a private jet, taking you somewhere exotic and romantic," Rae said over the phone early that afternoon.

Rylann was in her office, talking with the door shut while eating lunch. Naturally, she'd told Rae all about her big date.

For a brief moment, it struck Rylann how surreal it was that a private jet was even a possibility. Sure, she'd seen the penthouse and the two-thousand-dollar suits, but for the most part she didn't think about Kyle's money. Frankly, since they'd spent the majority of their time as a couple inside her apartment, the fact that he had millions of dollars, and would one day inherit a half-billion more, hadn't mattered all that much.

But now that she was thinking about it . . .

Wow, that was a shitload of money.

"I'm guessing no on the private jet," she told Rae. "Airplane travel requires security clearances and passenger lists. We're going incognito on this."

"Lists, schmists," Rae said dismissively. "Rich guys do

these things on the sly all the time. You think they fly coach on United with their mistresses?"

"Hey. Am I the mistress in this situation?"

"No, just the lucky bitch who has a hot billionaire heir whisking her off someplace secret tonight. Oh, wait—did I say that out loud again?" Rae chuckled. "So what are you wearing?"

That had been a particular challenge, seeing how a certain somebody had given her zero hints about where they were going. Rylann had decided to keep it simple. "A black wraparound dress and heels. If he takes me white-water rafting or cow wrangling, I'm screwed."

Rae laughed. "Oh, please let it be the cow wrangling! I can just see you, riding horseback in your heels and twirling a rope over your head, while on your cell phone threatening to subpoena somebody."

"If it's the cow wrangling, this will be my first—and last—date with Kyle Rhodes."

"Please. One flash of those dimples and I bet that man could talk you into just about anything."

And the scary thing was, Rylann was beginning to suspect that might actually be true.

PER THE "INSTRUCTIONS" Rylann had received via text message earlier, at four thirty she walked out the revolving door of the Federal Building, briefcase over her shoulder, and began heading north.

Her cell phone rang just as she hit the first intersection. "Okay, Dimples," she answered. "Now what?"

Kyle's voice was whiskey-rich in her ear. "Walk two blocks to Monroe and turn left. There's an alley behind Italian Village—you'll see me there."

"Whatever this is, you get bonus points for making it very cloak-and-daggerish," she said, dodging a pothole in her heels as she crossed the street.

"Never met an ex-con in a strange alley before, Ms. Pierce?" he teased.

Indeed, she had not. After hanging up, Rylann walked the two blocks and then crossed the street. She spotted the restaurant, Italian Village, and headed to the alley. When she turned the corner, she slowed her step at the sight before her eyes.

An elegant black limousine waited for her.

A driver stood at the rear right-side door and nodded as she approached. "Good afternoon, miss." He gallantly opened the door for her.

"Thank you." Rylann bent her head and saw Kyle sitting inside, wearing jeans and a white button-down shirt casually rolled up around his forearms.

He gestured to the windows. "Tinted, for privacy. And you don't need to worry about the driver; he's worked with my family for years. So your secret is safe." He held out his hand. "Shall we?"

With a smile, Rylann took his hand. She climbed in, slid across the seat, and set her briefcase on the floor by her feet. "Come on. *Now* can you tell me where we're going?" She buckled her seat belt as the limo began to move.

Kyle stretched his long legs out in front of him. "I don't know. I like keeping you guessing like this."

"I hope I'm at least dressed okay."

His eyes slowly traveled over her, taking in the V of her dress and her bare, crossed legs. "A helluva lot more than okay, counselor."

Her body went warm from the look in his eyes. "No cow wrangling, then."

The edges of his mouth twitched. "You? I'd pay a half-billion dollars to see that." He put his hand on her knee, caressing her skin lightly with his fingers. "So about tonight . . . I've been wondering if this is one of those ideas that sounds better in my head than it is in actual execution. I hope you won't be disappointed."

"If that's the case, I promise I'll fake excitement so well you'll never know the difference."

"I appreciate that. Okay, here's the deal: you probably don't realize this, but exactly nine years ago on this very day,

May 16, I spotted a certain dark-haired, sassy, first-year law student across a crowded bar. Seeing how it's our anniversary, of sorts, I thought we should go back to the proverbial scene of the crime."

It took Rylann a moment. "You're taking me to Champaign?"

"Yep. I rented out the second floor of the Clybourne." Kyle reached up and brushed a lock of hair behind her ear. "I promised you a date when I left your apartment that night, Rylann." His eyes held hers meaningfully. "I might be almost a decade late in delivering on that, but here we are. Finally."

Tiny sentimental tears sprung to Rylann's eyes.

And here he'd been worried that she'd be disappointed.

She smiled softly, then leaned forward to brush her lips over his. "It's perfect."

A LITTLE OVER two and a half hours later, the limo pulled to a stop in the alley behind the Clybourne. Kyle took out his cell phone and dialed. "We're here," he said when the voice on the other end answered.

He hung up and saw Rylann watching him with amusement.

"More with the cloak-and-dagger routine?"

"You wanted to stay off the radar." Kyle pointed to the bar. "So here's how this will work. Dex used to be the manager here, and knows the guy who's now in charge. That guy is going to take us up the back employee staircase, and then we'll have the whole second floor to ourselves."

"It's the last week of school—the upstairs bar would normally be packed. Do I even want to know what you had to do to arrange this?" she asked.

"Let's just say that the manager and I came to an understanding." Actually, he'd told the manager that he'd give him half the bar's expected food and beverage sales for the night plus 20 percent, *plus* an extra five thousand bucks for setting up the place per his exact instructions. But she didn't need to know that.

He saw the back door to the bar open, and a guy in his early twenties waved at the limo. Kyle looked at Rylann. "Ready to go back in time?"

She laced her fingers through his. "In case I forget to tell you later, this was the best first date I ever had."

"Did anyone ever tell you that you can be really sweet when you want to be?"

"I try not to let too many people know about that. It cuts against the bad-ass prosecutor reputation."

He tugged her hand and pulled her closer. "I've already seen the Bozo the Clown hair, counselor. We have no more secrets." With a quick kiss, he pushed open the door of the limo and stepped out. After checking to confirm that the alley was empty, he helped Rylann out and led her to the bar's back door.

The manager grinned as he shuffled them through, then extended his hand to Kyle once they were inside. "Joe Kohler. I've been stoked about this all week. Frankly, I thought the whole Twitter thing was hysterical." He shook Rylann's hand next. "And the mystery lady." He pointed to Kyle. "Whoever you are, you better treat this guy better than the last girl did." He gestured toward the stairs behind them. "Follow me."

Kyle shrugged when he saw Rylann's bemused expression. "One of the high-fivers." With his hand in hers, they followed Joe up the narrow staircase to the second floor.

"I brought in one of the waitresses to help me set up the place according to your instructions," Joe told him. "Figured we could use a woman's touch with this sort of thing."

Rylann raised an eyebrow at Kyle as they got to the top of the stairs. "Instructions?"

Joe led them around a short corridor, into the main bar area. "Hope you like it."

Kyle rounded the corner with Rylann, pleased when he saw they'd gotten it just right. White pillar candles—over a hundred of them—covered the tabletops and bar, casting the entire space in a warm, romantic glow. In the far back corner of the bar was a table covered with a white linen tablecloth, two crystal glasses, and an ice bucket that chilled a bottle of

Perrier-Jouët Fleur de Champagne Rosé—a recommendation from his sister, the wine expert.

With a stunned expression, Rylann took it all in. "This is . . . incredible." She walked over to the table with the champagne, then looked over her shoulder at Kyle. "This is the table I was sitting at that night."

Nodding, Kyle headed over. "I'd watched you for a while before making my move. There was a guy with red hair sitting across the table from you, and I was trying to decide if he was your boyfriend."

Rylann smiled. "That was Shane. God, I haven't spoken to him in years." Her eyes swept over the place, the flickering candles having transformed the normally semi-seedy college bar into a romantic setting. She stepped closer and curled her fingers into his shirt. "Thank you," she whispered.

Kyle brushed the hair out of her eyes. "Anytime, counselor."

"I CHOSE POORLY," Rylann said, eying Kyle's plate from across the table. "I should've gone with the curly fries instead of the regular."

"Yep, you should've." Kyle picked up one curly fry and generously set it on her plate.

She looked offended. "One fry? That's all I get?"

"You've got to live with the consequences of your decisions. How else are you going to learn?" He smiled and popped another curly fry into his mouth.

The Perrier-Jouët had begun to take effect, bringing a pretty flush to Rylann's cheeks. While normally not a huge champagne drinker, even Kyle had to admit this one wasn't half-bad. True, one probably didn't often pair a three-hundred-dollar bottle of bubbly with cheeseburgers and French fries, but that was about as fine as the dining got at the Clybourne.

Kyle's cell phone buzzed with a new message, and he checked to make sure it wasn't Sean, the executive from Silicon Valley he'd hired to be his second in command at Rhodes Network Consulting. "Sorry. My business line has been flooded with calls ever since the Twitter announcement," he said to Rylann. "Sean's going through all the messages now. I told him to call me if there's anything that can't wait until tomorrow."

She leaned in interestedly, reaching for her champagne glass. "So what's the next step for you?"

"I set up meetings and begin pitching to potential clients. The two graduates I hired from U of I start work on Monday, and then we'll be ready to rock and roll. After that, I cross my fingers and hope there are some people eager to get in bed with the Twitter Terrorist." He flashed her a cheeky grin. "Metaphorically speaking."

Rylann cocked her head inquisitively. "I've been curious about something. What was it that made you change your mind about the corporate world? Back when we first met, I remember you saying that you wanted to teach."

It was a perfectly innocuous question. And Kyle knew he could answer it vaguely, the same way he'd answered that question many times before. But as he sat across from Rylann, one day away from the nine-year anniversary of his mother's death, he thought maybe it was time to open up about that part of his life. He kept telling himself that he wanted all of Rylann— perhaps, then, he needed to let down a few of his own walls.

So he cleared his throat, trying to decide where to start. "My perspective on things changed after my mother died. It was a rough time for my family," he began.

KYLE. THERE'S BEEN an accident.

For as long as he lived, he'd never forget those words.

He had known instantly from his father's voice that it was serious. His grip had tightened around the phone. "What happened?"

"It's your mother. A truck hit her car when she was coming home from a drama club rehearsal. They think the driver might have fallen asleep at the wheel—I don't know, they haven't told me much. They brought her into the emergency room thirty minutes ago, and she's in surgery now."

Kyle's stomach dropped. *Surgery.* "But . . . Mom's going to be okay, right?"

The silence that followed lasted an eternity.

"I've sent the jet to pick you up at Willard," his father said, referring to the university's airport. "A helicopter will meet you at O'Hare and take you directly to the hospital. They said we could use the heliport."

Kyle's voice was a whisper. "Dad."

"It's bad, son. I feel like I should be doing something, but they . . . they say there's nothing . . ."

Shock began to set in at that very moment, when Kyle realized his father was crying.

The drive to the airport, the forty-minute flight to Chicago, and the helicopter ride to the hospital's rooftop had all been a blur. Some hospital staff member—Kyle couldn't have picked his face out of a lineup two minutes later—rushed him to a private waiting room in the trauma surgical unit. He'd burst through the door and found his father standing there with an ashen expression.

He shook his head. "I'm so sorry, son."

Kyle took a step back. "No."

A tiny, drained voice spoke out from behind the door. "I didn't make it in time, either."

Kyle turned and saw Jordan standing in the corner of the room. She had tears running down her cheeks.

"Jordo." He grabbed her and pulled her into a tight embrace. "I just spoke to Mom yesterday," he whispered against the top of his sister's head. "I called her after my exam." She'd been so damn proud of him.

His heart squeezed painfully tight as his eyes began to burn.

"Tell me this isn't happening," Jordan said against his chest.

There was a knock on the door, and a doctor dressed in blue surgical scrubs entered the room.

"I'm sorry to interrupt," he said in a somber tone. "I wanted to ask if you would like to see her."

Jordan wiped her eyes, then turned around to face the doctor. Both she and Kyle looked expectantly at their father.

He said nothing.

"Some people find it comforting to say good-bye," the doctor offered kindly.

Kyle watched as his father—a self-made mogul praised for his business acumen and decisiveness, whose face had been on the covers of *Time* and *Newsweek* and *Forbes*, a man whom Kyle had never once seen hesitate in any decision—faltered.

"I . . . don't . . ." his father's voice trailed off. He ran his hand over his face and took a deep breath.

Kyle put his hand on his father's shoulder, then turned to the doctor with their answer.

"We'd like that. Thank you."

Kyle quickly realized, right from those very first moments in the hospital, that his dad was having a hard time handling the many decisions that needed to be made with respect to his mother's wake and funeral. To help alleviate that burden, he moved into his father's house and took over most of the arrangements. It was a grim, emotionally draining time, and certainly not something he'd ever envisioned himself going through at the age of twenty-four—selecting readings and prayers for his mother's funeral, and the outfit she would wear in the casket—but together, he and Jordan managed to do what needed to be done.

After the funeral, his original plan had been to stay at his dad's place for another week or so, helping him sort through all the phone calls, sympathy cards, flowers, and e-mails that flowed in every day. Given the empire Grey Rhodes had built, there was an incredible outpouring of people who wanted to offer their condolences, and Kyle and Jordan did the best they could to keep up with all of it.

But when that first week passed, things still seemed no better. His father showed little interest in receiving visitors or speaking to friends and family on the phone, preferring instead to spend the days alone in his study or go for long walks around the estate grounds.

"Maybe he needs to talk to someone. A professional," Kyle said to Jordan one night when they were sitting at their parents' dining room table, picking halfheartedly at a lasagna someone had dropped off the day before. They could feed a small nation for a month with the number of casseroles, lasagnas, and baked macaroni and cheeses they had stacked in the refrigerator and freezer. No matter that their father could practically *buy* a small nation.

"I already tried suggesting that to him," Jordan said. "He says he knows what's wrong: that Mom's dead." Her eyes filled with tears, but she quickly shook them off.

Kyle squeezed her hand. "It's just the grief talking, Jordo." He had half a mind to march into his father's study right then and tell him to pull his shit together for Jordan's sake, but he doubted that would help. And he certainly understood his father's pain; they were all struggling to make sense of their mother's death.

He decided to stay in Chicago for another week. And then two weeks became three. There weren't really any good days, just bad days and slightly better days. Eventually things progressed to a point where his father was willing to see friends and family, which Kyle assumed was a good sign. But his dad continued to show absolutely no interest in his company—and the business-related calls, voicemail messages, and e-mails began to pile up, all unanswered.

Thus, it came as no surprise when, three weeks after his mother's funeral, Chuck Adelman, the general counsel of Rhodes Corporation, called Kyle and asked to meet with him. In addition to working for the company, Chuck was his father's personal attorney and had been one of his best friends since college. Kyle agreed to meet him for lunch at a restaurant only a few blocks from the company's downtown headquarters.

"Your father isn't returning any of my calls," Chuck led in after they ordered.

"From what I can tell, he's not returning anyone's calls," Kyle said matter-of-factly.

Chuck spoke in a quiet tone, his eyes kind. "Look, I understand. I was there when your parents first met—it was Hash Wednesday, and we were on the quad. Your father spotted your mother sitting under a tree, on a blanket with her friends, and said, 'That is one totally groovy chick.' He walked over and introduced himself, and that was it for both of them."

"Oh my God. My parents told Jordan and me that they met in a bookstore, fighting over the last Classical Civilizations textbook. They were *stoned* at the time?" Having gone to the University of Illinois for six years, Kyle knew exactly what people did on the quad on Hash Wednesday.

Chuck paused. "Of course, a bookstore. It's all coming back to me now." He pointed. "The calculus textbook. Now that's a cute story."

"Classical Civ."

"Probably best if we never mention this part of the conversation to your father."

"Agreed," Kyle said. "Now, aside from scarring me for life and ruining every sanitized, wholesome image I had of my parents' first meeting, why else did you want to meet today?"

Chuck rested his arms on the table, getting serious. "He can't do this, Kyle. He's the CEO of a billion-dollar company."

"And as CEO, I would think he's entitled to some personal time," Kyle growled protectively. "My mother just died three weeks ago."

"I'm not trying to drag him into the office. But if he could at least make himself accessible. Pick up his cell phone once in a while. Let people know that he's still in command," Chuck said. "The other board members are starting to wonder what's going on."

"Surely they understand these are unusual circumstances."

"They do. But that doesn't change the fact that this is a privately owned business. Your father *is* Rhodes Corporation." He shifted in his chair, as if debating how to continue. "As general counsel for the company, I'm obliged to mention that in the event your father was ever to become incapacitated, he named you as his legal representative. Which means that you would be in charge of running his affairs, both personal and business—including the controlling management of the company."

Kyle felt the burning in his eyes. He'd known, obviously,

that his father had always wanted him to work for Rhodes Corporation but had had no idea that he had this much faith in him. It was an honor, and also an incredible responsibility, but most of all he could not believe that things had gotten to the point where he and Chuck needed to have this conversation. True, his father wasn't himself these days. But no matter how messed up the situation was, there was one thing they needed to get straight, right then and there.

"*No one* is declaring my father incapacitated," Kyle said, looking the general counsel right in his eyes. "That man built an empire—he's a genius and an extremely powerful businessman. I dare anybody to say otherwise."

Chuck's expression was sympathetic. "I'm not the enemy here, Kyle. I'm trying to help. You're right, he did build an empire. And now somebody needs to start running it. Otherwise, people will begin to say all sorts of things, whether you and I like it or not."

Kyle got the message, loud and clear. And during the thirty-minute drive along Lake Michigan back to his father's north shore estate, he debated what approach to take. Ultimately, he decided the direct one was best.

When he got back, he walked straight into the study and found his dad sitting at his desk, scrolling listlessly through photographs of an older-model car on his computer. Since his mother's death, his father had expressed some interest in restoring a classic car, something he used to do as a hobby before his company had exploded with the Rhodes Anti-Virus.

"Find anything?" Kyle asked as he took a seat in front of the desk.

"A guy up in McHenry is selling a '68 Shelby," Grey said in a subdued tone.

Every time his father spoke, it struck Kyle how *unlike* his father he seemed. Dispirited. Listless. Somber. A stark contrast to the dynamic, almost larger-than-life man Kyle had known for twenty-four years.

"McHenry is only about an hour away. Maybe we can drive out there tomorrow and take a look at it," Kyle said.

"Maybe."

Kyle had been suggesting excursions like this for the last three weeks, none of which had come to fruition. Although his dad talked about rebuilding a car, he didn't seem to have much interest in taking any steps to actually pursue that. Then again, he didn't have much interest in anything.

Grey turned to Kyle with a tired smile. "Maybe you could drive out there and look at the car for me. You need to get out of this house as much as I do."

"Actually, I did go out today. I met Chuck Adelman for lunch."

Grey's face went flat. "Really. And what did Chuck have to say?"

Kyle decided it probably wasn't the best time to bring up the Hash Wednesday revelation. Frankly, the image of his father wearing bell-bottoms, smoking a joint, and calling his mother a "totally groovy chick" was wrong on so many levels he wanted to erase the whole thing from his memory. "You need to start returning calls and e-mails," he said bluntly. His father was a grown man—perhaps a little tough love was in order.

"Chuck is overstepping his bounds. He shouldn't have gotten you involved in this."

"I think it would be good for you to get back to work, Dad. It'll be something to take your mind off things."

"I don't want anything to take my mind off things."

Kyle sat quietly for a moment. "It's not dishonoring Mom if we move forward with our lives. That's what she would want us to do."

Grey turned back to his computer. "I gave up so much for that company. Not anymore."

The comment took Kyle by surprise. Because his father had grown up with little money, he'd always been particularly proud of his success. Talk to the man for five minutes, and he would find some subtle way of bragging about the fact that the Rhodes Anti-Virus protected one in every three computers in America. "What are you talking about? You love that company."

Grey shook his head. "Not as much as I loved her. She was . . . everything. I just hope she knew that."

His father began crying. Kyle started to rise from his chair, but his father immediately held out a hand.

"Don't. I'm fine," Grey said. He wiped his eyes, quickly composing himself.

"Dad—"

"I put off so many things," Grey said, cutting him off. "That safari trip, for example. How many times did your mother talk about that? She did all the research and planned this two-week vacation to South Africa and Botswana for us. What did I say? That things were *too busy* for me and that we would go next year." He struggled to control his emotions. "Guess I broke that promise, didn't I?"

After a moment, he cleared his throat. "She also wanted to take a couples cooking class at six o'clock on Tuesdays and Thursdays, but that was tough for me to do with the traffic coming back from the city. So I told her we'd do it next year instead. I could go on and on about all the missed moments." He looked over at Kyle, his face filled with regret. "I know what you're trying to do, and I appreciate it, son." His eyes were a distant, cool blue. "But the whole damn company can rot for all I care. None of it means anything without her."

Kyle knew from his father's quiet but firm tone that the conversation was over.

He left the study and called Chuck, and outlined his plan to the general counsel. Once his father was thinking clearly again, he could do whatever he wanted with Rhodes Corporation. He'd built the place, so if he ultimately wanted to sell it and spend the rest of his life rebuilding 1968 Shelbys in his five-car garage, that was his prerogative. But that decision was not going to be made by the man currently sitting behind his father's desk—because *that* man was not Grey Rhodes.

Consequently, the following afternoon he met with the company's eight executive vice presidents. He deliberately chose to meet with them in his father's office and, just as deliberately, sat behind his father's desk while he explained what the plan would be for the foreseeable future.

"The eight of you will carry on with the day-to-day responsibilities of your divisions," he told them. "Any decisions that need to be made by the CEO should be presented to me, with your recommended plan of action. I'll make sure my father responds."

Kyle doubted that any of the executive VPs in that room actually believed that *Grey* Rhodes would be making such decisions, but they had all worked with his father for years, respected him, and were fiercely loyal. Without any dissent, they offered their support to Kyle and said they would help in any way they could.

In many ways, being the de facto CEO of Rhodes Corporation was not as difficult as Kyle had imagined. Granted, he had Chuck's advice and counsel, as well as that of the executive VPs, but he was surprised by how much he enjoyed taking on a leadership role—even a covert one.

"You could really do this, you know," Chuck said to him one evening at the weekly "state of the company" meeting Kyle had set up for the two of them. For convenience, and to avoid the questions that might arise if they met too often in Grey's office, they were back at the restaurant where Chuck had first approached him about taking over for his father. "You have great business instincts."

Kyle flipped through a report he'd received earlier that day from the vice president of content security, detailing the initial sales results of a new subscription-based endpoint and e-mail protection service they'd recently launched. "I'm just the computer geek. Jordan's the one who got the Rhodes business gene."

Chuck looked pointedly at the open report Kyle held. "You sure about that? You've had your nose stuck in that sales report so long, your steak's getting cold."

"Maybe I'm just watching my girlish figure."

Chuck chuckled. "Or maybe that business gene got passed on to both Rhodes twins."

Things continued on this way for several weeks. The party line at Rhodes Corporation was that the CEO had decided to work from home and spend more time with his family following his wife's passing. Kyle kept in contact with the executive team behind the scenes, often responding to e-mails or reviewing proposals and reports in the late evening while working out of one of the guest suites in his parents' house. On several occasions, he attempted to broach the subject with his father, but got no further than he had on the day his dad told him to let the company rot.

When August rolled around—the month Kyle normally would've been returning to grad school—and *still* nothing had changed with his dad, he decided enough was enough. Neither rational arguments nor tough love could convince his father to get professional help, so that meant there was only one option left.

The guilt trip.

Kyle huddled with Jordan one night in the kitchen as they devised their plan. "It should be you," he whispered, keeping one eye out in case his dad walked in. Since the man never left the house, he was always around somewhere. "And you need to lay it on thick, Jordo. Quivering lip, big crocodile tears, whatever it takes. Dad never could say no when you cry."

Jordan looked indignant. "When have I ever tried to manipulate Dad with tears?"

"Oh, I distinctly remember a time when somebody cried for days after being told she couldn't have a Barbie Dream House because it was too big for her bedroom."

"We were *seven* at the time," Jordan said. "The circumstances are a bit different now."

"Did you get the Barbie Dream House?" Kyle asked pointedly.

With a mischievous smile, Jordan shrugged. "Santa came through for me." She glanced in the direction of their father's study, turning more serious. "Okay, I'll do it. I just hate that it's come to this."

"He needs help, Jordo. You and I simply aren't enough to fix this." Perhaps that was one of the reasons he and Jordan had let things drag out this long—neither of them had wanted to admit that.

An hour later, Jordan emerged from their father's study

with a reddened nose and a relieved smile. She gave Kyle the thumbs-up sign.

Later that week, their father had his first appointment with a psychiatrist, who prescribed an antidepressant, set up weekly counseling sessions, and also referred him to a local grief support group. The changes didn't happen overnight, but slowly Kyle began to see more and more glimpses of the old Grey Rhodes. First there was the quip about the number of lasagnas still stored in the freezer, then there was the day Kyle came back to the house after a meeting with Chuck and found his father on the phone with the director of a battered women's shelter, making arrangements to donate their mother's clothes.

One evening shortly thereafter, Kyle sat at the kitchen counter, eating Thai takeout and reviewing the August financials the CFO had sent over. Sales of the new endpoint and e-mail protection service had continued to climb steadily since its launch, and customer feedback had been overwhelmingly positive.

"Are those the most recent financials?"

Kyle turned around, so surprised by the voice he nearly choked on his shrimp pad thai. His father stood by the sub-zero refrigerator—how long he'd been there was anyone's guess.

Kyle swallowed the pad thai. "Yes." He took a sip of the evening cocktail he'd poured himself—vodka on the rocks—and tried to look nonchalant as his father took a seat on the bar stool next to him.

Grey turned to him with a keen gleam Kyle recognized well. He pointed to the financials. "Maybe you should show me what the hell you've been doing with my company all summer."

Kyle grinned. *Thank fucking God.* Without further ado, he handed over the financials to his dad. "About time. Reading this stuff is as much fun as watching paint dry."

Grey chuckled. Shaking his head, he looked at Kyle for a long moment . . . then reached out and pulled Kyle in for a hug so tight he nearly fell off his bar stool. "Thank you, son," he said in a choked voice.

"You're welcome." And Kyle would have been lying if he didn't admit that he was pretty damn misty-eyed, too.

Not surprisingly, the next thing Grey wanted to talk about was school. "I know your classes started a couple weeks ago. It's probably time you thought about heading back to Champaign."

"I already called Professor Sharma and told him that I won't be returning this semester."

"No way. You've put your life on hold for too long already."

Kyle had known that this moment would eventually come—at least he'd always hoped it would—and he'd thought a lot about his options. He could return to Champaign and spend the next few years in a cornfield, getting his PhD. Or, if he didn't want to be so far away from his family, he could transfer to the University of Chicago, albeit a school with a less prestigious computer sciences program, and continue his studies there.

And then there was option C.

"You're right—I have been putting my life on hold for too long," he said. "Maybe it's time I put these mad skills of mine to work. Luckily, I happen to know a guy who owns a company that might have something right up my alley."

Grey's eyes lit up with unmistakable pride—and then he stifled it. "I appreciate the offer. But we both know that's not what you really want."

The truth of the matter was, Kyle's views on what he wanted had changed a lot over the last three and a half months. He, Jordan, and his dad were a team now. He had no doubt there would be more rough times ahead—he was already dreading this upcoming holiday season—but whatever happened, they would stick together. Working at Rhodes Corporation would give him the peace of mind of knowing that he was by his dad's side, every day, even if his father didn't need him. Not to mention, he knew it would make his father happy—and the guy deserved a little happiness right then.

But his motives weren't entirely altruistic. Shockingly, over the past couple months he'd realized that he actually enjoyed working for Rhodes Corporation. Admittedly, the power had been illusory while he'd temporarily assumed his father's role, but he found the thrill that came with being at the top and leading others to be rather . . . appealing.

"It's too late. Two days ago, I applied for the open network security manager position. Between you and me, I think I'm a shoo-in." Kyle stretched out confidently in the bar stool. "Assuming you can meet my salary demands."

Grey raised an eyebrow. "Salary demands?"

"Hey, these mad skills don't come for free."

Grey shook his head, although his lips curved up in a smile. "Why do I get the feeling that this is going to be the first of many demands from one frustratingly stubborn Kyle Rhodes of the Network Security Department?" He pointed, trying to look stern. "You earn your way up the ladder like everyone else."

Kyle gripped his father's shoulder. They would undoubtedly butt heads many times over the course of their careers at Rhodes Corporation, but on this point they were in total agreement. "I'd expect nothing less."

RYLANN DIDN'T SAY a word as Kyle told his story; she simply sat there at the table and listened. She sensed that he kept some of the most personal details to himself—it was obvious that he was very protective of his father's privacy—but he told her enough to give her a clear picture of the lengths he'd gone to for his family nine years ago.

And that picture completely blew her away.

Twitter Terrorist, billionaire heir, ex-con, computer geek, bad boy—none of those terms came close to describing Kyle Rhodes. He was, simply, a *good* person, and a confident, intelligent man to boot, and she found that combination absolutely irresistible.

She'd told him—and herself—from the beginning that she wasn't looking for a relationship. Nevertheless, these past couple weeks they'd spent together had led her to one inescapable conclusion.

That Kyle deserved the best damn girlfriend out there.

He deserved a woman who wouldn't try to hide the fact that they were together. A woman who wouldn't hesitate to go to her boss and tell her that she was dating the Twitter Terrorist. A woman who would never have any regrets, even if that decision impacted the career she truly loved.

And the sixty-four-thousand-dollar question was whether *she* was that woman.

"You look so serious, counselor. Too heavy a story for a first date?"

Seeing the genuine look of concern in Kyle's eyes despite the teasing tone, Rylann quickly shook away her thoughts. She reached across the table and slid her hand into his. "Only if you don't want me to come away from this date thinking you're a really incredible guy."

He brought her hand to his mouth and kissed her fingers. "Nope. I'm okay with that."

LATER THAT EVENING, Rylann nestled against Kyle in the back of the limo as they drove back to Chicago.

The driver had discreetly left the privacy partition up, and soft jazz music played through the speakers. When Norah Jones began singing "Come Away With Me" and Kyle slid his hand to her lower back, Rylann tilted her head and felt a sharp tug at her heart when his mouth met hers.

He kissed her softly, his lips brushing lightly over hers, and for once there were no words between them. After a long while, he pulled back and she opened her eyes, and the look they shared felt more intimate than any other moment in all the nights they'd spent together.

Later, when they entered Rylann's apartment, she took his hand and led him to her bedroom. Slowly, he undid the tie of her dress at her waist, then pushed it off her shoulders and to the floor. He picked her up in his arms and carried her to the bed.

His hands and mouth moved tenderly over her body until she ached for him. When he finally settled between her legs and entered her, filling her completely, he tangled his hands in her hair and whispered huskily in her ear.

"You're mine, Rylann."

Thirty-one

THE FOLLOWING MORNING, Rylann dressed for work as Kyle fielded a steady stream of phone calls in her living room. He finally took a break and walked into the bathroom just as she finished straightening her hair.

"From the sound of things, I'd say there are *lots* of people eager to get in bed with the Twitter Terrorist," she teased.

"It's like an orgy at this point." He slid his arms around her waist and nuzzled her neck, the scruff along his jaw scraping gently against her skin. While he'd already commandeered an extra toothbrush he'd found in her bathroom, they hadn't yet had The Talk about him keeping a razor or any of his other things at her apartment.

When he pulled back and met her gaze in the mirror, she knew from his mischievous expression that something was up. "What's going on? I recognize that look."

He grinned broadly. "I got the cover of *Time*."

Rylann did a double take. "Wait—*Time* magazine? You. On the cover."

"Yep. The reporter I've been talking to just called to say his editor signed off on it. They plan to run my picture with the caption 'The New Face of Network Security.' Let's just hope they don't use my mug shot," he joked.

"The cover of *Time*," Rylann repeated. Then she turned around and planted one right on his mouth. "That is *awesome*."

"Perfect timing, too, with the launch of my company." He shrugged. "I had to agree to talk about the Twitter thing—Tijuana, my conviction, prison life, the whole nine yards—but I figure it's worth it."

Instantly, Rylann got a sinking feeling in her stomach. She was beyond thrilled for Kyle and knew what a great opportunity this was for him. But the interview would thrust the details of his arrest and conviction once again into the spotlight, and she'd been hoping, perhaps naïvely, that everyone could just . . . move on from that.

Kyle had been very blunt about his feelings over the way his case had been handled by her office, including the fact that they'd called him a "terrorist" and sought the maximum prison sentence. It was inevitable that the reporter would inquire about those subjects. And if Kyle answered the questions candidly, she feared the U.S. Attorney's Office would not be cast in the most positive light.

She could already picture the scene a week from now. Her, walking into work the morning the *Time* story hit the newsstands, the other AUSAs gossiping about it in the hallways. Cade dropping by to talk, annoyed about being cast as the villain, and Cameron very possibly frustrated that the integrity of the office she'd been working hard to rebuild since her predecessor's departure was once again called into question.

And behind the scenes, Rylann would be in the middle of it all.

Yes, she could always ask Kyle to not cast any aspersions on her office during the interview. But doing that felt wrong. Whether she agreed with him or not, he should have the right to express his opinions on the subject—especially since she knew that Cade had, in fact, been told to go after him particularly hard because of his last name and financial status.

And so the situation between her and Kyle grew that much more complicated.

"Are you okay?" Kyle touched her chin. "You're making the serious face again."

Rylann forced herself to plaster on what she hoped looked like a genuine smile and went for a joke. This was Kyle's moment, and she wouldn't ruin it for him. "Sorry. I just got a little starstruck there. It's not every day I get to rub elbows with someone whose face is on the cover of a magazine."

He held her gaze. "It could be an everyday thing, you know."

Rylann's heart began to race. Suddenly, it seemed they were about to have The Talk after all. And judging from her body's reaction, she was either excited to take their relationship to the next level . . . or about to have a panic attack.

Then Kyle's cell phone rang again, interrupting the moment.

He swore under his breath. "I should take that. Sorry things are so crazy right now."

"It's okay. You do your work thing." She exhaled unsteadily when he left.

She finished getting ready for work and was in her kitchen, pouring cereal into a bowl, when Kyle hung up the phone and walked over from the living room.

"I should get going," he said. "I need to run home, take a quick shower, and head into the office. According to Sean, we've already received thirty calls on the business line this morning." He pulled her closer. "I'm going to dinner tonight with my family. It's a tradition Jordan and I started eight years ago, as a way of making sure my dad wasn't alone on the anniversary of my mother's car accident. Can I call you afterward?"

Rylann nodded, thinking that it probably wasn't such a bad idea for them to spend the evening apart. Clearly, she had a lot of thinking to do. "Sure." She touched his face. "Is it hard, today being the nine-year anniversary of the accident?"

"It's gotten easier over the years." He kissed her good-bye, long and deep, then groaned and pulled back. "I'll never get out of here if I keep that up."

"I was just about to kick you out, anyway. I'm in front of the grand jury later this morning."

"Ooh, sexy. Now I get to picture you doing your lawyer thing all afternoon. What kind of case?"

"A secret one."

"Right. What happens in the grand jury room stays in the

grand jury room. I remember the speech well." With a wink, he turned and left her apartment.

Rylann stood there for a moment after he left, her smile slowly fading as the weight of her dilemma sank in. Forcing herself to push the issue temporarily aside, she grabbed her spoon and cereal bowl. She took a seat at the counter and had just fired up her iPad to catch up on the morning's headlines when there was a knock at her door.

Perhaps Kyle had forgotten something, she mused. With that in mind, she slid off the bar stool and left the kitchen. She cut through her living room and opened the door, expecting to see a pair of piercing blue eyes and dimples.

Instead, she froze.

Standing there on her doorstep, inexplicably, was *Jon*.

He held out his arms. "Surprise."

Thirty-two

RYLANN BLINKED IN shock. "Jon. What are you doing here?" She ignored the outstretched arms, not exactly in a place to hug it out right then.

After a moment, he dropped his hands back to his sides. "Okay, so much for hoping for a warm reception. I'm here because I'd like to talk."

"Do they . . . not have telephones anymore in Italy?"

He pointed, grinning. "Ah, there's that sarcasm I missed. I tried the telephone, remember? You hung up on me."

Technically, she'd said good-bye first, but this was hardly the time to get caught up in semantics. "Because I didn't think there was anything else we needed to say." But now, judging from the fact that he was suddenly *there*, on her doorstep, she'd been quite wrong in assuming that.

He shifted awkwardly. "Look, I just spent ten hours on a flight from Rome. After everything we've been through, are you really going to leave me standing out here in the hallway like some stranger?"

Rylann actually considered that for a moment. Then she stepped back from the doorway and let him in.

Jon smiled. "Thanks."

She watched as he entered her living room and checked out the apartment. He looked mostly the same as he had the last time she'd seen him, although he'd cut his hair a little shorter and had a healthy tan. The Italian lifestyle seemed to suit him well.

"Cute place," he said. He looked over at the counter, his eyes holding on the lone cereal bowl and iPad. Breakfast for one.

Before she got rolling on her cross-examination, there was one preliminary matter Rylann needed to get to the bottom of. "How did you find me?"

"Kellie and Keith. You gave them your forwarding address when you moved out here."

When he turned around and faced her, seemingly finished with his assessment of the apartment, she decided to cut to the chase. "Do you want to tell me why you're here?"

He looked her in the eyes. "I think I made a mistake. About us. Italy has not turned out to be what I thought it would." He stepped forward, his voice turning softer. "I really miss you, Ry."

Hearing the words, Rylann felt a mixture of emotions right then—regret, sympathy, and even some sadness.

But not love.

"We can't do this, Jon. It's over. We agreed on that when you left to get on the plane to Rome. I've moved on now."

His hazel eyes flickered with emotion. "Are you seeing someone?"

She paused, then nodded. "Yes."

"Is it serious?"

Such a complicated question. "It could be."

Jon flinched, then looked at the ceiling. "Wow. I hadn't been expecting that." He took a minute, and when he returned his gaze to her, his eyes were misty.

Seeing that, Rylann wasn't sure what to say. Whatever was going on with her ex right now, he was obviously confused and not in a good place. "Jon, I'm sorry."

He ran his hand through his hair. "I'm just tired. Long flight. Maybe I could get a glass of water?"

"Of course." She went into the kitchen and grabbed a bottled water out of the refrigerator. When she shut the door, she saw that Jon had followed her and was standing by the counter. "Oh. Here you go." She handed him the water.

"Thank you." He cracked it open and took a sip, then set

the bottle on the counter. "Just tell me one thing. When we were together, were you happy?"

Yes, she was. They'd obviously had their issues, like every couple, but they'd dated for three years, they'd lived together, and she'd even wanted to marry him. But then she'd gotten over him with the six-month plan—something that had probably been easier to do than it should've been.

And that said a lot.

"Yes, I was happy, but—"

He put his finger over her lips, cutting her off before she could finish. "Then it doesn't have to be over. I know I hurt you that night at Jardinière. There you were, thinking I was going to propose, and instead I blindsided you with my grand plan to move to Rome. I was an idiot, Ry, and I am so, so sorry. But we can start fresh. I want a second chance."

Rylann reached up, took his hand, and moved it away from her mouth. Whether he wanted to hear it or not, there was something she needed to say. "There isn't going to be a second chance, Jon," she said quietly but firmly. "I'm not in love with you anymore."

He grabbed her wrist when she tried to let go of his hand. "Wait, if you'd just let me—"

"You touch her again and you're gonna be sorry about a lot more than that night at Jardinière."

Rylann looked over and saw Kyle standing in the kitchen doorway, his blue eyes flashing angrily. He looked angry and tense and ready to rumble.

"Kyle," she said in surprise as Jon instantly dropped her wrist.

His gaze turned to her, and for a moment he looked so unlike the devil-may-care charmer she knew that she wondered, with a sinking feeling, if he was mad at *her*. She had no clue how much he'd heard, and from his perspective, the scene he'd just walked in on could've looked bad—particularly to a guy who'd been cheated on by his last girlfriend.

But then he moved into the room and stood close to her side. "I think Rylann has made her feelings perfectly clear," he said to Jon.

Jon blinked, recognition lighting in his eyes. "Holy shit, I know you. You've been in the news all week." He shot Rylann a look of utter disbelief. "You're fucking the *Twitter Terrorist*?" He laughed humorlessly. "You, the star assistant U.S. attorney, and an ex-con. You want to tell me how that's ever going to work?"

"If I remember correctly, that's none of your goddamn business anymore," Kyle growled.

"Uh-oh, looks like I struck a nerve there," Jon retorted.

Rylann stepped between them. "Okay, clearly we've got a bit too much testosterone in the room right now." She put her hand on Kyle's arm. "Can I talk to you out in the hall?"

He glared at Jon for a long moment—looking far more like an ex-con than a billionaire heir or computer geek—then turned back to Rylann and nodded. "All right."

They stepped out her front door and into the small internal landing that fit barely more than her welcome mat and their two bodies. At the opposite end of the landing was a staircase leading down to the first- and second-floor apartments.

First things first. "What are you doing here?" she whispered after shutting the door behind them.

Kyle folded his arms across his chest. "Are you kidding me? I find you in the kitchen, with your ex-boyfriend declaring his undying love for you, and you ask *me* what I'm doing?"

"Well, I assumed your cross-examination was going to be quite lengthy, so I figured I'd get all my questions out of the way first."

He pointed. "Don't try to be cute when I'm pissed like this. And for the record, I came back because I forgot my watch on your nightstand. I heard a guy's voice inside your apartment, and the door was unlocked, so I walked in."

Did he now? "When you're feeling a little less prickly, we should probably have a talk about boundaries and this whole possessive side of yours."

"Fair enough. The next time I hear a strange man inside your apartment and find your door mysteriously unlocked, I *won't* check to make sure you're not being robbed or held at gunpoint by some lunatic felon that you've prosecuted."

Rylann paused, thinking that over. "Perhaps this wasn't the best time to take issue with the whole possessive thing."

Kyle hooked a finger into the waistband of her skirt and pulled her closer. "Now it's time for my cross-examination. First question: when's the dickhead leaving?"

She cocked her head. "You're not mad at me?"

"Oh, I was furious when I first walked in and saw you two standing there with his finger on your lips." His expression relaxed a little. "But then I heard what you told him, about not being in love with him anymore." He held her gaze. "Is it true what he said? That you wanted to marry him?"

Rylann hesitated, but she didn't want to lie. "Back when Jon and I were together, yes, I thought we were going to get married." When she saw Kyle clench his jaw, she continued on. "But that feels like a lifetime ago now. So much has happened since then."

He seemed a little more appeased by that. "That brings us back to my first question: when is he leaving?"

She stepped closer, not wanting to fight about Jon. "He'll be leaving soon. I promise. But he flew overnight on a plane from Italy to talk about this—I'm not just going to toss him out on the street."

"Fine. I'll do it for you."

She reached up, sliding her hands up his chest. "Kyle, seven months ago a woman treated you like shit and acted with no regard for your feelings. I know the circumstances are different, but I'm not that callous. I can't just slam the door in Jon's face without giving him whatever closure he obviously needs." She peered up at him. "Besides, you can trust me."

He stared at her for a long moment before finally nodding. "Okay."

Rylann exhaled in relief. Whether they were officially a couple or not, they'd just survived their first fight and had come out okay. Maybe better than okay, even.

Until Kyle changed the game on her.

"But your ex needs to understand that we're together," he said definitively. "In fact, I think it's time everyone understands that. No more hiding out in your apartment, no more secret dates. If we're really going to do this, let's do it right."

And just like that, they were having The Talk.

"**YOU WANT TO** have this discussion *now*? Right here?" Rylann asked him.

"I was hoping there wasn't much to discuss." Kyle studied Rylann's face. "Now I see I was wrong about that."

Admittedly, his timing probably wasn't the best. But seeing how she had a guy waiting in her kitchen whom she'd once wanted to *marry*, a guy who now wanted her back, his possessive side was coming out with a vengeance.

He wanted all of her, plain and simple. And this time, he wasn't going to settle for anything less.

"You knew when we first got together how complicated things are because of my job," she said.

"I thought things had changed. Especially after last night."

Her expression softened. "Last night was great. I told you, the best first date I've ever had."

"It could be that way every day, Rylann." Kyle put his hands on her shoulders, sensing that it was now or never. He wasn't great at expressing himself, and frankly, she pretty much sucked at it, too. Quips and jokes were their usual modus operandi. But there were times in life when a man needed to suck it up and say what needed to be said.

And this was that moment.

So he peered down into her eyes. "After everything that happened with Daniela, I told myself I wasn't going to get serious with anyone for a long time. But then you came along and changed everything. I don't want to be some guy you're fooling around with anymore, Rylann. I want to be with you all the way."

Because I'm in love with you.

But when the words rose to his lips, he held them back.

Not because he didn't mean them—far from it. He knew, as he looked into those gorgeous amber eyes that he'd never forgotten, just how true they were. But he also saw the uncertainty on Rylann's face and realized, with some dread, that he wasn't entirely sure how this conversation was going to turn out. And once he said those words, *I'm in love with you*, something he'd never before said to anyone, they'd be out there forever.

So he fell silent, waiting for her answer.

"I want to be with you, too," she said.

Kyle smiled and pulled her closer . . . until he realized she wasn't finished. "But?"

"But I need more time. You're all over the news with your new company and the Twitter thing, and now there's going to be the interview in *Time*. This is not the week to go public with the fact that we're dating. Let's wait it out a few weeks, or a couple months, and then when things cool down—"

"A couple *months*?" He pulled back and said nothing for a moment. "You're really that embarrassed to be seen with me?"

Rylann pointed. "No. Not embarrassed. Just aware of certain facts. Mainly, that I'm a federal prosecutor and you are . . . well, you."

Gee, thanks for clarifying. "So let me make sure I have this right: Rylann, the woman I met nine years ago, wants to be with me. But Prosecutrix Pierce just wants to fuck. Is that how it works?"

She threw up her hands in frustration. "What do you want me to say, Kyle? Shutting down Twitter may have been funny to some people, and I know you have your high-fivers, but you are, in fact, an *ex-con*. And I've been up front with you from the beginning—that presents challenges for me."

Kyle stepped back, his tone dry. "Wow. And here I thought I'd never feel more like a thug than the day they threw me behind bars at MCC."

Rylann's expression softened. "I didn't mean it like that. It's just that you're pushing me for answers I don't have. We had an unexpected visit from my ex-boyfriend this morning, and now, suddenly, you're throwing down the gauntlet. But this is so new—we've only been dating for a couple weeks. Why can't we wait a little longer to figure things out?"

Ah . . . finally, Kyle understood what was going on here.

She wasn't sure how she felt about him.

For years, he'd played the field, always keeping things fun and casual, never taking the time to get too serious with any woman. Even with Daniela, he'd held back, not truly letting her in. But that wasn't the case with Rylann. Their relationship hadn't been all about wining and dining—it had been *real*. He'd opened up to her, had even told her private things about his family, and now here he was, putting his cards on the table—and hoping that what she'd seen these past few weeks had been enough to win her over. Because, for him, these past few weeks had been perfect—and everything he never knew he always wanted in a relationship.

And yet, seemingly, it still wasn't enough for her.

Not much else a man could say in these circumstances.

He stepped closer and gently cupped her chin. "The difference between you and me, counselor, is that I don't need more time. I know how I feel. You love your job—I understand that. It's one of the things I admire most about you. But I haven't waited thirty-three years to find something real, only to settle for always being second place in your heart. I want more than that."

Rylann put her hand on his, her eyes filled with emotion. "Kyle . . . don't do this. I never said you were second place."

"You didn't have to say it, Rylann," he said softly.

Because he knew it anyway.

So he lowered his head and kissed her forehead in goodbye. Then he steeled his heart, not looking back when she called his name, and walked out of her apartment for good.

Thirty-three

LATER THAT EVENING, Kyle walked into EPIC, a loft-style restaurant located in the city's River North area, and spotted his family—future brother-in-law included—sitting at a table near the back.

Jordan had called him earlier and had mentioned that she'd invited Nick to join them for dinner. She'd said it hesitantly, as if worried he might be offended that she'd included him in their yearly tradition.

"You don't have to run it by me, Jordo," he'd said. "Nick and I are cool now."

"Aw, you two really have bonded," she'd said teasingly. "That's so cute."

"Yeah."

There was a long silence on the phone.

"That's it?" Jordan had asked. "No sarcastic response?" Her tone immediately turned worried. "What's wrong?"

"Nothing. I'm just distracted with work," he'd lied. "I'll see you later, at the restaurant." Then he'd hung up the phone before she could ask any more questions. He simply wanted to get through the dinner with his family as painlessly as possible, so he could get home and try to forget what a royally shitty day this had been.

As he approached the table, he put on a smile and acted casual. "Sorry I'm late. Traffic on the Drive was murder." He sat down at the empty seat between Nick and his father and picked up the menu in front of him. "So what looks good?"

When nobody answered him, he peered over his menu and saw three pairs of eyes staring incredulously at him.

"You're really going to make us ask?" Grey said.

Kyle shot Jordan a look of death from across the table. *What did you tell Dad?*

Nothing, she glared back. "Your deal with Twitter?" she prompted him.

Oh. Right. He'd forgotten that he hadn't spoken to either his sister or father about that yet. They'd called as soon as the press release had gone out, but he'd been busy talking to prospective clients and, later, on his date with Rylann.

Hard to believe that was less than twenty-four hours ago. Last night had been incredible, and then within the blink of an eye, everything had changed.

Better to know now where you stand with her.

Yeah, well, that was what he was telling himself, anyway.

"I came up with the idea when I was in prison," Kyle said, in response to their question. "Four months behind bars gives a man a lot of time to brainstorm." He took a sip of water.

Grey laughed. "That's all you're going to say? You're not usually so modest."

Jordan eyed him suspiciously. "You're never so modest." She threw him a look. *What's going on?*

He frowned. *Nothing. Go away.*

She cocked her head. *What did you do now?*

He made a face. *Thanks for the vote of confidence.*

Sitting between Jordan and Kyle, Nick raised an eyebrow, looking over the FBI agent right then. "What's with the looks?"

Hearing that, Grey peered up from his menu. "Are they doing the twin thing again? Used to freak Marilyn and me out when they were younger. They'd have entire conversations like that at the dinner table." He waved his hand dismissively. "You get used to it."

The conversation moved on—thankfully—and Kyle distracted his family by filling them in on the details about his meeting with the CEO of Twitter. Nick then talked about his promotion to special agent in charge of the FBI's Chicago division and how that meant he would no longer be doing undercover work. When he smiled at Jordan and squeezed her hand after saying that, Kyle got the impression this had once been an issue for them.

"That's great to hear, Nick. So does this mean you're going to make an honest woman out of my daughter anytime soon?" Grey asked, out of the blue.

Jordan's eyes went wide, appalled. *"Dad."*

Kyle watched with amusement as Nick squirmed in his chair. He tipped his drink to the FBI agent. "Welcome to the family."

Grey turned to him. "Oh, I wouldn't get too comfortable there if I were you. You're in the hot seat next."

"What did I do?" Kyle asked.

"Who's this brunette bombshell you've been cozying up with?" Grey asked.

Damn Scene and Heard. "Don't believe everything you read in the papers, Dad," Kyle grumbled. Although that particular bit had been very true.

"Fine. How about what I *see* in the papers? A few weeks before the brunette bombshell, there was the pretty assistant U.S. attorney. The one whose chest you're staring at in that photograph." Grey looked at him pointedly. "You're a CEO now, Kyle. Maybe it's time you thought about treating your personal life as seriously as your professional one."

Kyle took a deep breath, silently counting to ten. It was the same lecture he'd been hearing from his father for years. Normally, this was the part where he grinned and said, *Sure, Dad*, then left dinner and called whatever girl was the flavor of the week on the way home.

But not tonight.

"First of all," he began, "I wasn't staring at the pretty assistant U.S. attorney's chest. I was looking at her eyes. And in hindsight, that's probably the moment I should've first realized I was totally screwed. As for getting serious, well, here's a shocker for you: I tried that. Thought I had something really great. But guess what? She doesn't want to get serious with *me*. Figured that out just this morning. So if tonight, for once, we could all skip the That Kyle Sure Is a Funny Asshole routine, I would really, really appreciate it."

Grey's face fell, turning immediately chagrined. "I'm sorry, Kyle. I didn't realize."

Jordan reached across the table, her expression one of genuine sympathy. "What happened? I thought things were going great with Rylann."

Kyle knew his family meant well, but this was worse than the sarcasm. Expressing emotions and getting in touch with his softer side hadn't worked out so well for him that morning, and the last thing he wanted to do was relive the experience. So he stood up from the table. "You know, I'm not really in the mood for dessert. You guys go ahead and order without me. I think I'll step outside for a few minutes—I've got some phone calls I need to make."

KYLE STOOD AGAINST the brick wall on the far end of the restaurant's rooftop lounge, looking out at the striking nighttime view of high-rise buildings that towered all around him. He scrolled through the voicemail, e-mail, and text messages he'd received during dinner—and got pissed at himself when he realized he'd been hoping one of them would be from Rylann. He hadn't expected her to call after the way he'd left things, but nevertheless his mind had begun conjuring up all sorts of ideas about what might've happened after he'd left her apartment. And none of them were good.

Perhaps he should've thought about that *before* throwing down the gauntlet while the guy she'd once wanted to marry was waiting in her kitchen.

As he was ruminating over the genius of that particular strategy, he suddenly heard footsteps behind him.

"I appreciate it, Jordo," he said without turning around. "But I'm not in a very talkative mood right now."

"All right. How about a drink instead?"

Surprised by the voice, Kyle turned around and saw his dad holding two rocks glasses. He offered one to Kyle. "I had them open a bottle of Macallan 21 especially."

With a slight smile, Kyle took the glass. "Nothing but the best for Grey Rhodes."

"Nothing but the best for *Kyle* Rhodes," Grey corrected him. "The man of the hour." He took a spot next to Kyle along the wall. "Any particular reason I had to read about the launch of Rhodes Network Consulting in the papers, like everyone else?"

Ah, yes. *That.* "I meant to call you after the press release went out, but the day just got away from me." Kyle paused, trying to decide how best to explain. "And before that . . . this company was something I needed to build on my own. Without any input from the mighty business entrepreneur Grey Rhodes."

Grey pulled back, seemingly indignant. "It's *your* business plan. It's not like I would've shoved unsolicited opinions down your throat."

Kyle raised an eyebrow. "Do you remember the conversation we had about five minutes ago, about me getting serious with my personal life and Nick needing to make an honest woman out of Jordan?"

Grey conceded that with a smile. "Fine. So I may, perhaps, have a few occasional thoughts that I vocalize when it comes to you and your sister." He pointed emphatically. "You ever seen *Keeping Up with the Kardashians*? Well, I have. Caught an episode once, in a hotel room. Gave me nightmares for weeks. God forbid I drop the ball and you two end up like that."

Kyle fought back a grin at that one. "They ever have an episode where one of the Kardashians hacked into Twitter and went to prison for four months?"

"Still not okay with the jokes from you about that."

"Sorry."

Grey looked sideways at Kyle. "Although you did one helluva job turning things around." He raised his glass in a toast, his blue eyes twinkling mischievously. "To the new face of network security."

Kyle cocked his head at his father's choice of words. "That's going to be the *Time* cover. You know about that?"

"Sure do. The reporter called me this afternoon, asking for

a quote for the story. Mostly, he wanted to know how I feel about the fact that my son is starting his own consulting business."

"What did you tell him?" Kyle asked.

His father's expression turned to one of pride. "That I knew nine years ago that you would make an excellent CEO. And that it was a blessing, and a privilege, to walk into my office every day and have you as my right-hand man." He smiled cheekily. "I also added that I hoped you would continue to recommend Rhodes Corp. products to all your clients, seeing how we protect one in every three computers in America."

Kyle laughed—of course his father had managed to work that in. "Thanks, Dad."

They each took a sip of the scotch, and then there was a long pause between them.

Grey leaned in. "You know this is the part of the father-son moment where I'm supposed to ask about this Rylann girl, right?"

Kyle set his drink on the ledge and shoved his hands in his pants pockets. "Yep. And now *this* is the part where I say thank you but that I think I've said all I want to say about her tonight. Which will conveniently be followed by the part where a waitress walks up and asks if we'd like anything else to drink, eliminating all further discussion on that topic."

Just like that, there was a voice from behind them.

"Excuse me, can I get either of you gentlemen something else to drink?"

His father looked over his shoulder, saw the blond waitress standing behind them, and stared at Kyle in astonishment.

Kyle smiled. "I paid her two hundred bucks to come over as soon as I put my hands in my pockets. I knew you and Jordan couldn't stay out of my business for long."

ACROSS TOWN, RYLANN sat next to Jon at a wine bar a couple blocks from her apartment. It was the first chance they'd gotten to talk all day. After Kyle had left her standing on her doorstep earlier that morning, she'd unfortunately had no time to wallow in her sorrows. Instead, she'd gone back inside, told Jon that she would call him later, and left to get ready for her grand jury hearing.

Shortly after arriving at the wine bar, Rylann had taken the lead with the conversation. She explained to Jon, in the gentlest of terms, that their relationship was truly, definitely, absolutely over. He listened this time, and though he looked upset and hurt and even a little frustrated, he finally seemed to accept what she was saying.

"So I blew it, then. For good." He ran his hand over his mouth. "I guess that's the price I have to pay for being a selfish ass seven months ago."

Rylann studied him. "Jon, don't take this the wrong way, but what's really going on here? I know I should be flattered that you hopped on a plane to try to win me back, but . . . can I be honest?"

He smiled wryly. "You always are."

"This whole thing feels more desperate than genuine. You seem kind of lost."

He swirled his wineglass, saying nothing at first. "I don't know. I just feel like there's something missing. Italy was great for the first couple months, but then the excitement wore off. I guess I thought that if you and I could get back what we used to have, at least that part of my life would feel right again." He looked at her over the glass. "I am sorry, you know. We had a good thing going, and I ruined it."

It was tempting to let him take all the blame. And, no doubt, he deserved *a lot* of it. But as Rylann sat there, looking at the man she'd once genuinely believed she wanted to spend the rest of her life with, she realized, for the first time, that she shared a tiny bit of the responsibility for the demise of their relationship as well. "It wasn't just you, Jon."

He cocked his head. "What do you mean?"

She sighed. "There *was* something missing. I don't think either of us realized it at the time, and frankly, I'm still not sure I can put my finger on it. On the outside we seemed happy, but there had to be something wrong, right? Otherwise, you would've never wanted to leave for Italy without me, and I . . . would've tried to make you stay."

He considered this, then gave her a half smile that was bittersweet. "And we both know how tenacious you can be when you want something."

She laughed softly, acknowledging that. "Very true."

They talked for a long time after that, about old times, Italy, and Rylann's new life in Chicago. Afterward they walked outside and said good-bye on the sidewalk.

"You're going back to Rome tomorrow, then?" she asked.

Jon nodded. "Temporarily, at least. I took the week off from work, hoping that I'd be spending it with you." He shrugged. "Maybe now I'll use the time to figure things out. Decide what I want to do with my life when I grow up."

"Whatever it is you're looking for, I hope you find it," Rylann said in all sincerity. "I want you to be happy."

"You, too, Ry." He touched her cheek in good-bye, then climbed into the taxi that would take him back to the hotel he'd checked into for the night.

Rylann stood there on the sidewalk, watching Jon drive off. She remembered a similar day seven months ago, when they'd said good-bye outside the apartment they'd shared in San Francisco. Only that time, the taxi had taken him directly to the airport and to his new life in Italy.

Once the cab disappeared from sight, she walked the few blocks to her apartment, her mind drifting back to everything that had happened that morning. Several weeks ago, she'd told Rae that she'd never once considered going to Rome with Jon because doing so would've been crazy, and she didn't do crazy. But that wasn't entirely true. These past couple of months, with Kyle, she'd been doing a lot of things that didn't make the most sense from a practical perspective. For him, she'd been willing to bend the rules, to go against logic, and to simply follow her heart.

And truthfully, that scared her a little.

She'd guessed, from the moment that she'd met Kyle, that he could cause her all sorts of trouble. She'd sensed it from that very first smile. Once they'd reconnected, she'd told herself that she was being careful, that they were just having fun. But these past few weeks had gone way beyond fun and had shown her how truly amazing it could be to have Kyle Rhodes in her life.

Earlier that morning, when he'd made the comment about her being embarrassed to be seen with him, she'd just felt . . . bad. While the sneaking around had been a little exciting, she knew he deserved better. But she'd been caught off guard when he'd forced her hand on the issue right then and there.

So now it was decision time. She could let Kyle walk out of her life a second time and preserve her perfect reputation as Meth Lab Rylann, the star AUSA who had never taken a misstep at work and who'd fought hard to establish herself as a woman who should be taken seriously in a profession that often failed to do so. Or she could accept that her crown would forever be tarnished, potentially diminish herself in the eyes of her boss and coworkers, and come out of the closet about the fact that she was dating the Twitter Terrorist, her former witness and the most infamous ex-con to be prosecuted by her office in recent history.

Mulling this over, Rylann let herself into her apartment and threw her purse and keys on the kitchen counter. She went to her bedroom and stripped out of the gray skirt suit and heels she'd worn that day. In the closet, she hung up the suit next to the others, the row of black, navy, gray, beige, and brown jackets forming a neat, orderly line. Then, instinctively, her eyes went to the shoe box on the top shelf near the back, the one with Kyle's flannel shirt. She thought of something she'd said to him that night, right after she'd kissed him.

I thought I'd fly by the seat of my pants for a change.

The only question left was just how far she was willing to take that.

Thirty-four

THE NEXT MORNING, Kyle sat at his desk at the downtown office of Rhodes Network Consulting, staring distractedly out the window at the view of the Chicago river.

When his cell phone rang, he blinked and quickly checked the caller ID, quelling a pang of disappointment when he saw that it was Sean.

He answered, and the two of them discussed the following week's itinerary. Monday was the official start date for all company employees, which currently included Sean, Gil and Troy, two administrative assistants, and a receptionist. Judging from the volume of calls Kyle had already received since the Twitter announcement, however, he doubted they'd be able to operate for long with a six-person team—especially once the *Time* article came out.

As his father had said last night, from a professional perspective he had indeed turned his life around. And he was proud of those accomplishments. But they did little to ease the dull, empty ache he'd felt since leaving Rylann's apartment.

He'd pushed her, and in the end he'd gotten the answers he'd needed. Just not the answers he'd wanted.

When his business line rang, another potential client wanting to set up a consultation, he forced himself to stay focused on work. Shortly after he finished the call, his cell phone buzzed with a new text message.

From Rylann.

AT SOME POINT, DIMPLES, DO YOU PLAN TO HAVE ANY
ACTUAL CONSULTANTS AT RHODES NETWORK
CONSULTING?

It took Kyle a half second, then he got up from his desk.
He walked out of his office, going past the empty cubicles
and workstations, and turned into the reception area.

Standing there, waiting at the front desk and looking very
businesslike in her trench coat and heels, was Rylann.

"I hope you take walk-in appointments," she said with a
smile.

Hmm.

Kyle knew that smile well by now. But Prosecutrix Pierce
would not find him so easily charmed this time. She could
throw around all her wiles and quips, and flaunt whatever
sexy skirt suit she had on underneath that trench coat of hers,
and he would remain decidedly immune to all of it.

"How did you find me?" he asked.

"I went to the website for Rhodes Network Consulting and
looked up the address," she said matter-of-factly. "You'd mentioned that you were planning to get a jump on things at the
office today."

He remembered that now; he'd said something about it on
Wednesday night, during the limo ride down to Champaign.

"How's your ex?" he asked dryly.

Rylann shrugged. "Okay, I guess. All things considered.
He's currently on a plane back to Rome, trying to decide what
he wants to do with his life." She looked him over. "You look
tired."

"I didn't sleep well last night."

She nodded, then shifted awkwardly. "Do you think we
could go to your office and talk? I feel strange standing here
by the reception desk."

Kyle paused, thinking about that, then gestured behind
him. "Follow me."

They said nothing as they walked back to his office—
probably the longest the two of them had ever gone without

speaking. Out of the corner of his eye, he saw her checking everything out.

"The place looks great," she said when they got to his office. "How much did you have to change before moving in?"

He leaned against his desk and shoved his hands in his pockets, not exactly in the mood to make idle chitchat. "Why did you come here, Rylann?"

She reached into the pocket of her trench coat and pulled something out. "To give you this."

When Kyle saw that it was his watch, his heart sank. And here he'd been hoping . . . well, obviously it didn't matter now.

"You forgot it, again, when you left my apartment yesterday morning," she said.

Kyle took the watch from her and slid it onto his wrist. "Thanks for returning it."

She held his gaze meaningfully. "And I also came here to tell you that you're wrong." She stepped closer. "I do want to be with you, Kyle. More than anything."

He remained motionless. "I'm waiting for the 'but.'"

She shook her head. "No 'but' this time. I'm in, all the way." She took a deep breath. "I'm going to tell Cameron about us this afternoon."

In so many ways that was exactly what Kyle had wanted to hear. But he remembered her hesitation yesterday all too clearly. "Rylann, I'm crazy about you—you know that." He held her gaze, laying it on the line. "But if we do this, I worry that one day you'll regret it. And that would kill me."

"I won't regret it," she said. "I promise."

"You say that now, but what about later?"

Suddenly, to his utter surprise, tears sprang to her eyes.

"I will never, ever regret stopping you from walking out of my life a second time, Kyle," she said in an emotional voice. "And I can prove it." She reached for the buttons on her trench coat and undid them, one at a time. Then she opened the coat and let it drop to the floor.

And even if she didn't say a single word more, Kyle knew he would never again doubt the way Rylann felt about him.

She was wearing his flannel shirt.

"You kept it," he said softly. "All this time."

She nodded. "For nine years, I've held on to this darn shirt, literally dragging it across the country and back."

Kyle touched her cheek, gently brushing away a tear with his thumb. "Why?"

She paused hesitantly, and then with a tender smile, finally put it all on the line, too. "I guess I always hoped you'd come back for it someday."

Fuck, that completely undid him. His chest pulled almost uncomfortably tight as he pulled her into his arms. "I love you, Rylann." He cupped her face, peering down into her eyes. "And now I finally have a good answer to the one question everyone always asks me—why I hacked into Twitter. I didn't know it at the time . . . but I did it to find you again."

She leaned into him, curling her fingers around his shirt. "That may be the best justification I've ever heard for committing a crime." She looked up at him, her eyes shining. "And I love you, too, you know."

He smiled, lowering his mouth to hers. He did know that. It may have taken nine years, and a whole lot of wrong turns along the way, but their story felt complete at last.

Because, finally, she was his.

Thirty-five

LATER THAT AFTERNOON, Rylann stood in front of Cameron's door.

She paused, took a deep breath, and then knocked.

A voice called from inside. "Come in."

Rylann opened the door and saw Cameron at her desk. The U.S. attorney smiled and gestured to the open chairs across from her. "Rylann, hi. Have a seat."

Rylann shut the door behind her, trying to gauge the other woman's mood. She'd worked with Cameron for two months now, and had nothing but positive things to say about the experience. While young for her position, Cameron was driven, fair, and an excellent trial lawyer. As the U.S. attorney for one of the largest districts in the country, she commanded significant power within the federal criminal justice system and had, in particular, garnered a lot of favorable attention over the last several months by prosecuting one of the most notorious crime syndicates in the country.

She was, in other words, a woman Rylann respected very much.

Rylann took a seat in front of the desk, trying to decide where to begin. *Funny story, Cameron. Nine years ago, I let a perfect stranger walk me home from a bar . . .*

Probably not there.

She cleared her throat. "I need to speak with you about a personal matter."

Cameron looked concerned. "I hope everything's okay?"

"Yes, thank you. But there's something you should know,

and I wanted you to hear it directly from me." She paused before coming out with it. "Kyle Rhodes and I have been exploring a relationship in a nonprofessional capacity." She cocked her head. "Wow. That sounded a lot less lame when I practiced it in my head. Let me try that again, without the BS." She looked her boss in the eyes. "I'm dating the Twitter Terrorist."

Cameron said nothing for a moment, and then leaned back in her chair. "Okay. First things first. Was this going on while he was your witness?"

"No," Rylann said firmly, wanting to make sure they were clear on that.

Cameron nodded. "Of course. Had to ask, though."

Rylann sat forward earnestly. "Look, Cameron, I realize this is unusual. We put the guy in prison and called him a terrorist. And because he's such a recognizable figure in this city, it won't be long before someone sees us together and links me to this office. I realize, when that happens, that our relationship might raise a few eyebrows. More than a few, probably. Trust me when I say that for those reasons, this was not something I entered into lightly. But regardless, Kyle is part of my life now. And I'm ready to accept whatever fallout comes with it."

"That's quite a speech," Cameron said.

Rylann exhaled. "Thanks. I'm a little nervous here."

Cameron studied her. "Are you worried that I'm going to *fire* you over this?"

Rylann shook her head, being direct. "No. But I am worried that this will put a strain on our working relationship. And that you'll question my judgment going forward." And while both would be tough pills to swallow, she nevertheless didn't regret her decision. She'd told Kyle that she was committed to this, and she'd meant it.

Cameron rested her elbows on the desk. "I appreciate your honesty, Rylann. So I'll be candid as well." She gestured to her door. "I realize that the door says 'U.S. Attorney' on it, but only six months ago, the word *Assistant* was in front of my name, too. And if things were different, and Silas had still been in charge, I have no doubt that he would've held the fact that you're dating a man this office recently prosecuted as a big-time strike against you. But you know what? Silas was an ass. He ran this office like a dictator, and the only thing he cared about was his public image. Whenever one of the AUSAs had an important victory, he took all the credit. If something bad happened, he let us take all the blame. Not to mention the fact that he was taking bribes from the biggest organized crime boss in Chicago and essentially tried to have me murdered—but that's a whole other story."

Rylann blinked. Okay . . . safe to say things had been a *lot* different under the previous U.S. attorney.

"The point is," Cameron continued, "when I took over this office, I vowed to do two things: first, clean up the corruption, and second, be the kind of U.S. attorney that I wish had been in charge when I was an AUSA. So yes—the fact that you're dating Kyle Rhodes *is* a little weird. When word gets out, are there going to be people who find it unusual that I've got a prosecutor dating the Twitter Terrorist? Probably. But in comparison to everything that was going on around here when Silas was in charge, I think I can handle it. We're a team in this office, Rylann. You're a fantastic trial lawyer and incredibly dedicated to this job. *That* is what's most important to me."

Rylann took a deep breath, feeling as though a huge weight had been lifted off her chest. "You have no idea how relieved I am to hear that, Cameron."

"You really were nervous about this," Cameron said with a chuckle.

"It's just that if I were in your shoes right now, I'm sure I'd be wondering why a woman in my position would choose to pursue *this* relationship."

Cameron smiled. "Oh, I understand that better than you think. These things work in mysterious ways. Three years ago, an FBI agent went on national television and declared that I had my head up my ass." She checked her watch. "And strangely, in about twenty-eight hours, I'm going to marry the guy."

Rylann held out her hands in surprise. "Oh my gosh, I hadn't heard. Congratulations."

Cameron's eyes sparkled happily. "We've been low-key

about it. I just started telling people today—I figure the cat will be out of the bag on Monday anyway, when I show up for work wearing a wedding band. Neither Jack nor I wanted a lot of fanfare. Just a few friends and family, a small ceremony, and dinner on the terrace at the Peninsula hotel."

"That sounds lovely."

The way Cameron's face had lit up said she couldn't agree more. "It's the place where Jack and I reconnected. Sort of. Another long story."

"Well, I won't take up any more of your time, since you obviously have a lot going on." Rylann stood up. "Thank you for being so understanding."

"What can I say? You caught me in a really good mood today. If it had been last Friday, I might've fired you." Cameron laughed when she saw Rylann's eyes widen. "Just a little U.S. attorney humor. Enjoy your weekend."

After Rylann left the office and stepped out into the hallway, she closed her eyes and exhaled.

She'd survived.

Now, she had only one mea culpa left—after that, everyone else could hear about her and Kyle in whatever ways these things inevitably came out. With that in mind, she headed down the hallway to Cade's office. She stopped in his open doorway and knocked.

Sitting at his desk, working at his computer, Cade looked over and smiled. "Hey, you. You're a bit early for Starbucks."

"Got a second?" Rylann asked.

"Sure. Come on in."

Rylann stepped inside, shut the door behind her, and took a seat in front of his desk. She crossed her legs, resting her hands in her lap. "I need to talk to you about something. And I'm warning you now—it's going to be a little awkward. Maybe a lot awkward."

He didn't seem too surprised by this lead-in. "I think I know what this is about. The rumors, right?"

Rylann cocked her head. "Rumors?"

"That you and I are hooking up." Cade held up his hand. "I swear, I had nothing to do with it."

Rylann blinked—she'd assumed Jack Pallas had been making that up to flush out Kyle. "Great," she said dryly. "Now there will be *two* scandals floating around the halls about me."

He raised an eyebrow curiously. "Scandal? What have you done, Ms. Pierce?"

"Well, remember that thing you read in the Scene and Heard column, about the brunette bombshell that Kyle Rhodes is seeing?"

Cade looked at her for a long moment, waiting for her to say something else. Then it clicked. "Get out of here. *You* are the brunette bombshell?"

"I suppose 'bombshell' may have been a little overboard, but you don't have to look that shocked by the description."

"That's not what I meant."

"I know, I was going for a joke. Trying to ease over that awkwardness." She saw his guarded expression. "Probably going to take a lot more easing."

"When did this start?" he asked.

"A few weeks ago. After the Quinn case pled out." Rylann tried for a smile. "It's weird, I know. I just told Cameron, and it was weird then, too. But I wanted you to hear it from me."

"I called your boyfriend a terrorist."

"Good thing he wasn't my boyfriend at the time. Then this would've been *really* awkward."

Cade sat back in his chair, still with the cautious look. "A couple months ago, I told you some things about Kyle's case. About the fact that Silas asked me to go for the maximum sentence in order to make an example out of him." He looked her dead in the eyes. "Did you tell Rhodes about that?"

"Of course not. That was something you told me in confidence. I'm still the same person you go to Starbucks every day with, Cade. Just . . . with an ex-con boyfriend you once called a cyber-menace to society."

He wasn't quite smiling yet, but he wasn't staring at her as though she'd sprouted a second head anymore, either.

"You know that everyone's going to be talking about this, right?" Cade asked.

"Oh, I have no doubt about that," Rylann said. She wasn't pleased about that fact, but she'd deal with it. She'd have to.

Cade studied her for a moment, then sat forward in his chair. "Seriously, what *is* it about this guy? He's just a rich computer geek with good hair."

Rylann smiled. "I think there's a little more to it than that."

"Christ, you are smitten." He threw up his hands. "What is going on with everyone these days? Sam Wilkins is babbling about a meet-cute, Cameron's sneaking off to get hitched, and now you're all starry-eyed over the Twitter Terrorist. Has everyone been sneaking happy pills out of the evidence room when I'm not looking?"

"No, just some really good pot."

Cade laughed out loud at that. "You are a funny one, Pierce. I'll say that."

"So does that mean we're still on for Starbucks later today?"

He studied her suspiciously. "You're not going to want to talk about Kyle Rhodes the whole time, are you?"

"Actually, yes. And then we'll go shoe shopping together and get mani-pedis." She threw him a get-real look. "We'll talk about the same stuff we always talk about."

With a grin, he finally nodded. "Fine. Three o'clock, Pierce. I'll swing by your office."

AT SIX THIRTY that day, Rylann packed up her briefcase and left the office, one of the last people there that Friday evening.

As it turned out, the world had not ended with the revelation that she was dating the Twitter Terrorist.

Granted, only two people in her world—other than Rae—actually knew this information, but seeing how they were two of the people whose opinions she cared most about, she was willing to call that a victory.

But she wasn't naïve. As Cade had mentioned, there was going to be gossip. A lot of it. From this point forward, her claim to fame would no longer be that she'd once climbed into a hatch and scaled down a rickety fifteen-foot ladder in a skirt suit. Instead, people would have a far juicier tale to tell.

Nevertheless, while Meth Lab Rylann may have been a little sad to see her legendary status go, Prosecutrix Pierce had no regrets about her decision. Despite the inevitable whispers in the hallways and the raised eyebrows, nothing changed the fact that she was a damn good lawyer. And now she was a damn good lawyer who could come home after a long workday, good or bad, to a man she admired, who challenged her, and who made her heart beat faster with one smile.

And that was something Meth Lab Rylann never had.

As she pushed through the revolving doors and cut across the plaza in front of the Federal Building, Rylann decided to treat herself to a cab ride instead of taking the L. She texted Kyle with the message that she'd talked to Cameron and would call him with the details when she got home.

Twenty minutes later, when the cab was a block away from her apartment, Rylann's cell phone rang, and she saw that it was Kyle.

"How did it go?" he asked after she'd answered.

"Better than expected," she told him. "I only told Cameron and Cade, but they were the two people I was most worried about."

"Please tell me the look on Morgan's face was as priceless as I'm imagining it."

"Does that mean you two won't be drinking beer together at the U.S. Attorney's Office annual Fourth of July picnic?" The cab pulled in front of Rylann's apartment, and she pulled out her wallet.

"Is there actually an office Fourth of July picnic?" Kyle asked.

"So I've been told. Kids, spouses, significant others—the whole nine yards." Rylann handed cash to the driver. "Keep the change." She stepped out of the cab and shut the door.

"Ooh, I saw a flash of leg there," Kyle said slyly in her ear.

Quickly, Rylann looked around.

Across the street, there Kyle stood, leaning against an obscenely expensive-looking silver sports car.

That was . . . quite a sight.

Rylann hung up the phone and walked over, briefcase in hand. With his arms folded across his chest, Kyle watched with obvious appreciation as she approached.

"You do wear that trench coat well," he said.

She stopped before him and pointed. "This is your car?"

"It is." He watched as she checked it out, then grinned. "Well, look at that. You like the car."

Damn skippy she liked the car.

"It's not bad," she said nonchalantly.

"Coming from you, that's quite a compliment." He pulled her closer, so that she stood between his outstretched legs. "So do they allow significant others who have prison records at the U.S. Attorney's Office annual Fourth of July picnic?"

She chuckled at the thought. "Let's get through next week first. See how things go after the *Time* article comes out."

Kyle cocked his head, as if realizing something. "You're worried about what I'm going to say during the interview."

Well . . . yes. "You say whatever you want." It was his job, his business, and thus his right to handle it his own way. Just as the same rules applied to her career.

He touched her chin. "I'll be circumspect, counselor. We're in this together." His blue eyes were warm as he peered down at her. "So what would you say to going out for dinner tonight?"

"A second date? This is getting serious," she said coyly.

"Just name the place. The sky's the limit." He slid his hand to the nape of her neck. "I could spoil you rotten, Rylann. If you'll let me."

Heady words, indeed. As they leaned against his superfancy sports car, she brushed her fingers across a lock of dark blond hair that had fallen across Kyle's forehead. Then, suddenly, she realized she had one mea culpa left.

Oh, boy.

He saw her look. "What?"

"I'm wondering how I'm ever going to explain you to my

mother. If you think I'm a burr up your ass about the ex-con thing, just wait until you meet her."

"Maybe we could take a lesson from my parents and give her the sanitized, wholesome version of the story. One that emphasizes my numerous fine qualities." Kyle mused this over. "Something like . . . 'Once upon a time, I met a guy in a bar who was wearing a flannel shirt and work boots, and he turned out to be a prince in disguise.'"

Just then, a car slowed to a stop in front of them, filled with five guys in their late teens. The driver stuck his head out the window.

"Yo, Twitter Terrorist!" he called out. "How's this for a tweet? 'Kiss my ass, dickhead!'" The entire group laughed as a guy in the backseat stuck his bare ass out the window, mooning them, then the car peeled away.

Kyle and Rylann stood on the street, saying nothing for a moment as the car drove off. Then he turned to her with a sheepish grin. "Obviously not one of the high-fivers."

Yes, she'd caught that. "What am I going to do with you, Kyle Rhodes?" She slid her arms around his neck and peered up at him.

His hand moved to the side of her face. "Whatever you want, counselor. Stick with me, and I promise you that life will always be an adventure."

And as he lowered his head and kissed her, Rylann decided that was the best plan of all.

Loved *About That Night*?

Read on for a preview of Jordan and Nick's story in

A Lot Like Love

by Julie James
Now available from Berkley Sensation!

THE CHIME RANG on the front door of the wine store. Jordan Rhodes came out of the back room, where she'd been sneaking a quick bite for lunch. She smiled. "You again."

It was the guy from last week, the one who'd looked skeptical when she'd recommended a cabernet from South Africa that—gasp—had a screw top.

"So? How'd you like the Excelsior?" she asked.

"Good memory," he said, impressed. "You were right. It's good. Particularly at that price point."

"It's good at any price point," Jordan said. "The fact that it sells for less than ten dollars makes it a steal."

The man's blue eyes lit up as he grinned. He was dressed in a navy car coat and jeans, and wore expensive leather Italian loafers—probably too expensive for the six to eight inches of snow they were expected to get that evening. His dark blond hair was mussed from the wind outside.

"You've convinced me. Put me down for a case. I'm having a dinner party in two weeks, and the Excelsior will be perfect." He pulled off his leather gloves and set them on the long ebony wood counter that doubled as a bar when Jordan hosted events in the shop. "I'm thinking I'll pair it with leg of lamb, maybe seasoned with black pepper and mustard seed. Rosemary potatoes."

Jordan raised an eyebrow. The man knew his food. And

the Excelsior would certainly complement the menu, although she personally subscribed to the more relaxed "drink what you want" philosophy of wine rather than putting the emphasis on finding the perfect food pairing—a fact that constantly scandalized her assistant store manager, Martin. He was a certified level three sommelier, and thus had a certain view on things; while she, on the other hand, was the owner of the store and thus believed in making wine approachable to the customer. Sure, she loved the romance of wine—that was one of the main reasons she had opened her store, DeVine Cellars. But for her, wine was also a business.

"Sounds delicious. I take it you like to cook," she said to the man with the great smile. Great hair, too. Nicely styled, on the longer side. He wore a gray scarf wrapped loosely around his neck that gave him an air of casual sophistication.

He shrugged. "It comes with the job."

"Let me guess—you're a chef."

"Food critic. With the *Tribune*."

Jordan cocked her head, suddenly realizing. "You're Cal Kittredge."

He seemed pleased by her recognition. "You read my reviews."

"Religiously. With so many restaurants in this city to choose from, it's nice to have an expert's opinion."

Cal leaned against the counter. "An expert, huh . . . I'm flattered, Jordan."

So, he knew her name.

Unfortunately, a lot of people knew her name. Between her father's wealth and her brother's recent infamy, rare was the person, at least in Chicago, who wasn't familiar with the Rhodes family.

Jordan headed behind the counter and opened the laptop she kept there. "A case of the Excelsior—you've got it." She pulled up her distributor's delivery schedule. "I can have it in the store by early next week."

"That's plenty of time. Do I pay for it now or when I pick it up?" Cal asked.

"Either one. I figure you're good for it. And now I know where to find you if you're not."

Okay, so she may have been flirting a little. For the last few months her family had been living under an intense spotlight because of the mess with her brother, and frankly, dating had been the last thing on her mind. But things were finally starting to settle down—as much as things could ever settle down when one's twin brother was locked up in prison, she supposed—and it felt good to be flirting. And if the object of said flirtation just so happened to have polished, refined good looks, well, all the better.

"Maybe I should skip out on the bill, just to make you come look for me," Cal teased back. He stood opposite her with the counter between them. "So, since you read my restaurant reviews, I take it you trust my opinions on restaurants?"

Jordan glanced at Cal over the top of her computer as she entered his wine order. "As much as I'd trust a complete stranger about anything, I suppose."

He laughed at that. "Good. Because there's this Thai restaurant that just opened on Clark that's fantastic."

"Good to know," Jordan said pleasantly. "I'll have to check it out sometime."

For the first time since entering her wine shop, Cal looked uncertain. "Oh. I meant that I thought you might like to go there with *me*."

Jordan smiled. Yes, she'd caught that. But she couldn't help but wonder how many other women Cal Kittredge had used his "Do you trust my opinions on restaurants?" line on. There was no doubt he was charming and smooth. The question was whether he was *too* smooth.

She straightened up from her computer and leaned one hip against the bar. "Let's say this—when you come back next week to pick up the Excelsior, you can tell me more about this new restaurant then."

Cal seemed surprised by her nonacceptance (she wouldn't call it a rejection) but not necessarily put off. "Okay. It's a date."

"I'd call it more . . . a continuation."

"Are you always this tough on your customers?" he asked.

"Only the ones who want to take me to Thai restaurants."

"Next time, then, I'll suggest Italian." With a wink, Cal grabbed his gloves off the counter and left the store.

Jordan watched as he walked past the front windows of the store. She noticed that a heavy snow had begun to fall outside. Not for the first time, she was glad she lived only a five-minute walk from the shop. And that she had a good pair of snow boots.

"My god, I thought he'd never leave," said a voice from behind her.

Jordan turned and saw her assistant, Martin, standing a few feet away, near the hallway that led to their storage room. He walked over, carrying a case of a new zinfandel they were putting out in the store for the first time. He set the box on the counter and brushed away a few unruly reddish-brown curls that had fallen into his eyes. "Whew. I've been standing back there, holding that thing forever. Figured I'd give you two some privacy. I thought he was checking you out when he came in last week. Guess I was right."

"How much did you hear?" Jordan asked as she began to help him unpack the bottles.

"I heard that he's Cal Kittredge."

Of course Martin had focused on that. He was twenty-seven years old, was more well-read than anyone she knew, and made no attempt to hide the fact that he was a major food and wine snob. But he knew everything about wine, and frankly he'd grown on her, and Jordan couldn't imagine running the shop without him.

"He asked me to go to some new Thai restaurant on Clark," she said.

"I've been trying to get reservations there for two weeks." Martin lined the remaining bottles on the bar and tossed the empty box onto the floor. "Lucky you. If you start dating Cal Kittredge, you'll be able to get into all the best restaurants. For free."

Jordan modestly remained silent as she grabbed two bottles of the zin and carried them to a bin near the front of the store.

"Oh . . . right," Martin said. "I always forget that you have, like, a billion dollars. I'm guessing you don't need any help getting into restaurants."

Jordan threw him an eye as she grabbed two more bottles. "I don't have a billion dollars."

It was the same routine nearly every time the subject of money came up. Because she liked Martin, she put up with it. But with the exception of him and a small circle of her closest friends, she avoided discussing finances with others.

It wasn't exactly a secret, however: her father was rich. Very rich. She hadn't grown up with money; it was something her family had simply stumbled into. Her father, basically a computer geek like her brother, was one of those overnight success stories *Forbes* and *Newsweek* loved to put on their covers: after graduating from the University of Illinois with a master's degree in computer science, Grey Rhodes went on to Northwestern University's Kellogg School of Management. He then started his own company in Chicago, where he developed an antiviral protection program that exploded worldwide and quickly became the top program of its kind on the market. Within two years of its release to the public, the Rhodes Anti-Virus protected one in every three computers in America. (A statistic her father made sure to include in every interview.) And thus came the millions. Lots of them.

One might have certain impressions about her lifestyle, Jordan knew, given her father's financial success. Some of those impressions would be accurate; others would not. Her father had set up guidelines from the moment he'd made his first million, the most fundamental being that Jordan and her brother, Kyle, earn their own way—just as he had. As adults, they were wholly financially independent from their father, and frankly, Jordan and Kyle wouldn't have it any other way. On the other hand, their father was known to be extravagant with gifts, particularly after their mother died nine years ago. Take, for example, the Maserati Quattroporte sitting in Jordan's garage. Probably not the typical present one received after graduating business school.

"We've had this conversation many times, Martin. That's my father's money, not mine." Jordan wiped her hands on a towel they kept under the counter, brushing off the dust from the wine bottles. She gestured to the store. "*This* is mine." There was pride in her voice, and why shouldn't there be? She was the sole owner of DeVine Cellars, and business was good. Really good—certainly better than she'd ever projected at this point in her ten-year plan. Of course, she didn't make anywhere near the 1.2 billion her father may or may not have been worth (she never talked specifics about his money), but she did well enough to pay for a house in the upscale Lincoln Park neighborhood, and still had money left over for great shoes. A woman couldn't ask for much more.

"Maybe. But you still get into any restaurant you want," Martin pointed out.

"This is true. I do have to pay, though, if that makes you feel any better."

Martin sniffed enviously. "A little. So are you going to say yes?"

"Am I going to say yes to what?" Jordan asked.

"To Cal Kittredge."

"I'm thinking about it." Aside from a potentially slight excess of smoothness, he seemed to be just her type. He was into food and wine, and better yet, he *cooked*. Practically a Renaissance man.

"I think you should string him along for a while," Martin said. "Keep him coming back, so he'll buy a few more cases before you commit."

"Great idea. Maybe we could even start handing out punch cards. Get a date with the owner after six purchases, that kind of thing."

"I detect some sarcasm," Martin said. "Which is too bad, because that punch card idea is not half-bad."

"We could always pimp you out as a prize," Jordan suggested.

Martin sighed as he leaned his slender frame against the bar. His bow tie of choice that day was red, which Jordan thought nicely complemented his dark brown tweed jacket.

"Sadly, I'm underappreciated," Martin said, sounding resigned to his fate. "A light-bodied pinot unnoticed in a world dominated by big, bold cabs."

Jordan rested her hand on his shoulder sympathetically. "Maybe you just haven't hit your drink-now date. Perhaps you're still sitting on the shelf, waiting to age to your full potential."

Martin considered this. "So what you're saying is . . . I'm like the Pahlmeyer 2006 Sonoma Coast Pinot Noir."

Sure . . . exactly what she'd been thinking. "Yep. That's you."

"They're expecting great things from the 2006, you know."

Jordan smiled. "Then we all better look out."

The thought seemed to perk Martin up. In good spirits, he headed off to the storage room for another case of the zinfandel while Jordan returned to the back room to finish her lunch. It was after three o'clock, which meant that if she didn't eat now, she wouldn't get another chance until the store closed at nine. Soon enough, they would have a steady stream of customers.

Wine was hot, one of the few industries continuing to do well despite the economic downturn. But Jordan liked to think her store's success was based on more than just a trend. She'd searched for months for the perfect space: on a major street, where there would be plenty of foot traffic, and large enough to fit several tables and chairs in addition to the display space they would need for the wine. With its warm tones and exposed brick walls, her store had an intimate feel that drew customers in and invited them to stay awhile.

By far the smartest business decision she'd made had been to apply for an on-premise, liquor license, which allowed them to pour and serve wine in the shop. She'd set up highboy tables and chairs along the front windows and tucked a few additional tables into cozy nooks between the wine bins. Starting around five o'clock on virtually every night they were open, the place was hopping with customers buying wines by the glass and taking note of the bottles they planned to purchase when they left.

Today, however, was *not* one of those days.

Outside, the snow continued to fall steadily. By seven o'clock the weathermen amended their predictions and were now calling for a whopping eight to ten inches. In anticipation of the storm, people were staying inside. Jordan had an event booked at the store that evening, a wine tasting, but the party called to reschedule. Since Martin had a longer commute than she did, she sent him home early. At seven thirty, she began closing the shop, thinking it highly unlikely she'd get any customers.

When finished up front, Jordan went into the back room to turn off the sound system. As always at closing, the store felt eerily quiet and empty without the eclectic mix of Billie Holiday, the Shins, Norah Jones, and Moby she'd put together for this week's soundtrack. She grabbed her snow boots from behind the door, and had just sat down at her desk to replace the three-inch-heel black leather boots she wore, when the chime on the front door rang.

A customer. Surprising.

Jordan stood up and stepped out of the back room, thinking somebody had to be awfully desperate to come out for wine in this weather. "You're in luck. I was just about to close for the . . ."

Her words trailed off as she stopped at the sight of the two men standing near the front of the store. For some reason, she felt tingles at the back of her neck. Perhaps it had something to do with the man closer to the door—he didn't look like her typical customer.

He had chestnut brown hair and scruff along his jaw that gave him a dark, bad-boy look. Right off the bat, something about his demeanor, the way he commanded one's attention, made her think he was a man used to getting his way. He was tall and wore a black wool coat over what appeared to be a well-built physique. He was good-looking, no doubt, but unlike Cal Kittredge, he seemed rather . . . rough. Unpolished. Except for his eyes. Green as emeralds, they stood out brilliantly against his dark hair and five o'clock shadow as he watched her intently.

He took a step forward.

She took a step back.

A slight grin played at the edges of his lips, as if he found this amusing.

She wondered how fast she could make it to the emergency panic button underneath the bar.

The shorter man, the one wearing glasses and a camel-colored trench coat, cleared his throat. "Are you Jordan Rhodes?"

She debated whether to answer this. But the blond man seemed safer than the tall, dark one. "I am."

The blond man pulled a badge out of his jacket. "I'm Agent Seth Huxley; this is Agent Nick McCall. We're with the Federal Bureau of Investigation."

This caught her off guard. "The FBI?" The last time she'd seen anyone from the FBI had been at Kyle's arraignment.

"We'd like to discuss a matter concerning your brother," the blond man said. He seemed very serious and slightly tense about whatever it was he needed to tell her.

Jordan's stomach twisted in a knot. She forced herself not to panic. Yet.

"Has he been hurt?" she asked. In the four months he'd been in prison, there had already been several altercations. Apparently, some of the other inmates at Metropolitan Correctional Center figured a wealthy computer geek would be an easy mark.

Kyle, being Kyle, assured her he could hold his own whenever Jordan asked about the fights during one of her visits. But every day since he'd begun serving his sentence, she'd worried about the moment when she got a phone call saying he'd been wrong. And if the FBI had come to her store on the night of a blizzard, whatever they had to tell her couldn't be good.

The dark-haired man spoke for the first time. His voice was low yet smoother than Jordan had expected given his rugged appearance.

"Your brother is fine. As far as we know, anyway."

That was an odd thing to say. "As far as you know? You make it sound like he's missing or something." Jordan paused, then folded her arms across her chest. Oh . . . no. "Don't tell me he's escaped."

Kyle wouldn't be so stupid. Well, okay, *once* he'd been that stupid, actions that had landed him in prison in the first place, but he wouldn't be that stupid again. That was why he'd pled guilty, after all, instead of going to trial. He'd wanted to own up to his mistakes and accept the consequences.

She knew her brother better than anyone. True, he was a genius, and assuming there was a computer anywhere within reach of the inmates, he could probably upload some code or virus or whatever that would spring open the cell doors and simultaneously release all the prisoners in a mad stampede. But Kyle wouldn't do that. She hoped.

"Escaped? Is there something you'd like to share about your brother, Ms. Rhodes?" Agent McCall asked in an amused, perhaps mocking, tone.

Something about him rubbed her the wrong way. She felt as though she were facing off against an opponent holding a royal flush in a game of poker she hadn't realized she'd been playing. And she wasn't in the mood to play games with the FBI right then. Or ever. They'd charged her brother to the fullest extent of the law, locked him up at MCC, and treated him like a menace to society for what, in Jordan's admittedly biased opinion, was simply a really bad mistake. (By someone with no criminal record, she noted.) It wasn't like Kyle had *killed* anyone, for heaven's sake; he'd just caused a bit of panic and mayhem. For about fifty million people.

"You said this is about my brother. How can I help you, Agent McCall?" she asked coolly.

He stepped farther into the store and leaned against the bar, seeming to make himself right at home. "Unfortunately, I'm not at liberty to fill you in on the details here. Agent Huxley and I would prefer to continue this conversation in private. At the FBI office."

And she would prefer to say nothing at all to the FBI, if they weren't dangling this bit about Kyle over her head. She gestured to the empty wine shop. "I'm sure whatever it is you have to say, the chardonnays will keep it confidential."

"I never trust a chardonnay."

"And I don't trust the FBI."

The words hung in the air between them. A standstill. Agent Huxley intervened. "I understand your hesitancy, Ms. Rhodes, but as Agent McCall indicated, this is a confidential matter. We have a car waiting out front and would very much appreciate it if you came with us to the FBI office. We'd be happy to explain everything there."

She considered this. Agent Huxley at least seemed to be somewhat more amiable than his partner. "Fine. I'll call my lawyer and have him meet us there."

Agent McCall shook his head firmly. "No lawyers, Ms. Rhodes. Just you."

Jordan kept her face impassive, but inwardly her frustration increased. Aside from her general dislike of the FBI because of the way they'd treated her brother, there was an element of pride here. They had come into *her* store, and this Nick McCall person seemed to think she should jump just because he said to.

So instead, she held her ground. "You're going to have to do better than that, Agent McCall. You sought me out in the middle of a blizzard, which means you want something from me. Without giving me more, you're not going to get it."

He appeared to consider his options. Jordan got the distinct impression that one of those options involved throwing her over his shoulder and hauling her ass right out of the store. He seemed the type.

Instead, he pushed away from the bar and stepped closer to her, then closer again. He peered down at her, his brilliant green-eyed gaze unwavering. "How would you like to see your brother released from prison, Ms. Rhodes?"

Stunned by the offer, Jordan searched his eyes cautiously. She looked for any signs of deceit or trickery, although she suspected she wouldn't see anything in Nick McCall's eyes that he didn't want her to.

A leap of faith. She debated whether to believe him.

"I'll grab my coat."